TOYS OF GLASS

TOYS OF GLASS

Martin Booth

SIMON & SCHUSTER

LONDON · SYDNEY · NEW YORK · TOKYO · SINGAPORE · TORONTO

First published in Great Britain by Simon & Schuster Ltd 1995
A Paramount Communications Company

Simon & Schuster Ltd
West Garden Place
Kendal Street
London W2 2AQ

Simon & Schuster of Australia Pty Ltd
Sydney

A CIP catalogue record for this book is available from the
British Library

ISBN 0-671-85199-3

Typeset in Garamond 12/15pt by
Hewer Text Composition Services, Edinburgh
Printed and bound in Great Britain by
Butler & Tanner Ltd, Frome and London

for Helen

Life is a toy made of glass;
it appears to be of inestimable worth,
but in reality it is very cheap.

Pietro Aretino: 1537

What is divine escapes men's notice
because of their incredulity.

Heraclitus: circa 500 BC

Since I last looked, the trunk of the dead *barriguda* tree has shifted and now leans at a slightly greater angle than before: the swollen river is undermining it. It has slipped down through space, possibly by as much as three degrees, from the right-hand edge of the spreading kapok tree on the far bank to settle squarely over the young *paxiuba* palm in the stilt roots of which a three-toed sloth has sought cover.

Perhaps thirty minutes have passed. There is no way of telling.

Time moves so slowly here. The single beat of an eagle's wing high above the jungle seems so leisurely. The wild bees which swarm to the hive hover as if in slow motion. Even the huge butterflies travel with a leisured pulse through the dense undergrowth. Every hour ambles by like an old cart-horse which has had enough, waiting with the stoical patience of a beast heading for the knacker's yard of which it knows nothing but instinctively senses will one day come.

It has been raining continuously for two days, not a light drizzle but a steady, incessant downpour which beats out a monotonous tattoo on the tin roof of the hut and patters loudly on the elephantine leaves of the jungle plants which grow right up to the rear wall providing within a green twilight by day whilst, at night, affording a pitch blackness as deep and oppressive as any to be found in a subterranean vault. There being no gutters on the hut, the water pours down all round like a fluid chain link curtain hung from the eaves. Every common jungle sound is stifled – if you will forgive a morbid cliché, drowned – by the cacophony of the rain.

When it rains this hard and long, which it does with a

dreary regularity, I can neither read, work, nor scarcely think: it is impossible to concentrate for more than a minute or two with the constant din. I had hoped, after an hour or so, I would have grown to ignore it as a commonplace, much as a man who lives by a busy road does not hear the ceaseless hum of passing traffic, yet I cannot push it from my consciousness.

For a few hours, I had lain on my camp bed, trying to catch up on the sleep which had evaded me during the night, but the rain would not let me so much as doze. Eventually, restive and peevish, I swung my legs over the side of the bed and went out on to the porch to sit just inside the prison bars of the rain.

Across the clearing, I could vaguely make out the line of native long-houses, their thatched roofs sodden and bedraggled. And dull. The rain robs the jungle of its vibrant colours, reducing the whole world to a series of uniform greys and khakis.

In one of the wide doorways, a fire flickered before which, from time to time, a figure passed to momentarily obliterate the orange flames. Steam rose from the thatch above the fire as if the house was being slowly boiled like some vast, dun-coloured pudding. Not so much as a pi-dog ventured out and the space under the huts, between the stilts, where usually the children played or the pigs rooted about or the dogs scratched or squabbled amongst themselves, was empty.

'Where in God's name does it all come from? How the hell can it rain like this for so bloody long?'

I spoke out loud, my voice flat in the warm, moist air. No sooner had I spoken than I regretted it: I have resolved not to speak aloud to myself. Never. That is, I consider, a sign of weakness, of self-indulgence: it is also a form of punishment of which I am deserving or far worse. Yet, deep within me, I am more afraid it might be a sign of gradually impinging insanity.

A man came to stand at the long-house doorway. Even at a distance and in the poor light, I could see he was stocky, strongly built, strangely powerful in the way primitive men can be. It was not a matter of brawn or stance but of presence.

It might have been Keewei, the shaman or Chuhi, the hunter. It was hard to tell through the rain. I stood up, raising my arm by way of greeting but the native was not looking in my direction and made no response. Sitting again, I stared blankly into the rain and allowed my mind to wander: not at random for that, too, might smack of the start of lunacy. I recalled the first time I met Chuhi.

From the very day of my arrival, the people of the clearing accepted me, if at first with a sense of polite curiosity. They could not understand my circumstance, why I and my companion had, without prior warning, appeared in their midst to occupy Dr Suarez's galvanized tin hut which had been abandoned for longer than they could remember. They watched our every move with a fascinated detachment but they very quickly came to approve the situation and trust me. My companion's presence helped, laughing with them, showing them we were eager to be their friends. It was once this trust was established, perhaps on the third or fourth day, that Chuhi paid his surprise visit.

He announced his arrival by making a noise like a spider monkey only much louder, a sort of high-pitched gibbering whistle halfway between the mewling of a randy alley-cat and the musics of the gods. His appearance was quite sudden. One moment, the clearing was empty with an uninterrupted view of the river's brown flow, the waterlogged dug-out and the unstable jetty: the next he was standing in full view. Not a branch in the undergrowth agitated nor leaf twitched. He was not there and then he was there, materialized from the jungle, dressed in tattered denim shorts and nothing more. The fly was open showing his genitals wrapped in a little bark pouch. Over his shoulder he carried a small hessian sack with his bow and a tube of arrows whilst at his side hung his little sporran made of the pelt of a howler monkey in which he stored his poison and darts. His blowpipe was in his left hand.

I guessed he was in his late twenties, about five foot three or four tall with a broad, flat nose, narrow almost Oriental eyes and a particularly slender, feminine neck around which he wore a necklace of cheap glass trader's beads interspersed with some creature's teeth. His arms were long and his legs short as if evolution had not quite finished with him. Otherwise, he was well proportioned, competently muscular, expertly constructed for his life. His dark brown skin was the colour of an old walnut case, his hair cut in a fashion reminiscent of the early days of the Beatles, as if someone had placed a gourd on his head and cut off all that showed. He eschewed extensive permanent body decoration, only painting lines on his chest and face with vegetable dyes: decades of missionary teaching had, I assumed, entered his subconscious just as the foreign aid doctors' hypodermics had pierced his skin to leave no visible mark.

Yet the drugs of the white man's civilization course through him, and he can do nothing about it.

The visit lasted no longer than fifteen minutes. In the distance, gathered in the shadows of the long-houses, I could make out the rest of the population of the clearing studying our meeting. It was plain to me Chuhi was on an ambassadorial, fact-finding mission.

He stood immobile for a short while before approaching the hut, stepping almost daintily. I made myself visible on the porch: this, I had been forewarned by Dr Suarez in Santo Antonio do Içá, was the etiquette of the tribesmen. It was a practical civility: enemies hide, friends come out in the open. That much was common between us: as it was in Cavendish Square so was it in the clearing. I positioned myself on the edge of the porch shadow – it was around noon when Chuhi turned up – and he advanced to about five metres from the hut. There he halted and, looking me straight in the face, smiled broadly to show his white teeth, the incisors filed to points like those of a predatory fish. This greeting made, he removed a gift from his sack and placed it on the ground. It consisted of a lump of amber and a gob of beeswax into which had been stuck half a dozen exquisite, iridescent feathers.

'Chuhi!' he exclaimed, his fist balled and jabbed into the air.

I, assuming this to be a colloquial greeting, replied, 'Chuhi!' and clenched my own fist.

He looked momentarily nonplussed then grinned expansively. His teeth shone with a defined and terrible menace. '*No. Me llamo* Chuhi. *Hay solamente uno.*'

His Spanish was heavily accented and it was some seconds before I had translated the words. Then I, too, grinned, understanding my stupidity. '*No soy Español. Soy Inglés,*' I said, speaking slowly, aware my own accent was far from perfect. '*Me llamo* Lyall. Dominic Lyall.' Again, I formed a fist and punched it upwards. Chuhi smirked with pleasure.

'*Do-me-neek Lie-yall,*' he tested the name. '*¡Muy bien! Es como Santo Domenico.*'

I stepped forward and, bending, picked up my gift. A sudden, terrible misgiving came over me: at that moment, he could quite easily have smashed his fist down, broken my neck and have had my head shrunken as a talisman. Certainly, such trinkets still existed. Dr Suarez had three, not one of them over a decade or two old. The newest of them, he was convinced, was a man he knew whom he had employed as a guide in the summer of 1970.

When I stood up, Chuhi was gone, swallowed up once more by the jungle. I did not see him again until he rematerialized across the clearing, to the side of one of the long-houses.

In the hut, I placed the amber nugget and display of feathers on the shelf above my *Gray's Anatomy*, Wright's *Applied Physiology*, White and Humphrey's *Pharmacopoeia*, the Air Brazil calendar, a line of miscellaneous non-medical books and a few other odds and sods I had brought with me yet which were useless save to remind me of my various human follies.

Now, sitting at the table and glancing over my shoulder, the amber still stands on the shelf. I can see it glimmering like a huge, rough jewel in the twilight. Beside it are the books, their bindings warped by the jungle humidity, the covers mottled with mould.

For the first months, I kept the calendar marked, rather as a prisoner might in order to keep sight of his release date or a child at boarding-school counting down the hours of tedium and bullying to the end of term, as if there was a finite, unannounced day on which I might bale out the canoe, quit the clearing and drift with the current back down the river. Yet, after a while, I stopped fooling myself and let the calendar go. I cannot recall its fate: I may have burned it with all my other papers. Perhaps the termites ate it. Perhaps it simply rotted away. Whichever is the case, it does not matter. There is no going back for me, for a man who has played god.

I return to my bed, remove my trousers and wrap a flannelette towel around my waist, sarong-style: somewhere in my memory I can hear my mother saying, 'Never sleep with your belly bare. You'll catch your death.' Lying on my back, I face up at the beams and, beyond them, to the grooves of corrugated iron.

Close to one of the cross-trees hang a cluster of half a dozen bats. When I first encountered these creatures, I was afraid they might be vampires and tried to drive them out of the hut with a palm frond. They steadfastly refused to be evicted into the daylight. Once they had left at dusk, I closed the windows and doors tight to prevent their return but, when I awoke the next morning, they were back in the roost, squeaking as they settled to rest. I checked my ankles and wrists, ear-lobes and armpits but there were no bite marks. As the weeks went by, I ignored them, only recognizing their presence when I had to clean up their mess in the corner of the room.

I shut my eyes. The roof disappears, to be replaced by a late evening sky such as was beloved by eighteenth-century English landscape painters – Constable, say, or the young Turner – a wash of dying day hanging over the straight, definitive line of the horizon and reflected in the mirrored water of willow-lined rhynes and unhurried rivers, still mill-ponds and lazy weir pools. From some indeterminate place comes the last of the day's cawing in a rookery high in a copse of winter elms: the first darting flash of a pipistrelle dropped from a crack in an ancient stone wall: and there is a whispering breeze, a cool zephyr blowing off a northern ocean, one to make me shiver and pull an imaginary overcoat closer about my shoulders.

Gradually, the tumult of the rain seems to subside and the breeze quietens. I hear voices. They are not speaking in the dialect of the people of the clearing, nor in the pidgin Spanish of this remote area, but in English. I cannot make out exactly what is being said but I can ascertain the tone of the conversation – it is light-hearted and carefree yet assertive and sure of itself. I try, as if I am an eavesdropper, to recognize the voices but cannot. Only one is familiar: it is my own voice.

I sit up as if, by doing so, I might comprehend what I am saying but it is a wasted exercise.

The rain increases momentarily, as if the clouds are wringing out their last efforts. The sudden pelting din serves only to drown out the voices and remind me of how hard it rained that miserable Friday when fate set its claws into me and rolled my dice.

◆

My surgery was situated in a quiet mews north of Oxford Street, in the part of London which is a hinterland between the snobberies of Mayfair and the pretensions of Marylebone. It was a convenient location. The mews, being a cul-de-sac, was anonymous, afforded parking for my patients and bore a dignified address. Beside the mahogany door was a brass plaque: *Dr Dominic Lyall – Consultant Gynaecologist*. That was all. No letters of qualification, no ostentatious justifications. In private medicine such things are unnecessary. My neighbours lent an added cachet: a famous and ennobled actor, a retired foreign secretary, a former governor of the Bank of England and an eminent psychiatrist specializing, as he diplomatically put it, in the foibles of the entertainment world.

The premises were large: my surgery, operating suite and laboratory occupied the ground and first floors whilst the top floor and part of the mews cottage next door made up my apartment. I permanently employed three laboratory technicians, two nurses and a receptionist: other specialists, such as an anaesthetist, were taken on as and when required on a temporary basis.

It did not take me long to establish my reputation. In those heady days, when the world was an optimistic place owned by the greedy and the wealthy, the hungry and the hopeful, anyone with an expensive car and a costly watch, a refined accent and an address in central London could not fail to do well in his or her chosen profession. I had served my time in medical school, tramped the wards of an urban hospital for long hours, stitching up the split scalps of drunks, stomach-pumping suicides and tending to ODs and the victims of RTAs, brought in by the police, often suffering horrendous wounds with various fragments of automobile embedded in them.

When the opportunity came to specialize, I chose gynaecology and urology and, once qualified, settled into the routine of a hospital obstetrics department. After a while, however, fortune smiled upon me in the form of an inheritance and I got out: I had, I believed, paid my debt to public medicine and was ready to move on. I took an additional specialization in human embryology and within eighteen months from completion, I had all the trappings of success – a Porsche 911 Turbo and a platinum and gold Vacheron Constantin watch. And the mews property.

It was not that I wanted to deliberately abandon the casualties of society, disregard or dismiss the sad and the lonely, the victims of drunken drivers and brutal husbands, the ranks of mothers-to-be and the drearily painted walls of the delivery room, merely for some mercenary or pecuniary motive. It was more I felt hamstrung by the public health service, unfulfilled and unable to visualize any future which did not involve ninety-hour working weeks, sleeping like a dog on a trolley in the rest-room or dozing off between the slamming of the door and the next dying whine of a siren pulling into the emergency bay.

My life seemed governed by flashing blue strobe lights and hurried surgery, exhausted ambulance drivers and harassed midwives who would have looked quite pretty if they had been given the time to change into jeans or a short skirt and put on a modicum of make-up. It was just all so sleazy and soul-destroying.

In part, I suppose I wanted also to be my own boss, not have to bow to an asinine administrator with a mediocre business studies diploma, working a forty-hour week and provided by the health authority with an expense account and a BMW sports saloon. I wanted to achieve something, branch out into a field of my profession, move on to the cutting edge of medicine beyond a dependency upon fiscal restraints and ministerial whim, government interference and political expediency.

Looking back, I believe I was afraid, scared of a weakness in myself. I was frightened the drudgery and tedium of my life would dent, perhaps erase, the commitment I felt. My only escape route was into private practice.

My patients were rich. Rich and unhappy. Despite their Ferraris and fur coats, they were miserable because they were unlucky. Providence had smiled on their businesses, their bank accounts and their share portfolios but tribulation had blighted their lives: they were unable to achieve what they thought was the simplest thing in the world, to have children.

I was the one who offered them hope. From their failure was created my success, my fortune, my considerable renown and a life-style to which many aspired but which very few achieved: yet I admit to succumbing to pride and a sense of warm achievement when called upon in the early hours to deliver a child in the making of which I had been instrumental.

The practice had been going for about three years when the day arrived, a Friday in May when fate spun its wheel. At the time, it was nothing out of the ordinary. I had been to dinner the night before with friends who lived in Amersham and had not returned to town until the early hours. Normally,

I checked through the appointments list for the next day before retiring. Molly, my receptionist, always placed it on my desk, neatly typed out on a sheet of headed A4 paper. Yet this time, I did not. There had been a burst water main on the A40 and traffic had been detoured through the dismal suburbs west of London. I became lost and by the time I reached the mews was tired and went straight to bed.

Fridays were exclusively a consultation day, my first patient the wife of a French industrialist for whom a visit to my surgery was more therapeutic than medical: she had miscarried several times, had no faith in her Parisian gynaecologist and hinted more than once she felt her husband was poisoning her so she might not go full term. Being a staunchly Catholic family, they already had four children and he was loath, she reported, to spawn more, though whether from a sense of sound economics or moral ethics I could not ascertain. On more than one occasion, the woman in fine flow with hardly a pause for breath between sentences, I was inclined to refer her to my colleague down the mews.

By the time she left, after an hour's consultation of which I doubt fifteen minutes had concerned her reproductive organs or cycle, I was numbed. Molly ushered the pestering woman out and brought me a cup of *cappuccino*.

'Is the next appointment here?' I enquired, sitting behind my desk and sipping at the hot froth speckled with dark chocolate.

'Yes, doctor. Mr and Mrs Cordiner.'

It is an unusual name and yet it did not register even when the door opened and Molly showed them in. He was tall, well built and very handsome in the way either the wealthy or the well educated tend to be; she was shorter, a blonde, pretty woman verging on the beautiful. I came round from behind my desk to welcome them.

'How do you do?' I said formally. 'Will you have a coffee?'

I indicated the suede leather settee by the coffee-table: I conducted my consultations without a desk as a barrier between my patients and myself although, in the case of the Frenchwoman, I frequently considered making an exception. It was not unknown for her to absent-mindedly stroke my knee by way of emphasizing her latest concern.

'Thank you,' the husband replied, his eyes smiling: his wife nodded and Molly took their order.

'Please, do sit down.'

They sat side by side on the settee, both of them suddenly on edge, the smile gone from his eyes. They reminded me of candidates for a job interview.

It was then I noticed the rain. It was lashing against the window, obscuring the view of the little courtyard at the rear. The geraniums in the window-box tossed to and fro, scarlet petals breaking free, momentarily sticking to the window before being washed away.

'A particularly foul morning,' I remarked, noticing as I did so his highly polished shoes were dulled with rain. 'I do hope you've not had far to come?'

'You don't recognize me, do you, Dom?' the man said.

I looked squarely at him. His eyes were smiling once more.

'I'm sorry . . .'

'Add a full beard.'

'And longer hair,' his wife interjected. 'And jeans. And, quite possibly, beads.'

It was then the name registered.

'Brian?' I half-exclaimed.

He grinned and asked, 'Still have your Harley?'

For several years, when I was serving my time in a London teaching hospital, Brian Cordiner and I had been close associates. I was a doctor under pressure of long hours and lack of sleep, he was a dentist with either a social conscience or a strong sense of self-destruction: he could have gone straight from dental school into a suburban practice but instead he had chosen to wander the wards with me, dosed up on caffeine pills and struggling to keep at least a semblance of alertness about his person. When I had stitched up the drunks, bandaged the fighters or sedated the car crash victims, I passed them over to him to work on their cracked or shattered teeth, remove the debris from their mouths caused by a parking meter, a policeman's truncheon or a steering-wheel.

'No,' I answered. 'The caution of years, a dislike of wet leather trousers and a face stung by grit has me graduated from a motor bike to a sports car. And you? Still have your Triumph?'

He pretended to smile disarmingly and said, 'Still got it. Just don't ride it much. It sits at the back of the garage under a tarpaulin. Pressure of work and . . . ' He glanced at his partner. 'My wife Larry.'

I looked down at their file card: *Brian and Larissa Cordiner – age 34, 29 – dental surgeon, housewife (formerly art historian)*. Their address was given as *Dell Cottage, Harbury, Somerset*.

'He will spell it with a *y*, too. I prefer Lari, with one *r* and an *i*. It's a bit unfair, don't you think? Rather unfeminine having a boy's nickname,' she said, smiling a little sheepishly. 'You can't really shorten Brian, can you?'

Molly entered with a *café au lait* and another *cappuccino*, handing my cup to me over from the desk.

'You can see what I've got up to since our purgatorial years,' I began, leaning back in my chair across the coffee-table from them. 'What about you? How are the teeth of the good yeomen of Harbury?'

'Harbury's little more than a hamlet,' Brian responded. 'We bought the cottage after we married. All of seven years ago. As for the local yeomanry, my practice is in a nearby town. The usual catalogue of dental disasters. I do one night a week in a local hospital, too.' He smiled wanly. 'Once addicted . . . '

He sipped at his coffee. A sudden squall pelted the rain against the window. Glancing over, I noticed the geraniums had lost all their petals. It was an omen. I know that now.

One of those little signals in life which one does not recognize or ignores at one's peril.

'I do a fair bit of bridge-work,' he went on, 'crowns, some cosmetic work. Most of the business is run-of-the-mill National Health stuff. Lot of pensioners in Somerset, retired lieutenant-colonels and rear admirals, colonial civil servants – you know the sort of thing. Arrogant when-eyes with dumpy wives bemoaning their loss of batmen and amahs abound in the lanes.'

'When-eyes?' I repeated.

'When-eyes,' Larry explained. 'When I was in Barbados, When I was in Rhodesia . . . Brian doesn't like them,' she added unnecessarily.

'I allow they do provide the occasional private patient,' Brian admitted.

For a while, we made small talk about our respective lives then, inevitably, the mood changed subtly over the space of a few minutes to come round to the reason for their visit. They were childless.

'We have been trying,' Larry said, almost apologetically. 'For several years. When we first met and married, I was on the pill. Since stopping them – well, since then, nothing's happened. We could adopt, but . . . '

She left the option hanging. She did not want to own another's cast off but hold her own progeny in her arms, breast-feed her own infant, go through the discomfort and pain, the risks and rigours, the lottery of human birth.

For half an hour I questioned them about their sexual habits. At first, they were reticent as so many couples are but, gradually, they unwound. There was nothing unusual in their relationship. They made love twice, perhaps thrice weekly, her menstrual cycle was more or less regular and not abnormal. Neither of them smoked, nor were they on any relevant medication and had not dabbled in drugs other than Brian who had, as I had, indulged in innocuous cannabis cookies which were all the rage for a while in the nurses' home when we were indentured slaves to the National Health Service. Neither of them had suffered any disease which might have affected their fertility.

Towards the end of our meeting, the inevitable question was posed. Larry asked it: the wives usually did. 'Do you think you can do anything for us?'

'I'm sure I can try,' I replied. 'Nothing is certain at this stage but, as you'll know, advances in the field of infertility have raced ahead in recent years. I can make no promises but I'll take you on as patients and we'll go from there. I shall require a copy of your full medical records from your family doctor and ... Well, this may be a long and exhausting – by which I might more accurately say frustrating – process. At the end of it, we may still have got nowhere.'

It was my standard speech and they, like everyone else, either did not hear it because it hinted at failure, or dismissed it in their eagerness to try.

The patient registration formalities over, my introductory pamphlet about *in vitro* fertilization given to them and my next appointment not due until the early afternoon, I sent Larry off to wander the stores of Oxford Street whilst I made a start by examining Brian.

'How many days since you last made love?' I enquired.

'Tuesday.'

'And you went to a public school, didn't you?'

He nodded, a puzzled look on his face, and said, 'Yes. Lancing.'

I rang the bell on my desk: Angela, my senior nurse, knocked and entered. I introduced them.

'We need a sperm sample,' I went on. 'As large as possible, hence it's better to take it a few days after sex. And it has to be fresh. That's why it helps if you went to a posh school. You'll have had the practice.'

I smirked: it was always best to either regard this moment in early treatment as a not-too-smutty joke or with clinical detachment. Dealing with a fellow medical man, I judged the former to be invariably the more appropriate.

'Angela,' I continued, 'will show you to the sin bin upstairs. It's a bit cramped but, I'm sure, a good deal more luxurious than the bogs at Lancing or the bushes behind the proverbial bike sheds. You'll find a few aids under the table, should you need them. Mostly Dutch and all illegal. The wonderful thing is my accountant has fiddled a tax rebate on them. Professional publications . . . '

When Brian had provided his sample and departed, another consultation arranged in a week or so to coincide with Larry's menstrual cycle, I went into the laboratory. Phillips, my senior technician, had prepared the sample, allowing it to liquefy before suspending it in a culture medium of HAMS F10.

'What's the count?' I enquired.

Phillips checked the seminal fluid analysis card on his clipboard.

'Low, about 28. And we only collected 1.8 millilitres: that was the whole sample.'

A normal reading would be anything up to 120 million spermatozoa per ml of fluid: a normal sample could be expected to be up to 5ml in volume.

'Motility?'

'Progressive motility 25, normal forms the same, sir.'

I bent to the microscope. A healthy human spermatozoon looks like a tadpole: it has a head about 2mm long, a mid-section of about 6mm and a flagellum, or tail, about 50mm in length. In Brian's case, although there was a reasonable number of healthy-looking sperm present there was also an inordinate number of abnormal ones: two- and three-headed sperm, tailless sperm, immobile sperm or ones which hardly wriggled their tails, twin-tailed sperm, sperm with blunt heads which would never be able to penetrate an oöcyte.

'Antibodies?' I asked.

Phillips ran his finger down the card and said, 'Not a problem.'

The sample was small but I decided to process it in any case, Phillips centrifuging the suspension of semen, adding it to a Percoll gradient, repeating the process several times in order to separate the normal sperm from the abnormal, bacteria and cellular debris. By mid-afternoon, we were in possession of a concentrated pellet of normal spermatozoa. These were then mixed with a cryoprotectant of egg yolk and glycerol, placed in minute quantities in colour-coded straws, thin tubes of non-toxic PTFE plastic then quick frozen to dehydrate them. This done, the straws were labelled and placed in the freezing unit of liquid nitrogen at –197°C. Only one in three men have sperm which will come through the freezing process: in time, we would discover the survivability of Brian's sample.

◆

Life is given to us, we earn it by giving it.

Only a sage could have said such a thing, a poet, a man with a vision beyond his own tiny horizon.

I can recall quite vividly the day I first heard those words. It was in a lecture theatre crowded with first-year medical students. We were an eager regiment, bright-eyed and bushy-tailed nineteen-year-olds, ready to go out and fight, conquer disease and liberate the world from hurt. Each of us carried a smart ring folder filled with pristine pages upon which we were to draw our plans of action, learn our tactics and stratagems, plot the advance of our armies across the battlefields of the human body.

At ten o'clock, our general arrived. The room fell hushed with reverence and awe. He was not what we had expected. The door to the side of the dais opened and an old, bent man entered, climbing to the platform with measured, frail steps. His horny hand grasped the side of the lectern for balance. A marked tic twitched the lumbrical muscle. I could not believe it possible such twisted, arthritic talons had delved into the delicate, secret places of hearts or brains.

'Gentlemen,' he began, then he looked around the room from beneath dense eyebrows, 'and ladies,' he added as if it was an afterthought, 'you are embarking upon a terrible journey. One of pain and suffering, much of it your own. A voyage of anguish and misery, of failure and frustration tempered only infrequently by all-too-brief moments of the ecstasy of success or achievement. You will see, in the various ports of call along your way, such sights as a normal man would shy away from, turn his face to the wall to avoid, pretend did not exist. Your peregrination will introduce you to the worst of the human condition. And your ship will be a messy vessel, no sleek cruise liner but a rust bucket with slopping bilges and decks awash with . . .'

He paused. A few cast uneasy glances at their neighbours. Fingers fiddled with pencils, with Parker ball-points, with gold Sheaffer pens given by proud parents to their successful surgeons-to-be.

'For all that, gentlemen – and ladies – you will be amongst the most privileged of men for you will be in command of the greatest gift a man may bestow upon his fellow.'

The pens and pencils stilled. All eyes were to the front once more.

'Tagore,' he continued, his voice suddenly louder as he scanned the room, his eyes as bright as a rodent's under his heavy brow.

We looked at each other as if this was the first medical term we were to encounter. The young woman next to me wrote down *Tay gore* on the first page of her folder and glanced nervously at me.

'Rabindranath Tagore,' the old man went on. 'An Indian mystical poet, friend of Yeats, one of the Georgians . . .'

It was then he quoted those words.

The vivid image of ships wallowing in oceans of blood vanished. We saw our general not as an infirm ancient but as a man with whom we would gladly march, beside whom we would man the barricades until we dropped. The introductory lecture over, I remember leaving the building filled with a dedication which would have done a crusader proud: indeed, it was the same kind of zealot's furnace which burned within me, the flames of decision, of undiluted righteousness, of sheer certainty.

Time and reality have dulled some of the vision he installed that early October morning in a cold lecture theatre in a cold city cowering under the first stinging wind of an early autumn, yet I came to live by the doctrine he espoused: but, more, I moved far beyond it. For what he considered life was the easing of physical anguish, the curing of disease and the setting of bones. Although the research was well advanced at the time, I am sure he did not realize how close science and technology were bringing us to the art of what, in another general lecture later in the year, he passingly referred to as extra-uterine formulation.

There is no greater act a man can do than create his own kind: not merely by putting the sexes together and allowing nature to run her course but by manoeuvring the raw materials, arranging the circumstances of nature, selecting the right genes and the best chromosomes, tipping the scales of chance in a favourable direction. Fixing the wheel of fortune.

To this I dedicated my life, rigging the deck and manipulating the odds to the advantage of those to whom nature had dealt a cruel hand.

What I chose to ignore was the old realization that for every action there is an opposite reaction, for every lucky winner there has to be a miserable loser.

And I did not know of Tagore's other maxim: *Life, like a child, laughs, shaking its rattle of death as it runs.*

◆

How little are we different.

Just as Chuhi sometimes hangs himself about with glass

beads when occasion demands it so Keewei, as shaman, bedecks himself in a jaguar skin pillbox hat which, like Chuhi's haircut, is a vague reminder of sixties fashion. He also wears, if the circumstance is one of considered importance, a pair of very derelict Reebok training shoes with violet trim. The laces are long since missing so how he manages to walk through the jungle and keep them on his feet is a source of wonderment to me. The shoes are size ten, his feet not six.

When I know in advance we are to meet formally, I also dress accordingly. I drape my stethoscope around my neck and don my white lab coat. If the meeting is of Reebok status, I put two brightly-coloured ball-pens in my breast pocket. One is green, the other red. Both no longer work. Additionally, I pin my old hospital identity badge on my lapel. It is a toughened formica oblong with my name incised in white on a black background. Beneath it is a square made of silver foil covering a layer of sensitized thermoluminescent plastic surrounded by a canary yellow frame. It was my clinical x-ray dosimeter. Now it is an obsolescent piece of jewellery worn to impress a witch-doctor.

We are both medical men, Keewei and me. In our own ways. I am a Mendelian – which is to say a realist. He is an Aristotelian. He does not know it but he is. He and the father of civilization share the same conclusions and misconceptions, the same dreams of wisdom.

Through laboured conversations in pidgin English and Spanish, often convoluted in the same sentence and spiced with the odd word in Huambas, not to mention sign language, sketches on paper or in the dust and much pointing to or touching of objects, I have deduced Keewei believes the father is the pattern of the unborn child and the mother merely a source of sustenance. A manioc seed produces a manioc plant and this, in his opinion, is how it is throughout creation: why a man should be any different from a plant does not occur to him. Just as a father passes on his wealth and reputation, tribal honour and peccaries, dogs and scrubby hens, so does his seed pass on his image, his personal guile, the intricate dark corners of his primeval soul.

He also believes in spontaneous generation. This he explained to me by tugging on a creeper hanging down from a bough leaning over my hut, hissing and flicking his tongue in and out, weaving his head from side to side like a Siamese court dancer, then finally stroking the bare belly of a little girl who happened to be sitting next to him. From this, I opined he believes lianas give birth to snakes. He went on to display his conviction that the green algæ in the jungle pools is the precursor of leeches and lice are created from the flakes of skin which peel from the scalp. The fleas from which his dogs suffer are the children of the dust in which they roll.

I have made no attempt to disabuse him of his beliefs. It is no longer my place to try and convince others of their ineptitudes and ignorance. Besides, Hippocrates believed humans were made by a blending of seminal fluids. He saw the liquid appear in the case of men and assumed it existed in women. It was only a short step to guessing that, as he put it, droplets in both liquids commingled with the final form of the child dependent upon whichever was present in the larger volume. And he was not so wrong. He had the vector right, it was just the detail of which he was unsure. There is sufficient generosity in my mind as to allow Keewei may have the inkling of truth in his concept of which I, the sophisticate, am blissfully unaware.

If only it were so simple, that the fire-bird was made of flame and the humming-bird fashioned from the petal of an orchid which broke free and took flight as it fell through the jungle canopy. If I knew no better, I would be at liberty to believe these myths and they would provide me with a way out of my dilemma. Yet one cannot turn back knowledge any more than one can time, one cannot shape what is past any more than one can what is to come.

With my microscopes and my petri dishes, my ultrasound scanner and my pulse oximeter, I was a wise man for whom nothing was beyond the bounds of possibility.

And that was my undoing.

◆

It was never easy telling a man he failed to measure up: when the shortcoming concerned what his ego considered to be the purpose of his life, it was all the more difficult. Some men cried openly, others sat stunned as if they had just had a death sentence passed upon them. A few became angry with me, with their god, with the sheer bloody bad luck of it. Strangely, very few demanded a reassessment of the results. If it was their heart or lungs I had been doubting, their kidneys or their pancreas, they would have screamed for a second opinion, criticized my competence, judgement, suitability for the job at hand. Yet they did not. The cause was never doubted, only the effect.

Brian accepted my news stoically and Larry was sympathetic: my examination of her had shown no adverse conditions. The common problems of infective damage created by chlamydia or the scarring of the Fallopian tubes causing the destruction of the cilia which waft the eggs down the tube were absent.

I explained the next step was to obtain some oöcytes – eggs – from Larry for *in vitro* fertilization, returning them to her and hoping nature subsequently might run its course.

Handing Larry a calendar chart, we worked out when day 21 of her menstrual cycle would fall and I prescribed then supplied her with buserelin, a luteinising hormone releasing hormone, in the form of a nasal spray.

'What if I get a cold?' she enquired.

'You don't have to sniff it in,' I advised her. 'Just squirt it up your nostril and pinch your nose. Don't sneeze for a minute or two. The hormone is quickly absorbed through the nasal lining and it shouldn't give any serious discomfort.'

'And if I get a cold,' Brian said, 'I guess I'd best not mix it up with a Vick's decongestant. One blast of that and I'll grow breasts and walk with a mince.'

He grinned at his joke and we laughed. Yet I could tell he was still trying to come to terms with his perceived inadequacy.

Upon day 1 of the next cycle, Larry visited me on her own and I administered the first FSH injection, a follicle stimulating hormone called Metrodin. It is derived from the menopausal urine of Italian nuns and is a major source of income for many a rural convent, a fact I find both obscene and hilarious. This done, I taught Larry how to inject herself: the shots needed to be taken twice daily for a week.

Removing an orange from a stainless steel kidney dish, I said, 'Now, this is how you inject yourself,' and I started to press the hypodermic needle through the skin. 'There is a resistance in your epidermis which you . . . '

'I'm not a citrus fruit,' she interrupted, smiling grimly, 'and I'm not squeamish. Just show me where to stick it in.'

Admiring her, I demonstrated a subcutaneous injection on myself then presented her with a box of measured doses in phials with a supply of needles and syringes.

'I feel like a junkie,' she remarked as she placed them in her capacious leather handbag.

'Let's hope,' I said, 'we can give you the right fix, then.'

On day 8, she returned in the late morning and I conducted an ultrasound scan of her ovaries, took a blood sample and gave her a 6000IU injection of oestradiol.

'How do things look?' Larry asked as she sat in the recovery room, a blanket up to her neck and a cup of tea at her side.

'Very good,' I reported. 'You have five follicles in one ovary and four in the other. They're all between ten and fourteen millimetres in diameter so we seem to be on course.'

She reached for my hand. Her fingers were cool and smooth. She pressed my hand to her lips and kissed it. I was not surprised. This was not the first time a woman had kissed me under such circumstances, not the first to see a vague, temporary love shining through the mists of tears or sedation. For a short while, I was their man. I had delved in their most private places, looked closely at what made them women and was not, therefore, taken aback by their reactions. After all, I had gone farther into their bodies, into their psyches, than ever their husbands could.

For a short time, I was their god and, until Larry came along, I was content in my temporary deification: but she changed me, or the circumstances of my association with her changed me. For that I can never forgive her although it was not her fault, just nemesis turning its wicked drum.

Another scan on day 12 showed nine follicles, six of them mature at between 18 and 21mm in diameter. The criteria for oöcyte collection being attained at 3 mature follicles, I administered a subcutaneous injection of 5000IUs of HCG, human chorionic gonadotrophin, and started the clock running for 36 hours.

◆

About three kilometres from the clearing is a waterfall. It is not a grand affair like the Iguassú or Ñacunday Falls, kilometres wide with white torrents plunging in steps thirty metres high. The water drops a mere fifteen or so metres on a front of not more than three hundred metres: and it is not virginal white but tanned with mud and punctuated with forest flotsam. Nevertheless, Chuhi refers to it as *el humo* – the smoke.

The track to the fall follows the river. It is one of the few permanent thoroughfares in the forest for the men of the clearing use it to gain access to the next native settlement twelve kilometres above the fall or take it to reach further into the forest for hunting. The women go this way to a clear spring from which they draw our drinking water and, half-way to the fall, there is a rocky outcrop from which the people sometimes fish.

For the first five hundred metres, the way runs parallel to the bank but some distance in from it, weaving through the green twilight between the boles of the trees. It looks idyllic, a pathway through paradise, but every hectare of forest is a microcosm of the whole world, rich with exquisite beauty and wonder, alert with impeccable pain and death. Even the benign, all-sheltering trees hold their own peculiar dangers. The *tucumá* palm trunks are ringed with vicious spines, inches long; closer to the river are a number of *pau dẻ novato*, novice trees, the domain of vicious stinging ants which are the trees' guardians.

I go to the falls once or twice a week. It is my means of taking exercise and, as soon as I leave the clearing, am unlikely to meet another human except in passing or at the rocky outcrop where the men may be gathered with their fishing spears. This solitude is precious to me.

At every step, something remarkable catches the eye. A grey mottled tree frog hugs a twig; a rhinoceros beetle waddles through leaf debris like a miniature dinosaur; a bizarre caterpillar bedecked in orange hairs loops up a stem; an emerald grasshopper, the exact shape of the leaf upon which it squats, moves to give away its presence; a brilliant canary yellow and jet black poison arrow frog hops from a rock; a ten-centimetre flatworm slides over the moist surface of a huge petal. Here, nature is either small and immaculate or gigantic and arrogant.

At the fall, I sit upon a particular rock which juts out into the water, a worn hollow in it giving me a comfortable seat. If the breeze is strong, it occasionally carries an invisible, cool mist over me but, being in the sunlight for much of the day and therefore hot and dry, I am not pestered by gunpowder ticks, leeches or ants. Even better, there are no flies, the *humo* deterring them.

Sometimes, I absent-mindedly watch the silver flick of fish, become mesmerized by the wings of butterflies shimmering as they gather to drink from the mud bank downstream of the rock, captivated by the white-winged swallows on their mid-river perch upon a log stump or amused by the bizarre, prehistoric design of an *hoatzin* perched clumsily on a bough.

So it is on the better days. At other times, I spurn all creation under the dancing sunlight and the bright scar of sky, concentrating instead upon the dark shadows between the tree trunks, under the vast leaves, beneath the rocks. And in my own soul.

At one point, near the outcrop, the track divides. One way goes along a narrow creek at the head of which is an area of huge boulders covered in mosses and undergrowth: once there, it turns back to the main pathway. The other keeps to the river bank crossing the creek where it enters the river by means of a small, swaying bridge made of entwined creepers and a length of scarlet plastic rope.

Despite my fear of falling from the bridge, I rarely take the boulder route. There was a time I kept to it but, now, this is out of the question. I do not want to see any ghosts, gliding in the trees or slipping their torment into my mind.

◆

As I scrubbed up, Angela switched on the theatre equipment and arranged all the tools of my trade to one side of the operating table while Roger, my anaesthetist, readied his own machinery and drugs.

We did not have to prepare ourselves as if undertaking major, invasive surgery: I wore a theatre gown but Angela remained in her uniform, Roger merely removing his jacket and donning a rubber apron. Of course, we all wore gloves but there was no need to cover our hair or mask our faces. When all was set, Larry entered dressed in a light blue cotton smock-like gown and lay upon the black slab of the table. Angela gently parted her legs and placed them in the raised chromium-plated stirrups.

Larry did not speak: it is surprising how seldom patients talk at this juncture. One would think they would chatter to disguise their embarrassment, the indignity of it, the fear every woman has of being so blatantly exposed, but they do not.

Roger inserted an intravenous drip into Larry's arm and placed the Ohmeda pulse oximeter clip on the middle finger of her left hand. The ECG pick-ups were attached by small suction cups lubricated with a transmitting gel.

'We are going to sedate you,' Roger said, his voice soft and calm: one would never think he played rugby for the Barbarians. 'You won't go to sleep. In fact, you'll be conscious throughout but you won't remember anything afterwards. I'll also give you a pain-killer although this is more of a precaution than a necessity.'

I watched as he began the flow of Propafol and Alfentinil, his eyes moving from the drip to the digital read-outs on the pulse oximeter and the oscilloscope on the ECG. After a short while, he nodded to me.

Whilst I inserted a speculum into Larry's vagina, Angela placed the rubber sheath around the ultrasound scanner and coated it with some of the transmitting gel. Next, I tore open the sterile packaging on the Steri-reel stainless steel guide and attached it to the probe, carefully aligning the aspirating needle and attached catheter in it.

'Larry,' I said quietly, 'we're going to start now. You may feel a little discomfort. If you feel any pain, just let us know.'

'Yes,' she replied distantly, like a person in a deep reverie, 'I'll do that.'

In reality the human body does not look as it appears in medical books: outside of pregnancy, the uterus is not a vast cavity but a mere channel, the sides of which are kept apart only by a thin film of mucus, and the ovaries do not hang free in the body cavity like bizarre, pendulous fruits but hug the wall of the vagina. To recover oöcytes is, therefore, relatively simple unless there are unforeseen complications. It merely requires piercing the vaginal wall with a needle, flushing out the contents of each follicle and that is more or less it. Very little bleeding occurs, no intrusive action is taken into the body and the whole process takes only a matter of minutes by a skilled gynaecologist.

I slipped the scanner through the speculum and studied the screen on my right. In the monochrome picture, liquid shows up as black, tissue as white. Moving the probe forward, as if I was flying a tiny aircraft by radar into the skies of Larry's body, I saw the first mature follicle. Carefully manoeuvring the needle to the vagina wall, I pierced it and entered the follicle. Checking the pressure on the read-out to be 100mm of mercury and ascertaining again the Spül-Automatik auto-flushing system was set to meter out exactly 3.6ml of HAMS F10 as an aspirant, I pressed my shoe against a foot switch. The electronic aspirator pump hummed and clicked. A blackness appeared on the screen then disappeared. A small glass container on the pump filled with a pinkish liquid.

None of us spoke. Angela removed the container and passed it through a hatch into the laboratory. I saw Phillips' hand reach out and take it. We waited. Twenty seconds passed like half an hour before his head appeared at the hatch.

'Positive,' he reported.

Extracting the needle, I shifted the scanner probe and located the next follicle, repeating the process over again. In just under three quarters of an hour, I had aspirated all six mature follicles: only the third and largest caused a problem and had to be flushed out three times before we managed to collect the oöcyte.

I stood up, wriggled my legs and eased my back as Angela took Larry to the recovery room. Although I sat throughout the procedure on a low stool and did not have to crouch to operate, I still ached in every muscle. It was the tension of the work which caused it, the excitement I always felt when embarking upon a journey into human tissue.

In my office, I sat behind my desk and waited, a cup of Kenyan coffee steaming before me. In a quarter of an hour, the internal telephone rang.

'We've graded the eggs, sir,' Phillips' voice said. 'Three are 1 or 2A, but the rest are 3.'

'Destroy the 3s,' I instructed him unnecessarily, 'and I'll be down in twenty minutes.'

Larry was sitting up in the recovery room, perched upon a large, soft cushion with a colourful mug of tea in her hand. She smiled weakly as I came in.

'How was I?' she asked.

'Perfect,' I replied, 'and your body has behaved itself immaculately. We have three top-notch eggs and, all being well with Brian's sperm, we'll be ready to transfer all of them to you in a day or two. I'll be in touch.'

For the rest of the morning, I attended to my correspondence, fielded a call from the abominable Frenchwoman then, at noon, I walked to my favourite restaurant, ate a light lunch of poached salmon with a glass of Vouvray followed by a *crème brûlée* and Turkish coffee, returning to the surgery just after two o'clock.

In the laboratory Phillips and his two underlings were busy with test-tubes and spectroscopic microscopes.

'Are we ready?' I asked.

He looked at his watch. 'We've had four hours,' he responded then beckoned to Janet, his senior assistant, who opened the freezer and removed a straw of Brian's sperm, checking its identity by a row of dots placed upon the plastic.

Whilst the sperm was thawed, I studied the oöcytes. There appeared to be no abnormalities.

At the next microscope bench, Phillips grunted. My nerves steeled. When he grunted it could mean intense pleasure but also deep disappointment.

'How are they?' I enquired.

'Not as good as they might be,' he replied.

He swung round the ground-glass viewing screen on the top of his microscope. It was full of spermatozoa but only approximately a third of them were active, wriggling and threshing their tails. The rest were immotile or moved very sluggishly and were not at all promising. A successful spermatozoon has to be strong enough not only to swim towards an oöcyte but to penetrate its outer layers; no mean feat despite the pointed head.

'How many straws have we?' I asked.

Janet checked her records and said, 'Just four.'

'Are we doing the usual three oöcytes, sir?' Phillips asked.

I nodded and said, 'All three of them.'

Phillips grimaced and Janet retrieved the three straws which were thawed. One contained hardly any motile spermatozoa, but the others were like the first.

'We'll have to use all the available sperm,' Phillips commented.

I nodded. It was not an ideal situation: it was always best to have some in reserve in case of a mishap but we were, in my opinion, left with no alternative.

We put the sperm and oöcytes together at four o'clock in the afternoon and set the laboratory digital countdown alarm at 18 hours. The next morning, we inspected the oöcytes: I was afraid the sperm would not be up to the job or, as sometimes happened, we might find an aberrant cell but all three contained the normal two pronuclei. The sperm had seemingly succeeded against the odds and what I saw down the microscope were no longer oöcytes but embryos.

It is possible for cells to divide parthenogenically for two or three cell divisions so, although I called Larry and requested she come in for embryo transfer the following afternoon, I kept an eye on them. The process of cell division is slow at first. Forty-eight hours from fertilization there may be only four or eight cells in each embryo: at six days, the embryo will be thousands of cells in size and have become a blastocyst. Yet there was no cause for concern. I felt certain these embryos were dividing as a result of fertilization and, looking at them the next day, my confidence was justified for each embryo contained at least sixteen cells.

Larry arrived punctually for the embryo transfer operation and came into the theatre. She looked around herself as if this was her first visit, her eye moving across the scanner, the pulse oximeter, the ventilator, endoscopic endolight and steel flasks of oxygen and nitrogen dioxide.

'I don't recall any of this from the last time,' she remarked.

'You were sedated,' I told her. 'You saw it all but you won't have a memory of it.'

She lay on the table and Angela helped her put her legs in the stirrups.

'We don't sedate you this time,' I said, slipping on a pair of surgical gloves. 'You'll feel no pain and little if any discomfort.' I held up the equipment I was going to use. 'All I shall be doing is inserting this fine plastic catheter through your cervix, then injecting down it into the uterus using this small syringe. It's little different from the type used by diabetics for their insulin shots. I shall be doing this three times as we are to implant three embryos. All of your eggs have fertilized satisfactorily. The whole business won't take ten minutes.'

Phillips passed the first embryo to me in a catheter. I injected this into Larry and he then checked the catheter under a microscope to ensure the egg was successfully transferred. It was. The other two went in as smoothly. I gave Larry an injection of 2000IUs of HCG and helped her to sit up on the edge of the table.

'That's it,' I said. 'With a bit of luck you're pregnant. We'll know in a fortnight when you take an ordinary proprietary pregnancy test.'

Angela leaned over to have me sign the necessary paper-work. When I looked back, Larry was crying. Tears were streaming down her face, dripping on to the cotton gown where they formed dark marks in the light blue material. Her hands were demurely folded in her lap: I wondered if this was somehow symbolic, as if she was trying to hold her minuscule would-be infant in place.

'Thank you, Dom,' she whispered huskily then, deciding perhaps to risk it, she put her hands to her face and began to shake with weeping.

◆

The other morning, as I made my way back from the waterfall, I came upon a group of children from the clearing. Aged between four and ten, they were playing in a shallow pool just upstream from the rock outcrop. A dozen or so splashed about and one tried to swim, whilst a group of boys engaged themselves in floating a piece of wood on the current, trying to hit it by throwing hard fruit cases at it.

I stepped behind a palm trunk and, unknown to them, observed their play. There is something unfathomably beautiful yet at the same time utterly terrifying about a company of children: they exhibit such pristine innocence yet this can change in a split second into an awesome display of primeval violence.

The ringleader of the fruit-throwers scored a direct hit on the wood. He whooped with pleasure at his prowess and spun round, his arms outstretched to invite approbation. His fellows shouted their congratulations: his face aglow with pleasure, the leader turned again to hurl another missile.

At this moment the swimmer, a boy of about six, turned in the water and splashed with his feet. The wood target was pushed out into the faster currents, whipped round and started to vanish. The hurled fruit case missed.

For a moment there was silence. The ringleader then shouted something in a high-pitched voice, redolent with anger. He pointed at the swimmer, who was now standing up to his waist in the river, a crestfallen, anxious look in his eyes. His every cell seemed cowed, afraid. The boys dropped their ammunition of fruit cases and started to close upon the swimmer who cringed down towards the water, raising his

31

arms ineffectually before him. The others encircled him and the ringleader, pressing his hands on the swimmer's head, thrust him below the surface. I mentally counted to five. Still the boy was under the water and the rest of the children were crowding round, shouting and yelling. The instinct of the pack was upon them and the god of innocence had abandoned them.

At the count of ten, fearing the child might drown, I stepped out from my hiding place and went quickly down the path to the pool. For a moment, my appearance had no effect: the boy was still under the water, his arms threshing to rise. Then a girl on the edge of the crowd saw me. She said nothing but she nevertheless transmitted my presence to the others, the clamour and shouts quickly subsiding. The child under the water rose gasping and heaving for air.

The ringleader stared at me. I carried on down towards the pool. As I approached, the children drew back towards the outcrop, moving closer together. My arrival cemented a common bond of fear. They were no longer two dozen frolicking children picking on a weakling but a single unit facing a shared fear. I reached the bank and stood on the edge of the muddy sand.

'¡No!' I remonstrated. '¡Es malo!' I mimicked ducking the boy and shook my head. '¡No! Debe respirar.'

The children stared at me. I was reminded of how animals follow a passing predator with their eyes transfixed on it.

Suddenly, the leader shouted. He was looking straight at me but he was addressing his companions. '¡Es él que escucha a los espectros!' he yelled.

There was a tense moment, then all the children whirled round and fled screaming for the outcrop, churning up the water with their little legs, small fish leaping free of the surface to avoid them. They reached the rocks, scrambled out of the river and disappeared shouting towards the clearing. The jungle soon stifled their cries.

I stood alone. For those few moments, I was their bogey-man and wondered if perhaps their parents sometimes used me as a threat to ensure compliant behaviour. I could readily imagine one of the old women, exasperated by a lively child, warning it of me. *Beware*, she must say, *eat your food* or *go to sleep* or *stop your noise* or somesuch *lest the one with the white coat who listens to ghosts will come and get you.*

◆

In the second month of Larry's pregnancy, I was invited to spend the weekend at Harbury. I drove down on the Saturday afternoon, the motorway busy with holiday-makers heading back from the channel ports, their roof-racks laden with suitcases covered in plastic sheeting, caravans towed behind cars too under-powered or too old for the task. The further I drove from London the less busy and wide became the roads, the last ten or so miles of my journey being on side roads and in country lanes. I had to stop three times to check the rough map Larry had sent me. It was not until seven o'clock on a glorious evening, the sun warm and still high, the air cooling in the shadows and alert with midges dancing in a column just in front of the car, their infinitesimal bodies catching the sunlight, that I swung the Porsche in through their gate and switched the engine off.

Dell Cottage was much as I had expected with a trim lawn, tidy beds of standard rose bushes, a small paved patio beside which was a barbecue made of bricks and a modern garage tucked away behind a hedge of conifers. Upon the grey stone wall by the door grew a dense wistaria.

Larry came out to greet me as I pulled my overnight bag from the space behind the seats. She looked admir-ingly at the car and ran her finger along the curve of the roof. It was painted black with a custom-made grey leather interior.

'It's rather swish. It's what Brian calls a CC.'

I thought for a moment. 'Consular corps? Only Saudi diplomats have Porsches.'

'No,' she corrected me. 'Consultants' Car.'

There was no resentment in her words. She was not envious of my German speedster although, I thought as I closed the door, should the pregnancy fail to go full term, she might develop the rancour which childless couples nurture in middle age, foster with as much care as they would have lavished on a child and often do lavish upon the surrogate, a King Charles spaniel or a Siamese cat.

'Brian's out,' Larry said as she led me through the house. 'Emergency treatment . . .'

The sitting-room was cool and dark, beams lining the ceiling, the floors flagged. Across the far end was a vast fireplace surrounded by deep settees and armchairs. The staircase was made of stone, the narrow steps polished by aeons of climbing feet. Half-way up, as the stairway turned, I had to duck to avoid striking a beam.

'How old is the house?' I enquired.

'About 1720. It was three cottages but they were knocked into one at the turn of the century. By the local doctor, as it happens. It was thatched originally. We've a picture . . . ' She pointed to a sepia photograph of the house in an oak frame. The roof was thatched and, by the door, stood a dumpy woman in an Edwardian matron's dress. By her side was a nondescript black dog and a small boy in a sailor suit. 'The doctor's wife and son,' Larry said. I sensed a tiny pull on the last word.

'Well,' I said, 'I'd rather not bring Mrs Macawber there back to life, nor her hell hound, but . . . '

There was no need to say more. Larry understood and I wondered how often she had passed the photo and had exactly the same thought.

'I'll show you your room,' she half-whispered and took my hand.

It was a large bedroom with a substantial double bed, a pine dressing-table and wardrobe. I dropped my bag on the floor by the bed and gazed out of the window. The gardens were trim and classical: the flower beds were edged, the lawn mown in stripes, the apple trees heavy with fruit. Beside a thatched summer-house, swallows dipped over a small pond in the centre of which a fish was rising to take insects. Beyond a low line of box was a neat vegetable and herb garden, whilst over the beech and hazel boundary hedge at the far end of the property was an open pasture with several Jersey cows lying in it. It was, I thought, the garden of a woman with time or longing on her hands.

We ate alfresco that evening, Brian cooking steaks over the barbecue. The dessert was a concoction of bananas, chocolate and orange curaçao cooked over the fire and flambéd with brandy.

'If you're as good a dentist as you are a chef,' I remarked, 'you should be in private practice.'

'Possibly,' he replied, 'but then I'd have to live in London to make the big money, commute, join the Friday race down and Monday crawl back. I wanted a quiet place, a quiet practice and a still peace in the evenings.'

The sun was down below the horizon. Some way off rooks cawed as they settled in a tall stand of elms. In the field, a cow lowed intermittently.

'Mind you,' he continued, 'dentistry can be boring. Same old problems day after day: a filling here, a polish there, Mrs Grumble's dentures or Mr Groan's crown. I'm not complaining but there are days when I celebrate an abscess.'

'All the more reason for going private,' I declared. 'Get paid well for the boredom. A filling in a rock star's mouth is more exciting than a farmer's abscessed maw.' I looked into the sky. High overhead, against the washed light, two V formations of gulls headed westwards. An owl hooted across the fields.

'What are the chances, Dom?' He spoke quietly, in the way people whisper in churches, afraid that, by asking, he might be tempting fate.

'As you'll know from my pamphlet, about the same as in nature. Thirty per cent of IVF patients get pregnant at the first attempt, twenty-five per cent go full term. Twelve per cent miscarry, usually in the first twelve weeks. Where the statistics are loaded against you – or for you, depending on your point of view – lies in the fact you've a one in four chance of twins and one in twenty-five of triplets. Wheeling a three-seat baby buggy through the supermarket is a bit of a chore.'

Larry appeared, a blue angora sweater draped about her shoulders, carrying a tray with a pot of coffee, cups, brandy glasses and a bottle of cognac balanced upon it.

'Why did you go into fertility work?' Larry enquired as she poured the coffee.

'I suppose I found – I find – it interesting,' I replied. 'And it's rewarding. Not just financially. It's pleasing to see a healthy baby as a result of my work, especially rewarding to deliver a baby after cycles of trying. It's like backing an outsider in the Derby and watching it romp past the post.'

'Surely it's more than just pleasure at beating the odds?' Larry scolded me.

'Of course. There's also the satisfaction of knowing I've beaten nature. Loaded the dice of life.'

'There are some,' Brian remarked, handing me a brandy, 'who would say you're playing craps with God.'

'And they may be right,' I allowed. I had heard this argument before and it pleased me for, yes, it was true. I was competing with God, and I was winning.

A handsome tabby cat appeared padding across the lawn. It paused to study a blackbird then made straight for Larry's chair, jumping up to squirm itself into her lap.

'This is Napoleon,' Larry said, stroking the cat. 'Say hello to Dom, Napoleon.' The cat took not the least notice of me and curled its tail against its side, the tip twitching.

'There's more to it than winning against the odds, or rigging the game,' I went on, warming the balloon of brandy in my hands. 'My work has me living on the boundaries of the last mystery of humanity.'

'What do you mean, the last human mystery?' Brian asked.

'What I say,' I continued. 'We've conquered leprosy, TB, cholera, bubonic plague and eliminated smallpox. We're still hunting down cancer, motor neurone disease and so on: it's only a matter of time. But we know virtually nothing of the mechanisms of creation.'

'What of genetics?' Brian argued.

'True,' I concurred, 'but we've only scratched the surface. The human genome is being mapped, discoveries being made monthly: for example, the genetic fault which causes cystic fibrosis has been virtually identified. It's known to be on chromosome 7. But that's minute compared to the complete strand of DNA.

'As for the actual processes, we know precious little. We understand the sperm swims up the Fallopian tube and fertilizes the egg, lodges on the uterus wall and placental tissue begins to form. But what chemical signals give the instructions to the egg cells to divide? Does the sperm carry a signal? Perhaps. But eggs will divide on their own accord if artificially pierced. As for foetal development . . . ' I sensed I was getting carried away but felt I needed to tell them. It was not a matter of justifying myself but of explaining the drive in my life.

'Brian,' I carried on, 'you see teeth every day. What's new about them? Very little. There are developments in dentistry, new technology, new materials to plug holes, cosmeticize crowns. But that's about it. Now I see vaginas and uteruses every day, testicles and penises. Basically, when you've seen one uterus you've seen them all just as a molar is a molar. It may be damaged or diseased, just as your molar might be but you have only three recourses. Fill it or crown it or pull it. And nothing new to learn. But in every uterus complex chemical actions are going on, hormonal influences I cannot guess at. And I want to know . . . ' I fell silent. Against the night sky, I saw a bat flicker.

'Why have you never married, Dom?' Larry asked, changing the subject. 'Has your job ruined you for . . . '

I laughed quietly and sipped my brandy. I knew exactly what she was thinking: I had often been asked the question and behind it had been the same query. It had been assumed my quest for the mystery of life, looking at the sexual organs of women every day, had removed the mystery of sex and love.

'No, nothing to do with the job,' I told her. 'Not directly. After all, Brian still kisses you after a day prodding about in other people's mouths. I suppose I'm a bachelor because I've grown accustomed to it. I like my town house, my Porsche, my holidays in the Virgin Islands, my Yves Saint Laurent shirts and Savile Row suits, enjoy being . . . ' I searched for the appropriate word, ' . . . unencumbered. Besides, I don't believe I'd make a good husband.'

Larry stood up, the cat falling to the patio and looking up at her with a belligerent, dismissive stare. 'I think you're totally wrong,' she declared. 'You'd make a super husband. You understand women.'

'So do hairdressers,' I retorted. 'Would you marry one of them?'

'You know what I mean,' Larry replied. 'You know what makes a woman tick.'

I laughed loudly and finished my brandy. 'No, I do not understand women,' I said. 'I comprehend how their bodies work, at least the reproductive bits, but I have not the merest inkling of how their minds operate.'

'That,' Brian announced, grinning broadly, 'may be the greatest mystery of all.'

Later, as I helped clear away the dishes, Larry remarked quietly, 'We owe you so much.'

'You owe me nothing,' I insisted. 'I've done my job and you've paid me for it.'

She gazed down the garden, dark in the early night. Her cheeks were lit up by a sudden lick of flame from the dying charcoal on the barbecue. 'We both feel you've been a friend for years,' she said.

◆

Some way down river from the clearing is a range of low hills in the jungle. The loftiest summit is not one hundred and fifty metres above the water and the slopes, though quite steep, are covered in dense forest. A path wends its way up the highest hill from the river bank and is, like that to the falls, kept open by the men of the clearing. As most pathways do, it gives access for hunting, but there is another reason for the route: it leads to the old tribal cemetery.

Nowadays, when one of their number dies, the people of the clearing give the corpse a vaguely Christian burial. It is wrapped in a shroud of either cloth or bark, according to the supply of either material at the time, interred in a grave dug in the earth and a wooden cross, which rots to dust in less than a year, is placed at the head of the tomb. No prayers are offered nor hymns sung and the interment, in the jungle, is soon forgotten and never revisited.

However, not many decades ago, the dead were given a traditional ceremony at which large quantities of *masato*, a foul-smelling home-brewed beer, was consumed and coca leaves chewed in the presence of the festering cadaver. At the height of the ceremony, amidst dances and chanting, the body was taken to this hill and placed upon a natural rock ledge. Dressed in a finery of beads and feathers, snake or animal skins, it was left to decay. Needless to say, red-headed turkeys and yellow-headed vultures were quick to arrive on the scene, soon to be followed by king vultures and, if there was much left over from their feast, black-collared hawks. Perhaps a jaguar joined in the bounty. The flesh mostly consumed, ants and beetles, small lizards and fly larvæ finished off the remains until, in less than a month, all that was left was a disjointed collection of bones as clean and as odourless as a laboratory skeleton.

From time to time, I go to this funerary hill. The people of the clearing always seem to go by boat, landing near the hill on a wide meander but I, lacking the skill of handling a dug-out canoe and fearful of the off-chance of being seen, take a lesser-used route through the forest.

I am no longer afraid of the jungle. I am beyond fear now. There are many dangers, most of them caused by near-invisible reptiles or totally invisible bacteria, but I have grown inured to them. My only real fear is of being discovered.

The walk to the hill takes about three hours. I am obliged to carry a pocket compass and a razor-edged machete for the path often disappears and I have either to reinstate it or cut a new way through. The journey is also made with a cheap plastic cigarette lighter presented to me by Dr Suarez. Although I am not a smoker, the item is essential jungle equipment for it is the only effective means by which one may remove the ticks and leeches which climb up one's legs or attach themselves in the briefest of moments as one brushes against a leaf.

At the foot of the hill, I pause and drink from my water bottle. Despite the humidity in the jungle, one rapidly gets thirsty and it is essential to maintain a high level of body fluids. I know this as a doctor: so too does Chuhi who, on a long journey, refrains from urinating in order to keep his liquid content high.

My drinking over, I set off up the pathway from the river. It does not go straight up the hill, but twists and turns between the boles of the trees, passing displays of bizarre fungi shaped as if born from the mind of a horror fiction writer. Many of them, despite a macabre beauty, give off the most evil stench. Two, in particular, are obscenely noxious: one is constructed like a dome of scarlet netting whilst the other, as if to mock my profession, is shaped very much like a tumescent human penis. The unsightly presence of the fungi is annulled by the exquisite blossoms which flower everywhere. Vivid yellow stars sprout from dull-looking lianas, peach-coloured trumpets with fluted outer petals stand out from thick, scaled pods whilst epiphytic lilac orchids hang like artificial waxed blooms from the twigs of the trees.

Sitting with the sun overhead, sharing the stone ledge with a few splinters of bone and the ghosts of generations of forest people, I let my mind wander over my own brief history, more especially the last decade or so.

And it is then I think of Ruth and the pathway she set me upon.

◆

Thomas Arkassian ran his obstetrics practice from an opulent third floor apartment in Boscobel Place, Belgravia. An Armenian by birth and in his mid-fifties, he was a dapper, immaculately dressed man of impeccable taste. His surgery was more like an art collector's salon than a doctor's work place. Abstracts by Polyakov and Malevich, Kandinsky and Lanskoy hung in reception whilst, in his consulting room, a huge canvas by Arshile Gorky filled the wall behind his desk: like most *émigrés*, he needed something to remind him of home, no matter how far away it was or impossible his return there. Even his lavishly equipped operating theatre had a Braque view of a harbour and boats mounted above the instrument table, protected by a perspex box for the sake of sterility. The furniture was modernistic, his desk made of chromium plated steel and perspex, the chairs sumptuously deep and crafted in white, tooled leather.

From time to time, we referred cases to each other. Thomas' reputation was considerable and his sending clients to me enhanced my own standing whilst my passing on patients to him spread the word I was associated with this doyen of high society doctors.

In keeping with his high profile, Thomas and his wife entertained frequently. Marie Arkassian was at least half her husband's age, the fourth of his wives, all of whom had been as exotic as himself: Marie was part Swedish, part French and part Japanese, Sorbonne educated and endowed with the sort of looks women would kill for. She was taller than Thomas, thin and agile but not scrawny in the way of fashion. Her skin was smooth and lightly tanned, her hair dark brown and tressed to her shoulders. His pet name for her was Modi and, indeed, she had the calm, sensuous air of beauty to be found in the better of Modigliani's portraits: she reminded me of the artist's *Seated Nude* in the National Museum at Antwerp.

An invitation to an Arkassian party was not to be turned down. Unlike me, he did not live above his practice but owned a town house overlooking the Thames at Richmond. The interior was quite unlike his surgery. Here were no Russian abstracts: the drawing-room contained water-colours by Turner and John Crome, oils by Constable and sketches by Gainsborough, eighteenth-century furniture and Axminster carpets. Only the sitting-room which gave on to a terrace and short garden leading down to the river, contained modern works and then these were all British – Graham Sutherland, Paul Nash, Ceri Richards and two sculptured compositions by Henry Moore, one in bronze, the other Cumberland alabaster. It was as if, at work, he was still the immigrant made good but, at home, he was the Englishman he had grown to become.

The guest list for a party was as catholic as the host's artistic tastes ranging from pot-smoking rock singers to merchant bankers, artists to models, explorers to engineers. The provision of food and drink was fabled throughout London, even in those selfish, party-going times: Beluga caviar, sterling silver buckets of chilled Bollinger and Montrachet, porcelain bowls of peeled quails' eggs, oval platters of smoked salmon or minuscule tandoori-pickled octopi and ice-filled tureens of Irish oysters.

I enjoyed these bacchanals. They usually began late on a Sunday morning, after Thomas returned from the Russian Orthodox church he attended, and ended early on Monday. Some continued after he had departed for his surgery, his wife being left responsible for politely ejecting those who had outstayed their welcome.

The people I met there fascinated me. It was not just a matter of becoming acquainted with them and widening my own social circle but also of observing them, of watching how the human animal behaved when the strictures of morality or propriety were removed. Over the years, I saw Tory cabinet ministers cuddle petite pop singers (and share their joints and later, no doubt, their beds), lithe models and fat entrepreneurs play strip poker with the latter always losing, a very famous artist draw the portrait of an equally well-known film star's pet Vietnamese pig and, on one occasion, I observed a noted London madam, tipsy as a Turk, smoke a Gitanes cigarette with her vagina, blowing smoke rings through the labia by the rapid contraction of her abdominal muscles. Being fairly drunk myself, I asked her to restrict her future consumption to filter-tips as a precaution against cervical cancer: my recommendation, of which I was subsequently ashamed when informed of it, was greeted with peals of laughter.

It was at an evening party Thomas gave to celebrate Guy Fawkes' Night I first met Ruth.

The guests arrived at just before seven, to be welcomed by Thomas dressed in seventeenth-century costume, his wife decked out as a serving wench in a full skirt and flounced blouse with her bosoms pressed high in a Victorian stiffened brassière. Waitresses, all of them blonde Scandinavians and dressed like their mistress, served hot buttered rum in mugs. We were guided on to the terrace and stood about in a chill damp wind until a quarter past seven when a barge moored in the river erupted into light and we were treated to a grandiose and most impressive fireworks display. The last Roman Candle extinguished and the final Catherine Wheel reduced to a spinning disk of charred wood, we were ushered indoors to a superb stand-up banquet of roast goose, wild boar and ptarmigan. I positioned myself in the drawing-room and sat on a long settee, my plate and glass of champagne on a low table before me. I had just begun to eat when Thomas approached.

'Dear Dom,' he said cheerily, 'what did you think of the fireworks?'

I made no effort to reply: Thomas never let a simple sentence go without embellishing upon it and never asked a rhetorical question without immediately supplying the answer.

'They were magnificent, were they not?' He went on, 'And the incredible thing is, the *maître de feu*, or whatever one would call a pyrotechnician in polite circles, is a public schoolmaster! And, to top it all, a priest! What irony, eh? A man of the cloth who dabbles in the arcane sciences of hell. An alchemist of our modern times.' He chuckled in his characteristic manner. 'A charming man whom you must meet. He'll be along soon. In the meantime, I have someone else I wish you to talk with.'

He became suddenly quite serious and sat in a chair opposite the settee. I wondered if he was going to pass on to me a particularly sensitive patient although we had always kept business out of our socializing.

'Not a patient,' he said, reading my thoughts, 'but a professional who seeks our advice. Or, more especially, yours. I'm afraid I can't be of much assistance.'

It was not unknown for either of us to be approached by people hunting information. Only the week before, a producer had contacted me to request details of the procedure for embryo transfer which he required for the making of a medical drama movie.

'I don't see what I can have you don't,' I replied.

'Skill, Dom. You are the IVF man whilst I am not. Now, wait here with your food and I will fetch . . . '

The door to the dining-room opened, a hubbub of conversation bursting through, and a young woman entered. She was of average height, dressed in a plain black skirt and an embroidered blouse under a cashmere sweater. Her blonde hair was cut short and curled in at her neck.

'Ruth!' Thomas called, rising from his seat and turning to wink at me. 'She's pretty, wouldn't you say? A very pretty girl.'

She crossed the room and slid her plate on to the table next to mine. Noticing she did not have a drink, I courteously rose to my feet.

'Ruth, let me introduce you to Dr Dominic Lyall. But call him Dom. He's the man you want. Dom, this is Ruth Schroeder. Also doctor.'

'How do you do,' I said and shook her hand.

The skin of her palm was surprisingly hard and I wondered if she was a musician: I had only a few minutes earlier shaken the hand of a famous guitarist to discover his fingertips to be as callused as the sole of a bushman's foot.

'I'm fine, thank you,' was her response.

'Now,' Thomas ordered, 'you two sit down and get to know each other.'

He guided her into his chair and nodded with his chin at me. I lowered myself to the settee and picked up my glass. I was about to ask if I might fetch her a drink when Thomas observed she was without one.

'You've no bubbly, my dear,' he exclaimed. 'One cannot talk business with a handsome man like Dom unless one has.'

Not asking for her choice, he beckoned to one of the waitresses hovering at the door with a tray, placed a glass of champagne by Ruth's plate and winked at me once more before leaving us alone.

'Do you live in London?' I enquired.

'No, sort of Headington. It's a suburb of Oxford.' She spoke with a soft American inflection, not stridently confident like a New Yorker's or filled with braggadocio like a Californian's but with a lilt, the possible remnants of a Southern accent.

'And where are you from?'

'Virginia, originally. But I've lived in the UK some years now.' She picked up her fork and looked about the room. 'Tell me, are those genuine Turners?'

'Yes, they are,' I assured her. 'Thomas has rather a weak spot for nineteenth-century English painters.'

She looked around and, lowering her voice a fraction, asked, 'Is he very rich? I mean, seriously rich?'

'Yes,' I informed her, 'Thomas is seriously rich and this is only a part of it. I assume you've visited his practice?'

'No.' She shook her head. 'Is it . . . ?'

'Seriously opulent,' I confirmed, 'only there it's all Russian abstract painters. And one Armenian. Thomas is – rather, was – an Armenian.'

'I'd guessed as much from his name.'

She meticulously cut through a slice of ptarmigan, spreading a thin layer of gravy and cranberry sauce across it with her knife. She might have been a surgeon, so careful and controlled were her actions, yet her hard hands confused me. A surgeon must keep his hands supple in order to feel every nuance and condition of flesh through the barrier of surgical rubber.

'What branch of medicine are you in?' I asked.

'I'm not a medical doctor,' she replied. 'Not exactly. I have a doctorate but I was trained as an archaeologist, more precisely an archaeological primatologist. Since then I have specialized as a palaeo-biologist.' She smiled. 'It is a bit of a mouthful.'

'No more than *in vitro* fertilization gynaecologist,' I answered, returning her smile.

'I've recently been visiting a dig in Syria. It accounts for my rough hands. Creams and such aren't that much use when you're grubbing about in dirt all day. I sensed,' she added as an afterthought, 'you felt them.'

'You're very perceptive,' I complimented her.

'In my line of work, one has to be. Just as, I suspect, you are. A tiny detail in the soil, or in the flesh, can tell a complex tale or explain a quandary. I can see the corner of a flint tool the size of a fingernail in a clod of earth just as you can recognize a disease from a few damaged cells under a microscope.'

We ate our food for a minute or so. She seemed somehow reticent to volunteer any further conversation. This surprised me, for anyone whom Thomas knew or invited to a party was usually an extrovert of the first order.

'Have you known Thomas long?' I asked, trying to force a new line of communication between us.

'I've never met him before. I wrote to him to ask his advice.' She did not look at me as she spoke, as if there was some embarrassment in her admission. 'I'm not sure why, not now. I needed to talk to someone who . . . I'm not sure how to put this.' She paused, as if drawing upon some inner reserve of courage. 'I was told – I had heard – he was not averse to carrying out . . . Well, I need something doing . . . It's all a bit difficult.'

'What exactly do you mean?' I enquired.

'It's like this. I had been led to understand that . . . That Thomas has been known to . . . Well, to sail close to the medical wind. As it were.'

She was most flustered but I could not for the life of me discern why. I wondered if perhaps she required an abortion but could not believe she was unaware such an operation was comparatively easy to obtain, even under the National Health Service. There was no need to seek out a private practitioner.

'Are you perhaps,' I ventured, 'in trouble?'

She looked at me for a moment then broke into a nervous laugh as the implication of my question dawned on her. 'Oh, no! I'm not in any trouble. It's nothing like that at all.'

'So?' I rejoined quite sharply. I was finding her hesitancy somewhat annoying. 'What is it I have, and Thomas does not, which you require?'

She pushed her plate away, her food virtually untouched. 'Might we go outside? I'm a little reluctant to talk in here.'

I picked up my champagne and followed her through the sitting-room and on to the terrace. The river was black and cut with the jagged bars of light reflected from the houses opposite and the traffic crossing Richmond Bridge. The fireworks barge had heaved anchor and was gone but a small launch was making heavy way against the current, its bright green starboard light glowing like a beast's eye against the darkness of the bank.

'Do you read the scientific press, Dr Lyall?' she asked.

I leaned against the varnished wooden rail which ran

around the terrace. 'Yes, in so far as it directly affects my own discipline. Outside that, I'm afraid I don't. Life is too short to keep abreast of every development. And please,' I added, for I felt she needed putting at her ease, 'call me Dom.'

'It makes you sound rather like a monk. A holy man,' she said, smiling.

The light from the picture window to the sitting-room cast across her face. Thomas was correct: she was, I realized, quite a pretty woman. Her cheek-bones were high and her lips full without being fulsome: the skin of her hands might have been hard but her cheeks were soft. She was not what I would class as beautiful – the beautiful people were mingling in the rooms behind us – but I did find her attractive.

'I assure you,' I replied, 'I'm not a holy man. Unless you would rate gynaecology as a religion which, I have to say, some of my patients may well do. For a few of them,' I thought of the accursed Frenchwoman, 'I am a mixture of medical practitioner, father confessor and high priest.'

'And would you say you are a moral man?'

I was taken aback by her directness. All hint of her hesitancy seemed to have evaporated into the night air.

'Yes,' I said abruptly. 'I would say I am. I don't seduce my patients, I don't carry out illegal abortions, I conduct my practice strictly within the ethics of my profession and the law as laid down by the HFEA and the relevant acts of Parliament.'

'The HFEA?' she enquired.

'The Human Fertilization and Embryology Authority. The watchdog of my trade, so to speak. I don't transgress their rules.'

For a long moment, she was thoughtful. I wondered what on earth it was she had expected of me and was inclined to probe her for the information, but there was no need. She was unable not to proceed on her quest. 'May I tell you something and then put a proposal to you?' she asked.

'On the condition I'm not bound by it, you may say what you like,' I replied and I sipped my champagne.

'My area of archaeology is the study of early humans,' she began. 'It covers anything from what you would call ape men up to the Bronze Age, about 1000 years ago. Hence primatologist: I'm concerned with primates rather than just strictly humans. I'm employed at a small research laboratory near Oxford: I would rather not say which at present. It is not an archaeological research facility nor is it affiliated with the university. It is a private affair funded by a multi-national drugs company for whom we are working on a number of fronts, mostly research into possible drug treatments of diseases which have existed in men for thousands of years. For example, arthritis.'

Two other guests came on to the terrace. I saw her glance in their direction and stare for a moment at them. Turning, I saw one of the intruders on our conversation was an internationally famous baritone. They saw us and, assuming they were encroaching upon a tryst in the making, smiled and went down the steps from the terrace towards the river. When they were gone, she continued.

'For our work, we receive specimens of human tissue from all over the world. Whole Egyptian mummies, Roman skeletons, Mongolian tribesmen baked to death in the sands of the Gobi desert, Amer-indian remains: we had for a while a Danish bog person . . . Yet there is always a problem with these. The mummies have had their viscera removed and been subjected to embalming as have, on occasion, the Amer-indians. The skeletons are just that and the Mongolians are usually as desiccated as flaked coconut. The bog person we had only for a matter of weeks and it was naturally preserved with tannin. Although we learn much from these remains, we are always hampered by the effects of time or high priests.

'Recently, however, we have had the remarkable fortune to receive a complete and comparatively undamaged specimen. It is a Bronze Age man dating back to the middle Bronze Age, about 1300BC.'

'How long have you had this specimen?' I asked.

'Just a few weeks. And I have him for only another nine for

the time being, though I'll get him back at a later date. A number of institutions, those who have funded the preservation, have possession of him in turn in order to carry out research in our own specific disciplines.'

'I'm surprised,' I went on, 'there has been no mention of the discovery in the press. They usually latch on to something so unique as this.'

'It's been hushed up,' she replied enigmatically. 'Everyone involved, even those who found him, have been ordered to keep quiet. It was felt journalists should be kept in the dark until the research is done. Even archaeologists are not being informed unless they are on a team with specific access. No one is allowed to publish a paper or anything like that and we are all sworn to keep the secret.'

'He,' I said, adopting her personification of the specimen, 'must be regarded as of great importance to you – other than as a relic of the past.'

'Oh, he is most important to us for two main reasons. The first is he is a full-blooded European whereas all of our previous tissue specimens – I don't count the Roman bones, of course – have been otherwise. As you will appreciate, our funding company are primarily interested in developing drugs for the First World and that means people of broadly Caucasian extraction.'

I sipped my champagne again and said, 'That is somewhat immoral. Drugs should be developed for all men. Besides, medicines which cure a white man still work upon Africans, Chinese and the rest. A human is a human.'

'That's correct,' she defended herself, 'and I am not behaving immorally nor, I believe, is the funding source. The point is we are better able to work with European material because we know more about the life-style of the material than we do those of other ethnic groups. It is accepted diet plays an important part in many diseases so we need European material to relate to a known database of knowledge.

'For example, if we knew ancient Europeans had a high rate of miscarried pregnancies and they ate a lot of wheat in their diet, and Aztecs or Incas miscarried far less and ate no wheat, we might deduce a line of enquiry. What is in the European wheat?'

'That's simple,' I interjected. 'The wheat would be affected by ergot. We know ergotinine is an unstable alkaloid in ergot, especially of rye, and it can cause termination. It's used today in migraine cures but not prescribed to pregnant women for the obvious reason.'

'Yes, I know that,' she said, and I detected a hint of impatience. 'I was just giving an example. What I mean is we have studied Europeans and Mediterraneans more than any other race and we know more about their history. Therefore, to have a European specimen is very valuable indeed.'

'You have not told me what the second important reason is.'

'The second reason is he is complete and frozen solid.'

'By which you mean,' I replied after a moment's thought, 'well preserved.'

'Better preserved than a leg of New Zealand lamb in the supermarket.'

My brain was whirling with the possibilities this information prompted in my mind. It was in the realm of science fiction to assume he could be brought back to life like some twentieth-century Frankenstein's monster but if his tissues were no more damaged than is usual in the process of freezing then he would be a unique research opportunity. I was fascinated by the idea this young and pretty woman had at her disposal the body of a man over three millennia old.

Yet no sooner had these thoughts occurred to me than I saw the pitfalls.

'What if he were frozen some time after death?' I enquired. 'Some degree of decomposition would have set in.'

'He was killed in a blizzard. At least, this is the most likely scenario. No part of his body was crushed or distorted at death which precludes his being caught in an avalanche or similar catastrophe. And it is certain he died very quickly and was frozen within an hour or two. He was almost certainly surviving in sub-zero temperatures prior to his death as two of his toes are frost-bitten, suggesting he had been in the snow for some time.'

'Before you tell me more,' I interrupted her, 'I fail to understand why you should be reporting all this to me. I am not a forensic doctor nor am I a pathologist.'

She did not look at me as she replied but stared at the river, the lights coruscating on the surface. From the direction of Richmond Park, a rocket soared into the sky to explode into an orbed flower of green rays.

'Would you care to come and see him?' she asked softly.

I had no alternative but to accept her invitation: by now, my curiosity was aroused not only by the thought of the ancient corpse but also by what it was she envisaged as my involvement in her research.

◆

Chuhi had lost his blowpipe: either that or, more likely, it had been damaged, for he spent four days fashioning a replacement. He stationed himself outside his long-house and gave his undivided attention to the task, pausing only to eat hurriedly and sleep, which he did in the doorway of the building.

On the second day, I went to him and asked why he slept in the doorway.

'*Señor*,' he replied, not looking up from his work and speaking quickly, '*si me duermo, mi alma puede montar guardia con la cerbatana y asegurar que ningún fantasmas pueda entrar.*'

To this reply, I enquired where these evil spirits might come from. He waved his hand about in a vague fashion.

'*El aire*,' he said. '*Del cielo.*'

Contrary to my expectation, the pipe was not made from a hollow stem such as bamboo but from two lengths of dull grey wood placed against each other. The process of manufacture fascinated me for, despite the presence in the clearing of metal knives and tools, he worked entirely in what must have been traditional methods.

First, he erected a framework of stakes in the ground, hammering these into the soil with a smooth stone from the river, the whole construction under the wide eaves of the long-house. At the top of each stake, he cut a notch with a stone blade the like of which I had not seen before. It was made from obsidian and was loaned to him, he told me, by Keewei who was its guardian. Into the notches he wedged a three-metre length of the grey wood cut in cross-section like a *D*, the curve on the lower surface. Along the straight surface he smeared damp sand then placed a thin pole of incredibly hard wood, longer than the grey wand and as straight as a die. This, too, was temporarily removed from Keewei's ownership. On top of it was placed an identical grey wood length, the straight edge facing down.

For hours on end, Chuhi sat in the shade of the long-house, twisting and sliding the rod backwards and forwards between the lengths. Every so often, he paused to tighten the wedges and insert more damp sand. As the rod bored out a channel in the opposing lengths of grey wood, he bound them with a cord woven from a tough but thin and elastic liana which hangs from a tree the other side of the manioc beds inshore from my hut. No one spoke to him and he laboured in a state of near trance.

On the fourth day, he suddenly stopped and, snapping out of his muse, took the assembly to pieces, running his finger along the opposing grooves. Then, glancing up, he saw me gazing across the clearing at him. *¡Bien!*' he called to me, '*Muy bien. Muy recto.*' He pushed his flattened right hand through the air, beckoning to me with his left.

I put down the trousers in which I was sewing a rent caused by a *tucumá* spine and walked over to him. He held out the two halves of the blowpipe. They were surprisingly lightweight, still warm from the incessant friction of the hardwood rod. The bore was slightly wider at the muzzle end. I gave him a thumbs-up of approval and he smirked gleefully.

'*Ahora a ver, Señor Dom.*'

He took the two lengths back and I squatted in the shade next to him. With a strange triangular tool made from a tough mussel-like shell mounted in a wooden handle, he planed the outside surfaces until they were smooth, finishing off the surface with a soft stone like pumice or coral, the source of which I could not guess. I had seen nothing like it in the locality. This done, the two halves of the pipe were stuck together with a glob of resin brought to him in a pouch of leaves by Yetze, his wife, bound with lianas and heated over the family's cooking fire. As it cooled, a stain of some sort was rubbed into the wood, giving it a dark polished hue like mahogany. Finally, from a pocket in his tattered denim shorts, he removed a circle of carved bone, yellowed and smooth with age. '*La vieja,*' he remarked, pressing it to his pursed lips and blowing through it.

I nodded knowingly and he offered it to me. I did likewise, tasting his spittle upon the surface.

At the breech end of the blowpipe he inserted the bone mouthpiece, ramming it home with his finger. It was a tight but perfect fit: the tolerances would have pleased an engineer.

'*Se acabó,*' Chuhi remarked and he stood up.

I also made to rise but found my muscles cramped, my right ankle quite numb. Time had passed by and it was near sunset and yet I had not noticed the hours slip away: sometimes I wished the battery in my cheap Seiko would die and leave me to count time as the people of the clearing do. They use a stick drilled with holes into which are inserted little pegs made of fish teeth. Every day they remove one until all the holes are empty: then they fill them again and start over. I could keep track of fortnights in a similar fashion. Beyond that, I no longer have an interest.

Chuhi entered his long-house. I was about to set off for my hut when he reappeared, a dart in one hand, his new blowpipe in the other. He placed the dart in the pipe, put his lips to the mouthpiece and did not so much blow as spit. The dart flew with such speed I did not see its passage through the air.

'¿*Donde está?*' I asked and pointed roughly in the direction of his aim.

Chuhi pointed to my hut and, taking my hand as if I was a child, led me across the clearing, on to the porch and through the door. The dart was stuck firmly into the spine of my *Gray's Anatomy* where it stood on my shelf. He tugged the dart free and we parted company. As he left, I realized again he could, without any effort, kill me. My realization did not fill me with dread. Living with these simple people and being trusted by them, I am obliged to abide by their ways, their laws. It is preferable to living by those which, prior to my arrival in the clearing, governed my life.

◆

I drove down to The Harmon Institute on a Friday morning. It was not what I had imagined. Located deep in the Berkshire country south-west of Oxford, I had expected it to be either a small stately home converted into laboratories or one of those modern boxes of aluminium and glass thrown up within a landscaped business park where the lawns were as sterile as the laboratories and the strategically placed trees barely more than saplings. Instead, it was contained within what appeared to have been an old army store depot surplus to requirements since VE Day. The only modern construction to be seen from the lane outside was a new set of concrete posts strung with gleaming razor wire and hung every twenty-five metres with polite notices warning trespassers off, advising of the voltage of the fence and the sharpness of the wire blades. Every fifty metres was a bank of spotlights and a sophisticated television camera mounted on a high pole.

At the gatehouse, from its architecture clearly once a guardhouse but now tarted up with new windows and security devices, I stopped the Porsche before a barrier and gave my name into a speaker set into a steel bollard. A uniformed minion appeared and walked round my car with a mirror on a stick with which he inspected the underside, requested I open the bonnet on the luggage compartment and rooted about in it, opened the passenger door and looked about the interior, spoke into a walkie-talkie then handed me a plastic visitor's identity badge. Finally, with instructions to find the car-park, he pressed a button, raised the barrier and waved me through: I noticed a video camera on the guardhouse roof filming the car. Careful not to exceed the 15mph speed limit, I drove by long, low, old-fashioned barrack buildings and across what had obviously been a parade ground. Were it not for the fact the buildings had been painted white and all the windows and doors replaced, I might have been on the set for a war movie: the roadways were even still lined by stones although these were no longer painted but had been weathered to their natural colour.

As I parked in a space marked for visitors' vehicles, Ruth Schroeder greeted me, ushered me through a comfortable but spartan reception area and down a maze of corridors, some of recent construction, joining building to building. The air had a tang of cleanliness and Dettol, the floors smooth tiled and quiet underfoot.

'This reminds me of a provincial hospital,' I said. 'One yet to receive its improvement grant.'

'It was a hospital before we bought it,' she replied. 'They built a new one some miles away. More secure. It was a psychiatric unit. Prior to that it was an army barracks and, once, a prisoner-of-war camp for Italians.'

'It seems pretty secure now,' I remarked. 'Is all the hi-tech fencing and closed circuit TV necessary to guard archaeological remains?'

'Industrial espionage,' she said. 'Our treasures are in our files and databases. And our brains, of course.'

We reached a door marked *Dr R. Schroeder: Palaeobiology Unit 4*. She opened it with a slip of plastic like a credit card.

The buildings may have looked obsolescent but the laboratory was far from outmoded. We walked past ranks of new benches, stereoscopic microscopes, dissection tables, autoclaves and complex equipment with which I was not familiar. Personal IBM computers were dotted about the room, all switched on with their screens competing for attention with oscilloscopes and digital read-outs. We entered an office behind a glass screen at the far end.

'I'm afraid it's not quite Harley Street,' she remarked, pointing to a padded typist's chair in front of a computer.

I sat on the chair. It gave slightly under my weight, a spring creaking in the pedestal leg. The cursor on the screen winked at me from the last point it had reached in a long sequence of blocks of letters:

TAACTAGCC
TAACATGCC
TAAACTGGC
TAATCAGGG

I realized it was a partially sequenced DNA chain. A counter at the side of the screen showed the computer had reached line 1008. By a sink in the corner, a coffee percolator bubbled.

Ruth perched on the edge of her desk, her white lab coat open and her shapely thigh showing beneath the hem of a tight, short skirt. 'I suppose you are still interested in my Bronze Age hunter,' she said.

'I would have to be to drive all this way into the sticks, not to mention subject myself to a security system which would do a mad despot proud.'

She laughed but I sensed there was little humour in it. 'Some of us call the facility here the concentration camp.' She turned to the percolator. 'We're locked in to concentrate. Would you like a coffee?'

I nodded and she stood up to pour out two mugs, putting a milk bottle and a 100ml Pyrex beaker of sugar on the desk. I tested the drink: it had the sour taste of coffee which had been too long on the boil. As there was no spoon in the beaker, I poured in what I guessed to be two spoonsful.

'I want to show you something,' she continued. Going behind her desk, she opened a drawer pulling out a perspex box which she placed by the telephone. In it were a pair of twisted blackened sandals with crossed thongs. 'These are his footwear. And this,' she slid her hand over the desk towards me, 'is his axe.'

I picked it up. It was surprisingly heavy, about fifteen centimetres long with a six centimetre wide blade. The top was beaten into a reverse blade with two side walls.

'More properly,' Ruth said, 'it is not an axe but a celt. This type is known as a palstave celt according to the means of fastening it to the haft. Of course, it's made of bronze. The shoes are in an evacuated box as are his other clothes. He was wearing a fleece-lined cloak, a leather skull-cap type of hat, a woollen tabard-cum-smock affair and a cross between a loincloth and a pair of Y-fronts. And he wore a pair of woollen socks. The clothes are now with an anthropological museum for preservation. We here no longer have an interest in them.'

'Then why keep the shoes?' I wanted to know.

'They're made of leather,' she explained, 'and we're still testing them. For pollen deposits, seeds, soil samples.'

'Did he carry no real weapon?' I enquired. I knew enough to be aware a celt was more ceremonial than practical.

'He did have a yew bow and leather quiver of arrows in addition to a short bronze knife. He was also carrying a shoulder-bag containing little pouches of herbs, barks, dried fungi and flowers. I'm not sure what else. These are all in another department here. He carried no food except for a piece of what looks like jerky.'

'Where was he found?' I asked.

'Northern Italy, on the Swiss border. In the Alps. I'm not at liberty, I'm afraid, to divulge the actual location. But the area below the find site was comparatively densely populated in prehistoric times and is famous for its prehistoric sites. Ironically, he was discovered by an alpine rescue team hunting for a lost skier. They arrived a few millennia too late.'

I turned the celt over in my hand. The metal was deep green with the exquisite patina found on ancient bronze.

'I still don't see how I can be of assistance to you,' I said, handing the object back to her. 'My knowledge of archaeology is limited to television documentaries and childhood visits to the museum. Nor,' I added, nodding in the direction of the computers in the laboratory, 'am I a geneticist.'

She sat down in the chair behind her desk and leaned forward. 'You're very observant,' she remarked. 'You would make a good archaeologist.' She picked up the box containing the sandals, looked at it then replaced it in the desk, flicking a switch on her telephone. 'Now we shan't be disturbed.' She sipped her coffee.

I knew she was building herself up to start telling me what she wanted. I think she was also sizing me up, considering whether or not, at the final moment before committing herself, I was the right man for the job. Perhaps she was also pondering on how much I might charge for my time.

'I'll come clean with you,' she said at last, lowering her mug to the desk, fitting it meticulously on to a ring stain left by a previous mug. 'I've not told you everything, not been entirely honest.'

'I have guessed as much,' I replied, 'but I'm not doubting your honesty. On the other hand, your motives . . . ' I left it hanging in the air and she gave me a sheepish half-smile.

'We aren't just investigating possible medicines and the like here,' she commenced. 'We're at the forefront of science and it's . . . I'd better start at the beginning, I suppose. If I'm a little patronizing, please forgive me. I've,' she half-smiled again, 'been practising this speech ever since the fireworks night.'

I settled as comfortably as I could in the typing chair, leaning back in it. Another spring twanged ominously.

'As you must know, all living things share the same gene pool. All life originates from the same source and has in common the same DNA. Or deoxyribonucleic acid, from which genes are made. DNA is a complex, spirally-shaped, double helix of molecules. Think of a ladder which is twisted around its long axis. The side bars are made of alternate phosphate and sugar molecules – the sugar is deoxyribose – and the steps are made of pairs of nitrogenous bases joined together. There are four of these, known by their letters G for guanine, T for thymine, C for cytosine and A for adenosine.

'Because of its structure, DNA can self-replicate. I'll not bore you with the mechanisms. It is capable of three incredible proprieties: it can store and transmit information faithfully, it copies itself accurately and it can mutate.

'In the bases of DNA lie the instructions for the cellular building and operation of every living thing which has ever existed. In our DNA, in every cell in our bodies, lie the instructions – no longer valid – for making not only us but also anything from an ant to an elephant. Every time a cell divides, the DNA replicates.' She paused as if lecturing me, allowing time for the facts to sink in. I finished my coffee, a revolting sludge of brownish sugar remaining in the bottom of the cup.

'We are currently sequencing DNA here,' she continued. 'That is to say, we are attempting to read the instructions, understand the codes. As the code is the same in every living creature, once we know it for one, we know it for all. In other words, if we can decipher the code which makes a cell in an embryo become specialized – say, a lymph cell – then we will have the code for the manufacture of every lymph cell in the world, be it in an aardvark or a zebra.'

'Or a man,' I interrupted.

'Yes,' she replied, her voice a little distant as if she was dreaming. 'Or a man.' She sipped at her coffee once more, not from thirst but because the action helped her return to her theme. 'At present,' she continued, 'there are 9000 scientists working on human DNA sequencing in 36 countries. This group is working on the Human Genome Project and they – we – are seeking to map the human genome – the whole DNA code. When we crack it, we will have the ability to find out how human life, and all life come to that, is determined.'

To the accompaniment of springs, I eased my back in the typist's chair and leaned forward on to the desk myself. 'As I understand it,' I said, settling my elbows on a pile of computer printout sheets, 'this is a considerable undertaking. There are, I seem to recall, over 100,000 genes. Only two per cent are known. The reaction, interaction and so on of 100,000 units is impossible.'

'Not with technology and computers,' Ruth replied. 'DNA sequences are read by sequencing machines and computers work on the sequencing. But it is a mammoth task. For example, there are, we believe, about 30,000 genes relevant to human brain function. We here at Harmon are just a cog in the investigative wheel. However, we are also going off on our own path at the same time.

'You see, the power which will be unleashed when the code is understood will be vast. We could create life with such knowledge. The odd genetically engineered tomato or pea we have already begun to develop will be as nothing. We are at the border of an entire new science, an entire new era in human evolution. Let me give you this . . .' She rummaged under some papers in a tray and handed me an envelope. I opened it and removed a number of what looked like photographic negatives. Holding them up to the light coming through the partition from the lab – there were, I now noticed, no windows in the office – I saw they consisted of what looked like fuzzily-printed bar codes such as one saw on food packaging, though much longer.

'They're photos,' she said, divining my thoughts. 'Each line is a piece of a strand of DNA. These ones come from the fruit fly, *Drosophila*. It's used extensively in genetics research. The pictures could just as readily be a part of human DNA.'

'What if you had a complete DNA sample from an animal?' I asked. 'Could you recreate it?'

'Yes,' she answered bluntly. 'Give me the complete DNA from a dog and, in principle, I could make a dog. Give me the complete DNA from an extinct bee and I'll bring it back to life. The stuff of science fiction writers and film makers. Mind you, we are a long way off such an event but, in theory, it's perfectly feasible.'

'How?' I questioned. 'You need a living cell.'

'That's not so difficult. We've already taken DNA from frozen tissue and put it into microbes which have replicated it. Or, rather, it has replicated itself within them on a petri dish. It's not so much more difficult than growing a culture of, say, cholera bacteria in order to make a vaccine.'

Her lecture on DNA manifoldly increased my curiosity. I wondered why she was telling me all this when it was not a part of my scientific discipline and therefore not something over which she would be likely to seek my advice. Besides, it was obvious her knowledge was as up-to-date as it might be. Whatever it was she wanted of me, it could not be related to the structure of DNA or some science fiction-like experiment. Considering it time our intercourse moved on, I decided to ask her outright the one question I was most eager to learn. 'And what,' I asked, 'is your exact work?'

I could not have been more blunt and her reply could not have been any less direct. 'I'm looking for the mechanism which instructs initial cell division.'

I sat back to the tune of creaking springs. This pretty girl with firm thighs was seeking to uncover the very basis of my own world. How often had I watched through a microscope as a sperm penetrated an oöcyte and, after a while, the cell divided: the first step in the making of a baby, constructing a human being. To say I was awed would be to stretch the limitations of litotes. I was utterly fascinated.

'I thought you'd find it incredible,' she said. 'I find it unbelievable myself sometimes, but I think I have it in my reach to make this ultimate discovery. It won't happen this year. Nor maybe the next. Yet it will one day. I may not be the first either: I don't see a Nobel prize looming my way. But . . . '

So many thoughts started to move into play in my head: with complete bee DNA you could make a bee; with the knowledge of cell division, so many battles could be fought and won against disease. I thought back to my weekend in the summer with Brian and Larry . It was no longer just a matter of recognizing the genetic fault which caused cystic fibrosis: now it was a matter of being able to eliminate it at source – along with every other ailment. Yet one word Ruth had spoken kept running through my mind: *frozen*.

'I know what's going on in your head,' she declared. 'What I need you to do is to assist me to obtain the frozen sperm out of my Bronze Age man. I could do it, but I'm no expert and I'm certainly not familiar with the interior workings of a testicle. Being frozen, there are also tissue deformations which I could not understand or accommodate even if I was to read up testicular structure.'

Under normal circumstances, I would have laughed at such a line from a pretty young woman. Yet this was no laughing matter. 'You mean,' I said, 'in not so many words, you want me to get raw and possibly complete, undegenerated DNA out of your dead ancient mariner?'

'Yes.'

'So you could replicate it?'

'Yes.'

'And make a living Bronze Age man?'

She stared at me, put her hand on mine and then laughed quietly, half mockingly. 'No. I don't think we have such a technology to hand.'

'So why . . . ?' I started, but she interrupted me, serious once more.

'Because it's never been done. No one has ever obtained a complete DNA sample from a prehistoric man. Not that I know of, anyway. Or historic, come to that. They've never been preserved like this. Of course, tissue has survived – in Egyptian mummies, those bog people and so on – but I've never felt I could trust it. There's no way of telling what degradation might have occurred. My axeman, however, has the nearest possible standard of purity about him. He was quick frozen.'

I thought for a moment and admit my mind was not dwelling on what it should have, upon the ethics of our conversation, the morality, the rights and wrongs of it all. Like her, I was suddenly captivated by the possibility. I was, like so many men and women in white coats before me, blinded by the pure science of it and unwilling to consider the applied applications. The Curies and Rutherford had not envisaged nuclear warfare, nuclear waste from leaking power stations, nuclear disasters in central Russia which contaminated land in Scotland: they only saw the sparking glow of radium, the magic atom splitting in two.

'Why?' I asked, 'don't you call in one of your colleagues? Surely there are medical doctors by the dozen in your concentration camp.'

'There are,' Ruth admitted, 'but this is my work.'

I thought then of the old adage: nothing so spiteful as a woman wronged. Or a scientist robbed of his laureate. Everyone in the world wants to make their name at something. In her case, it was in a fashion much grander than a railway station or a book of poems, a painting of sunflowers or a machine which sowed wheat.

'Where is he, your Bronze Age axeman?'

She tipped her head at a closed door behind her desk and said quietly, 'Next door. Will you consider doing it?'

Of course, I should have declined. It was the proper course to take, the ethical, the moral. Yet I did not.

◆

The man lay on his back in a large perspex box rather like a giant incubator into which one places premature babies: the difference was, at one end, there was an airlock. Along each side were arm holes containing fixed, airtight rubber gloves. Several rigid pipes entered the box at the opposite end, attached to a small vacuum pump and a number of gas bottles connected through a centralized bank of pressure meters. Mounted along the top of the box were metal filaments of the sort one might find at the rear of a domestic fridge except that they were not frosted over.

The man himself was about 1.6m tall and of average

proportions. His legs were together, his arms straight by his sides as if he was standing to attention when he died. His hairline had receded and he was bald on top but the tresses which hung down the sides of his head reached his shoulders. He was not a muscular man but possessed a kind of ethereal strength which seemed to reach out to me through the thick perspex. There was no way of telling, but I felt a strange charisma from him, as if his soul had not yet departed the body but was still frozen therein, waiting for release.

'As you can see from the gloves, the box,' Ruth said, 'has been partially evacuated. What atmosphere exists in there is utterly sterile. We toyed with filling it with nitrogen or carbon dioxide to reduce the chances of decomposition but decided against it. There may well be anaerobic bacteria present in the body. He is still more or less frozen, but we have him at only $-2°C$. The temperature is closely monitored, of course.'

'Has his body been cleaned?' I enquired.

'No. It's much as it was when it arrived.'

His skin was deeply tanned as if he was used to living either in bright sunlight or in the snow-fields of the Alps where he had died. Pressing my face to the perspex, I could see quite clearly a little dirt under his fingernails, his eyelashes standing erect from the eyelids and a growth of several days' stubble on his chin.

'The ice was removed very carefully with a heated prong a bit like a soldering iron,' Ruth said over my shoulder. 'There may have been a little thawing of the epidermis but not much more.'

Standing up, I gazed into the case. It was then I noticed the eyes still extant.

'I wonder what those eyes last saw,' Ruth half-whispered behind me.

'It's remarkable they have lasted,' I said.

'That's an indication he was quickly frozen to death. If the body had taken hours to freeze, the eyes would like as not have sunk.'

I walked around the perspex box, studying the body from every angle. It was in astonishingly good condition. I could clearly make out the hairs on the forearm, the whorls of the fingerprints and the lines on the soles of the feet. As the minutes past, I felt more and more excited and yet, at the same time, calmed by this dead stranger. I could not get over his quality of preservation: in my hospital days, I had seen cadavers in far worse condition seventy-two hours after death, stored in a drawer in the mortuary. What lay before me now, I realized, was something quite unique. The chances of there being another body like this anywhere in the world were remote indeed and the opportunities for study virtually non-existent. The axeman was a one-off, a freak of chance and circumstance, a fragment of ancient time caught by a coincidence the mathematical probability of which was infinitesimal. The more I thought of this, the more my one doubt begged a question. 'Are you sure,' I asked at length, 'this isn't a hoax? An Alpine Piltdown Man?'

'Quite sure.'

'It would be a simple matter to plant a corpse in the mountains with a few Bronze Age artefacts on it.'

'Yes, it would but whenever there's a hoax, there's a hoaxer looking to gain from it. Gain reputation, gain monetary reward, gain a good laugh . . . '

'And this one?'

'As I've said, the body was found by chance on a mountain rescue mission. Besides, it was so remote. No trickster would have resorted to such lengths: a hoax is only good if people discover it. Besides,' she added as if this was the least important piece of information, 'we've had a piece of his shoe carbon-dated. He's genuine.'

Turning my attention back to him increased my awe. When I had a niggling doubt he was a marvellous curiosity: now, all incertitude dismissed, he was incredible almost beyond the point of belief.

'Is this,' I enquired, 'the position in which the body was discovered? The posture?'

'Exactly. The body was in fact removed from the mountain *in situ* in a block of ice. It was not removed from the ice until it reached here. Transportation was in a lorry used for continental meat deliveries.'

With this knowledge, I gazed at the man's eyes. They were blank with death and yet I felt, at that moment, this was not a hunter who had been lost in the mountains, or a foolhardy traveller caught out in a freak blizzard. It was the body of a man who had gone to the mountains to die, who had sacrificed himself for some reason I could not and would never be able to appreciate.

His genitalia seemed to be in as good a state of preservation as the rest of him. His penis was flaccid between his thighs, with a lean towards the left. I could not see his testicles but assumed they would be complete. It was interesting to note he had been circumcised, the foreskin non-existent and the glans prominent.

'Can you do it?' Ruth enquired. Her voice was little more than a whisper, husky with tension.

'I think so. The most obvious course, I think, is to aspirate the epididymis. This is an accessory organ which lies on top of the testis. Spermatozoa are made in the testis and pass into the epididymis. Here, they mature into active sperm and are also stored until ejaculation. The storage can last a very long while. If our patient had not had sex for a while before death, and I would think it likely if he was alone in the high mountains, then we should find a concentration of sperm. This, in turn, will give you a fairly concentrated extract, if I may put it like that, of DNA-rich material. There is, however,' I concluded, 'one necessary condition.' I glanced at Ruth's face. A mix of emotions showed in her eyes, her quick mind running over the options: my payment, my demand for shared recognition in the published paper, my cut of her fame.

'What is it?'

'He'll have to be thawed,' I said, 'at least in the area around his genitalia. I can't aspirate frozen tissue.'

She smiled with relief and, returning to her office, picked up the telephone. I followed to hear her punch out a three-digit number then issue a curt instruction to someone called Barry.

A minute later, there was a knock on the door. Ruth, using her plastic card which was essential not only to enter the building but also to exit from it, tripped the electronic lock to allow a laboratory technician to enter.

'This is Barry,' she introduced me. 'He's the best.'

I noticed she did not afford Barry a knowledge of my name.

'How d'you do,' he replied and shook my hand. His hand was soft and delicate, almost effeminate, yet his fingers clasped my own in a vice-like grip. I was reminded of the hands of undertakers, forensic laboratory staff and mortuary porters who could be so gentle with a corpse but also had the strength to prise open the results of rigor mortis.

'We need our man thawed a bit, Barry,' she ordered. 'Not too much. Just one area.' She looked at me. I took a pad from her desk and drew a diagram of the region I needed unfrozen.

'You want him thawed right through?'' Barry enquired.

'Just the sexual organs,' I requested.

'And you want these warm or still chilled. I can do him blood heat if you want.'

'No,' I said. 'Just so the tissue is relaxed. I don't need it up to body temperature.'

'No problem,' Barry declared and he passed into the axeman's quarters. 'Take me a couple of hours. Blood heat would have been a lot longer.'

Ruth and I spent our lunch in the Institute social club. It was a meagre building with a few tatty snooker tables, a reasonably stocked bar and a small cafeteria serving mediocre food. Our conversation pointedly avoided the subject of our impending work. Ruth was reluctant to discuss her project in even such a restricted place and I felt as if I was less a visiting specialist and more a conspirator.

At two-thirty, we returned to the laboratory. The technician had thawed the body as requested but it was still contained in the perspex chamber. The partial vacuum, however, had been replaced by an oxygen/carbon dioxide mix at atmospheric pressure.

I did not require complex equipment: a few catheters for the aspiration, a syringe, some tubing, a suitable sterilized liquid and sterilized glass containers. These were placed, suitably sterilized, in the air lock at the end of the chamber which was then evacuated and allowed to fill with the O_2/CO_2 mixture. I washed my hands in a nearby sink, dried them thoroughly and dusted them with talcum to prevent them sticking in the rubber gloves mounted in the chamber walls. Whilst I was busy prepping myself, the technician placed my equipment in the main part of the chamber, next to the man's thigh.

'I may need a little help,' I told Ruth. 'Will you assist me?'

She made no reply but nodded and, sitting on a stool across the chamber from me, inserted her arms into another pair of gloves. Around her head she had placed a thin pipe microphone of the sort airline pilots use: across the room was a voice-activated cassette recorder. Having attended to my immediate needs, the technician set about erecting a video camera. I settled myself on a stool and pushed my hands into the gloves, the rubber cool and tight-fitting.

Then I paused. In front of me lay the corpse of a man over three thousand years old, his head to my right and his feet to my left.

I had dissected humans before. Or, more often, parts of them. In medical school, I had been presented in anatomy classes with an arm or a leg from which to dissect out the brachioradialis or peroneus brevis muscles, perhaps a lung to investigate or a cerebellum to section. I had on many occasions been afforded the opportunity of attending the dissection of some part of a complete cadaver: in my third year of study, a group of four of us were assigned a complete body of our own which, over a period of weeks, we completely sundered. Yet I had never attended to a body which was uniquely mine. My first was this remarkable person before me. I felt he should have had a name.

Before picking up a catheter, I tentatively reached out. He might have been alive, a breathing patient, so gentle was my movement. I felt a tingle of excitement course through me as if he had given off some invisible charge for which I was the conductor.

Where the body had been thawed, the skin was remarkably supple and although not truly life-like it did not appear as dark as if still frozen. Very gently – more so, perhaps, than if he had been a living patient – I took hold of his penis and moved it up and to one side away from me. His pubic hair was coarse and resilient, like wire wool. This movement of the penis caused the testicles to rise a little higher from between his thighs. I felt for the testis nearest to me. It was so firm and soft I could roll it between my finger and thumb. With extreme caution, I inserted the catheter through the upper part of the scrotum, guiding it into the epididymis by feel. The sharp point easily penetrated the skin.

All the time, as I was working, I could hear Ruth's voice murmuring like a woman at prayer in a church. From over my shoulder came the quiet buzz of the camera.

The needle in place, I fitted a 20ml syringe to the catheter and depressed the plunger. The liquid ran into the body, slightly distending the top of the testicle. I gently massaged the scrotum with my fingers then pulled the plunger up. For a moment, nothing happened then there was a rush of grey, almost milky fluid up the catheter and into the syringe. It actually stared like semen although it was not.

Disconnecting the syringe, I placed the liquid in the first glass container and sealed it with a tight plastic clip, making sure the liquid did not come into contact with the top. Sterilized glass carries no threat to sperm but some plastics can be poisonous. This done, I passed the container to Ruth who stood it in a perspex rack.

I aspirated the same epididymis twice more, the liquid becoming less milky each time. This done, I repeated the procedure on the second testicle and, in half an hour, I was finished. 'That's it,' I said as I withdrew the catheter for the last time. 'Whatever there is in there which might be of value to us is now removed.'

There is no way I can account for my next action. The axeman's left hand lay by his side, the palm facing up and the fingers slightly bent, the thumb apart from them. I slid my hand over his thigh and placed it momentarily in his. The tissue was hard and cold through the rubber but I felt a great sense of strange companionship. It was almost as if I had known him.

My simple equipment was removed to the airlock with the sealed bottles standing upright in the rack. The airlock was closed, several blocks of solid carbon dioxide placed close to the body by the technician. Ruth and I left the room and sat in her office, the door shut.

At first, we did not speak. She labelled the cassette tape she had made of her running commentary. I sat looking at the bottles. Eventually, she broke the silence. 'I think we'd better have a look,' she said quietly.

Together, we took the rack into the laboratory. My hands were shaking but not with the cold which had started to affect the genital area of the body towards the end of my work, seeping in from the surrounding frozen tissue: I was excited. Excited and incomprehensibly afraid.

Ruth peeled the sterile packaging off a pipette as I opened one of the bottles. There was a momentary hiss: the atmospheric pressure in the perspex chamber must have been slightly lower than normal. She inserted the pointed end into the liquid, put the mouthpiece to her lips and cautiously sucked up about half a millilitre of the liquid, dripping small globules on to a row of microscope slides, slipping a cover slide over it, the liquid spreading out and sucking the thin glass down to itself. This done, she flicked on a monitor screen to one side of the bench at which we were standing and pressed a switch on a powerful microscope. She stared at me then. Her eyes were deep, intense. She had the look of a person about to plunge into an abyss. There was fear present in her but also an intense longing. I wondered if this was how parachutists looked just before their first jump.

Taking one slide, she fitted it into the retaining clips under the lens and started to turn the vernier scale knobs on the microscope body.

I watched the screen.

At first, there was only a grey snow but, gradually, cells came into focus then, beneath them, unmistakably, spermatozoa.

I do not recall what I said, nor what exclamation Ruth uttered. We were both too involved with our thoughts to notice.

As the screen focused, my first thought was what an incredible thing I had achieved: my next was an overpowering sense of foreboding, of having not exactly transgressed any law, broken any ethical barrier but somehow done something momentous, something I might live to regret. This deep apprehension was, however, quickly superseded by a feeling of euphoric happiness. I had, I thought, achieved the impossible and was inordinately proud.

The sperm were dead. I was not surprised at this but I admitted to myself a slight disappointment. It would have been unbelievable if, on thawing, they had become motile. Ruth, however, was silently jubilant. She stepped back from the microscope and stared at the monitor screen.

'There's your DNA,' I said.

She made no comment but turned to kiss me hard and full on the lips, her hands on my shoulders pulling me towards her.

◆

The people of the clearing have held a festival. Preparations began late in the afternoon when Chuhi and his half-brother, Mayno, arrived carrying two howler monkeys trussed with creepers. Both creatures had been darted and I thought they were dead but as Chuhi dropped them to the ground, one of them let out a squeal like a piglet and thrashed its head from side to side. One of the women, standing by a hearty fire which had been lit in the centre of the clearing, grabbed the animal by its hind legs and, without so much as a thought, swung it in an arc over her shoulder to bring its head crashing down on a large, flat river stone close to the flames. I could hear the skull crack like a walnut.

By dusk, the fire was roaring with two spits placed over the flames. The monkeys were gutted but not skinned, their entrails thrown to the dogs. Instead, they were singed over the fire, their body cavities held open by sticks. Herbs of some sort were rubbed into the raw meat.

The men of the clearing dressed up for the occasion. Chuhi placed a sprig of macaw feathers in his hair and painted several lines upon his face. The other men, according to their rank, followed suit, Keewei draping a rather moth-eaten jaguar skin cape over his shoulders, donning his pillbox hat and Reeboks, and slipping on a necklace made of monkey incisors and, where a central jewel might be, a Coca Cola bottle top.

I watched the festival get under way from the porch of my hut. Keewei made a chanting pronouncement and threw what looked like small bones into the fire, the people responding with a part of the incantation. This was followed by fifteen minutes of dancing, each adult taking a turn at prancing around the fire tossing sticks into the heat. The children stood back in a huddle, guarded by the oldest who kept them in check. The cavorting over, the men disappeared into a long-house, the women cooking large thin pancakes of manioc flour, flicking them over on a flat iron griddle and piling them up on a wooden platter. The placing of the howler monkeys on the spits appeared to be a signal to the children who all ran forward and, for some minutes, tossed twigs into the fire and frolicked about in imitation of their elders. I watched from the hut in a detached manner. From time to time, one of the women looked across at me but I was otherwise ignored, allowed to be an indifferent spectator at their feast.

Night fell. The fire was kept high. The orange flames flickered upon the trees and the bats, quitting my hut, flashed out to swerve away with alarm. Their usual flight-path across the clearing was no longer viable. The rather enticing scent of roast monkey drifted across to me. Suddenly, the men appeared. In their midst was a youth, stripped naked, his brow garlanded with woven leaves. He walked awkwardly and, as he approached the fire, the light shone on his thighs: it took me a moment to realise his legs were smeared with blood. He was placed close to the flames and I saw his penis had been tied with a length of coarse twine. The women stopped cooking and the children fell silent.

Positioning himself behind the youth, Keewei grabbed him firmly by his biceps and, intoning in a high-pitched voice, thrust him briefly into the flames, then dragged him away. The youth's head lolled. I wondered if he was about to lose consciousness but, when Keewei stopped and finally tugged him several steps from the heat, letting go of him, he remained standing. Two women then went to him, helping him to sit on the ground upon a blanket whilst a slightly younger boy stood as stiff as a sentry by his side.

Chuhi broke away from the gathering and came towards my hut. He raised his hand, signalling to me. '*Ven a comer, Do-me-neek Lie-yall*,' he invited me, grinning broadly, the lines on his face accentuating the curve of his cheek-bones.

'*¡Gracias!*' I replied and followed him to the fire.

The people were now seated around the fire in a circle. The flames were dying down but there remained a substantial volcano of embers. Chuhi announced my arrival in Huambas and the people murmured a greeting to which I replied *gracias* again.

The food was handed to the men by the youth, the twine around his penis a tourniquet: he had been circumcised in the long-house. All the women were served by the guardian boy, the meal beginning with the pancakes.

'*Pai-joo*,' Chuhi said, taking a torn scrap of pancake smeared with a dark paste. '*Me llamo Chuhi. Se llama pai-joo.*' He handed it to me. The paste was made of pulverized fish mixed with some kind of smooth oil. It did not taste unappetizing and was followed by plantains which had been cooking in clay on the edge of the embers: they were tart and gritty. Finally, the two monkeys were removed from the spits and cut into chunks by Keewei. Each person, regardless of sex, was presented with a piece by the youth. I received a forearm. The flesh was crisp, the hand on the end charred. It reminded me momentarily of a baby I had once treated in my hospital days, a poor mite badly burned in a house fire. It had died. I put the arm to my mouth and bit into it. There was a surprising amount of meat on the little limb and although it was roasted almost dry on the outside, within it was still succulent and moist. It had the texture of lamb, being striated, but was quite without fat.

'*Debes chupar la mano*,' Chuhi ordered. '*Te da habilidad en las manos.*'

It took me a moment to translate his words: when I understood them I felt I had no choice but to obey. I placed the burned monkey's fingers in my mouth and sucked. They tasted of charcoal. The whole assembly of people clapped and laughed, looking from one to the other with approval. Chuhi placed his hand on my shoulder and pinched me hard. He, too, was laughing and I wondered if I had fallen for an old jungle joke but he then took the arm from me, sucked the fingers himself and passed the limb on. Everyone had a suck.

The meal over, the detritus thrown into the remains of the fire, the women departed with the children. I made to leave also, thinking the masculine gathering would not require my presence. However, Chuhi signalled I should remain.

At this juncture, I had expected home-made beer to be served. Several days before, I had observed the women making *yamanachi*, skinning manioc roots and cooking them, taking hunks of root out of the pot, chewing hard on them for a minute or so then spitting them into a big clay calabash: every so often the women charged their mouths with water and added this liquid spittle to the brew. The masticated mush was kept stirred by an old woman using a paddle-like spoon. She chanted in a low, near inaudible voice as she worked like an automaton, the flesh of her arms sagging with age and her hands intermittently shaking so badly she could not maintain the circular stirring motion.

Yet no gourds of *yamanachi* appeared. Instead, Keewei rose from his place and walked around the fire, dabbing a red spot of *urucú* dye in the centre of each man's forehead: he included me. This done Mayno, sitting two places from me, produced a hollow stick like a miniature blowpipe into which he inserted something I could not see, working it into his neighbour, Q'eke's, right nostril. He blew hard on the pipe. The other man sniffed hard, removed the pipe and snorted. He then, in turn, did the same favour for his neighbour. Quite soon, the pipe reached Chuhi who did the same for me.

The pipe was filled with a pinch of greyish powder. On the spur of the moment, I wondered if it was cocaine but dismissed the thought. Cocaine is highly addictive yet none of these people were addicts: this was the first time I had seen this behaviour in all the months since I arrived in their midst.

Chuhi blew quite hard. I was taken by surprise. The powder stung my sinuses and I gasped for breath as it hit my lungs.

All of us dosed on the drug, I sat waiting to see what might happen. There was a bitter taste in my throat but nothing more.

Q'eke stood up, his arms jerking. He stared at the glowing ashes, took two steps back and barked like a dog. Saliva dripped from his mouth. His eyes rolled and he curled up on the ground, circling round on the spot like a dog before dropping to the dirt. One of the long-house mongrels, attracted by the realistic bark, came over, sniffed at Q'eke then curled up beside him in the warmth of the fire. The man next to him started to flap his arms, his mouth squawking like a jungle parrot. The next rose and, with infinitely slow motions, started to walk away from the fire, his neck outstretched and his head turning slowly from side to side. He had grouped his fingers into two bunches: I guessed he was a sloth.

One by one, as the men became creatures, I wondered what would happen to me, what animal might be born within my soul. Would I become a delicate bird or a hissing snake like Tee-an, three seats from me, who writhed spitting on the ground? What beast lurked within me, trying to get out? As the drug began to affect Chuhi, I became terribly afraid. The influence swept over me with such rapidity I was, in my last lucid moment, astonished. It was as if I was suddenly possessed by something which gripped my very soul. My face grew incredibly hot and my fingers, when they touched it, were like icicles against the skin. I felt as if they were boring into me and tore them away with a second pair of hands I had somehow developed. Perhaps, I thought, I was turning into a centipede. Or a god, one of those found in the Orient, with umpteen arms.

Somewhere in my body, a tree was growing. I could look inside myself, as if into a vast red cavern, and watch it spread its leaves which were alight with a green fire like neon shining through imperfect emeralds. Flowers hung from the walls of my body cavity, orchids with complex petals, wax-like and reminiscent of fat tissue. From deep within me emanated a curious bird-song.

Gradually, it altered pitch until it became an incomprehensible woman's voice. She was crying then laughing, muttering then shouting. I felt my lips moistened as if by someone's tongue trying to thrust itself into me. At the same time, a furry hand – or so it seemed – caressed my genitals and slid between the cheeks of my buttocks to toy with my anus.

The woman's voice transformed itself into a tolling bell which seemed to come from a bird perched high in the tree inside me. Beneath the tree stood a man. My inner vision concentrated upon him and I closed on him as if flying through the sky contained within my torso.

The man was me. I was dressed in a smart suit. My gold Vacheron Constantin glinted on my wrist. In my hands I held a small glass bottle containing a whitish liquid.

There was a tap on my shoulder. I turned round slowly. There was a smile on my face. I could feel the muscles tightening to form it as well as see them moving one against the other like plates of crimson steel dotted with black rivets.

Standing behind me was the Bronze Age man.

When I awoke, just as dawn was breaking, I found myself propped in the chair on my porch. The memory of all I had experienced was as vivid as if I had lived it and my head was clear. In the centre of the clearing, the last wisps of smoke were rising from the fire. All the men had disappeared save one: as if to confirm the night had not been a dream, Q'eke still lay on the ground with his canine companion.

I went to stand. My knees were weak, I was cold and I had shat myself.

◆

As we sat after my aspiration of the dead man, numbed by the success of the operation, Ruth broached the subject of how much I would charge for my time, stating she was sure she could meet my minimum fee from her expenses: I waived any emolument. At that point, she suggested I dine with her in Oxford before returning to London. A dinner invitation was, she insisted, the least she could do by way of thanks: besides, she assured me mischievously, she would put that on her Institute expense account instead.

We left the laboratory about six o'clock. I followed her elderly Volvo in my Porsche to a faceless suburban street in Headington. She was renting a flat in the upper storey of a semi-detached house constructed, I would guess, in the building boom years of the early fifties. It was a poky apartment consisting of a colourless sitting-cum-dining-room, a reasonably large bedroom, a small kitchen and a smaller bathroom which reminded me of the digs I had occupied during my second year at medical school. She had done her best to decorate the place to her taste, painting over the wallpaper, filling it with her own furniture, hanging pictures on the wall but this only provided a veneer. The garden outside was weed strewn, the lawn unkempt, the trees unpruned. The wooden back garden fence, where it was lit by a stark light from the downstairs flat, was leaning and lacked several slats. The street lights cast a meagre glow over the chipped paving stones and uneven kerb.

We took it in turns to wash in the cramped bathroom. A pair of tights hung from the shower curtain rail; the side of the bath needed repainting and the lavatory was a different colour porcelain from the sink. I could hear Ruth humming in the bedroom whilst through the floor rose the strains of the signature tune of an early evening soap opera mingled with the stink of frying fat. The whole place depressed me intensely. At seven-thirty, I drove us both into the centre of Oxford, parking in the cobbled solitude of Merton Street.

The restaurant was tucked away down an alley, a discreet place with beamed ceilings, dim lighting and dark walls covered with eighteenth-century prints of the city and university. We had hardly spoken since leaving the Institute and it was not until the waiter had taken our order and served us each a martini she broke our near silence, raising her glass. 'To him?' she suggested.

I needed no explanation and touched her glass with mine. 'To him,' I repeated.

'It's unbelievable,' she said softly, looking around the restaurant as she lowered her glass. There were only two other occupied tables. It was mid-week in late autumn.

'It is remarkable,' I replied. 'I had, to be truthful, not expected anything quite so – so perfect. I was quite prepared to cut into the testicle to obtain samples of seminiferous tissue. It is there spermatozoa are generated. Germ cells divide to form spermatids which, in turn, divide to give spermatozoa. If we had been unsuccessful . . .'

'But we did it,' she interrupted. 'Or rather, you did it.'

I sipped my martini. I could not drive from my mind's eye the picture focused on the monitor. 'Will you publish the results of today's little experiment?' I enquired.

'No,' she replied without hesitation. 'Not yet. There's a lot to be done with the material before I start to consider learned journals.'

'What are your first steps?'

'Initially, to extract the DNA. Then I want to compare its structure with a sample from a modern man. If there are significant differences over three thousand years . . . ' She paused and gazed at a print on the wall but I could tell she was not seeing it. 'Now that will be worth a piece in *Nature* or *Scientific American.*'

'I would rather,' I said, 'you didn't mention me in your paper.'

'Why on earth not? You are instrumental to the whole thing and you deserve to be known for the achievement. Besides, I owe you that.'

'I'll settle for this dinner and your company,' I answered. 'As for being known, I already have a reputation which may well not be enhanced by my patients thinking the hand which, albeit gloved in surgical rubber, probes their own private regions had on at least one occasion tinkered about with those of a pre-Christian cadaver. I appreciate your concern and generosity but, I think, leave me out of it.'

'Well, if you insist. But I think you should take credit where credit is due.'

'I'd rather have my practice and my Porsche than scientific approbation,' I declared. 'One cannot live off scientific fame or notoriety.'

'Do you never want more than just your personal success?' she asked after a moment's pondering. 'I mean, do you not feel there should be more to life than just being a doctor? Something more – more satisfying?'

'My work's very satisfying,' I told her. 'And I don't just mean in the pecuniary sense. I make human life possible, bring happiness to couples for whom misery is the order of the day because of a physical disability. Some doctors heal paraplegics and get them to walk, carry out cataract operations so the blind may see, restructure an inner ear so the deaf may hear. I am in their league.' I sipped my martini again, adding, 'I often wonder how many marriages I save with my expertise.'

She made no reply. The waiter brought our hors d'oeuvres and a bottle of chilled Muscadet which he left propped in an ice bucket with a napkin draped around the neck.

'This is not a comment on your work,' I said, thinking perhaps she had taken my speech as a criticism. 'I appreciate as much as any doctor the need for pure scientific research. After all, it was a boffin in a white coat who first succeeded in fertilizing a human egg in a test-tube. Without such research, my expertise would not exist. And, of course, I like to keep up with developments and, on occasion, I fill in reports for independent researchers working in the field of artificial insemination, fertilization and so on. Yet, at the end of the day, I prefer to see my results with a little more immediacy.'

'That's a little puerile,' she responded. 'To want immediate gratification.'

'Not quite immediate,' I replied, smiling. 'It takes nine months for my results to manifest themselves. But I appreciate what you say. Research can often only yield a result after years of often repetitive and boring study. And many failures.'

'Do you never fail? Is that what worries you about pure research?'

'In no way,' I said, rather curtly. 'I'm not afraid of failure and, indeed, I often fail. Sometimes because of my own faults, sometimes simply because I misconstrue nature or nature contrives against me. I recently spent an entire afternoon in microsurgery trying to reconnect a *vas deferens* from which a section had been cut. My patient had undergone a vasectomy when it was dangerous for his wife to conceive. She, poor woman, was subsequently killed in a riding accident and he remarried and wanted children with his new wife. For reasons partly of my own making and partly because the patient rejected the implanted replacement tube, I was unable to successfully carry out the reconnection. I failed him.'

My tone must have been sharper than I had intended for she felt silent again for a while and, throughout the rest of the meal, she prattled about some of her colleagues, told me stories of her student days on a long archaeological dig in the Hebrides and ventured a few oblique remarks on what she thought of the government and its policy towards research and development in the pure sciences: she was unable to understand how the prime minister could be so blind as to let the sciences down with government underfunding. I parried her observations, mainly for the sake of argument, playing devil's advocate to her political statements. She became quite heated at times. It was not until we had nearly finished our meal she realized I was toying with her and her attitude changed.

'You are a tease,' she accused me, her eyes bright.

'And you are gullible,' I rejoined.

'Over dinner, perhaps,' she allowed, 'but not in my laboratory.'

'Agreed,' I acquiesced and, although she remonstrated with me, I paid the bill for the meal.

As we slipped into our coats at the restaurant door, she put her arm in mine and said, quietly, 'Do you have to go back to London tonight? The roads will be icy.'

Looking up, I saw a narrow strip of sky scattered with a bright spatter of stars. Her breath misted in the air. I was not surprised at her indirect propositioning and it was not the first time such an approach had been made to me. In my hospital days, brief affairs were commonplace between doctors and their colleagues, between nurses and physicians. They were all so involved in their work they took any opportunity that arose for a relief from the tedium of long nights on the wards, the anguish of watching children die and men weep. They shared so much it seemed almost a natural progression they slept with each other, hid their fears and exhaustion in each other's arms and caresses. In many ways, I suppose, they slept together because of the camaraderie they participated in together. And that was what we were, this slim American palaeo-biologist and me – comrades, co-conspirators who owned a secret. Perhaps she thought sleeping with me would seal our clandestine contract, ensure the secrecy remained intact, inviolate.

'No, I don't,' I answered. At the same moment I knew I could not return to her drab lodging above the television set and the smell of frying food. 'But I feel neither should I come to your flat.' She looked momentarily crestfallen and let go of my arm. I took her hand and placed it in the crook of my elbow. 'I have had far too much to drink,' I went on as we walked down Bear Lane by the light of old-fashioned street lamps and into Oriel Square: we might have been a Victorian couple, 'and I don't feel either willing or competent enough to drive a fast car through the streets.'

'Then you can hardly drive to London,' she retorted. 'We can take a taxi . . .'

'Alternatively,' I suggested, 'I can book us into the Eastgate Hotel at the end of Merton Street.'

I felt her hand tighten slightly on my arm and took this to be acceptance of the plan. It being November, the hotel was not fully booked and I checked us into a double room at the rear of the hotel. Leaving Ruth in the room, I returned to the car and drove it the few hundred metres to the hotel car-park for safekeeping.

Just before I locked the car, I checked in the glove compartment; nestling behind the owner's handbook, an AA membership guide and a small dictaphone I used sometimes when travelling, wrapped for protection in a windscreen demister cloth, was a small bottle. I picked it up. The cloudy liquid looked unchanged: no doubt, the pure atmosphere inside the container and the partial vacuum would help to preserve it, if preservation was required. To be additionally sure, I placed the cloth hard against the windscreen which was already becoming lightly glazed with frost.

Ruth had run a deep bath whilst I had been out and we took it together. She was a hungry, rapacious lover: there was desperation about her. It was not, I felt, she was making up for lost time but was trying to live as much as she possibly could in the present, as if there might be no future. I felt sorry for her that night and, after we had sported in the bath and, later, in the double bed, I held her in my arms as she fell asleep.

I did not, I recall, sleep that night. Instead, I lay next to this pretty girl and thought over my actions of the afternoon, of the little bottle in the Porsche. And, over and over again, I saw the Bronze Age man's face frozen in ice and the repose of death, felt his hand in mine.

◆

I do not know why I did it.

Throughout my life, I have never stolen. Not even as a child, mixing with peers who helped themselves to chocolate bars or gobstoppers from the corner shop when old Mr Hawkhurst's back was turned in response to a spurious request for stock we knew he did not keep, did I thieve. I have always meticulously maintained tax records, indicated to shopkeepers if my change has been excessive; once finding a wallet in Hyde Park, I handed it to the police.

And yet, despite this, I stole the container of aspirated liquid.

It was so easy. As Ruth stared in exultant wonderment at the monitor screen and its portrait of dead spermatozoa, I slipped one of the bottles into my pocket. They were yet to be labelled, yet to enter into scientific history. Some instinct told me as I did it she would not notice one missing.

My motivation puzzles me.

The contents of the bottle were scientifically valueless without an established provenance. They were financially worthless for there is hardly a market in prehistoric sperm, documented or otherwise and I could hardly boast of their ownership to others for I considered it essential my name not be linked to the matter. In many ways, I was like the owner of a stolen work of art, smug in the knowledge of my possession but quite unable to share it with others for fear of discovery. Perhaps that is why I wanted the bottle. As a work of my art. Just as the painter retains his favourite picture from the exhibition, or the sculptor keeps the first cast of his coveted bronze, so I wanted to possess this unique specimen.

I returned to London the next morning, dropping Ruth off at her flat. It was Saturday and she asked me to stay the weekend but I politely refused. Partly, I did not want to embroil myself in an affair but mainly I was just as anxious to get back to my practice as she was to return to her laboratory and commence work on the axeman's DNA.

Arriving in the mews, I parked in my allotted space and entered the practice by my private door. There was no one about. I went up the stairs to my apartment, entered the kitchen and temporarily placed the bottle in the refrigerator. Then I took a shower, changed into some fresh clothes, went down to my office and quickly checked my mail. Molly had sorted out the important correspondence but there was nothing requiring immediate attention. Taking the bottle from the refrigerator, I walked through the consulting rooms and into the laboratory. Phillips had left one neon light on, as he was instructed, the venetian blinds lowered as a means of security. At the far end, the storage freezers hummed.

Not raising the blinds, I prepared a bench with the equipment I required – pipettes, sterilized straws, a bottle of cryoprotectant and an embryo storage bottle made of PTFE plastic.

I decided against centrifuging the sample for there was no way I could tell what might happen to the sperm under such increased gravitational forces. Using a Percoll gradient was out of the question: that was really only of use to sort out motile sperm.

Very slowly, I removed the top of the bottle. It hissed as the other had done. With a micro-pipette, I extracted a tiny drop of fluid, placed it on a slide and switched on a microscope. The sperm were there in comparatively large numbers. As the sample had not been mixed with semen, it was fairly concentrated although there was present a fair amount of miscellaneous cellular debris. I did not, however, feel I had to separate this: it was quite plain to see which was which in the sample. I had risked the material being contaminated or affected by the plastic seal: it had been impossible for me to keep the bottle upright. I was pleased to notice, however, no effect seemed to have occurred.

Over the next four hours, I painstakingly reduced half the sample to minute amounts held in a series of yellow and green plastic straws, the original liquid mixed with cryoprotectant. This done, I decanted the remainder of the liquid into the embryo storage bottle. My next step was to cover my tracks.

Going to the office, I took down a telephone directory and searched for an unlikely and, hopefully, unique surname, at the same time ensuring it did not look too bizarre: Zuncheddu or Przalskiya would stick out. It did not take me long before my eye picked up on *Mouette*. I switched on the computer, checked through the database against the million-to-one chance there was a patient of the same name on my books and settled down to invent a childless couple. The result was a file card printout with their details:

Mouette – Jonathan and Sylvia
Address: 41, Havingdene Rd, London SE28.
tel: 081 444 3452 (ex-directory)
Married: aged 31 (m) and 29 (f)

I checked in the A-to-Z gazetteer there was no Havingdene Road in London. In addition to the file card, I printed out a file cabinet docket slip and opened a file on them. Manipulating the database, I copied a medical history across from another couple, printed out a set of reports and placed these in the file. Next, I falsified egg, sperm and embryo storage and subsequent use consent forms, noting on each sheet no permission was given for their use with a third party, and put them with the records. Returning to the laboratory, I coded the straws and plastic bottle, entered the codes in the file and on the database, quick froze the samples in the usual manner and placed them in the storage freezer.

It was done. The Bronze Age axeman was now Mr

Mouette of the suburb of Thamesmead. Anyone looking through my files would see nothing out of the ordinary: Phillips, coming upon the material in the freezer, would simply dismiss it as a patient I was no longer actively treating. If he or Molly wondered if the material was available for another patient they would see from the file it was not: the integrity of the axeman's sperm was therefore safe.

I cleared up the laboratory, placed the glass bottle in a sink, wrapped it in several layers of absorbent towel and smashed it with a Bunsen burner tripod, dropping the splinters in the rubbish bucket.

It may have been vanity. It may have been a contradiction in myself: maybe I did after all want to claim my place in medical history. Be that as it may, I then sat down at the desk in my office and typed out a full account of everything to have occurred on the computer, from my first meeting with Ruth Schroeder. As a security measure against Molly or anyone else finding the file by chance, I apportioned it a hidden attribute. This meant, although it was on the hard disk in the computer, no one would see it if they called up a directory of the computer's contents. To discover the work, they would need to search for all the hidden files and remove their electronic cloak, so to speak.

◆

The Frenchwoman was back: according to her own diagnosis, her *ovrees are mis-function*. My assessment was the menopause had begun in her and she was not willing to accept the fact she was getting old. I could tell by looking at her this was the fear which ran in her blood. Her make-up was just a little too overdone, the hem of her skirt just a little too high for her thinning legs, her blouse just a little too low cut and her perfume just a little too powerful. She was running after her youth. I thought, as I searched for a vein in her forearm from which to draw a blood sample, that if she lived in Hollywood she would be visiting a cosmetician, not a gynaecologist. What she really wanted was liposuction and a face-lift.

Just as I found the vein, there was a discreet yet insistent knock upon the consulting room door. It had to be something serious: Molly knew never to interrupt a consultancy without good cause. I withdrew 10ml of French blood, removed the needle and called for her to enter.

'I'm sorry to disturb you, doctor,' she said. 'There is an urgent call for you.'

'Can you put it through?' I requested.

'Line one isn't working very well,' she replied.

It had to be bad. This was our little code to tell me the call was not to be overheard by a patient. I called Angela in, gave her instructions as to what else needed doing to the Frenchwoman and stepped into my office. Molly had already placed the receiver off the hook.

'It's Mr Cordiner,' she advised me.

I picked up the telephone.

'Hello, Dom?' I heard Brian say before I could greet him. 'I'm sorry to bother you mid-patient. I've rung . . .' He paused. I knew what he was going to say. Larry had miscarried. It was late in the pregnancy and I felt a thrill of anxiety rush up my back.

'When did it occur?' I asked.

'Three hours ago. We were going down to the coast for the day. Bracing breeze off the sea, blow the cobwebs away. It's cold but a clear blue sky down here. We . . . A lorry hit us. The car's a write-off but we were OK. Twisted chassis. Not even a window actually broke. We got shunted from the offside front. Not quite a head-on. Bit of a wham.' He was beginning to babble, the words postponing the moment when he had to tell me.

'Don't worry,' I said. 'Where are you?'

'A hospital. Dorchester. An ambulance brought us in. The lorry driver went through his windscreen. Lot of blood about. Bit like the old days, Dom. Anyway, we were in casualty. Just a check-up. Shock, that sort of thing. You know how they like to keep you under observation. Anyway, Larry suddenly got these pains. The baby . . . ' He stopped and I could hear him crying. I was not as worried now I had heard the cause was a car smash. The fault was not her body but external forces.

'I'm sorry, Dom. It's all . . .' Brian continued, his voice near to breaking.

'Right, Brian,' I said, putting on my best authoritative doctor's tone, 'don't worry. The miscarriage is not likely to affect future chances. Now – were there complications with the miscarriage?'

'No. None. It . . . He just came out.'

'I'm on my way,' I told him. 'Stay in the hospital. I'll put Molly on the phone – you remember my receptionist? – and she'll get all the details. Hold on a tic.' I turned to Molly and said, 'Who's in this afternoon?'

She consulted the computer screen on my desk and replied, 'Mr Stapleton's coming in for a sperm sample.'

'Have Angela deal with it. Explain to Stapleton I've an emergency. Get all the details from Mr Cordiner now and fill in a miscarriage report for me.' She waved the form in her hand. 'Good lass!' I exclaimed and removed my hand from the receiver. 'Hello, Brian? I'll just get shot of my patient and I've managed to cover this afternoon. I'll clear up here and I'm on my way.'

'Thanks, Dom,' he replied, his voice quiet with sorrow.

'Hang on, chum,' I said as cheerily as I could, 'here's Molly.'

I arrived at the hospital about 4.30. It was already dark and the clear sky of the day had been replaced with mean drizzling sleet. I introduced myself to the casualty receptionist and requested to speak to the doctor who had dealt with the Cordiners before going in to see them.

The doctor was in his mid-twenties, as harassed as I recall being myself at a similar stage in my career, slouched on a PVC chair in a rest-room-cum-office with his feet hanging on the open drawer of a filing cabinet in which I could see an assortment of jars of instant coffee, Ovaltine and sugar.

He stood up as I entered and hung his stethoscope down his chest: it had been slung over his shoulder. We shook hands and I questioned him about the miscarriage.

'There were no problems, no complications. It was just one of those things, induced by trauma.'

'May I see the foetus?'

He nodded and I followed him along corridors lined with trolleys and invalid chairs to a door marked *Pathology Dept – Medical Staff only*. We went in and he spoke to a technician. The foetus lay in an enamel tray.

'We're waiting for the chaplain,' the technician explained. 'The parents have signed a release but want a prayer or two first.'

'And then?' I asked: it was not unusual for foetuses to be shipped to medical schools.

'Then it'll be sent to the incinerator.'

'No coroner's objections?' I enquired.

'None,' the doctor said. 'And we've written a report for the legal eagles in case of an insurance claim through the traffic accident.'

At the time, a foetus under twenty-eight weeks was regarded as not yet living and, in the eyes of the hospital and the law, nothing more than any other organ removed in an operation. There was, therefore, no objection to my investigating it. I put on a pair of gloves and borrowed an apron.

The foetus was about twenty weeks old and, as Brian had said on the telephone, was male. By that stage of development, it was a perfectly formed if ill-proportioned human about 15cm long. Its skin was pink, its hands and feet bore the requisite number of digits and showed no signs of any malformation. Taking a scalpel, I made a longitudinal incision down the chest then, with a pair of bone cutters, split the sternum, opening up the body cavity. At first inspection, all the major internal organs – heart, liver, lungs – seemed to be present and appeared quite typical. I was convinced the foetus, had it gone to parturition, would have been a normal, happy baby.

Delving more deeply, however, shifting the small intestines aside, I noticed one kidney was well advanced but the other was virtually non-existent. This caused me some concern so I set about looking more closely at the foetus. It was then I discovered it had no eyes.

It was a shock. I stepped back from the table and sat on a stool. Had I been a religious person, I would have offered up a prayer not to the god of stillborn infants but to the controller of car crashes and runaway lorries, thanked him for his timely intervention. For decorum's sake, when I was done, I sutured the incision shut and removed the gloves and apron.

'Have you seen him?' Brian asked as soon as we had greeted each other. He looked none the worse for the accident, the only physical marks on him being a contusion on his forehead above the left eye and a bandage on his right arm, yet his hands were unsteady and he was ashen faced.

'Yes, and there were no abnormalities,' I lied. 'That probably gives you no comfort but it tells me, save for this tragic accident, you would have had a healthy infant. It bodes well for our next attempt.'

'It won't affect our chances?' he asked, his eyes searching mine.

'None whatsoever. If the miscarriage had occurred out of the blue, I would have been very concerned indeed but it did not. It was induced. I'm sure Larry will conceive again with just as much ease.' I put my hand on his shoulder. 'It's a bugger, Brian,' I commiserated, 'but it's not the end of the world. We'll overcome it.'

We walked towards a general ward. Larry was in a side-room of four beds, only one other of which was occupied by a young woman still under sedation from, the ward sister informed me, an appendectomy.

'And Mrs Cordiner?' I enquired, as Brian went ahead of me into the room.

'She's comfortable. We'll keep her in for a few days just in case and the psychiatrist's going to have a word with her. The chaplain's been in.'

'Injuries?'

'Nothing too serious. No concussion but she is shocked. The miscarriage was occasioned by the lap seat belt digging hard into the stomach on impact. She then seems to have slid forward under the belt and it created a lot of upward pressure on the stomach, probably dislodging the foetus.'

'Internal haemorrhaging?'

'None unexpected and everything's stabilized now.'

I entered the room, bent over Larry's bed, kissed her cheek and held her hand as I perched on the edge of the mattress. I told her the same as I had Brian. She was tearful but I could see she was determined this was not going to lessen her resolve.

'I didn't carry anything heavy. Next time, I shan't drive, either,' she declared and managed a weak smile.

As I left the hospital, I was very optimistic about the chances of a second pregnancy but concerned about the foetal defect. It might have been a one-off, a chance in a million: on the other hand, there might well have been something seriously wrong with Brian's sperm. As I drove back to London, I wondered what it might be: perhaps he had been lax over x-ray procedures in his dental practice, not donned his lead-lined apron or left the room when photographing mandibles and impacted molars. There again, perhaps he had somehow absorbed too much mercury from the amalgam used in fillings. Both could cause serious problems of this sort. I worried it over in my mind but realized there was nothing I could actually do. I was loath to tell Brian he had an inherent problem. There was no solid proof. Babies are born deformed and he was, quite possibly, just unlucky.

My prognosis for an easy second attempt was correct: seven weeks later, Larry was back in my consulting room to produce five mature eggs. To overcome the loss of any of Brian's sperm as had previously occurred through freezing, I decided against freezing but planned to take his contribution to the process on the day I collected the oöcytes. I planned, therefore, to simply purify the sperm collected and immediately fertilize the eggs.

All seemed to go well, but there arose then a major problem. Brian's sperm count had dropped drastically from his first consultation. Whereas it had been about 28 on his previous visit, it was now down to 16 and, although the semen sample was bigger at 2.8 ml, the progressive motility was down to 11 with a very marked reduction in normal forms. The sample he had given was, I felt certain, insufficient to ensure fertilization, information I kept from them.

While Larry lay in the recovery room, I suggested to Brian we go out for a drink: it was not long after New Year and my invitation did not seem amiss. We walked through streets busy with shoppers to a wine bar I knew of in a quiet street. It being early evening, the place was not yet crowded with pre-theatre or after-work drinkers and we had a table to ourselves in a corner.

For a few minutes, we talked of the car crash. The events of the day were, weeks later, ordered in his mind: the lorry had, inexplicably, suddenly veered towards their car. He had frozen momentarily then spun the wheel; the vehicles had hit each other; the steering-wheel struck his arm and Larry slid forward, half under the fascia. He was, he said, glad she had not broken her legs, thankful they had been slowing to turn into a lane to the beach. He did not mention the miscarriage, but sipped his wine at the point the ambulance arrived in his recounting. 'Anyway,' he said, his spirits rising a little, 'we're back on course now. It's just a temporary setback, isn't it?'

I nodded and then I lied.

'Only temporary,' I agreed. 'Right now, the eggs are in their containers and your little tadpoles are doing their stuff.'

He grinned then his face grew sad. 'We were going to call him Richard Dominic,' he half-whispered. 'The hospital chaplain used the names in his blessing. Richard, you see, was my father and . . . '

I put my hand on his arm and said, 'Well, you must give the next one another name. You can't use the same one twice.'

He shook his head in agreement.

Half a dozen young executives entered, dressed in sharp

designer suits and carrying Gucci and Pierre Cardin brief-cases. They were raucous and brash. One was speaking on a mobile phone.

'Yappies,' Brian remarked. 'That's what Larry calls them. Not yuppies, yappies. Young arrogant pricks.'

I grinned, not only at her witticism, but also with relief for Brian's mind was moving away from the morbid and miserable back to his usual self.

'I expect,' I commented, looking at the group ordering a bottle of Moët et Chandon, 'they would have some difficulty in the sin bin.'

'On the contrary, Dom,' Brian answered, winking in the direction of the one with the phone, 'I bet they'd manage very well indeed. They're a load of wankers.'

We both laughed. It was a word from our schooldays, a dinosaur word which was both crude yet so very apt.

'If you couldn't manage it,' I said, 'what would you do? I have patients from time to time who simply can't. Not even with the tax avoidance smut.'

'I don't know. It doesn't arise.'

The hair on my nape tingled.

'Would you go for AID?'

'What is it?'

'Artificial Insemination Donation. Or Donor.'

'You mean have another man's sperm used?'

'More or less. We can go to a central bank for it or rely upon excess sperm from other patients of my own who've signed a release.'

Brian took a long swill of wine and wrinkled up his nose. 'I would never accede to that. Another man's sperm in my wife. All right, so it got there through a catheter, but so what? The resultant child would not be ours. Hers, but not ours.'

'But you've signed a release on your sperm,' I pointed out, 'and Larry's given permission for her spare eggs to be used for a non-ovulating woman.'

'That's different,' Brian replied sharply, 'I don't mind helping out a fellow man – or woman – but I'd not want such help myself. It would be no better than adopting. The child would still not be mine and, somewhere, there would be its real father, alive and forever posing a threat . . . '

'A threat?' I interrupted.

'A threat. A ghost the child might one day want to discover. A usurper waiting in the wings.' He drained his glass, refilling it from the carafe on the table between us.

I let the subject drop and mused upon the vanities of men. There was no question of my telling him what his sperm count was that day. He was in no mood to hear talk of his personal failure, his inability to produce what he considered to be the most vital aspect of every man's existence. Not for mere semantic reasons does the English language have the word seminal in its vocabulary. I topped up my own glass and considered what course of action I might take if, in eighteen hours, the oöcytes had not been fertilized.

◆

Chuhi and the other men have gone hunting as a band, taking the boy who was recently circumcised with them: for him it is a red letter day, the first hunt he has attended. They set off as a band not long after dawn armed with blowpipes and bows with extraordinarily long arrows, passing me as I stood by the river.

'¿Qué estás cazando?' I enquired of him as he passed.

'Tucuxi,' Chuhi replied enigmatically and walked away.

I did not understand the word and, being reluctant to admit to my ignorance, I assumed by asking how they caught it I might have a clue as to the identity of their quarry. '¿Como atraparlo?' I enquired.

'Nosotros se lo cantaremos a su muerte,' he said curtly and walked smartly off, quite bluntly ignoring me.

'¡Buena suerte!' I called after him, none the wiser: I could not hazard a guess as to what animal was killed by singing.

Chuhi neither turned round nor made any reply. It was

then I remembered Dr Suarez: they don't talk when going off hunting for fear their words will forewarn their prey.

The women and children also seem mostly to have vanished. An old crone, the one who paddles the *yamanachi*, remains. She is weaving in the shady doorway of a long-house.

For the last half an hour, I have been tormented by a *seringueiro*. It is an insignificant-looking bird not unlike a hen blackbird but with a longer tail. It has perched in or around a *sororoca* wild banana tree and incessantly whistled at me. I have tried to drive it away by pelting it with gravel but the bird is determined not to shift its ground. Now it has learnt, at the sight of me, to fly out of range into a higher tree: when I am gone, it returns to the *sororoca*. The creature's call is not a tuneful melody nor a low, monotonous call one may readily ignore. It is a loud, crude, drawn-out wolf-whistle which soon becomes tedious. If I were to lose my sanity here, this bird would be a significant contributory factor. Another would be my dwelling upon the past which I cannot escape. I suppose I had hoped, in time, it would disappear or fade like a failed love affair but it has not. When not being distracted by the people of the clearing, the river or this damned bird, I find my mind moving back in time almost as if it had a will of its own, a determination to reassess itself and perhaps find a way of undoing things. It looks for those moments when kismet gave its knife another twist.

My trouble was I was never a coward.

I followed the wrong dictum.

Instead of heeding Robert Browning's sound advice when the imp of misfortune danced into my life

> *Why comes temptation but for man to meet*
> *And master and make crouch beneath his foot,*
> *And so be pedestaled in triumph?*

I ignored it and followed instead my own lead. I fell into the same snare which entrapped Dorian Gray. He saw the opportunity to become immortal and he took it, with never a thought for the consequence, never once considering how for every contract there is a hidden clause, for every action there is an equal and opposite reaction, a law which applies not just to the physical but to the emotional world as well. Or, I might add, an unequal action for, as the innocents in Paradise discovered, a tiny bite of one apple can alter the shape of creation.

That is what I did. Bit the apple. Altered creation.

It was so easy. It always is. I remember a headmaster castigating me once: to be good is difficult but to sin is simplicity itself. I had stood before his desk, guilty of some infantile crime I have long since forgotten, and been forced to listen to his diatribe on right and wrong but all I recall now is that one statement which was drilled home, beaten in with a short length of linoleum strapped across the palm of my left hand three times. I should have listened to the old pedant but I did not. I remembered his lesson well enough but I was too smug, too artful to learn from it.

How stupid I was, how arrogant. My life was fulfilled beyond the expectations of most men. I had a comfortable wealth which had not grown, as a tycoon's might, to be a burden. My work was satisfying, both financially and intellectually rewarding. And yet I chanced it. I knew I was taking a risk the minute I agreed to see the axeman, the second I thrust my arms into the rubber gloves, the moment I held, just for the fleetest of seconds, the dead man's hand.

The ethical question was not lost on me. As I pressed the aspirant into the catheter, I knew I was doing wrong, was breaking the bounds of propriety, was carrying out an act any hospital or professional ethics committee would abhor and censure. If news of what I was doing leaked out, I was sure to be at best castigated and, quite feasibly, forbidden my licence to practise medicine. It even occurred to me I was invading the axeman's privacy. My conscience even had me cast a quick look at Barry's video camera to ensure I was not included in the frame and I felt a vague relief to see that the lens was closed up on the area of the thawed genitalia.

The reason why I did it has nagged me. Perhaps it was just intellectual curiosity, a need to know what was or was not possible. Every man wants to stretch himself when the time comes, see how far he might go, might extend his skills, might learn a new trick in his game. There again, it might have been a subconscious desire to have a place in the research history after all so that, a century later, I might be ranked with Ruth alongside Faraday or Edison, Fleming or Pasteur, and people might say when reading their history books or attending their lectures, they were the ones who did it first.

Whatever the real truth is, the scientist in me took over. I know that now. With so much order and knowledge at my command, I assumed a power I should not possess yet did, took upon myself a responsibility it was not mine to bear. It was God's.

Whenever I entered the laboratory, called by Phillips to view this sample or agree that decision, I could not help catching a glimpse of the freezing unit and think of the secret it held. It was almost as if the axeman was silently calling to me in his unknown language, asking me to act, to free him from his cage of ice, to set him alive once more.

At least once daily, I have questioned my motivation.

I did not act out of a sense of self-importance nor did I deliberately set out to challenge God. I was not seeking self-glorification, either: if I had wanted that, I would have given Ruth permission – indeed, I would have pressed her – to print my name in her paper, publish it so the world knew I was the one, with her, who had broken the barrier of yet another scientific possibility.

Science was not the motive, either. Not directly. Yet, indirectly, I suppose it was because I was toying with it, playing with the laws of nature to see if I might bring in a new play, a new stratagem to the game of life. In the vernacular of second-rate politicians and embittered trade unionists I was seeing if I, a mere spectator, could shift the goal posts on the main field.

With hindsight, I admit to curiosity which, in itself, is a

selfishness. I embarked upon my actions to see if it was possible to achieve the undreamt of.

At times, I tell myself I did it out of love and, in part, this is the honest truth. I felt for Brian and Larry, loved them in their misery with the compassion which divides humans from the animals, wanted them to achieve the happiness they so urgently sought, so desperately needed to fulfil themselves. I knew they would never have children of their own, created exclusively from their own bodies.

Yet I also did it for myself and I cannot escape the fact. I took up my knowledge and my tools and, like any artisan, I set out to create the unique.

It was Mark Twain who wrote the best protection against temptation is cowardice. That was my failing. A lack of cowardice, a conviction of bravery.

No god is ever afraid but I was, even if I did not admit it or was even conscious of it, for a while. And I was a god then.

Voices echoing from the direction of the river draw my attention. The hunters are returning, shouting excitedly to each other, calling ahead. The old crone has given up her weaving to waddle off towards them, her squeaky voice calling out. I have suddenly realized the accursed *sororoca* bird has ceased calling. Perhaps it has realized there are soon to be a large number of gravel-throwers in the clearing.

As the jabbering crowd of men arrive, I can see they are carrying a large animal slung from a pole between them. Coming closer I recognize what they have caught, much to my surprise, is a freshwater dolphin. Its sides and prominent dorsal fin are smeared with a rich ruby coating of newly-spilled blood. Chuhi beckons to me. I leave the hut and approach the jubilant hunters. The old crone is beside herself with excitement. She slaps her hand on the dead creature's solid flesh, making little whooping screams. The circumcised youth has a wide, complacent grin on his face. To have made such a kill on his first hunt of adulthood will, I should think, be long remembered and enhance his reputation with the ladies.

The dolphin is quite dead but, I should guess, not long so. Crouching I peer into its face and its almost human eye. Around the circle of the socket is a rim of tears. It occurs to me it cried as it bled to death because it succumbed to the magic of the hunters' sing-song voices, the terrible temptation to rise towards the music and on to the barbs on their fishing arrows. Like me, it fell for the wonders of the unknown, the possibilities of fortune: and, like me, it has suffered for its gullibility, its belief in its own providence.

◆

Deciding not to wait the eighteen hours, I set to work that night. It was not just a matter of secrecy but also of practicality. I would not be disturbed and needed all my attention for the task I had set myself.

Phillips had mixed Larry's five mature oöcytes with Brian's minimal sperm offering but, as soon as the practice closed and everyone had gone home, I removed these from the incubator and carefully separated out the oöcytes. Not one of them had been fertilized, for which I was grateful: the sight of the blind foetus was seldom absent from my thoughts. Furthermore, the sperm seemed even less motile than before despite being in an enriched environment of HAMS F10 and at a perfectly controlled temperature. Quite clearly, I believed, Brian's sperm were unsuitable and he was fast becoming completely infertile.

The procedure I was to embark upon was theoretically not difficult but it was intensely time-consuming and required a very high degree of concentration. A spermatozoon being basically only a DNA vehicle, it is not essential it pierce the oöcyte itself. With careful microscopic manipulation and a needle far thinner than a human hair, it is possible to assist nature by implanting a sperm artificially in the egg. It was this I intended to do but not with Brian's output.

With the equipment ready, I left the laboratory and,

unlocking the filing cabinet, removed a file. The catalogue slip read *Mouette – Jonathan and Sylvia.*

My hands shook. I remember that quite distinctly. And I broke out into a sweat, not fear or guilt but sheer excitement.

From the file, I withdrew the slip of paper which gave me the codes for the straws and took two from the freezer unit, thawing them in the usual manner. With the contents in one small petri dish and the oöcytes in another, I set about the delicate task of implanting one of the axeman's spermatozoa into each of Larry's eggs.

My hands no longer shook. I worked steadily, carefully, methodically. Through the microscope eyepiece, the first oöcyte appeared as a little two dimensional sphere, the cellular contents opaque and the cell wall invisible except at the edges of the image where it appeared like a line drawn with a fine pen dipped in indian ink. It looked exactly like an illustration in a textbook. With a single sperm captured in the hollow channel of the needle, I moved this slowly into my field of vision. It has never ceased to amaze me how man's ingenuity has succeeded in achieving such a wonder as a hollow tube only a few microns in diameter. With the needle close to the oöcyte, I sucked in my breath and held it, like a man about to fire a gun, who has the target in his sights and has taken up the slack on the trigger. I put the head of the needle against the cell and pushed. It was a tiny movement of my hand. Imperceptible. In the screen the end pressed on the outer cell membrane which gave but did not break. It was rather like forcing a finger into a balloon. My approach, I realized, was perhaps too gentle. My second attempt was more forceful. The cell membrane broke and the head of the needle slid in, displacing but not damaging the cellular material. It was a simple matter to eject the sperm head. It moved from the needle into the cell, a tiny translucent dot. I slowly withdrew the black line of the needle. The cell membrane closed the point of piercing. With the needle out of the field of vision, I continued to watch the cell. It was not that I was going to observe anything happening. Even if fertilization was to occur, it would not be an immediate process. There was no sudden cell division, eruption of activity.

I repeated the process with another oöcyte. It was just as successful. The sperm head entered without a problem. The third oöcyte did not work. After two successful attempts, I was perhaps getting a little blasé at my expertise or else the structure of the cell membrane was weak, the oöcyte not a grade 1 but a 2A specimen: whichever was the case, the membrane ruptured and some of the cellular contents escaped. I discarded it.

By just after two o'clock, I had impregnated four oöcytes with sperm from the fictitious Mr Mouette – the Bronze Age axeman.

As Phillips would be the person to check if fertilization had occurred, I had to cover my tracks so he would not suspect anything. Accordingly, I replaced the now fertilized oöcytes into their original containers and added to them the requisite amount of Brian's sperm. The chances of them fertilizing an oöcyte now was almost non-existent but, to make doubly sure, I killed all the sperm off by heating them to a temperature at which they could not remain alive before replacing them. Having discarded one oöcyte, I falsified the records to account for the lost one.

With all the containers back in the incubator, I returned the Mouette file to the cabinet and locked it. Taking a pad of notepaper from a desk drawer I wrote, in detail, everything I had done, checking it through and correcting it so I might not forget a single action or piece of data. When I was satisfied with my work, I typed it all into the computer as an extension to my original hidden file of notes on the aspiration. The pages from the notepad went through the shredder beside Molly's desk and into the waste bag beneath: they would soon be bedding for Angela's daughter's rabbits.

This done, I went to bed but not to sleep.

The enormity of my deed kept me awake. I felt no guilt but a mixture of intense pleasure at having assisted the Cordiners in their quest for a child and an exquisite excitement. That I had acted in direct contravention of all the laws and ethical codes of practice governing my profession, and had specifically disregarded Brian's wishes, did not concern me. Deep in myself, I knew what I was doing was for the best: Brian and Larry would have their child and there would be no ghost haunting the future, no living father lingering in the dark forests of time, waiting to jump out and claim his place.

At the same time, and for entirely personal motives, I knew I was pushing back those boundaries of science, taking another step nearer to unravelling the last mystery which was all that mattered. Once more, I had tipped the odds of nature my way, had played another card and trumped God.

At mid-morning, Phillips and I inspected the containers.

'I could have sworn we had five on the go,' Phillips remarked as he took the little plastic bottles in their rack out of the incubator.

My heart jumped. He checked the records and shrugged.

Two of the oöcytes had fertilized.

'Not as lucky as last time,' Phillips said, not taking his eye from the microscope screen, 'but then those sperm were distinctly dubious. They're all of them dead now.'

Early in the afternoon, Larry came to the practice and, with a hand as steady as iron, I inserted the catheter through her cervix and transferred the two fertilized oöcytes. 'There we are,' I confirmed, smiling. 'Better luck the second time around.'

Larry smiled back at me and, once again, took my hand. 'This time, Dom,' she said quietly. 'This time we will do it.'

I looked down at her hand in mine and thought what those same fingers had achieved in the dark, wicked hours of night.

◆

Chuhi's younger brother, Tieco, is suffering from *pian*, a form of syphilis. He has developed open sores and ulcers up to three centimetres in diameter on his neck, right arm, and thighs. The sores weep atrociously, staining his flesh with damp patches of plasma which harden on his dark skin to form crusts of yellow matter with the appearance of smeared candle wax. The thin black lines he has painted on his skin, either by way of decoration or as a charm against the *pian*, appear under this coating like sketches on the inside of cheap glass.

He has been to see Keewei who has diagnosed the disease correctly and treated it in accordance with the jungle pharmacopoeia he has in his head, dabbing a pungent brew of stewed leaves, river mud and crushed ants on the wounds. These have had an immediate curative effect: the leaves, I suspect, contain chemicals which promote some form of healing, the ground ants no doubt supply formic acid which burns out the infection and the mud acts as a poultice and bandage, keeping secondary infection at bay. Folklore obliges Tieco to abstain from sexual union whilst he has these sores because, as Chuhi has told me, *el alma puede salir por los poros de su piel y fuede entrar en un otro hombre – la locura sigue:* the soul can escape through these holes in his skin and enter another, driving them mad. It is, of course, a primitive means of avoiding infection: whilst he has these manifestations of the disease, he is highly infectious. Yet Keewei's medicine does not attack the bacterial cause of the disease. As soon as one sore is cured, another erupts and all Tieco can do is return time and again to the shaman, each visit costing him a hen or a basket of freshly-caught fish.

Last night, just before dusk, Chuhi suddenly appeared at the side of my hut. As is my habit, I was seated in the twilight on the veranda taking the evening air. I had been reading *David Copperfield* from a thick edition of all Dickens' novels in my modest library of books but had let the volume drop to my lap as the daylight faded. The print was too small to decipher by anything but direct sunlight. The sun was well below the trees across the river, the last birds squabbling as they established their night perches. From beneath the eaves the bats broke free and splashed momentarily against the sky.

At first, I did not notice him. It was not until he knocked softly on the corrugated iron hut wall I learnt of his presence.

'*Buenas noches*, Chuhi,' I said.

'*Cshatt, cshatt!*' he exclaimed softly and put three fingers over his lips which I took to signify the equivalent of *shush*. He glanced across the clearing before continuing, '*Buenas noches, señor. Me gusta hablar contigo.*'

The people of the clearing were not usually so secretive in their approaches to me and, wondering what might be amiss, I reached to light my oil lamp, but Chuhi *cshatt*ed again and I put the matches down. Assured I was not going to illuminate the porch, he crept onto it and squatted against the wall by the door. Once settled, he knocked on the floor planks and another figure slid into view, moving with the silent agility of a cat. '*Es mi hermano*, Tieco,' Chuhi announced in a half-whisper. '*Está malo.*'

'*Pués, debo examinarlo*,' I declared and once more reached for the matches.

'*No, señor.*' He nodded to his brother and they both slunk into the hut. I followed, closed the door and swung down the wooden shutters. I was then permitted to light a lamp.

Tieco's condition was apparent and I did not have to consult a textbook to diagnose his problem. I had seen it in Santo Antonio do Içá where Dr Suarez had gone out of his way to show me sufferers in the streets, briefing me on what medical conditions I might find amongst the jungle dwellers.

'*Mi hermano* ...' Chuhi began then, for the first time, seemed a little unsure of himself. '*Hace falta de pian see ling.*'

My Spanish is not good but I thought I had enough of a command to translate everyday conversation.

'*¿Qué falta . . . ?*' I queried.

'*Pian see ling,*' Chuhi repeated, then, after a pause, tried another version. '*Pian-isileena.*'

It was at least a minute before I realized what he was saying. Chuhi wanted penicillin for his brother because he assumed it cured *pian.* I smiled my understanding and prepared to give him a shot. I still had some supplies remaining.

Tieco looked apprehensive as I removed the needle and syringe from their sterile wrappers. He muttered under his breath to his brother who just nodded encouragement, sticking out his lower lip in a grimace as I extracted some saline from a bottle, added it to the penicillin, shook the powder vigorously to dissolve it and refilled the syringe.

'*¿Qué dice?*' I enquired, interested to know what Tieco was saying.

Chuhi shrugged as if to say – nothing, just give him the jab and be done with it.

I rubbed a dab of methylated spirits on Tieco's arm and popped the needle in. His skin was hard but the needle was up to it. He winced and jerked his head away. I wiped the spot again as I withdrew the needle. '*Se acabó,*' I told him.

Chuhi spoke in the Huambas dialect then added, '*Mi hermano no habla español.*'

I requested no payment but was given something in any case. Tieco produced three of the dolphin's teeth, each one exquisitely carved into the minuscule shape of a bird. I was enchanted by them and thanked him. He bobbed his head much as a Victorian maid might have done then, without asking me, Chuhi blew out the lamp and the two of them disappeared into the deep shadows of the last twilight.

After their departure, I sat on the porch again. The night was moonless. From the long-houses came a faint hubbub of voices and the cry of a baby. Firelight danced on the thatch and timber of the walls. I might have been living ten thousand years ago for there was no sign in the view of any of man's discoveries, inventions or artifice, save the fire.

For a while, I pondered on their strange approach to the hut and then went in to sleep but this morning, on going down to the river, I learnt why they had been so secretive.

On the bank stood Keewei. He was washing an aluminium pot in the river, scouring it with sand and gravel mixed with ashes from a fire.

'*Buenos días*,' I greeted him, but instead of his usual response he glowered at me. Even in the jungle, I realized, it is not done for one doctor to poach another's patients.

◆

Throughout her pregnancy, Larry paid regular and frequent visits to me. I kept a close check on her, monitoring her blood, her general health, her emotional state – in short, everything I felt was pertinent.

For the first twelve weeks, I lived in daily fear of a call to say she had again miscarried: as the three months drew to an end, I found myself dreading the ring of the phone, especially at night and on my private number. If I heard Brian's voice upon the line, my heart rate increased in a leap. Yet nothing happened. On the few occasions Larry caught a cold, she suffered it with no more medication than a menthol chest rub with Tiger Balm. She was determined there should be no risk at all to the foetus, even from as unlikely a source as an aspirin or a decongestant pill. Her diet was strictly controlled according to the latest fad on 'eating for two', approved by myself. On top of that, she carried nothing heavier than a tea tray, abstained totally from alcohol, assiduously avoided cigarette smoke (to the point of embarrassing both myself and Brian in restaurants) and maintained a strict regime of daily rest and nightly sleep.

As the foetus grew, I shared in almost every aspect of its development. My excitement was tremendous although I had to keep this suppressed to the levels expected of a friend and medical consultant: yet I was exultant, as if the child was my own. In a manner of speaking, of course, it was. I had planned it, formed it, set it on its journey and although its seed was not my own, it might just as well have been. I had arranged it all. I had been its creator.

At just over seven months, I conducted an ultrasound scan to ensure all was well. Larry arrived in the practice on a Tuesday. I remember it well and might have sensed the omen, had I not been so preoccupied with the anticipation of seeing the child for the first time.

It was raining heavily. Molly saw the taxi arrive at the appointed time and rushed down the stairs with a golfing umbrella but Larry was already out of the cab, the rain pattering on her head and her hair starting to gather into rats' tails.

'You really should take more care,' I remonstrated with her as she entered the consulting room, Molly taking her coat and shaking it in the corridor outside. 'You'll catch pneumonia.'

'Not a chance!' Larry retorted. ' I simply won't give it house space.'

We kissed, as friends do, and Molly brought in a coffee for me and a cup of thin Chinese tea for Larry: she had also forsworn coffee for the duration of her pregnancy.

'You have no idea, Dom, how much I look forward to the birth. As soon as my milk flows and I know all is well,' she sniffed the air, 'I shall have a huge *espresso* and a double gin and tonic.'

I questioned her. All seemed well. Angela entered to inform me she was ready and so we went into my operating suite where Larry undressed, slipped on a smock and cautiously lay down, a large pillow under her head and a soft, thick covering between her back and the cool black surface of the table. I undid the bows of tape which held the front of the smock closed and smoothed a transmitting gel on to her distended belly.

'You must admit I do look a bit – *cetacean*,' she commented as my hands moved smoothly over her skin.

Angela moved the monitor to a position where both Larry and I could see it together. The scanner was switched on and I placed it on Larry's stomach. The monitor screen jumped with patterns of curved white lines and dots. It resembled a rather poor negative of an astronomical time-lapse photograph, the lines traces of stars on the move.

'I can't make anything out,' Larry said.

Shifting the scanner down towards the top of her pyramidalis muscle there came into view on the screen the unmistakable outline of a human head.

All Larry said was, 'Oh!'

Angela pointed to the screen with her finger. 'That's its head and here,' she moved her finger as I moved the scanner, 'is its face. This is an arm and, if you look carefully, you just about make out two fingers.'

I showed no outward sight of emotion at all. It might have been just another baby, one of the hundreds I had transferred from plastic test-tube to uterus, had scanned and monitored and later received a Polaroid of to pin on the notice-board until it was faded or covered by others. Inside, however, my blood raced and my mind whirled. As the scan shifted around Larry's belly, I avidly watched the screen, interpreting every image, every curved line and dot, assessing what each was and looking out for anything which struck me as abnormal. There was nothing. Yet, as I returned finally to the head – mothers-to-be want to see the head more than little arms and legs – I could not help a shudder of anxiety at the thought this one also might lack its eyes.

When Larry was dressed, I asked her what she thought.

'I can't say,' she answered, her face glowing with pride. 'It's quite incredible. Seeing into your own body and . . . ' She looked into my face. She was not crying but her eyes sparkled. 'You were right. Second time. And we've done it!'

'Not yet,' I cautioned. 'The race isn't over until the horse is in the stable. Or the baby in the cot.'

'You don't anticipate any problems, do you?'

'None,' I assured her. 'The baby is perfectly positioned, head down and ready to go. Or come. But we must never count our chickens.'

She smiled and said, 'No. But then I'm not going anywhere until the car takes me to the hospital.'

It was agreed Larry would give birth in the local hospital about eight miles from Harbury. I would attend the birth if I could but was not worried in myself if I was absent. A midwife had been regularly visiting Larry at home, the hospital gynaecologist had been in touch with me and was in receipt of copies of all the documentation.

In the event, the baby was born at just after midnight on a Sunday morning. I was out for dinner at the time and returned home about one o'clock to find the green light on my private line ansaphone winking. I pressed the replay button and heard Brian's voice. 'Dom, this is Brian. The baby was born at zero-twenty-five hours. Six pounds, four ounces. Everything working. The midwife says it was an easy birth. I was there. It looked it. Larry's doing fine.' There was a click as he hung up followed by a buzz on the tape to announce another message. I let it run on. 'Dom, sorry! Forgot! It's a boy.'

I sighed and sat down. My hands felt weak. My whole body seemed drained. Then I had a long, slow drink and went to bed.

A busy two days prevented me from doing anything other than sending the usual congratulatory telegram and having a huge bouquet delivered to the hospital. It was not until the Wednesday afternoon I was able to travel down to Harbury. Larry had been released from the maternity ward the day before and was back at home. As the Porsche drew to a halt, the split stable-type kitchen door opened and Brian appeared, preceded by the cat which trotted smartly across the patio and out of sight: it moved with the alacrity of an animal usurped.

'What can I say, Dom?' Brian exclaimed, first shaking me by the hand then, after a moment's pause of uncertainty, hugging me.

'I'd say you've pulled it off,' I said.

'We, Dom! We pulled it off. He's a grand little chap.'

I reached into the rear of the car and handed him a magnum of Bollinger. 'Something to wet the baby's head with.'

He ran his eye appreciatively over the bottle. 'Drown him, more like.' He touched my arm. 'Thanks, Dom. It'll be consumed ere long.'

We entered the house, he put the champagne in the ice compartment of the refrigerator and, turning to me, said, 'You'll want to see him. Larry's got him attached to her upper structures at the present. But that's no problem. Let's go up.'

I followed him through the kitchen, across the dining and drawing-rooms and up the stairs past the photo of the dumpy woman and her son: I thought of Larry's description of the photograph and considered how the house now contained not a doctor's son, but a dentist's.

At every step, an almost unbearable excitement welled in me. By the time I reached the landing, I could feel myself sweating.

The master bedroom was large, the walls painted white and hung with Victorian rural water-colours, the windows framed by floral print curtains which matched the cushions in a bay window and the cover to the dressing-table stool. By the double bed was a cot: the coverlet on it also matched the rest of the décor.

Larry was sitting up in bed nursing the infant which was wrapped in a shawl. 'Hello, Dom,' she said quietly. 'He's arrived.'

I kissed her forehead. Brian looked on with the characteristic self-satisfied smirk of a new father. The baby was engrossed in suckling upon her left breast, its eyes tight shut as if it was concentrating hard upon the problem of feeding. Its left arm was raised with a tiny half-clenched fist with which it occasionally kneaded the breast.

I could do nothing but stare at the child, hardly believe it was there, alive and breathing. Until now, the whole matter had seemed somehow impermanent and improbable, still a thought rather than a deed. Even with my frequent checks on Larry's health, I had somehow distanced myself from it by my inability to fully realize the enormity of what I had done and what I might achieve. It had been, for nine months, a scientific possibility rather than a fact. Now, the child existed, not as a blurred scanner image or a regular thump in my stethoscope but as living flesh and bone, existing its independent life. The doting parents considered their child a miracle, given to them against cruel odds by kind fortune, but they had no idea of just what a miracle he truly was for Larry was holding in her arms not just a child but a milestone in evolution, the first prehistoric human to be born for over three thousand years. And, just as Brian and Larry wanted to advertise their success at starting a family so did I have a strong, nearly overwhelming compulsion to broadcast the truth about their son. Rising in me was the sheer exhilaration of what the child meant, of what possibilities it might hold and what these could provide for mankind. There was, I thought, so much we might learn from this small creature. Yet I held my peace. There was no conceivable way I could share my incredible secret with anyone.

'Well, what do you think of him?'

Brian's words cut into my reverie. It took me several seconds to get my reply shaped. My mind was racing, yet not with guilt, not with the subterfuge I had committed, giving him a child which was not his own.

'He's just wonderful,' I declared and thought how I had never spoken a truer sentence in my life.

'He's no bother at all,' Larry said, 'He has only woken twice each night so far and he sleeps like a baby.'

We looked at each other then all three of us laughed. Larry's cliché broke the swirl of thoughts in my head. The laughter caused the infant to stop suckling and turn its head. Its eyes opened and stared, in the myopic way the new-born have, straight into my face. A surge of indescribable excitement coursed through me. I felt I could see, in the tiny points of its pupils, back into time.

'I think he's had enough,' Larry declared, gently rubbing the infant's back and holding him out towards me.

Taking the baby from his mother and unwrapping him, I placed him on the duvet of the double bed to examine him as I would any other new-born. Touching him sent a thrill through me: I felt as I guessed Howard Carter must have felt as he lowered his hand, for the first time, upon the gold sarcophagus of Tutankhamun.

Putting the baby face down, he turned his head to the side and, on my gently running my finger up his instep, he fanned his toes. A light pinch on his heel made him retract his foot. Laying him on his back, his head turned aside again and he bent his arms and legs. Praying inwardly his sight was in order, I shone my small bright pocket torch into his eyes: he screwed them up. When I clapped my hands, he flung his arms out and wriggled them about. Next, I made a soft mewing noise like a cat: he stopped moving and tried to listen to me. Finally, I placed my index finger in his open hand. For a moment, he did not react then, quite suddenly, he gripped me with a strength I had not often come across in such a young infant. Holding me fast, he turned his head and looked at me again in such an intense way I was, momentarily, unnerved. I am sure I was imagining it but it seemed as if, for a second or two, this tiny soul was trying to communicate with me.

Removing my finger from his grasp, I embarked upon a thorough post-natal examination. Although I was aware the hospital would have checked everything, I wanted to satisfy myself all was well. Starting with his skull, I felt the fontanelles of his head then began to move down his little body. His heart sounds and femoral arterial pulse were strong, his lungs were good, he had no hernia or genital abnormality. I studied his back for spina bifida and checked against any congenital dislocation of the hips. Everything was perfect. All the while, the infant made no complaint but just lay calmly on the duvet, occasionally gurgling if I tickled him.

'So?' Larry enquired as I handed the baby back to her.

'Tip-top,' I said, smiling. 'Not a flaw.'

That night, I accepted an invitation to stay over and, after dining on a large Chinese take-away, we adjourned to the drawing-room, discarding the plastic spoons and paper

plates with which we had eaten: the lack of washing up
was Brian's idea. Larry pointed out it was because he was
responsible for all the household chores for a week: then,
she assured me, they'd be back to crockery. Her main fear,
she declared, was he might be bringing in paper clothes next
which required no laundering but were merely discarded when
dirty. He accused her of considering the use of towelling
nappies for the baby rather than disposable ones – only, he
declared, because she wanted him to have to soak and then
boil them. Their banter was light-hearted, the talk of two
people very much in love and recently equipped with a son
and heir.

Brian lit a fire, the flames dancing off the polished ceiling
beams and stone surround to the inglenook then left to open
the champagne. Larry sank into a deep black leather armchair
by the fire, placed a remote control baby alarm on the floor
and sighed deeply. I seated myself at the end of a voluptuous
matching leather settee.

'I never realized breast-feeding was such painful work,' she
observed, gently lifting her left breast inside her nursing bra and
resettling it again. 'He hasn't a tooth in his head but those bony
little gums. And he sucks like a jet engine.'

I made no comment but smiled my response. She closed
her eyes for a while and I returned to my thoughts.

Since meeting Brian and Larry at their first consultation,
I had been to visit their house only twice. Usually, with their
frequent trips to London, I had entertained them so we had
built up our relationship without my actually travelling to
their home. Now, with the baby born, I would hardly be
required.

Certainly, I knew we should remain in touch but I would
not see them as often as I had and I would certainly not see
the child with any degree of frequency. For some reason, I
had not considered my contact with the child after its birth:
it had been enough to get the fertilization to work and see
the foetus through to parturition. Now, however, I knew I
had to stay in its life, watch it as it grew, observe it and

note what I saw. It was no longer sufficient just to know I had achieved the unimaginable: I wanted to see the results as time passed.

Brian returned with the magnum balanced in a galvanized bucket of ice. 'Couldn't find anything decent which was large enough. Our silver cooler's too small.'

'It's not silver,' Larry commented without opening her eyes. 'It's EPNS.'

He poured the champagne into three fluted glasses and handed them round.

'To the baby,' I suggested and raised my glass.

Larry opened her eyes and sat forward in her chair.

'No,' she declared, 'to you, Dom. You have made possible a wish we never thought would come true.'

I felt an intense wave of guilt run through me. I knew I should tell them but I also knew I dared not. There was too much at stake now and not just in my life but also in theirs and in that of their child. For the first time, the enormity of what I had achieved struck home. And so, with all the modesty I could muster, I accepted their gratitude and sipped my champagne.

Larry only drank one glass before retiring upstairs. I could see the burden of the birth and the responsibilities of the first days of motherhood were tiring her out. Once she was gone, Brian and I sat before the fire, talked over our student days and sank the remaining champagne. By ten o'clock, we were talking only after long pauses during which we considered the flames in the grate, studied the bubbles rising in our glasses and listened to the silence of the old house.

'You know,' Brian said after a long silence punctuated by a creaking of a beam and his clumsily tossing another log on the fire, sending a cascade of sparks up the chimney, 'we've been talking. Larry and me. We think you live too much of a cloistered life in London. You're like a monk. You can't spend all your life living over the shop. It's unhealthy.'

'I'm quite satisfied with my existence,' I replied.

'Can't be. In London. All smoke and car fumes and garbage.'

'"When a man is tired of London, he is tired of life; for there is in London all that life can afford,"' I responded. 'Samuel Johnson.'

Brian humphed dramatically and said, '"London, that great cesspool into which all the loungers of the Empire are irresistibly drawn." Conan Doyle. Johnson was a humbug, Conan Doyle was a . . . a non-humbug.' He drank his glass empty and refilled it, observing, 'There's still an inch or two in the bottom. Anyway, we think you should get yourself a place in the country.' He spoke the words in one breath, slightly slurring them together.

Despite my having succumbed to the champagne, I recognized he had in one sentence answered my dilemma. I wanted to be near the boy but could hardly contrive to be forever hovering about in their lives. Now, unwittingly, Brian had invited me into their lives. My head was suddenly clear. 'You may be right,' I conceded. 'I could perhaps do with a pad in the sticks.'

'Nice property going in the village,' Brian continued after a moment. 'Just right for a confirmed bachelor. We could go and see it in the morning.'

When Brian eventually went upstairs, I sat for a long time in front of the dying fire and considered the future. I would buy a cottage in Harbury, visit as many weekends as I could and, in this way, I should be able to observe the boy as he grew. This arrangement would not afford me a continuous record of his development but it would certainly give me a considerable insight into his character and progress.

The next morning, accompanied by Brian and a sallow young man working for a local estate agent, I visited Cobb End, not a hundred metres from Dell Cottage. It was a detached, three-bedroom cottage occupied by an elderly woman for whom the upkeep was plainly too much. The walls were in dire need of redecoration, the window-frames were rotting and the electrical wiring was verging on the dangerous. The garden was unkempt and the gate leaned on its hinges. Her asking price was £88,750. I pretended to consider the situation, procrastinating in the best would-be buyer fashion, questioned the slate damp course, the drains, the condition of the roof. I even hoisted myself through a trapdoor and inspected the attic, filled with old steamer trunks covered by mottled P&O labels, the detritus of a colonial past. Eventually, pointing out the many defects in the property, I offered £84,000. Much to my relief, she accepted on the spot.

Larry was elated. She hugged and kissed me, poured out three espresso coffees and set them on the kitchen table. 'It'll be wonderful having you here,' she bubbled ecstatically.

'Only at weekends,' I reminded her. 'I've a practice in London.'

'All the same, it'll be wonderful. Here,' she handed me a cup, 'my first *espresso* in nine months and a week.'

'Dom,' Brian said, 'we'd both like you to be god-father. One of them. There has to be two, as you know. My partner in the dental practice, Roger Bates, will be the other. Can you make next Saturday? At St Anne's. That's the village church. You pass it driving from the main road.'

'I'm most flattered,' I replied, and I was. 'And, of course, I accept. However – you have yet to tell me what names you are giving him.'

'We only decided last night,' Larry admitted. 'He's to be Adam Dominic.'

As I drove back to London, the double irony was such it made me laugh aloud. I was, indeed, the child's godfather. And he was, indeed, Adam of a sort.

◆

I have in my occasional employ two of Q'eke's children, a girl of ten and a boy of about six. Her name is Urú and his Yammi. They are inseparable, the girl always on the lookout for her brother, assuring he does not step out of his depth in the river, does not stand on a bird snare set by their father, does not go too near the edge of the rocks on the spit below the waterfall. She does not molly-coddle him. Quite frequently, I see him engaged in a rough-and-tumble with other children and he often comes off the worse, his sister making no move to rescue him but, if they are walking along a path, she is ever vigilant for snakes, the webs of poisonous spiders or the hives of angry bees. In this way, she is teaching her younger sibling to fend for himself not in the human precinct of the clearing but the wild universe of the jungle. It is specifically Urú's vigilance which I employ but, as she is never apart from her brother, I have to take Yammi on as well. Her job is a reversal of that which she does for her brother: for me, she is my sentry against the world of humans.

If strangers are on their way to the clearing, Urú is the first to know of them. She does not necessarily see them, nor hear them. In some way I cannot hope to understand, she is almost able to divine their impending arrival. Just as Tonto could listen to the ground and tell the Lone Ranger the cavalry or the outlaws were so far off and travelling in such and such a direction, so can she foreknow who is coming, the direction from which they will appear and, fairly accurately, when they will arrive. Unlike Hollywood's Indian scouts, she does not put her head to the ground, sniff the air, or climb a promontory and gaze out over the prairie. She merely sits quite still for a minute or two, concentrates and then pronounces in the best Delphic fashion. Another mystery, of course, is how she knows when to apply her powers. There must be some kind of forewarning but what it is and how it manifests itself in her I cannot tell. She is even able to work out the arrival of people coming by canoe so she is not reliant upon the sound of breaking vegetation or cracking branches.

Urú does not exercise her skill merely for my benefit. She

warns Chuhi or Q'eke of impending visitors or the return of a hunter. She is also, incredibly, able to ascertain the origin of the visitor, capable of saying if he is a clearing person, a man from another tribe or a white man.

Early this afternoon, I was sweeping out my hut when I saw her and Yammi playing with several other children at one of their favourite pastimes. By the door to a long-house there stood a large pot of *yamanachi* fermenting in the sunlight. It was covered with a bark cloth but the scent of it was eking out and had attracted a swarm of large black flies. Either the smell of the intoxicating drink or a spillage down the side of the pot was affecting them and they were slower in their reflexes than usual. Without too much difficulty, the children caught the flies and tied long thin threads around their legs. The insects thus tethered, they were held in check by a stone on their leashes until the effect of the *yamanachi* was worn off. When they grew more active, they were taken up and the children, holding on to the threads, flew the flies about the clearing like little automaton kites. Races were held, and endurance tests, the children shouting with pleasure at their sport.

Pausing in my sweeping, I was watching this innocent cruelty when I saw Urú stop in mid-game to stand quite still. Her fly flew to the end of its range then stopped short in mid-air, lost momentum and fell to the ground. For about a minute, the child stood stock-still then, as if coming out of a trance, she turned to face my hut and started towards me, abandoning her insect which, seizing its chance, took to the wing and struggled towards the trees trailing its cargo of thread.

'*¡Señor!*' she called as she ran, '*¡Señor! Llega un gringo.*'

I had expressly asked her to watch out for the coming of white men and this alarm, her first for other than a jungle native, was bad news indeed. '*¿Cuántos son?*' I asked.

'*Uno,*' she replied with certainty, holding up her index finger.

'*¿Cuántas horas?*'

She pointed to the sun, lowered her hand and, pressing her thumb against her little finger as a demarcator, showed me the last joint.

I had no time to waste. Her indication was the shortest time unit to which a clearing person could relate. It might mean a minute, it might mean five. It certainly did not mean as much as a quarter of an hour.

With all haste, I went into the hut, thrust my broom to one side, grabbed a knife, a bottle of boiled water, a hat and my small binoculars, slammed the shutters down and bolted them then left, slipping the padlock on to the door. I did not head towards the river. The odds were the visitor would appear from that direction. Instead, I crossed the vegetable plots and positioned myself behind a huge tree trunk which had fallen months before. It was bedecked with mosses and lichens, decorated with small, bright yellow fungus clumps and inhabited by several lizards, a nest of leaf-cutter ants and more beetles than one could count.

I had not long to wait. Very soon, the children quit their fly game to run shouting towards the river bank. The sound of an outboard motor reached me and I realized it was the first noise I had heard from the industrial world for some months. Crouching, I observed the clearing through an archway formed by the trunk. I was in deep shadow and quite certain not to be seen: also the sun would not flash upon the lens of my binoculars which I focused on the shore.

A flat-bottomed canoe hove into view, turning in an arc upstream before steering in to the clearing. In it were seated two people. One was a native, stripped to the waist and wearing a band of feathers around his pudding-basin haircut. The other was a white man dressed in a khaki bush jacket and a wide hat shading his face. The outboard died, the native standing in the prow. As the canoe nudged the shore, he jumped out with a metal stake tied to a length of bright yellow nylon rope. The white man stepped on to the bank, removing his hat to wipe his brow with a blue bandanna. He was a stocky, but solidly built man with broad shoulders and a full beard. His long hair, which reached his shoulders, was unkempt with sweat. From a leather satchel over his shoulder, he handed out gifts of rock sugar to the children who clamoured around him like the flies around the *yamanachi*. Their hands reached up in supplication.

Chuhi and Mayno appeared out of a long-house followed by a woman carrying a woven basket. All the other adults held back and, as the man turned towards Chuhi, I saw he wore an automatic pistol in a holster on his hip.

They welcomed each other, Chuhi and the man touching fists rather than shaking hands: it is the greeting which precedes not friendship but business. The woman laid the basket on the ground and, chasing away the most persistent children, the men sat around it, cross-legged in the dirt.

Through my binoculars, I could see they were doing business over pieces of amber which Chuhi took from the basket and held up one by one. There was a good deal of haggling and, although I could not hear exactly what was being said, it was plain to see Chuhi was striking a hard bargain. There was much hand waving and flashing of fingers, gesticulating and grimacing. I could see the white man's face twitching with feigned pain at one offer, smiling and chortling at a settled bid. Every so often, he raised a piece of amber between his face and the sun, studying it as Chuhi indicated the creatures trapped in the petrified resin.

After about half an hour, of which I spent at least five minutes ridding myself of a wide bestiary of six-legged creatures and several leeches, the enterprise session seemed to end. The men stood and touched clenched fists again. The white man went to the canoe and, at the stern, produced from a low wooden chest a short-handled axe, three aluminium cooking pots and an iron griddle plate, some bolts of cloth, several small folding knives and a canvas bag which he rattled. The exchange was made, the amber taken to the canoe.

I hoped that was the end of the parley, for I had

just been discovered by another hoard of minuscule but viciously-tempered ants, but it was not. The white man spoke to Chuhi for a moment then walked to the side of the clearing and, standing in full view of the people, pissed into the undergrowth. He made no attempt to hide himself and seemed to take pride in his exhibitionism. I could see, as he finished urinating, his penis was erect. No doubt, he was hoping this might excite one of the younger women and have Chuhi offer him her pleasures for an hour, but it did not. The people of the clearing just looked stonily at him. He buttoned his trousers and then called out, '¡Señor! Quién vive en esta cabaña ruinosa? ¿Un ermitaño?'

To my dismay, he set off towards what he called my ramshackle hut, his heavy jungle boots flicking up dust with every step. He reached the porch and scuffed his boot on the planks. '¿Hay aqui un sacerdote?'

He was not on my trail specifically, but was just curious. Had he asked after a doctor or an anthropologist, I should have been concerned. But a priest! I smiled to myself at the irony.

'No, señor Rodriguez, no hay ningún sacerdote,' Chuhi shouted back.

He made sweeping gestures with his foot and called out, '¿Quién estaba limpiando el suelo? Iguanchi?'

Iguanchi was one of the first native words I had learnt. It means spirits or ghosts. His sarcasm was not lost on Chuhi who I could see was becoming annoyed. He shuffled his feet, a sure sign a clearing person was losing their patience. 'Las almas no limpian las casas,' Chuhi replied.

At that moment, Urú ran forward accompanied by Yammi. She jumped on to the porch and, with a switch of twigs, began to pretend to sweep the floor. The white man grinned at the children: I wondered if he was not only an exhibitionist but also a pederast. There was something about his beard which struck me as distinctly evil. He tried the door and shutters, checked the padlock and attempted to peer in through a crack in the window-frame. I knew I was safe. He could see nothing in the dark interior.

'*¿De quién es esa casa?*'

'*Del medico Suárez. De Santo Antonio do Içá,*' Chuhi replied. He had walked over to the hut. '*Es donde él reside cuando viene.*'

This explanation satisfied the white man: if it belonged to Dr Suarez it had a purpose he could appreciate. He returned to his canoe and, after several pulls on the cord, started the outboard motor. His native companion, who had played no part at all in the trading, squatting to one side of the canoe as if guarding it and watching the clearing people with suspicion, tugged the stake free and jumped on to the bow.

I waited in my hiding place for a further fifteen minutes, until Urú waved for me to come out. With alacrity, I broke cover and spent a few minutes dusting ants out of my trousers and hair, slapping larger examples off my arms and shirt and slicing a large, previously undiscovered leech off the back of my calf. Satisfied I was rid of most of the fauna of the log, I made for my hut.

'*Gracias*, Urú,' I said as I stepped on to the porch and unfastened the padlock. '*Gracias*, Yammi.'

The little boy's hands were sticky from the lump of rock sugar he was sucking, smoothing down the crystal edges of one side with his tongue.

'*Ahora, es momento para examinarlo,*' Urú declared.

'*Si,*' I agreed, adding in English, 'it is time to see.'

The two children entered my hut. I took down my copy of *Gray's Anatomy*, opening it at page 299 upon which was printed a full plate diagram of the muscles of the head, face and neck, each one of them colour-coded for identification. Urú stared at it for a long time, muttering quietly to herself in her own dialect. Every so often, her finger stroked the illustration then the corresponding part of her own head. Her brother paid not the slightest attention but sat on the floor and noisily mouthed his sugar. At last, sated with the picture, Urú turned and said, '*Bastante gringos para hoy.*'

I was relieved at the news. One visitor was sufficient, white man or otherwise: and I was still being pestered by the occasional ant roaming in the folds of my clothing. Ever since I first saw this extraordinary little girl exhibit her talent for prophesy, I have been burningly curious to know how she does it. As I closed the book, I decided to ask her. 'Urú,' I said, '*¿Comó sabes cuando vendran los gringos?*'

She thought for a moment before replying, '*Los Dioses con alas me hablan.*'

Gods with wings, I thought: she must have visions, see angels. Or they might be birds. Perhaps she was able to assess, from bird alarm calls or the way a stork or raptor flew up the river, the coming threat: and yet this would not account for her being able to differentiate between a white man and a jungle native nor foretell arrivals still half an hour off.

'*¿Son los dioses con alas los pájaros?*' I enquired, making my hands into the shape of wings and flying them in front of my face: to add meaning to my question, I also squawked in poor imitation of a macaw.

'*No son pájaros,*' she answered, grinning at my parrot call. '*Son dioses con alas.*'

She left the hut and walked away to the river where she washed her hands and then, taking Yammi with her, disappeared along the path leading to the waterfall.

I know it is inevitable. One day, the visitor will not be satisfied with a few lumps of amber and testing the padlock. He will demand to be shown where I am hiding. The people will refuse to oblige him, of course, but he will not let his gun rest in its holster. When that happens, it will be near the end.

◆

It was several months before I could move into Cobb End. A local builder and decorator had done a superb job on the property, installing central heating, re-wiring the entire cottage, re-installing the plumbing, painting the walls and building me a small garage at the end of the garden, approached by a new gravel driveway. I bought some suitable period furniture at an auction in Crewkerne but equipped the sitting-room with a more comfortable, modern suite in heavy oak. Before moving in, I advertised in the village post office for a housekeeper and gardener. Within an hour of the notice being posted, Mr Stoke arrived on my doorstep to fill the latter post. I took him on to trim the bushes, fell two scraggly fir trees, cut the lawn, plant beds of shrubs or perennials and generally tidy the place up. Mrs Maggs, a middle-aged woman in the village, agreed to act as my housekeeper and look after the place in my absence.

Starting in mid-March, I visited the cottage almost every fortnight, arriving early in the evening but arranging my appointments so I could be out of London before the rush-hour traffic began to build up. The drive down was surprisingly relaxing after a week of medical practice and I could be in the cottage within three hours of leaving the mews.

Brian and Larry were very keen to take me into their lives. They introduced me to their friends and acquaintances as the doctor who had given them Adam. Each time they imparted this information, I was embarrassed by their praise for my expertise and riddled with guilt. It became a pattern I would visit them on the Saturday afternoon for tea, remaining either for supper with friends of theirs or for a snack and a drink if no more formal gatherings were arranged. This arrangement was exactly what I wanted, affording me at least three hours observation of Adam. It was only natural I should pay him much attention: I was his godfather and made a point of showing I doted upon him through my role just as much as his parents did in theirs. I made a point every visit of bringing him a gift, making sure each one was something which would test the child or give me an insight into his behaviour.

At first, these were the simple things one gives to infants, brightly-coloured objects which make a noise, catch the light or move in a fascinating manner. I bought plastic balls with bells or chimes in them, rattles and interlocking rings in primary colours. Adam played with them, tossed them through the bars of his play-pen, drooled on them, rolled them on the floor and tried to get them in his mouth. It was not until I bought him one particular toy I noticed his behaviour differed towards it from the other items he had seen.

The toy was a transparent plastic orb about the size of a large grapefruit made of two halves welded together at a perimetric seam. It contained a bright green plastic fish which floated in what I took to be distilled water mixed with coloured beads. As the ball was rolled, the liquid slopped to and fro with the fish, an idiotic smirk upon its anthropomorphic face, rocking about with gay abandon, the beads swilling against the sides. When I first presented him with this, Adam was most puzzled. He did not touch the ball at all but sat squarely looking at it, his head moving from side to side as if he was trying to listen to it.

'You can't hear this one, silly,' Larry teased him. 'This hasn't got a bell in it.' She rolled the orb towards him. Adam did not move away from it so I was certain he was not afraid of it, but neither did he try to touch it. He watched it instead.

'He'll be a coarse fisherman when he grows up,' Brian predicted. 'He'll prefer to sit and wait for the fish to make a move rather than get out his fly rod and go for it.'

For half an hour, Adam looked at the fish ball. Every so often, he let his attention wander to another toy but, within a very short time, his eye was back on the green fish which, very slowly, gyrated on the water. At last, just as I was wondering what to make of his reaction, he touched the ball very gingerly and then, with his little fingers, sought to gently pry apart the welded seam holding the ball together. He did this with such concentration that, when Larry dropped a teacup on the patio and it shattered, the infant did not so much as look up. I was convinced he was trying to let the fish out and that his long observation had not been as a result of being captivated by the bright fish but by trying to work out how he might get at it.

That night, in the study at Cobb End, I wrote down in great detail everything I had observed during the day, listing Adam's reaction to the ordinary toys and contrasting it to his behaviour with the fish-in-a-ball. When I had completed my notes, I tapped them into a cheap computer bought for use in the cottage, storing them on a floppy disk and observations to date: this would be transferred to the hidden file in the practice computer on my return to London.

Over a few weeks, I contrived to hide the fish and brought Adam other toys which contained moving objects: there was a cube with a pyramid in it which dived about on a string, a number of balls with stars and fruit suspended in them and one rather expensive item I bought in Hamleys toy shop in Regent Street – a box with a series of mirrors and holograms in it depicting a car, a boat, an aeroplane and a bicycle. With all these, Adam played contentedly without trying to get into them. Yet as soon as the fish reappeared, he remembered it and tried once more to open the globe.

At the same time as watching his response to objects, I started to listen to what Adam was vocalizing.

In common with many proud parents, Brian bought a video camera to film his son growing up and, for a number of weeks, he took a few minutes' footage almost every day. At my request, he lent me the videotapes one weekend on the pretext I was going to judge which were the best sequences for Brian to edit into a one-hour film.

It was whilst watching these tapes I noticed, to my amazement, Adam had a specific vocabulary and that the sounds he made were not necessarily baby-talk nonsense. There were a large number of random cooings and chatterings but he also made specific vocal responses to the same situation. Whenever the cat came into shot, he would say, very precisely, *Muck*. The word caught my attention because it was nothing like *cat*, nothing like Napoleon, and was repeated exactly. Not only the cat elicited exact words: so also did the neighbour's dog, referred to as *bing*, the willow tree over the pond (*poat*), the cows in the field at the end of the garden (*kin*) and the horse a little girl rode down the lane every afternoon (*naga*). The latter surprised me because it was so like *nag*.

In my notes, I listed a glossary of Adam's sounds, the non-attributed and the assigned. Beside each, I gave a date, a quick description of the circumstances of the word and, as best I could, Adam's temperament at the time. I soon had a comprehensive dictionary and was able, when observing him, to sometimes understand what he wanted to say, react to or comment upon in his infantile way. If I was correct in my assumption the child was already forming distinctive words, rather than merely babbling, then my discovery was, I felt sure, unique. I could not recall any instance in child developmental literature where anyone had observed specific vocal sounds being used at such an early age.

Adam was also quick to crawl, moving rapidly across the floor and eager to attempt standing if placed on his feet, holding on to chairs or tables, Brian's leg or Larry's skirt. Inevitably, when he lost his balance he promptly sat down. I was astonished by this development: he was then six months old but had the motion skills of a child at least three months older.

At the same time as he began to explore standing, he also took to using tools. Over the space of a matter of weeks, he seemed to learn how to use a ruler to retrieve items fallen under the floor of his play-pen and, in the garden, he was quick to pick up sticks in order to prise over stones or wheedle into the crevices of the patio in a hunt for the woodlice occupying the cracks. Curiously, however, I noted he continued to spurn his spoon and preferred to eat with his fingers.

All my observations were done on the sly, so to speak. I could not be obvious in my study of the child but then, at the end of June when he was coming up to his ninth month, the opportunity arose for me to have a solid, uninterrupted four hours alone with Adam.

During the week, should Larry have to leave her son

whilst she went out, it was planned Marie, her cleaning lady, remain to baby-sit. This arrangement worked well except for one Saturday when Marie's sister, Harriet, was to be married. Harriet being the barmaid in the Crown Inn, it was not surprising virtually the whole village was invited to the ceremony and revels afterwards.

It was Larry who first broached the subject of the wedding with me. She did it in a most tentative fashion by remarking over tea the weekend before, how she hated babies crying in public. 'We were on a plane once,' she remembered, not looking at me but gazing into the distance of the garden. 'A package holiday Brian and I took in Tenerife. Coming in to land, there was this one child who screamed incessantly as soon as we began our descent. No doubt the poor little thing was alarmed at the pressure in its ears or something but I still cringed in my seat and thanked my lucky stars it wasn't my offspring.'

'I've had a similar experience,' I said, 'but one of the advantages now of bachelordom and wealth is I invariably fly club class where children are, mercifully, thin on the ground.'

'You mean in the air,' Brian joked.

'And in church,' Larry went on. 'When we were married Brian's cousin brought her two-year-old. Admittedly she didn't cry but she was exceedingly . . . ' She searched for a polite word. 'Eloquent.'

I had guessed by now where this conversation was leading and thrilled to the thought of the opportunity it afforded me. It was all I could do to suppress my excitement. 'If you are hoping I will baby-sit whilst the barmaid is wed to the ploughboy, or whoever the lucky rustic is who is to fall into her capacious bosom next Saturday night, the answer is an affirmative. I'd be delighted to mind the fort and the princeling.'

And so it was. I arrived at Dell Cottage a little after lunch – the wedding was at half past two – to find Larry and Brian dressed up to the nines, Adam fed, recently changed and asleep in his cot.

'Now you're sure you'll be all right?' Larry asked.

I shrugged and replied, 'I doubt it. I am only a doctor with limited knowledge of infants.'

'If you need us, you know where to find us,' Brian added.

'Indeed I do,' I confirmed. 'From two-thirty to three you'll be in the church and from three to five-thirty you'll be seated at, or lolling under, a table in the village hall.'

At two o'clock, they left the cottage and walked up the lane. I watched them go with much the same sense of expectancy as a child watches his parents go out two days before Christmas, leaving the wardrobe full of presents unguarded or a teenager observes them leaving so he may help himself to the cigarettes in the lounge or the condoms in his father's sock drawer.

With their departure, I went straight upstairs to the baby's room. He was still sleeping in his cot, a mobile of garish lambs swinging over his head in the breeze blowing in through the window. From my blazer pocket, I took out a 2ml syringe and needle. Cleaning his skin with a dab of cotton wool, I took a specimen of 1ml of blood from Adam's arm: he stirred but did not wake as the needle went in. It was so fine it left only the tiniest puncture mark and I was sure it would not be noticed by Larry: if it was, she would think of it as merely a scratch. Once the specimen was collected, I injected it into a small bottle of anticoagulant and slipped it back in my pocket.

Thirty minutes later, Adam woke. I went to his cot and, lifting him out, carried him downstairs and out to the patio where I sat him in his play-pen for safekeeping whilst I removed my blazer, hanging it on a garden chair and checking my pocket dictaphone and stopwatch were working correctly.

All this while, Adam sat leaning against the bars of his play-pen. He ignored the toys in it and instead watched me. It was as if he knew I was going to do something with him and was patiently waiting for my next move.

The dictaphone and stopwatch tested, I began my simple tests.

The first thing I did was to give him a new toy. I did not

remove it from its box but handed it to him still packaged. He turned the box over before him for about a minute, ignoring the garish illustrations on it. This done, he immediately opened the lid and removed the contents. The toy was an octopus with a beaming face. The body was made out of cloth but the various tentacles were each fashioned in an individual material with very different textures. One was made of finely ribbed rubber, another of smooth plastic, a third of closely knitted wool and so on. Adam took the toy and, one by one in a most methodical fashion, felt, pulled and studied the tentacles. He did not attempt to place any of them in his mouth which surprised me. Babies frequently want to taste new objects as well as touch them.

I did not seek to stop him playing. I was timing his attention span. He played with the octopus without distraction for eleven minutes. Since putting him in his pen, he had leaned against the bars and not once fallen to one side. So far, I reckoned, he had remained upright for about fifteen minutes despite having reached forwards to fumble with and open the toy box. So far, I had not spoken to him and only whispered into the dictaphone. He had made no sound at all save a gentle cooing I took to be the usual appreciation noise he was making in response to his present. Waiting a few more minutes, I suddenly said, 'Adam, do you like your octopus?'

He looked up immediately on hearing his name and gazed at me.

'Naga,' I said distinctly. 'The naga is coming.'

Instantly, he fell silent and kept quite still save for a slight angling of the head. He was obviously listening intently. For two minutes ten seconds, a very long attention span for an eight-and-a-half-month-old, he listened: then he placed his right hand on his head. 'Naga,' he said. 'Naga.'

I replied, 'Bing.'

Once more, he strove to hear the dog and even looked over his shoulder in case I could see it and he could not. There was no barking from the next garden. Satisfied the dog was not around, Adam looked at me again, put his right hand on his head and repeated the word *bing*.

The placing of the right hand on the head might have been coincidental and an adage my pathology tutor had given to his class years before came to mind: once is coincidence, twice is happenstance, three times is the bleeding obvious.

'Kin,' I said. 'The kin are in the field.'

He did it.

After listening to the summer afternoon, totally disregarding the distant ringing of the church bells to celebrate the wedding which I thought would have taken his fancy, he put his right hand on his head.

'Kin,' he replied, 'Kin.'

A word, allied to the hand motion, was a negative.

I sat back in the patio chair, pressing the pause button on the dictaphone. It was astounding. This tiny child had the ability to think conceptually. With his actions described on the dictaphone, and the tape turned over, I decided to test for an affirmative response.

Napoleon the cat appeared at the end of the patio. It was *en route* from the house to the end of the garden where a number of small birds were congregating to take caterpillars off an apple tree. I was certain Adam had not seen the cat arrive. It was at least five metres behind him, sitting down and intently watching its prey.

'Muck has arrived,' I declared. 'Muck.'

Without any hesitation, Adam placed his right hand against his cheek and replied, 'Muck, muck.'

I could not understand for a minute how the child knew the cat was there. It moved with feline caution, not wanting to alarm the birds. I checked behind me. Perhaps there was a window in which the cat had been reflected. I concluded Adam must have heard it .

The cat rose and slunk off in the direction of the feeding birds.

'Muck,' Adam stated and put his right hand on his head.

When Larry returned, somewhat jolly from the imbibing

of champagne, her first words were, 'Well, Dom, we can see you aren't cut out for parenthood. You look absolutely shattered.'

'Give you a hard time, did he, Dom?' Brian enquired with alcoholic *bonhomie*.

'Not in the least,' I replied, rising from the patio chair. 'He's been as good as gold.'

'So you got along all right then?' Brian went on.

Larry added, 'No problems?'

'None whatsoever,' I assured her. 'He's played quite happily the whole while.'

Larry bent down to the edge of the play-pen: I felt a quick twinge in case she noticed the needle prick but she did not.

'Hello, darling,' she said to Adam. He smiled at her. 'Did you have a nice time with Uncle Dom, then?'

Adam put his right hand to his cheek.

◆

I opened the door myself, as Molly was out for lunch. The express delivery rider was dressed in black leather with a metallic blue crash helmet and gauntlets which could have belonged to a medieval king had they been encrusted with gemstones. His powerful motor bike was parked just up the mews, the engine rumbling like the threat of a distant storm. Under his arm was a padded envelope the size of a paperback book.

'This Dr Lyall's surgery?'

'Yes, I'm Dr Lyall.'

A radio clipped to his lapel burst into cracking, incomprehensible chatter. He pressed a button with his medieval hand. 'Four-seven, four-seven. Drop-off W1. Goin' to E12 next. Over.'

He released the button and the radio gabbled again. 'Roger. Will do. Out.'

He turned his attention to me, taking out the padded

envelope, checking the label and handing it to me. 'Sign the receipt portion, please.' He fumbled in his leather armour and offered me a cheap ball-pen. I scribbled my initials on the pro forma label, he tore off a carbon copy and departed, his motor bike reverberating off the walls of the mews.

In my office, the door shut, I slit open the envelope. In it were several sheets of folded paper and a small glass bottle containing what was left of Adam's blood sample. I unfolded the letter and spread it on the blotter in front of me. It was on personally headed stationery with *Dr Stephen Collard* printed in cursive script. It began:

Dear Dom,

Many thanks for sending me this sample: as you requested, the residue is returned herewith.

My full report, hot from the IBM, is attached but, to summarize for you – knowing how busy you money-spinners are these days! – the results are as follows: the blood group is O pos and all seems well. I've tested for all the usual defects and there are none. This is the blood of a normal human.

However, as you requested, we also ran ELISA tests for antibodies.

I paused. My hand, where it held the edge of the letter, was taut, the muscles in my wrist aching with the strain. It continued:

These have thrown up some rather unusual data which you may wish to reconsider . . . Possibly, there has been a mix-up in the blood sample you sent and you may wish to check with your records and lab staff.

I was under the impression from your accompanying letter the sample was from an infant of about nine months. I find this hard to believe in the light of the fact that we have discovered antibodies present affording your patient immunity against bubonic plague, rabies, yellow fever and anthrax. These do not, as you will understand, occur naturally and lead me to think this is an adult blood sample drawn from someone who has at some stage been immunized.

I accept, of course, a mother's immunity to some diseases may be transferred to her offspring but this usually weakens in time and is only a mechanism to protect the new-born arrivee in the big dirty world.

More astonishing, however – if this is the blood of an infant – is the fact it has antibodies present against smallpox. Of course, I need not remind you we have eradicated smallpox from our planet and that no immunization has taken place for a few decades. There is no need for it. This, more than the other immunities, suggests to me you have – forgive me! – got your samples crossed and do recommend you have a scrutiny of your lab procedures.

Anyway – glad to have been of help. My bill's in the post! (Only joking!) Hope we get to meet in the not too distant future.

He had signed it *Steve* over his official title, *Consultant Haematologist*.

I picked up the little bottle and shook it. The contents pinked the sides then ran down to collect in the base. I set it on the desk and stared at it.

◆

I have found out Keewei is not antagonistic towards me because he feels I have stolen one of his patients. What has riled him is the fact I have come to live in the clearing and offered medical advice and treatment to the people but I have desisted from sharing my information or expertise with him.

When I construed Chuhi was being guileful when he brought Tieco to me I was only half correct. He was being particularly subdolous not in order to cheat on Keewei but on

135

the evil spirits lingering in the night on the look-out for the sick whom they may try to inhabit or kill.

It seems, or so I have been led to understand by Chuhi, Keewei considers me to be a shaman like himself, albeit one with a different bag of tricks, a different pantheon of gods on call and very different methods. On account of this, he does not see me as threat to his livelihood as I am not in competition with him.

Earlier this evening, Chuhi invited me to sit with the men about the fire outside his long-house. They were neither imbibing drugs nor consuming bowls of *yamanachi*. Instead, after they had eaten, they passed around a communal gourd of what I assumed was a concoction of juices made from fruits and squashed berries. It was hard to see into the container and my only clues to the contents were what I took to be pips and fragments of leathery peel. Few words were spoken and, after a while, one of the men produced a small instrument like pipes of Pan and commenced to blow a rather monotonous tune on it.

Sitting across the fire from me, Chuhi was paying most of his attention to something lying in his lap. Every so often, he looked up to see if any of the others were observing him but they were mostly either staring into the fire or sitting with their eyes shut listening to music. The gourd continued to do the rounds: in a bizarre fashion, it reminded me of port being passed around the table at a gentlemen's dinner. It even travelled anti-clockwise around the fire. At length, Chuhi looked up, seemed to steel himself and said loudly, 'Mye name ees Chu-hi.'

The musician stopped abruptly. The men all stared at him as, indeed, did I.

'Mye name ees Chu-hi,' he repeated, emphasizing the last word. 'Aye yam an . . . ' he checked in his lap ' . . . armar-ssonyan.'

'Amazonian,' I corrected him, adding, '*En Inglés, el río se llama el Amazon.*'

'Amarson. It ees good.'

The others realized he was speaking my tongue and applauded him, chattering briefly amongst themselves. Chuhi, gaining confidence and, I sense, startled I had understood him, took heart. 'Thee tree ees tall. Thee man ees tall.' He scrutinized the book for a moment. 'The mung-tayne ees tall.' He looked directly at me through the grey smoke. '¿*Qué es un* "mung-tayne"?'

I got to my feet and moved to sit next to him, glancing over his shoulder. He was holding a very dog-eared child's Spanish-English textbook.

'Mountain,' I told him. '*Montaña.*'

'¡*Ah, si!*' he exclaimed. '*Montaña.*'

He held the book at an angle to the fire. The flames had momentarily died down. Q'eke tossed another log into its heart.

'*Keewei es su amigo.* Keewei you f'iend ees,' Chuhi announced then he corrected himself. 'Keewei ees you f'iend.'

The old shaman, seated next but one to me, grinned expansively and leaned over to pat my arm, the feathers and animal teeth sewn into a band around his upper arm bouncing and rattling together. I smiled back at him and, in a return of amicability, put my hand on his. The skin was dry, almost horny. He beckoned to me and Manyo, sitting between us, stood up and took my former seat allowing me to be next to Keewei. I shifted towards him. The old man smelled of a strange perfume, not unpleasant but very heady and unlike anything I had known before. His eyes glittered in the firelight and, at this close range, I realized two of his teeth had been sharpened to points. We did not speak for we had no language in common.

From behind him, Keewei pulled a woven bag with a hinged flap to close it. He tugged a stick out from the weave and opened it, removing samples of roots, dried leaves and fungi, twigs and assorted desiccated frogs, lizards, snakes, bats and little shrew-like rodents, all split asunder and splayed with splints. These arranged before us, he began to point from them to me, touching various parts of my body then picking up a sample and holding it to me. I was soon to learn, through a mixture of sign language, native dialect and grunts, a small green lizard was good for mending broken bones, some stringy leaves cured headaches, a smooth bark infused in water cured toothache and a particularly pungent fungus was the best remover of warts and skin blemishes. Every so often, I muttered *muy bien* as encouragement to him: his instruction was fascinating for I was sure there was some basis to a number of his shamanistic treatments. The thin leaf looked like a variety of willow and it is known willow contains a form of natural aspirin.

I pointed to the dried frog and raised my eyebrows, the universal question mark. Keewei pointed to the trees, mimed shooting a bow and arrow then pretended to prick his finger. Although the amphibian had lost its colouring in death, it was plainly a poison-arrow frog. When I next enquired after the snake, Keewei leaned over his shoulder and called to the long-house. At his shout, there was a rustle in the building and an adolescent girl appeared, running for all she was worth to obey the shaman's bidding. When she reached his side, he lifted up the short skirt she was wearing and pointed to her pubis. I nodded. He then spread her legs apart, pushed his middle finger into her vagina, removed it, flickered his fingers in the air up and down her thighs then held the snake against her belly. I assumed the snake was either a cure for menstrual pain or had some power towards assisting labour or encouraging an abortion. There was no way of knowing.

When Keewei had explained all the samples to me, he put them back in his bag and, taking hold of my hand, tugged on it and pointed to my hut. He wanted me to share some of my tricks, treatments and panacea with him. Nodding my agreement, I rose and he followed me to the hut, waiting politely at the door as I lit the oil lamp and ushered him in, suggesting he sit on a chair. This he did, perching uncomfortably on the edge as a child might.

Putting on my white coat, hanging my stethoscope about

my neck and pinning my worn-out clinical x-ray dosimeter to my lapel, I showed him *Gray's Anatomy* and Wright's *Applied Physiology*. He held the volumes at arm's length, admiring them as one might a book of fine art reproductions, chuckling and muttering to himself all the while. When he tired of reading, I showed him a spatula and a kidney bowl, tucking it into his neck so he might see how it fitted. This he found both intriguing and amusing. When I removed the bowl, he took it from me and studied it closely. He fondled my stethoscope where it hung round my neck. I removed it and gave it him. The instrument puzzled him until I placed it in his ears and pressed the end to my chest. I coughed. He started back as if alarmed but I put my hand on his shoulder to comfort him. It was then he heard my heart. His jaw dropped open with awe and he stared almost reverentially at me. I smiled back and said, 'If only you could see an ultrasound scanner, my friend.'

Assuming I had now imparted a fair share of information, I began to put the books and equipment away but Keewei was not appeased. Not quite. He wanted to know one more trick. He stuck his arm out and mimicked sticking a hypodermic in it. Although my supply of hypodermics was not extensive, I decided I was honour bound to satisfy his curiosity so I removed one from its sterile pack and attached it to the syringe, breaking the plastic seal on the needle sheath. He watched my every move with the avidity of a hungry dog watching his master open a tin of meat. Holding it out to him, he took it in both hands, his arms rising as he accepted it: he must have expected it to be heavy, although why I cannot guess for it was only a disposable plastic 5ml syringe.

For some minutes, he turned it over and over in his fingers, studying it from every angle. He did not attempt to operate the plunger which I had deliberately left half out. At length, he handed it back to me and signalled he wished to receive an injection. I had no choice. He would have regarded it as churlish of me not to comply. After all, in his eyes, I had gone this far: the administration of a shot was to him nothing more than the prescription of a lizard or a pinch of crushed fungus. I poked about in my drugs box for something which would do him no harm and came up with a box containing 20 ampoules of vitamin B complex.

As if rolling up a patient's sleeve, I pushed his feathery toothed armlet up his biceps then, making a great show of the procedure, I set about cleaning his arm with a swab of meths, filing then snapping off the glass top of the ampoule and drawing out the contents, clearing the air from the syringe, squirting a little liquid out of the needle then, with a flourish a fairground magician would have been proud of, I pushed the needle through his skin. As with Tieco, the skin was harder than I had expected. He did not wince but looked closely as the needle penetrated him and I depressed the plunger. The vitamins injected, I withdrew the needle and wiped the spot once more. Keewei studied the site of the injection very closely, shaking his head with wonderment. He was quite satisfied now and stood up from the chair, said, 'Gracias, señor' in as stilted an accent as my own and, pushing down his armlet, walked out. In the clearing, I could hear him calling to the others, boasting of his achievement.

I sat on the edge of my bunk, looking around the spartan hut, at the mouldy books and the galvanized iron walls, the upright joists of bare wood and the roof timbers. A great emptiness swelled in me for which I could not attribute an immediate cause. Possibly, it was engendered by a feeling of isolation. There again, it might just have been a stirring of nostalgia for the days when I frequently administered injections in a luxurious consulting room not far from Wigmore Street.

◆

It was late autumn. I remember the weekend well for I had driven down to Harbury in the most atrocious weather. When it was not raining so hard the double speed on the windscreen wipers could scarcely cope, it was hailing. Pellets of ice ricocheted off the bonnet and smashed against the roof with such thunder I could not hear the radio. This would have been bearable had I not had a puncture and been forced to pull on to the hard shoulder of a dual carriageway, changing the wheel whilst being thoroughly sprayed by passing lorries. I arrived at Cobb End two hours late, soaked to the skin and in a foul mood. I made myself a hot drink and went to bed, not to wake until late the next morning.

The weather had turned and the day was one of weak autumnal sunshine with brisk, damp breezes not quite strong enough to be classed as winds. As usual, I walked down the lane to the Cordiners' house in the afternoon. Brian was in the garden, raking his lawn. The trees had been stripped of their remaining leaves the night before and the ground was strewn with them.

'No rest for the wicked,' Brian declared as he saw me approach. 'I should employ a gardener.'

'Old Mr Stoke will oblige you, I'm sure,' I replied. 'My garden's in good order. Mind you, the pixies might be doing that. I never see him and he's paid by Mrs Maggs.'

A call from the house alerted us and we turned to see Larry crossing the lawn, thrusting Adam in his push-chair before her, the wheels leaving ruts in the soggy grass. 'Hello, Dom. Adam here wanted to come out to watch you both.'

The child looked at me, his face breaking into a smile. Larry stood the push-chair on the lawn and snapped the brake on with her foot. 'Watch after him, won't you,' she commanded unnecessarily of Brian and me. 'He's just thinking of walking, Dom. Maybe you could give him a little stagger in a while? I'll fix tea.' She then kissed me lightly and returned to the house.

'He's very good,' I observed to Brian as Adam sat patiently strapped into his baby buggy.

'He is remarkable,' Brian agreed. 'He rarely throws even the tiniest tantrum, he can sit for up to half an hour watching things around him and he has taken a strong liking to the cat. They roll about together in front of the fire playing like kittens. We were afraid he might be allergic to Napoleon and we might have to get rid of him – the cat, that is, not Adam! – but all seems well.' Brian turned his attention to a pile of sodden leaves, placing them in a wheelbarrow and carting them off to a compost heap. I squatted beside the push-chair.

'Hello, Adam,' I said. 'Where's Muck?'

The child listened for a moment, looked around the garden then, putting his right hand on his head, repeated, 'Muck.'

'Good boy,' I praised him and he smiled again.

Brian walked back to us with the empty wheelbarrow. 'Now the filthiest landowner's chore of the year,' he announced. 'You might be advised to live in London in the autumn.' He pointed to the pond on which floated a carpet of dead leaves and tangled weed. With a rake, he set about lifting the leaves and weed from the water, dumping them in the barrow. Adam was watching a crow strutting across the end of the garden and it was not until the third rakeful was being dragged out he saw what Brian was doing. At the sight, he became very agitated, reaching forward from his seat but unable to move too far because of the harness restraining him.

'He wants a walk,' Brian said. 'You can take him out, Dom. He's a good little marcher if you hold his hands.'

I slipped the buckles open, lifted the child out of the buggy and, setting him on his feet, took his hands in my own, leaning over him. He immediately set off in the direction of the pond, five metres or so away. His steps were as unsteady as might be expected but he moved with what I thought was a solid determination. At the water's edge, he stopped. The pond was lined with flat paving stones on one side and he sat on these: I held fast to the collar of his coat lest he pitch forward.

'He likes to watch the fish,' Brian remarked from across the pond. 'But do keep a grip on him. He almost fell in once. Scared the lights out of us.'

The water must have been very cold and yet Adam reached down and thrust his fingers under the surface. At the same time, he made a strange purring noise in his throat. I thought he might be choking on something, or was about to vomit because of the angle of his leaning and pulled him up. He gave me a quick glance – it might have been to reproach me – then strained to reach for the water once more. I let him go lower, still grasping his collar. Once more, he thrust his fingers into the water and purred. It was such a low tone I am sure Brian could not hear it. It was only just audible to me, kneeling beside the child.

His fingers had been under the water for not more than ten seconds, and I was thinking of pulling them out because of the water temperature, when fish started to congregate about his hand. Not only the goldfish appeared, used to coming to the surface to accept food, but also half a dozen brown fish, a small striped perch, two tench much larger than any of the others and a school of minnows. They did not seem to be seeking to bite the child's fingers but swam very close to them, packing themselves together as close as they might.

I could not believe this behaviour. Perch, for one, are vicious predators and the proximity of so many minnows presented it with a glutton's banquet. No sooner had the fish packed into a wedge of wriggling fins and writhing bodies than I saw, beneath them, several frogs hugging the muddy bottom next to a flash of orange I took to be a newt. Adam made no attempt to remove his hand and I thought I should do it for him. The cold must have got through to him by now. Yet when I touched his arm, he whimpered and gave me a worried look. Deciding he would know best, for no child forfeits his comfort, I gave in. The fish remained close to his fingers. Across the pond, about eight metres wide at this point, Brian dragged the last of the weed and leaves free of the surface. The water beneath where he had been working was black with a suspension of sludge and bottom detritus.

'All done, Adam,' he called. 'All finished.' He set off with the wheelbarrow again. Adam left his hand in the water for ten seconds then stopped his purring sound. The fish immediately dispersed, the frogs kicking free of the bank, making for deeper water. The child removed his hand and I helped him stand up.

'Naga,' he said.

I strained my ears: sure enough, far down the lane, I could just hear the clop of hooves on tarmac.

Adam held my hands to walk back to his buggy, intent on being put in it. I lifted him in, utterly puzzled by what I had observed. Somehow, he had been able to attract the fish to his hand with, I assumed, the purring noise. They had come, disregarding each other's presence and the looming humans above the surface. It was, I thought, like the lion running with the antelope ahead of the bush fire.

That was it! I understood. Adam had been afraid for the fish which were, no doubt, in a degree of panic as Brian's rake intruded upon and drastically altered their world so he offered them safe sanctuary. No sooner had this explanation presented itself to me than I questioned it. There was, I thought, no way any human could be so skilled in communication with animals. Catch them with guile, yes: men can tickle trout and salmon from a stream but to draw them in – and a child just over a year old having such a skill – was unthinkable. And yet I had just seen it happen.

'I've had enough slavery for one afternoon,' Brian announced, walking towards us across the lawn. 'What do you say to a spot of tea, Dom?' He looked down at his son. 'Time for a drink of milk, Adam?'

We went towards the house. I pushed the baby buggy and I must have been very silent for, as we reached the patio, Brian removed his grubby gardening glove and put his hand on my sleeve. 'You all right, Dom?'

'I'm fine,' I said but not quickly enough.

'You sure? I mean,' he laughed briefly, 'shouldn't you see a doctor or something?'

'This physician can heal himself,' I replied. 'At least, diagnose himself. Don't worry, I'm – it's probably overwork. I've had a heavy week and a bloody awful drive down last night. Got up late, too. My constitution's just a little out of kilter. That's all it is.'

Brian went into the garage to remove his boots and put away some gardening tools leaning against the wall. I volunteered to remove Adam from his push-chair and carry him indoors. It was about five o'clock, darkness falling with winter rapidity. In the hedge by the garage, a blackbird was calling its night song whilst, in the copse of elms the rooks cawed. In the lane, the little girl from the rectory rode by on her horse.

'Naga,' Adam said again with a sense of delight, pointing at the animal.

'Naga,' I said in agreement and I bent to remove him from his buggy.

It was then Adam whistled. It is the best I can describe the noise. He did not actually purse his lips and blow but he made a sort of squeak-cum-whistle with his throat. The blackbird flew out of the hedge and landed squarely on the curved handle of the push-chair. It was so close I could see its thin toes gripping the slippery plastic. It totally ignored my presence and gave a blast of bird-song. From such close proximity it was piercingly loud yet extraordinarily beautiful with the most exquisite tones. Even when I moved to unstrap Adam, rocking the frame of the buggy, it did not fly off but shifted its toes to get a better hold. Adam squeak-whistled again and the blackbird responded with a low, near inaudible churring.

Brian came out of the garage. The bird, without the usual shrilling alarm call, flew off to the hedge where it settled and recommenced its evening song.

'They're very tame here,' Brian remarked as the blackbird zipped past him. 'Anticipating their winter seed supply starting soon. We always put out seed and nuts. Religiously every morning. Have done since we moved in. It's wonderful to see them in the bleak months.'

Sitting round the fire with scones and cups of Earl Grey, we talked of our week's work. Larry announced she had embarked upon a study of Etruscan vases: she felt she was letting her knowledge of the history of art atrophy and had decided to write a paper on some obscure aspect of design lost on both Brian and myself. I recounted a patient I had treated during the week whose husband had, to put it charitably, some peculiar notions of what excited his wife: I had been required on Tuesday to remove the smooth pop-on cap for a deodorant bottle from the woman's vagina and, on Thursday, sign an affidavit to the effect for her divorce attorney.

Brian's tale was of seventy-year-old Mrs Pargeter who owned an aged Jack Russell terrier called Bodger. The dog, into its early teens, and its owner were inseparable. What was more, since Mr Pargeter's death, the dog had become its owner's primary confidante and companion. Where Mrs Pargeter went, Bodger was sure – indeed, had – to follow. This caused a number of confrontations between Mrs Pargeter and various people around the town where Brian had his practice. First, she refused to allow the dog to be tethered outside shops whilst she entered: the dog, now being a human in canine form as far as its owner was concerned, had a right to accompany her as her husband had done. Second, the dog created an uproar on the local bus when Mrs Pargeter insisted it sit on a seat: the drawback from the point of view of the bus company was that, when a policeman was called, it was found the dog had had a ticket purchased for it.

The latest turn in Bodger's life had happened in Brian's practice. The dog had a loose tooth and its owner insisted a dentist, not a vet, remove it. No amount of coercion or persuasion would shift the woman's resolve.

'So what did you do?' I asked.

'I rang Keith Markham. He's the local vet and has treated the dog for years.'

'He wasn't touchy about you encroaching upon one of his patients?' Larry wanted to know.

'No. He's a good chap. Took it all in fun, really. So eventually, in the spirit of compromise and professional co-operation, I went to his surgery this morning and used his equipment to extract the dog's tooth. Didn't take long.'

'Who got the bill?' I enquired.

Brian laughed and replied, 'That's a private doctor for you! But, as it happened, I charged her the standard National Health Service fee for an extraction and split the proceeds with Keith. It came to more than he would have levied. So there, Dom, we public boys can occasionally pull one over on you cowboys.'

'Can I change the subject?' I suggested. 'I want to ask something about Adam.'

Brian poked about in the fire, settling the ash and adding a few split logs to the embers.

'What is it, Dom?' Larry asked. Her voice was just a little edgy.

I allayed her fears as quickly as possible. 'It's nothing to worry about,' I began, 'but can you tell me about Adam playing with Napoleon?'

'Don't you think he should?' was Larry's immediate response. 'I know you mustn't let cats go near cots for fear of suffocating the baby but I thought just playing under supervision was all right. I thought it would do no harm if . . . '

'It doesn't,' I interrupted. 'And, if you ask my opinion, I think it's good for a child to be brought up with animals. He isn't allergic to the creature so there can be, in my view, no harm. I just wanted to know what his relationship was with it.'

'Relationship?' Brian replied, sitting back in his chair and picking up his plate.

'I mean,' I said, 'does he talk to the cat as he plays with it? Does he ever get angry with it? Some children, even very young ones, find it fun to torment a cat or dog. It gives them an exercise in power.'

'They're the best of friends,' Larry assured me. 'They play . . . '

'Like kittens,' I butted in. 'Brian told me.'

'Adam's certainly never shown any antagonism towards Napoleon.'

'Never pulled his tail?' I proposed.

'Never.'

'Nor his ears? Never tried to stick his finger in the cat's mouth or – well, the other end?'

'Nothing of the sort. They just play together. When they get exhausted, they lie next to each in front of the fire. I put the fire-guard up, of course. They just snuggle in and the cat purrs like crazy. He likes Adam's company. I do take care Adam always lies with his face away from Napoleon. Just in case.'

'Why do you ask?' Brian quizzed me.

'I was just curious,' I lied. 'I was reading a paper lately which suggested infants who had animal friends early in life would grow to be pacific, calm children. Reasoned, level-headed. Probably all bunk. It was in an American journal . . .'

I fell silent, Larry and Brian exchanged looks. I wondered what was coming, what they were about to tell me. Perhaps they, too, had noticed something strange in Adam's behaviour. In one respect, I longed for them to share their information with me. I would incorporate it into my notes, use it to build up an even more solid picture of Adam. Yet, on the other hand, I prayed they had noticed nothing for, if they had seen something amiss they might well start to question things, look more closely at their son and make such discoveries as I had during the afternoon.

'Are you going to tell him?' Larry said.

Brian put his plate down and wiped crumbs from his hands on to the hearth. 'Well,' he began, 'talking of America, I've been offered a six-month exchange. It's part of a programme of international co-operation amongst dentists. I go to an American university and, in exchange for a salary and a quarter workload in the student dental service, I get to attend classes in the latest techniques and so on. Some poor sap of an American dentist comes here and takes my place for the duration, receiving my salary in lieu of his own vastly inflated income.'

'So,' Larry took up the conversation, 'we're going to Lincoln, Nebraska.'

'Congratulations!' I replied, as enthusiastically as I could. 'You had better pack your fur coats and snow-shoes. It's like the Arctic there for four months of the year.' In my mind, however, I cursed their good fortune. They were taking Adam out of my reach, just as I had found out he could charm fishes through the water and birds out of the undergrowth.

◆

Two weeks before Christmas, the telephone rang in my surgery between appointments. Molly said there was a young woman on the line but the caller refused to give her name, insisting on speaking personally to me. This was not an uncommon occurrence and I assumed I was about to hear from someone who sought a termination or was embarrassed about their infertility. It never ceased to amaze me how many were afraid to talk about their inabilities to conceive: it was, I suppose, on a par with mental illness, something they felt was their fault and should be hidden like a madness in the family. I put the receiver to my ear, readied my most doctoral and authoritatively understanding voice and heard Molly say, 'You are through now, madam.'

'Hello?' I said.

'Hello, Dom?' the caller replied.

'Who is this?'

'Ruth. Ruth Schroeder. Do you remember? It's two years . . .'

'Of course I do,' I said but I kept my tone as professional and as even as ever. It was just as likely she was contacting me as a potential patient, or for help, than as a long-lost acquaintance.

'Can we meet?'

'Certainly,' I agreed. 'Would you care to come to the surgery?' This would give her the chance to become a patient: I was sure that was on her mind.

'No,' she hesitated, 'not your surgery. This isn't a professional call. I mean . . . I don't . . . I'm not looking for treatment or anything. I need to talk to you. I need to pick your brains.'

'Again?' I queried.

'Again.'

From time to time, I had thought about Ruth, about how her work might be developing and how we had spent the night together in the Eastgate Hotel. And I had often remembered, stuck in traffic or lying in bed, the axeman prostrate in his partially evacuated box, his hand beneath my own. Yet I had never felt the urge to contact her, extend our relationship or ask after her project. I did not want to take on one of those encumbrances I wished to avoid and did not want her to assume I was seeking to elbow my way in on her research. Not wishing to visit her poky flat in the dull end of Oxford, I took the risk of inviting her to Cobb End. She accepted immediately and, I sensed, with a degree of relief.

As usual, I drove down on the Friday, stopping *en route* at a supermarket to stock up on food more suitable for entertaining. Mrs Maggs was instructed only to maintain a stock of the more basic foodstuffs in the cottage so I was seldom prepared for a house guest. On a whim, I also purchased a Christmas tree, a pack of decorations and a set of fairy lights. I spent the evening decorating the tree and went to bed just after midnight, having taken a light supper before the television, watching a banal late-night film.

The next morning, I shopped again for champagne and chopped some kindling, working up a sweat as I swung the axe and split the logs Mr Stoke had ordered in for me. I could not remember when I had last done any manual work and, by midday, my back ached and my arms felt jarred from the impact of blade on wood.

Ruth arrived in her derelict Volvo shortly after two o'clock, dressed in jeans and a large, loose sweater. Her hair was longer than when I had last met her and hung to her shoulders, giving her a tousled appearance.

'Hello, Dom,' she said, as I opened the car door for her. 'How've you been keeping?'

I noticed an overnight bag lying on the floor behind the driver's seat and tried to remember if I had, in fact, invited her to stay the weekend: I had not thought so but she must have guessed I had implied it. Her presumption momentarily annoyed me.

'I'm fine,' I said. 'And how about you?'

'The same. All work and no play makes Jill a dull girl.' Her voice had lost none of its diluted Virginian accent which I found simultaneously enticing and prosaic: she sounded like the stock heroine in the late-night film I had watched.

'This is a beautiful property,' she remarked as we entered the sitting-room. 'Cosy and old world.' She touched the low beams and the stone pillars of the fireplace. 'Is this your family home?'

'I bought it a year or so ago. On a whim, really. Wanted to get out of the city sometimes. Away from work.'

'I know exactly what you mean!' she exclaimed then, looking me straight in the eye, said, 'You could always have come to visit me.'

'My preference is to be alone,' I replied. 'I see too many people all week long so . . .'

'You mean you see too many women.'

I smiled to allow her the point, although it was not true.

'Let me show you around,' I suggested.

She followed me from room to room, exclaiming a strangely simplistic delight at the stone stairs, the low ceilings, the small windows with brass catches, the quaintness, as she put it, of the whole place.

'I never expected you to like such an old place,' she commented as we returned to the sitting-room. 'You don't seem like a man with antique tastes. More modern, somehow.'

Ignoring her observation, I guided her out into the garden, let her wander by herself along the trim beds now bleak in the winter as I watched her from a distance. I was trying to figure out why it was so urgent she see me. Her preamble seemed to portend something unpleasant. I do not know why I felt this way, yet I did: she was angling for something and I felt a tinge of apprehension tickle the nape of my neck.

When she was done touring my property, we went into the kitchen and I prepared tea, making smoked salmon sandwiches and unwrapping a box of luxury cakes, boiling the kettle and setting the spread out on the kitchen table. She did not assist but sat watching me, making small talk which increased my sense of apprehension. When she began to discuss matters concerning the Institute, the recent acquisition of the latest electron microscope, an increase in research funding, her succession of unsatisfactory lab technicians after the promotion of Barry to another department, I knew where she was heading – her Bronze Age protégé.

It was I who instigated the turn in our conversation: I could not put up with much more procrastination. 'How is your axeman?' I asked, going straight to what I was sure was the point of her visit.

'He's back with me and just dandy!' she said. I inwardly flinched at the expression. 'I've had him for a month now. All to myself.'

'I expect you've done a lot with him?' I was tempted to say *to* him but it seemed somehow cruel.

'Yes. I've had a very busy time with him,' she declared and sipped her tea: it was as if the drink was clearing her throat and mind. 'I don't really know where to begin.'

'At the start,' I suggested unnecessarily.

She took another sip of her tea.

'After your visit,' she commenced, 'I sent off the samples for DNA analysis and concentrated on the stomach. By the way, he is now thawed completely and permanently, kept just above freezing but warmed up if needed. This has not caused any deterioration as we are maintaining a partial vacuum/nitrogen atmosphere in the container. There was the question early on of anaerobic bacteria but once we had samples of them cultured, we overcame the problem.

'The stomach was fascinating. He had eaten not long before his death and I was able to identify his last meal. It consisted of crushed barley, linseed, knot-weed and a plant called gold-of-pleasure. And grapes. He had eaten what looked to have been like raisins. The knot-weed and gold-of-pleasure were gathered in with the harvest, not deliberate dietary items. There were also a number of small body-parts of bees present – a leg, a fragment of wing and part of a thorax from which I deduced his cereal was bound together or sweetened with honey.'

'No meat?' I asked.

'None but we found in his bag fish scales so he must have either had fresh fish with him or carried dried fish as a sort of Bronze Age K-ration.'

'Have you identified the fish?'

She picked up a sandwich, smiled and said, 'Salmon. It seems tastes haven't changed all that much.'

I poured out more tea and ate a sandwich myself as she went on.

'A pollen analysis of his clothing was interesting, too. It was a very rich result. Barley, twenty-three different grasses, walnut, chestnut, knot-weed, gold-of-pleasure, clover, grape. It seems as if he died in April or May because, in that part of Europe, late spring is when these flower.'

'And he died in a blizzard?'

'A late blizzard, yes. Tree-ring studies have indicated a number of harsh winters around the time of his death so it's highly possible.'

'How old was he?'

'In his mid-thirties. A good age in those days. If you saw forty-five you were a really wise old man. His teeth are somewhat ground down from eating primarily a cereal diet. Tiny grains of querns – flour milling stones – usually wore away the teeth by late middle age. I x-rayed his whole body shortly after you visited and this produced a fascinating piece of data. Wait just a moment: I've some things to show you.'

She went outside. I heard her car door open then close: she returned with a scratched, black leather briefcase. Clearing a space on the table, she put it down and snapped the brass locks open.

'He had broken his arm when he was in his late teens,' she said as she rifled through the contents of the briefcase. 'It was a nasty break. Not a clean snap but a jagged, oblique fracture to the long axis of the humerus.'

'It can easily be set,' I interrupted.

'That's true. Today. But in the Bronze Age bones were often not set. Records of healed breaks fill the books. But this one . . . '

She pulled an x-ray negative from her case and handed it to me. Evening was drawing in so I switched on the kitchen lights and held the photo-plate to one of the spot lamps. The bone had repaired well but through it, protruding from either side, was a sharp white line with terminals at each end.

'The bone had been pinned,' Ruth said. 'Not as well as a surgeon might do it now but, nevertheless, he had had someone fix his arm who had one hell of a knowledge. And that's not all.' From her briefcase she removed what appeared to be a nail. I took it from her, turning it over in my hand. It was made of bronze and weighed about ten grammes with a flat head at one end, a blunt point at the other, the metal dull but uncorroded. Indeed, it had a patina to it that suggested it had been polished not deliberately but by many hands stroking and fingering it.

'It's in remarkable condition,' I commented, 'considering it spent fifteen odd years in his body.'

'His one's still in place. This one was in his shoulder bag. My Bronze Age man was a bone-setter. Or, more precisely, a witch-doctor. I hadn't really considered the contents of his bag when we met. I was too wound up with his body. Since then, I've looked very closely into it, done a lot of reading, tramped a lot of museums and pestered a lot of people to open a lot of show cabinets.'

'And the result?' I asked.

'Here's what he had in his bag.' She took a sheaf of paper out of her case. 'You'll recall he had little pouches of herbs, barks, dried fungi and flowers. These consisted of willow and birch bark, dandelion and deadly nightshade flowers, laurel and hawthorn leaves, rowan and cherry twigs, common field mushrooms and puffballs, acorns and hazelnuts and, curiously, ground fish bones. And what we assumed at first was a piece of jerky. In fact, it is a piece of raw opium. In addition to all that and the bone peg we also have a stick with notches cut in it, some twine wrapped round it and a stone whorl. It seems to have been a weighing device of some sort, a bit like those used still by Chinese traditional doctors. In short, I'm convinced he was a Bronze Age shaman.'

I made no reply. The archaeological proof seemed to point to her hypothesis being more than true. The plants he carried all had known medicinal uses: dandelion is a diuretic, deadly nightshade contains belladonna and opium was the most efficacious natural narcotic and pain-killer known to man in pre-Christian times.

'Where did he get the opium?' I thought out loud.

'The Middle East, beyond doubt. That's one of the exciting details. It indicates trading around the Mediterranean well before the advent of the Phoenicians who did barter in opium which they obtained from Egypt, Persia and what we now call Syria.'

I began to clear the tea things away, emptying the pot down the sink and pressing the waste disposal button, placing the cups, saucers and plates in the dishwasher, storing the remaining cream cakes away in the fridge and eating the last of the smoked salmon sandwiches.

'And his DNA?'

'As remarkable as the opium. There is, of course, a long way to go before a complete analysis exists but I am finding some very strange diversities. You see, in all humans, regardless of ethnic origin, there are large sections of identical DNA. Naturally, there are also many places where it is different, where there is a fault which causes a disease or a certain different bio-type, but there are still marker sections where the DNA strand is the same in you, me and the man next door, even if he's a Nigerian or a Japanese. Or a woman. What is more, it's the same in DNA samples taken back at least three hundred years. In other words, these marker sections which we can recognize easily have not changed in recent evolution. However, in the axeman, they are different.'

Once more, she scrabbled about in her briefcase to produce a negative of two sections of DNA. 'The one on the left is from a tissue sample taken in an autopsy last February. An Italian, as it happens, the victim of a light aircraft crash. That on the right is the axeman.' She pointed with a ball-pen to the picture, sliding the point from one strand to the next. The hazy black bands were marginally thicker in one than in the other. 'This section of DNA in the crash victim reads

AACCTAGAC
TACACACCG
GCTTTTAAA
CCATATGAT

but in the corresponding section here in the axeman, it goes

AACTTAGAT
TACTCACCA
GCTTTTAAG
CCATATGAC

which is an anomaly. I can't tell how this difference may manifest itself in a living person. We are some way off such a capability but it augurs some incredible discoveries for the future.

'Just think of it,' she went on, putting down the negative and waving her arms about, her hands and the ball-pen emphasizing each point. 'Once we understand these fundamental differences and can perhaps work out how they are engineered and what their cause and effect is, we'll be able to manipulate genes to overcome genetic diseases, not just recognize them. We could actually cure Adenosine Deaminase Deficiency and through it Severe Combined Immune Deficiency. Think of it! No more ADA, no more SCID. And no more Duchenne muscular dystrophy, cystic fibrosis, Creutzfeld-Jacob disease, Huntingdon's chorea, Alzheimer's. Jesus Christ, Dom! Once we get to the therapy of genes, the sky's the limit! And it's only a matter of time.'

She was temporarily exhausted by her enthusiasm and let her arms drop as if they were too tired to support themselves. Slowly, she replaced all her papers and photographs in her case, letting the lid fall shut and clicking the catches down. 'Do you mind if I go take a shower?' she asked. 'I'd like to get the road off me. I had to change a wheel coming down.'

I showed her where the bathroom was and put fresh towels out for her, switching on the electric water heater. Ruth went out to her car and brought in the small overnight bag, which action I took to be not a little presumptuous but I made no response. It was obvious she was hoping to take up where we had left off at the Eastgate Hotel and although I was not against renewing our relationship on a temporary basis, I did not want her to become a part of my life.

As she ran the shower, I felt a sudden and intense protectiveness towards Adam. I do not know why it should have suddenly come upon me there and then, but it did, commingled with a grim sense of foreboding.

Returning downstairs, I started to prepare our evening meal, cutting meat, slicing vegetables and dicing fruit for a dessert. As I worked, I thought over all she had told me about Adam's natural father and considered the implications.

There was not a doubt in my mind the axeman was a shaman and this had to explain Adam's strange abilities. At first, I considered there was no possibility these skills could be inherited but the more I thought about it, the less improbable it seemed. Identical twins are able to communicate through some form of telepathy: there had been a number of studies of twins living thousands of miles apart sharing common experiences. I recalled one instance from my own practice. Her name was Geraldine Forsey: the wife of a national racehorse trainer, she was pregnant but there was a possibility of complications for she had miscarried twice. I nurtured her, examined her weekly, took an infinite number of tests and precautions with the result she went full term. On the day of the delivery, she gave birth to a healthy seven-pound daughter. And, simultaneously, her unmarried conservationist sister who was on safari in Tanzania and well beyond contact with her twin, was rushed by air ambulance to hospital in Arusha with sudden and unaccountable abdominal contractions. There was nothing wrong with her at all and, the pains subsiding after ten hours – the duration of Mrs Forsey's labour – she was released by puzzled doctors.

If that were not sufficient proof for me, I had to consider other allegedly inherited traits, where parent and offspring have shared talents which cannot be put down to social upbringing or environment. Artists, musicians, chess players, mathematicians, men and women with inordinate skills shared with their parents, some of whom died when they were in their infancy. It was possible. I was certain of it. As I cored the apples to put round the pork casserole and squeezed the lime juice on to the pineapple and guavas included in the dessert, I was utterly sure, without the merest incertitude, Adam had inherited his remarkable skill of calling fish and birds.

I stopped my cooking and sat down. As a doctor, as a scientist, I knew I should have demanded more proof before reaching such an unshakeable conclusion. One result does not determine the veracity of an experiment any more than one dose of codeine might cure a migraine or one shot of insulin save a diabetic. And yet I knew I was right, just as a detective is irrefutably sure when he has the guilty man sitting before him, although not in possession of the slightest scrap of evidence. How many times had I over the years looked at a patient and been able to exactly diagnose their problem without so much as asking them to unfasten a button or touch their flesh? It was not so much a matter of medical knowledge that strengthened my conviction as to their illness but an inner certainty born of what the detective would call his nose and I would term irrational experience. It was that which told me I was right about Adam.

Now convinced, my mind boggled at the implications. Adam had acquired skills most men no longer possessed, especially in the First World, the world of technology. Evolution had suppressed it, bred it out of them. After all, modern industrial man has no need to call up birds when he has guns to kill them from afar, poisons to bring them down, nets to throw over them and tape recorders to scare them away with the sounds of their natural predators. As for fish, I thought, why tickle them close when we can pollute or dynamite them. Or farm them.

My mind was streaking ahead now, filling with disjointed thoughts, spinning with excitement. Adam was a unique key to the past. Fourteen months old, he could charm animals. This being so, what skills he had yet to exhibit could be extensive, earth-shattering. He could give insights into the natural world no modern man could dream of and the use this might have in our understanding of nature, of animals, the implications this could have for conservation . . .

'Can I help?'

I was jerked out of my reverie by Ruth standing in the kitchen door. She had changed from her jeans into a tight skirt and sweater.

'No,' I replied, standing up, 'I was just having a break. And there's not much more to do.' I pointed to the fridge. 'Would you like a drink? I've some wine in there.'

She opened the door and removed a bottle of Sauvignon. I handed her a corkscrew and she poured two glasses, putting one next to me on the work top.

'Do you think intelligence is inherited?' she asked.

I started. She might have been reading my mind.

'I can't say. I've not considered it.'

'It's been an idea for over a century,' she said. 'Francis Galton was the father – if you'll pardon the pun! – of the eugenics movement in the 1860s. The idea then was to check the birth rate of the unfit and improve the race by furthering the productivity of the fit by the early marriages of the best stock. That was how it was put.'

'It smacks of the farmyard,' I replied. 'Selective breeding. Find the woolliest lambs and mate them for even woollier offspring. Hitler tried it with the Aryan youths and holiday camps. Not the stuff of moral humanity.'

'Sure, and the Americans tried it well into the 1960s at the Lynchburg Colony. I'm not questioning the morality of it,' Ruth went on. 'Just the scientific feasibility. Of course, get two muscular parents and the odds are most of their children will be muscular little toughs but I'm going beyond blue-eyed and blond-haired Teutonic super-kids. It must be possible to selectively breed people for physical characteristics. I'm thinking more of mental ones.'

I put the casserole in the oven and turned the knob to 350°. The fan started to whir as I slid the dish on to the oven rack and closed the door.

'Britain has been considering such a problem for decades,' Ruth continued as I stood up. 'It comes from having a class society. The upper classes have been afraid of mixing with the lower for fear of diluting their blue blood. At the same time as Hitler was breeding his blondes, it was believed in Britain the lower classes were breeding too fast and the general level of intelligence of the nation would fall as a result.'

'Watching the dozy, chinless wonders who inherit the benches of the House of Lords,' I remarked, 'this seems to be a bit of a *non sequitur.*'

She laughed for a moment but was soon serious again. 'As recently as 1958, Sir Peter Medawar – no fool, he – gave over his BBC Reith lecture to the concept national intelligence might fall off because the working classes were no longer dying quickly, thanks to free health provision, and were therefore too fertile. Even to this day, the argument still simmers that IQs may be inherited. And what of homosexuality? There are those who say this is an inherited trait.'

'Perhaps,' I replied, 'it's nature's way to stop us breeding. After all, gay couples don't have kids. If the gay gene, if it exists, is inherited, then you can see how it might be a natural check and balance.'

She looked at me for a minute. I busied myself peeling carrots.

'You're teasing again,' she said at length, but I could tell she was not too sure.

'I'm teasing,' I confirmed. 'I don't think nature is so stupid as to develop an inheritable gene to stop us breeding and then put it into people who don't breed. On the other hand, nature works in mysterious ways. You might argue AIDS has been developed by nature to cut down numbers, for the sake of the planet and the common good. We are over-populating mother earth at an alarming and unsustainable rate.'

'There are those who say AIDS is an invention of the laboratory test-tube.'

I looked at her to see if she was joking, but she was not. She was in deadly earnest. I wondered what she knew, what secrets were tucked away in her laboratory database, accessed only with a password, unbreakable and inviolate, present on a hard disk somewhere with a hidden attribute.

'This is very much a bachelor's house,' she said, suddenly changing the subject and looking around her. 'No woman in her right mind would keep such a tidy kitchen.'

'The kitchen,' I pontificated, 'is an extension of the mind. I am a doctor. I like things ordered and clean. This kitchen is, I suppose, a subconscious extension of my operating theatre.' I held my hand out. 'Serrated vegetable knife.'

She glanced around the walls and saw the chrome knife hanging from its magnetic bar. 'Serrated vegetable knife,' she repeated and slapped it into my hand.

Throughout our meal, we talked of different matters, of the village, of my neighbours, of her summer holiday in Italy, of politics and other petty affairs of paltry men. It was not until I served coffee before the fire she returned to our previous conversation.

'You know,' she said, 'humans benefit from their biological diversity.'

'How do you mean?' I rejoined.

'Take dogs. Take the dachshund. It was never invented like

161

that by nature. It was shaped by careful breeding, controlled evolution. And look at it now. Their backs dislocate because they're too long, they have hip trouble and their little peters – if they're boys – trail on the ground. Nature's not to blame for that. Humans are. Sheep give birth to a high proportion of mutants because they are inbred. But we are different. We are diverse, always mixing, breeding out of control. And this gives us a huge gene bank upon which to draw. Hybrid vigour. That's what it is. If a new disease appears, we can look through our genes to combat it, to develop a resistance.'

'That rather blows away any theories of eugenics,' I said.

'Of course. Eugenics is bunk. And yet . . . '

'And yet?'

'And yet we're not far off from being able to manufacture people. Not whole people. Not chance people such as you make in your *in vitro* fertilization lab. Just people with certain traits. Eugenics was a dream from a time before genetics. Now it becomes feasible. Once we map the genes and know what does what, we can alter the future of mankind.'

'And not just for the better,' I said. 'Not just to wipe out diseases.'

'No,' she concurred quietly, 'not just that. It's like any discovery. Nuclear power gives cheap electricity but it makes plutonium waste and bombs. But that's not my responsibility. The morality, I mean. It's for society to decide. If we always thought of what might be, what the effect of any action is, we'd never progress.'

She fell silent, stirred her coffee, put her cup on the table, reached out to a little dish of Bendicks mints and placed one in her mouth. 'Dom,' she then said, 'would you do another favour for me?'

'As on the last occasion,' I replied, 'it depends on what it is.'

She came right out with it. There was no beating about the bush. I was already her co-conspirator so she thought, I suppose, there was no need for delicate subterfuge and

162

argument. 'Will you implant one of the Bronze Age man's sperm into a living human egg?'

'Why?' I asked.

'Because if you did, and we let the cell divide for, say 18 divisions . . . '

'That would produce more than a quarter of a million cells,' I interrupted.

' . . . and we stopped there,' she went on, 'I would have sufficient material for a DNA study of . . . '

'Of what?' I enquired.

'Of a new kind of man. A modern man and a primitive one.'

I refused, politely but firmly. She questioned me as to my motive for refusal, tried to cajole me into changing my mind: she would not take notes, my name need not be mentioned as she had previously agreed with regard to the aspiration of the axeman. I still would not agree. She argued ethics were not involved for no human would be made. The embryo – she knew enough to recognize it would by then technically be one – would not be living, not have taken on a form. It would, she assured me, have no soul.

My continued rejection of her request then peeved her and she accused me of being afraid of the future, of progress, of scientific advance. She suggested I was a medical Luddite with my head stuck in the sand. This failing, she changed tack and tried to shake me on moral grounds, saying her work would lead to the elimination of disease, the *raison d'être* of my profession. Still not shifting my resolve, she accused me of intellectual turpitude, of being a materialist whose only interest was the fat fee collected from every patient.

Eventually, she surrendered and threatened, 'I can always do it myself.'

'Of course, you can,' I agreed affably. 'It requires no skill other than a steady hand and the right equipment and that is minimal. You just inject the oöcyte and incubate.'

'It would be better if you did it,' she replied.

'Why?' I retorted. 'Are you afraid of the consequences?'

She looked away.

'No,' she declared.

Yet I knew she was.

The refusal to oblige her request to implant the sperm clearly nettled her, destroying any romantic intentions she may have been harbouring. At eleven o'clock she left, taking her overnight bag with her. After her departure, I sat alone before the fire. The Chirstmas tree lights winked in the corner of the room and the fire danced its glimmer on the wooden beams.

It was then, I think, I finally realized the enormity of what I had done and the miracle which I alone had perpetrated – and the danger in which it placed Adam.

◆

The people of the clearing are gentle and generous. They have accepted me into their community without question. No one has pondered my motives for coming here, attempted to guess what happened to send an Englishman and his companion into their midst. My past has not been challenged, for which I am grateful to them.

The former results from the people being conservative and polite. Inquisitiveness is seen as rude and for all their primitivity, they are never in their own way discourteous or inconsiderate. The latter is because they have little concept of time and do not consider anything which happened over a fortnight ago to be of any relevance.

Fourteen days, or thereabouts, seems to be the limit of their conscious timespan. Anything further back occurred in the mists of antiquity or in the realms of myth. Birthdays are not celebrated, nor any other anniversary, and religious festivals are not prompted by date but by natural conditions. If a tree falls in the jungle nearby, if a caiman is trapped in a fishing net, if one of a certain species of bird is accidentally snared then this may prompt a festival or an appeasing of the spirits.

In their ignorance of time, they are fortunate. Their

simplicity of spirit is, I am sure, accounted for by their lives not being measured. Death is not something they anticipate but merely an event sure to come, like the sunset or the seasonal risings and fallings of the river.

For me, things are different. I would forget time if I could, eradicate all the history which lies in me, the deceits and failures, the arabesques of fate. Priests got it wrong when they said the sinner enters purgatory after death. He lives in it whilst he is alive, purgatory is another name for the passage of the hours.

One occurrence has, however, now happened which can, in a way, aid my loathing of time. I cannot erase the past but the future looks slightly more bearable. The battery in my cheap Seiko has finally expired. It has served me well since I was obliged to part with my gold Vacheron Constantin in exchange for it and tickets up-river to Santo Antonio do Içá: once the ticket inspector saw my wristwatch, money lost its value for him. He got by far the best of the deal for my tickets were little better than deck steerage passes and the Seiko is made of stainless steel with a scratched glass. Gradually, over a week, the digital numbers began to imperceptibly fade until, at last, they vanished altogether and the face was left blank, like a little green blackboard from which the master had rubbed out the lesson.

It being no longer of any use to me, and my not wanting to replace it even if I could, I prised the back off with a knife and removed the little battery. It was silver and no larger than a small pill. Knowing it must contain chemicals dangerous to the forest and the people – mercury, perhaps, the most insidious of killers – I placed the battery on the bookshelf until evening then, the fire in the clearing lit, I tossed it into the flames.

The children watched the spot in the embers where it had fallen. As no one had ever seen me toss something into the fire with such deliberation, this seemed to them to be a moment of some importance. The battery did not let me down. After burning with a neon blue flame for a minute, it exploded with a sharp crack. The children jumped then laughed with nervous pleasure. All the adults started except Chuhi who must have anticipated what might happen and Keewei for whom magic was a part of his and, he supposed, my life.

After that, I thought I was free of time. Yet I was wrong. For a few days, I kept wondering what time it was, what day it was: despite having lost the Air Brazil calendar a few months after my arrival in the clearing, I was aware of the day and date because the watch kept tally. I was temporarily lost, like an addict prevented from his next fix. I subconsciously looked at my wrist several times only to see just my skin, less tanned where the strap had been. After a week or so – perhaps seven or eight sunrises might be a more appropriate measure – I felt unaccountably afraid without the knowledge that it was whatever o'clock, on such-and-such a day.

Just as I was getting over my withdrawal symptoms, Chuhi set my rehabilitation back.

'*Señor*,' he addressed me one morning as I was tidying my hut, '*vente conmigo hoy a la selva.*'

'*¿Por qué?*' I asked.

'*Porque hay una plaza,*' was his enigmatic answer.

My curiosity was aroused by what kind of place this might be so I agreed and, not long after, we set off. He led the way along a path I had not previously travelled. After a mile or so, it began to grow faint and I grew slightly uneasy although I was sure Chuhi meant me no harm. If, however, I was to lose contact with him I would surely be lost. Keeping a sense of direction was out of the question. The path meandered to and fro, dividing and sub-dividing into animal tracks or even less frequented ways.

About midday, we arrived at a hill. The slopes rose sharply ahead of us, thick with forest and ficus trees which had sent out aerial roots to embrace and, in places, crack the boulders of the hillside. Chuhi made his way around a group of vast rocks then disappeared from sight. I was not looking at him the moment he vanished and, finding myself alone, all the fears of being lost welled up in me. The first thought to occur to me was, had I my gold watch, I could have used it as a compass to orientate myself: but, looking up, I could barely see the sun through the forest canopy.

'*¡Señor!*' It was Chuhi's voice, hollow and distant. I followed it to discover the mouth of a wide cave at least ten metres across and five high.

'*¡Señor! Entre.*'

Although the forest was in shadow, I had to wait a moment for my eyes to adjust. Chuhi was standing about ten metres into the cave which sloped gradually downwards, the roof lowering all the while. Rocks jutted out of the soil overhead but the floor was smooth and packed down. As I reached him, Chuhi struck sparks off a stone and lit a patch of dry moss taken from his pouch. With this, he ignited a firebrand. The rear wall of the cave took on a mottled fiery glow. It was, I thought, like looking into the boiler of a furnace through a flame-stained inspection window. The entrance to Hades might look like this from a distance.

'*Ámber,*' Chuhi declared.

I stepped forward and touched the wall. It was chipped and jagged in places, smooth as glass in others. Holding the firebrand closer, Chuhi showed me the face of the amber. The sputtering flames seemed to become dissolved into the cave sides as if the amber was sucking in their light and greedily feeding upon it.

Jamming the firebrand into a crevice, Chuhi removed a small steel hand axe from behind a fallen boulder and swung it at the amber face. Expecting a ring of steel, I flinched in readiness but the sound the axe made was a dull thud.

For perhaps a quarter of an hour, Chuhi swung his axe, working at a block of amber about the size of two clenched fists. He worked feverishly, in silence save for the grunt of exertion. The firebrand burned lower and began to extinguish at the edges. The roof of the cave was hung with a pall of black smoke which was leaking out at the cave mouth. The rocks at the rear of the cave, I noticed, were dark with soot whilst, nearer the mouth, this had faded with time: from its size and depth, I assessed the cave must have been at least a century old.

Just as the firebrand began to die, the lump of amber broke free and fell to the floor. Chuhi kicked the firebrand from its crevice and carried the amber to the cave mouth. For its size, it was not as heavy as stone. Placing it on a boulder, he raised his axe and struck the amber with the flat side of the blade. It shattered into half a dozen fragments, each about the size of a hen's egg. Quickly inspecting these, Chuhi handed one to me, indicating I hold it to a splinter of sunlight breaking through the trees above.

The amber was the golden colour of syrup, shot through with flaw lines, cracks and bubbles. I could not help thinking how old the air within them was: that, if I was to be able to break one open, I could breathe air untainted by a passage through human lungs. Between the imperfections was scattered in suspension a variety of dark pieces of prehistoric debris.

'*¿Qué hay?*' Chuhi asked, not taking his attention from a chunk he was holding up.

'*Ámber,*' I replied.

'*Sí, señor,*' he responded. '*¿Qué hay en el ámber?*' He beckoned to me to look at his own piece, pointing with a twig to the debris within. '*Sí, señor,*' he instructed me. '*Una hormiga, un escarabajo pequeño, el ala de un insecto.*'

For a moment, I could see none of these then my eye caught a shape and they all became clear. I studied my own piece of amber: set in the centre, one wing bent under its thorax, was a tiny moth.

'*Son niños del sol,*' Chuhi remarked, adding in a flat voice which might have been mercenary had it been sophisticated, '*el gringo Rodriguez va dar mucho por ellos.*'

He replaced his axe behind the boulder in the cave, waved his arms unnecessarily to dispel the last of the smoke and, gathering up the fragments of amber, put them in his pouch. I went to place my piece in with the others but he shook his head and pointed from it to me.

'*Gracias,*' I thanked him.

He said nothing but smiled, his dark eyes gleaming in the sunlight.

All the way back to the clearing, I could not help thinking how time holds all creation prisoner, stores up all its sins and vanities, its failings and its wonders until it feels the hour has come to finish them off.

◆

It was a quarter past four in the afternoon. Exactly. The clock on the shelf next to the filing cabinet had just finished its silver chiming, the sound still in my ears as the knock came on the door.

At the time, I was writing up my clinical notes on a patient who had been referred to me by one of the teaching hospitals. It was a most unfortunate case. The woman, in her mid-thirties, had born two children but lost one of them to a brain haemorrhage at the age of five. The other was, by all accounts, a sickly child of eleven. At the age of twenty-eight, she had suffered badly from endometriosis but had not been to her doctor until the problem had persisted through five or six menstrual cycles. Hormone treatment had been prescribed and had seemed to do the trick for a while but the condition returned. On the internal pelvic examination carried out in the hospital, it was discovered she had three malignant ovarian cysts, one filled with blood, a fairly sure sign of endometriosis. At this point, by chance, the woman's husband had come into a large sum of money and his wife had been transferred to my register.

'Come in,' I called out.

The door opened and Molly entered followed by two men dressed in suits and carrying briefcases.

'These gentlemen are here to see you, Dr Lyall,' she said. 'They are from the HFEA.'

I stood up and came round the edge of my desk, shaking hands with both of them. One introduced himself as Thomas Hodson, his partner as Andrew Scammell. They were both inspectors from the Human Fertilization and Embryology Authority.

'Please, sit down,' I invited them. They accepted. 'What can I do for you?'

'We would appreciate it if you would allow us to briefly inspect your premises,' the one named Hodson requested.

'This is a bit of a surprise,' I pointed out. 'One is usually afforded some warning.'

'Yes, sir,' Scammell agreed, 'but we also like from time to time to carry out a snap inspection. This implies no concern on our part at all and I must assure you there are no grounds for your being chosen for such a sudden visit. No allegations have been made or complaints received – nothing of that sort at all. And no improprieties have been drawn to our attention. It is merely policy in our office. Your name has been selected at random from the list of facilities in our area which covers a wide part of the south-east of England.'

He was clearly at pains to point out they were expecting to find no irregularities but I was aware of my heart fluttering faster.

'What can I show you?' I enquired.

'Nothing specifically, sir,' Hodson replied. 'If you would just let us have a wander round. You may guide us yourself, let one of your staff give us a conducted tour or leave us to our own devices. We are basically looking out for any lax procedures in administration, any lapses which might break the relevant legislation. We are not looking specifically to find fault nor to take a prosecution. This is an advisory rather than an admonitory visit. And there are three of us. We have a colleague waiting outside, an executive member of HFEA. He will join us if you are in agreement.'

'Of course,' I said, feigning joviality. 'I'll have my senior nurse show you around. I assume you'll not mind if I get on with my work in the meantime?'

To my relief, they said this did not concern them so they fetched their colleague as I called Angela in, introduced her to the three of them and watched them leave the office.

No sooner was the door closed than I removed the ficti- tious Mouette dossier from the filing cabinet and placed it in my briefcase for temporary safekeeping, thrusting it behind a number of case notes awaiting a meeting the following day at St Thomas' Hospital. I did not for one moment expect they would go through my filing cabinet but I wanted no chances taken. What if, I thought, their preamble was a polite fabrication and they had, somehow, been tipped off: there was no way I could know.

At the end of my desk, the computer screen flickered with a pattern of swimming cartoon fish, a screen saver which automatically cut in if the computer was unused for fifteen minutes. I touched the mouse and the image on the screen returned to the disc operating system program manager display. Taking a floppy disk from a box in my desk drawer, I copied the hidden Mouette file on to it and then, to be safe, erased the original from the hard disk. The floppy I placed in my briefcase with the file.

The inspectors and their colleague, a member of their organization sent with them presumably to see fair play, were by now in the operating theatre checking up whatever details they needed to ascertain, ticking these off on a report form. I slipped past them, smiling politely and, going to the freezing unit on the pretext of needing to check something, removed the straws of the axeman's samples, putting these in my jacket pocket.

My hand was still touching the straws in my pocket when a voice asked, quite severely, 'What are you doing, Dr Lyall?'

It was Hodson. He was looking directly at me, his left hand holding a clipboard before his chest, his pen poised in his right hand.

'I'm just making sure of a coding sequence on some straws,' I replied after what I hoped was an indiscern- ible pause.

'Should you not have a reference card in your pos- session?'

'I know the number,' I said, 'three-four-one-two.'

I removed my hand from my pocket. The hairs on my neck were prickling and I felt a bead of sweat move in the small of my back.

'I see,' Hodson remarked. 'Thank you.' He jotted a few quick notes on his clipboard and turned his attention to something else.

Returning to my office, I immediately went through into my apartment and quickly placed the straws at the rear of the freezer compartment of my fridge, behind a carton of Häagen-Dazs ice-cream and several packets of frozen vegetables and convenience meals. My hands were shaking and I felt light-headed. I took a bottle of ice cold soda water from the door shelf and splashed it into my hands, rubbing my face with it then, somewhat revived, went to my bathroom and patted my face with Dunhill aftershave, wiping my flannel around the inside of my collar. Somewhat calmed, I sat for a few minutes on the edge of my bed then, when I was satisfied all was safe for the time being, and my composure was regained, I returned to my desk to busy myself with some patient records.

I felt sure there was no need for such caution. The inspectors were not paying attention to the finer details of my practice: they were, it seemed, more intent on studying the layout of my rooms and talking to Angela, Phillips and Molly in reception. I could hear their voices but not the subject of their conversation.

After an hour or so, the inspectors entered my office. Hodson looked particularly tight-lipped, his clipboard gripped firmly in his right hand. 'Dr Lyall,' he began, placing several sheets of paper on my desk, 'we shall be sending you a full report in a week but we feel it is important the findings of our visit be made known to you now.'

A pull of apprehension tightened in me. They had not looked into my computer nor, come to that, the ice compartment of my fridge, but I knew one should never underestimate officialdom. Like police officers and tax inspectors, these were men trained to see what others missed, even those guilty of a skilfully contrived crime or a carefully disguised embezzlement.

Hodson looked at Scammell who said, 'Our recommendations are advisory at this stage. You are not bound to act upon them. However, we feel the shortcomings we believe we have discovered could be construed as a breach of the relevant legislation governing IVF practices.'

I could not believe they had seen my sneaking the straws out of the freezing unit: if that had been the case, I thought, I would have been apprehended at the time.

'We recommend, with immediate effect, you tighten up your administration,' Scammell continued. 'Doors are to bear notices explaining the function of the rooms into which they lead. Your laboratory area must bear signs reminding staff and visitors it is prohibited to anyone not directly involved in the IVF or related processes. As you must be aware, the law dictates no staff other than those involved in the IVF process may enter the laboratory area. We have noted your receptionist enters that facility. This is not to be allowed.'

'Furthermore,' Hodson interrupted, taking up the criticism, 'there should be lines of demarcation on the floor by doors to indicate their restriction. This is not essential but I have found it of use in some cases. The operating procedures of your staff are lax. Mr Phillips, your senior technician, was not aware the temperature increase warning light on your storage facility was broken. It is not sufficient to rely upon the warning buzzer alone.'

'You yourself,' Scammell added, 'are lax. You came in to check on some straws having committed the coding on those straws to memory. This is not good enough. You should carry with you the reference card or patient file so as to be able to cross-check yourself.'

They made a number of other, minor comments but that was the nub of it. They were trusting my integrity as a doctor, my ethics were not being questioned: they were more concerned with administrative trivia than moralities and principles.

I made apologetic noises, promised their suggestions would be followed to the letter and accepted their criticisms in good faith. In the circumstances, they could have accused me of being the Butcher of Belgravia and I would not have flinched. I was safe.

As soon as I was alone that evening, I returned the Mouette file to the cabinet, put the straws back in the freezing unit, re-entered the data into a new hidden file on the hard disk and arranged for discreet signs to be made for the doors. In addition, I made a back-up disk of the Mouette computer data to store at the cottage for safekeeping.

The HFEA inspectors' visit was not the only event to make the week memorable. Three days later, Brian telephoned.

I was sitting watching a drama on television, eating a seafood salad with a half bottle of champagne to accompany it, when the telephone rang. I pressed the remote control, dropped the volume and lifted the receiver.

'Hello, Dom, it's Brian.'

His words had the momentary pause and hollowness satellites give to the human voice.

'Hello, Brian,' I responded. 'How are you? And how's your exchange going?'

'Fine, just fine,' he said. 'In fact, better than could be expected. And the exchange has metamorphosed into – well, the main thing is we're staying over here for three years. I've got a contract with the university to teach . . .'

I was not listening. Their prolonged absence meant I should not see Adam until he was nearly five. Those fascinating years of development were to be lost to me. I felt a simultaneous disappointment and anger run through me.

'Dom! Dom? You still there?'

'I'm still here, Brian. And congratulations. But what about your partner,' I searched my memory for his name, 'Roger Bates, isn't it?'

'Sorted out,' Brian replied. 'He's got someone over from Australia who just wants a few years. One of those Aussie world traveller types. Look, Dom, can I beg a favour of you?'

'Certainly.'

'Can you keep an eye on the house for us? Fix up Mrs Maggs to do it over once in a while? I've arranged for an estate agent to let it on short-term agreements, but – well, you know. Can you liaise with him the next time you are down there?'

'Of course I can, Brian,' I said, but I must have sounded angry.

'You sure this isn't an imposition?' Brian went on. 'If it is – well, we know how busy you are.'

'Not an imposition,' I assured him. 'It'll be no bother. The agent will do most of it. I'll just see things don't get out of hand.'

'You're a good sport, Dom. We'll fix for you to visit us.'

'How's Larry?' I enquired. 'Adam?'

'Fine. Larry's going to do some work in the university. Art history stuff. They want her to do a spot of teaching and she's writing a book on Navaho pottery. Adam's getting along. He can walk now and is starting to talk.'

'What does he say?'

'Oh, the usual baby prattle. Mama, dada, that sort of thing. And he googles and burbles. His first full word seems to be Naga-saki. God knows where he gets it from!'

I made no comment but was prepared to wager with myself it was the word he uttered when cowboys on horses rode by.

◆

I came upon Chuhi standing on a boulder at the end of the rocky outcrop below the falls. From the pathway, he was in silhouette against the forest on the far bank, his light brown body contrasting with the bright sunlight on the foliage opposite. His arm was raised over his shoulder, grasping his six-foot-long fishing spear, a thin line of twine draping forwards over his shoulder.

Knowing the etiquette of fishermen the world over, I did not call out to him but remained in the shadows on the path to watch him. He was quite motionless for some minutes before, with a movement too rapid for my eyes to follow, he flung the spear into the river. It made not the slightest stir in the water until it rose again. He began to slowly pull on the line and, in a short time, hoisted on to the rocks a large, not particularly streamlined fish.

'*Ay, señor Do-me-neek!*' he called, catching sight of me and holding the fish up, twitching on the spear. The tip of black, hard wood had gone clean through its body.

'*¡Buenos dias!*' I shouted back.

He beckoned to me to join him so I left the path and scrambled over the rocks. By the time I reached his side, he had removed his catch from the spear and made an incision in its back, just behind the head, severing its spine.

'Eet ees a goot feesh,' Chuhi announced, grinning at both his prize and his attempt at English.

'It is a good fish,' I agreed and ran my finger along its side. Like most freshwater fish, it was a little slick and slimy.

Dropping his catch in a basket, he offered the spear to me. 'You, feesh.'

I shook my head and said, 'I cannot fish with . . . ' I touched his spear and added, 'a spear.'

He looked a little crestfallen so I took hold of the weapon and admired it. It was surprisingly light, perhaps made of a kind of strong balsa-wood, and very front-heavy on account of the tip which was unbarbed. I wondered how he managed to retain the fish on the spike. Chuhi felt my biceps and raised my arm over my head, grimacing and shaking his head. '*Si, no puedes lanzar,*' he agreed and, taking it from me, laid the spear on the rocks by the basket, beckoning to me to follow him.

We descended the rocks to the river's edge and turned towards the pool where the children swam. They were not about although, from time to time, I could hear puerile shouts from the direction of the falls. Going down on his haunches, Chuhi indicated I should imitate him. His bare toes just touched the brown water. I, too, squatted down.

'*Puedes pescar,*' he declared.

With the caution of a man testing the temperature of water, he slid the index and middle fingers of his left hand into the water, spreading them apart like an inverted V, his other fingers bent under his thumb. When I did not follow suit he grunted softly and nodded at my right hand. I copied him.

Taking hold of my free hand in his and gripping it tightly, his fingers intertwined with mine much as lovers' do, he began to whistle. I tried to imitate the sound but he stopped and shook his head.

'*Toco la música de los peces*,' he said in a near whisper.

The whistle did not come from between his lips or teeth but appeared to emanate from his nostrils. It was very high-pitched, like the sound of a dog whistle just tuned to the range limit of the human ear.

Something touched my fingers, brushing against it. I looked down but could see no movement in the murky water. It came again, followed by another. Chuhi's hand gripped tighter. A fin broke the surface by my knuckles. It was large and I judged the fish beneath it must have weighed at least a kilo.

Chuhi lowered his hand into the water, still whistling, then withdrew it very slowly. His hand had been bent into a cradle upon which lay a large black fish, its back humped like a carp. Its mouth was open displaying triangular, shark-like teeth.

'*Piraña*,' Chuhi said softly, briefly interrupting his whistling. He nodded at my hand and began to whistle. I bent my hand into a cradle and, sure enough, a fish came and settled in it. I raised my arm and discovered a brown catfish resting on my fingers. It was about sixty centimetres long with a broad brown body, its fins tipped with scarlet. It was all I could do to lift it clear of the water.

Chuhi shook his head and stopped whistling. '¡*Pirarara!*' he exclaimed pointing at my catch and, with a deft flick of his arm, tossed his *piraña* into the bushes where it came to life, flapping and thrashing against the low branches. I was about to do likewise with my catfish but it suddenly flipped and was gone.

We stood up. Chuhi took out his knife and killed the *piraña* with a spine incision. When it was dead, he handed it to me. It was not at all aerodynamic, the scales not smooth but somehow raised so that running a finger over it was like stroking a very full pin cushion. Its eye had an orange iris with a jet black pupil.

Leaving Chuhi with his spear, I set off in the direction of the falls to sit on a boulder close to the base of the falls, just inside the reach of the spray. It was cooling and gentle, like the touch of an experienced masseuse. Under the first cascade, children were cavorting, dashing through the curtains of water, screaming and laughing, tossing handfuls of moss at each other. Watching them, I saw in my mind's eye the figure of Adam at the age of one, dipping his hand in the garden pond and luring the fish to stroke his fingers.

◆

It was just over three years before I met the Cordiners again although we were in almost monthly touch by letter or telephone. A few problems arose with the letting of their house, to which I gave my attention, but otherwise our communication was of a purely social nature.

For Adam's birthday and Christmas, I sent gifts I thought would appeal to him and, at the same time, stimulate him. What his parents must have made of a large magnifying glass, a number of books on animals aimed at an age range of at least eight, a monocular, wooden do-it-yourself construction models of insects, a collection of fossils and a small tin box with a glass bottom to enable the owner to see into ponds, I cannot think. Yet they dutifully passed these on to Adam, writing to say how much he appreciated and used them. These comments, I believed, were not mere polite platitudes for I was certain the boy did enjoy them and, once he was shown what to do with them, used them.

From time to time, I was sent a photograph of Adam

with his parents. He was growing steadily and, I was assured whenever I asked, healthily. Indeed, Larry had put him into a pre-school kindergarten as soon as she could, to allow herself the opportunity to work and study. He was quick to relate to the other children, easy to get along with and was, she was told, the best behaved of the pupils.

Not being able to pose the kind of detailed questions to which I wanted answers was frustrating and annoying. On a number of occasions, I made tentative plans to visit them in their prairie home but these fell through either because of commitments they had or because I fabricated my own excuses in order not to go. There was little I could achieve by being present for just a week and I knew whatever I did learn would be negated by my having to leave without the chance of following up my discoveries. This would have frustrated me even further. I decided it was best not to see Adam until such a time as I could take up my observations of him in earnest.

After the expiry of Brian's contract with the university, the family took a two-month holiday travelling the world, their passage marked by the arrival of postcards from Tahiti, Osaka, Hong Kong, New Delhi, Athens and Rome. Each card heightened my anticipation, marking off the days until they would reach London.

The night before their return, I was unable to sleep for the excitement of seeing the boy again. I looked at the photographs I had of him, placing them in chronological order so I might have some idea of his physical development. In every one, he was a smiling child, clearly happy and ready for whatever life might pass before him. In one picture, he was shown with his arms around a neighbour's dog and I considered, whenever I looked at it, if he was merely playing with the animal or somehow communing with it as he had with the blackbird.

The photographs prepared me, to some extent, for the sight of him but, as they walked through the arrivals channel at Heathrow, I could not help being taken aback by the child's inordinate beauty. He was of average height for his age, his body well proportioned, his dark brown hair curly and soft.

Looking at his hands, I saw them to be long-fingered, almost simian. His face was handsome with his mother's smooth, high cheek-bones and small nose but his mouth was fuller than hers, his brows a little closer together. His skin was tanned from his travels but it was his eyes which caught my attention. They were dark brown, deep and strangely knowing: they were an adult's eyes in a child's face.

Brian, surveying the crowd of welcoming families, chauffeurs with name-boards, sweethearts and businessmen, caught sight of me and called out. I pushed through the throng, kissed Larry, shook Brian's hand hard then went down on my haunches to be level with Adam. I held out my hand.

'Hello, Adam,' I said.

He took my hand as if to shake it.

'Hello, Uncle Dom,' he answered. His voice was quiet and lacked the accent of the average American child. 'We've seen the Taj Mahal and the Acropilius.'

I smiled and replied, 'Did you, indeed! And have you also seen the Colosseum?'

'Yes,' he answered, 'and there were lots of cats there. And the guide said they were the ghosts of the lions and leopards which killed the Christians and the glad-eaters.'

Larry held Adam's hand and I took over her luggage trolley, leading them out to the car-park.

'Thanks a bundle for meeting us,' Brian said. 'Arriving *en famille* is such a drag. I trust you've not brought your Porsche?'

'No trouble,' I said, 'and I have hired an estate car. I expected you to be laden down with chattels.'

'You were a darling to watch out for the house for us,' Larry commented as I negotiated a roundabout and turned the car on to the motorway. 'Is everything all right at Harbury?'

'I doubt you'll notice any change,' I said. 'Harbury has hardly altered since electricity reached it. There are two new houses at the end of the lane, but they are not the distasteful sort of modern cube one sees. The telephone box has been relocated by the pub. The church has death-watch beetle –

you know the sort of thing. Mrs Maggs was really the one to run everything and I think she made a killing. Rumour has it she altered her fee for cleaning according to the gross national product of the tenant's home country. As the last one was a Japanese businessman and his family who had her virtually on beck and call twenty-four hours a day, she must have done well. She and her husband have, over the past three years, bought a new Ford Fiesta to replace their ageing Mini and have had a rather expensive conservatory built on to the rear of their cottage.'

As we chatted, I took glances at Adam in the driving mirror. He was engrossed, watching the countryside go by, observing cars as they passed us or gazing ahead through the windscreen. In a lull in the conversation, he suddenly spoke to me.

'Uncle Dom,' he asked, 'is the pond still there?'

'Yes,' I said. 'The pond is still there and it is a little bigger because the stream has been diverted.'

'And Napoleon?' he enquired.

Upon their departure for America, the cat had been passed to Mrs Maggs to look after. I had seen it on the odd occasion, wandering through the village, hunting sparrows in my garden or field-mice in the orchard behind it. 'Napoleon is fine,' I replied.

'He must be older,' Adam reasoned.

Looking in the mirror, I could tell he was pleased the cat had survived but I was also astonished he remembered it. So, evidently, were Larry and Brian.

'Do you remember Napoleon?' Larry asked.

'Oh, yes,' Adam said brightly. 'He was my friend. We used to roll on the floor together.'

I did not remain at Harbury for the night but, having dropped them off at their house and had a cup of coffee in Cobb End, immediately drove back to London. It was not until the weekend I returned, my excitement mounting as I drew nearer. The thought of Adam back in Britain filled me with anticipation, the years of his absence seeming of little consequence. It was true, I knew, I had missed much of his growing up and yet, I thought, this actually amounted to very little of considerable importance. The interesting time was to come, when I was able to not so much study his body as look into his young mind and see what hid there, what lurked in his thoughts and share them with him.

On the Saturday afternoon, I appeared as normal, knocking on the split door of the kitchen. Larry was baking, standing at the table with her hands covered in flour, a striped apron protecting her jeans and blouse. 'Hi!' she exclaimed, seeing me arrive. 'Just like old times.'

'Just,' I said and sprung the clip on the lower half of the door.

We kissed and I sat at the table as she continued with her cooking.

'The house is hardly changed,' she remarked. 'Now we've got all our goodies out of store, it's as if we never left. There's been no breakage of anything vital. Not even a stain on a table. You've been marvellous.'

'Don't thank me. I'm not responsible. Your estate agent chose good clients and Mrs Maggs kept them in line. Where's Brian?'

'He's out buying a new car,' Larry replied. 'We'll have to get used to little ones again. We had a huge Chevrolet in the States.' She busied herself for a minute or two, slipping one tin tray in the oven and removing another. 'Cookies,' she explained, placing hot biscuits on to a cooling rack. 'We've not become Americanized, I promise. But there are things over there . . . And Adam has a penchant for cookies.'

'How has he been?' I enquired, thankful she brought up the subject of her son. 'I suppose he's enjoyed himself. Disneyland and so on.'

'He's been super, Dom,' Larry answered, closing the oven door, adjusting the regulator and starting to sift flour through a sieve. 'He's a wonderful child. He never has a tantrum. And I mean never. He behaves so well with adults and yet also with his peers, making lots of friends in his nursery group. And yet, do you know, he didn't seem sorry to leave. It was as if he remembered everything about Harbury and just wanted to get back home. Since we've been here, he's been as busy as a bee fixing up his room, wandering the garden. He spends a lot of time outside. He's a real tomboy.'

She started on another pile of cookies, cutting the dough with a plastic ring. From overhead came the creak of floor-boards. 'He's upstairs in his room right now. I don't expect he knows you're here.'

I thought, I bet he does but made no comment.

'Why don't you go up and see him? He was talking all about you on the plane.'

'Really?' I said.

'Oh, yes. He was longing to get back to see his Uncle Dom. Your birthday presents have not gone amiss.'

'What's his health been like?' I asked.

'Excellent. He has had chicken-pox but it was a very mild bout indeed. Other than that, nothing apart from the occasional cold. He did have a terribly upset stomach after we returned from a week in Mexico but I think it was spicy tacos rather than food poisoning. Brian says we may have a problem with his teeth in due course. They are fine and healthy – he brushes them assiduously – but Brian thinks the molars are going to come through too soon and may have to be removed.'

I wanted to enquire about the children with whom Adam mixed. This was the one aspect of observation I was most sorry not to have had the opportunity to study. His interaction with his peers would have been fascinating, especially if he showed them how to charm fish and knowledge of this had got back to Larry by way of parental chatter at the school gate. By chance, my ponderings were answered.

'One curious thing, Dom,' Larry continued, 'is whilst the children Adam was with caught all sorts of other things, he stayed clear. There was a near epidemic of measles in the kindergarten but he was one of only three who didn't catch it. Three out of forty-one kiddies! Whooping cough hit about half the children but Adam didn't get so much as a tickle in his throat. He was the least affected of those who caught chicken-pox. Just a few spots here and there. Some of them were positively scrofulous.'

She laughed at the memory, set aside the cookies and began to work on some currant cakes. I smiled politely but my mind was well ahead of hers. If he was so immune, then his blood must be well worth a study, not to mention his DNA. When the technology caught up, Ruth, I considered, would have a field day with 5ml of it.

'There was one occasion we were quite worried,' Larry said, interrupting my thoughts.

I felt a sudden twinge of alarm. 'What was that?'

'Last winter, there was a terrible flu outbreak. China A variant H or something. You know how they give annual mutations names. Anyway, it hit poor Adam really hard. We were afraid he would get pneumonia. He was hospitalized and they kept him in for a week. But he pulled through.'

'What tests did they do on him?' I wanted to know what others might have discovered, what might have appeared in his medical records.

'Nothing really. Blood tests and so on. But he was otherwise fit as a fiddle.'

'There was nothing unusual?'

'Nothing at all.' She laughed lightly and went on, 'You do worry about him, Dom. Anyone would think you were his father.'

I smiled at the irony. 'I just take an interest . . .' I began but she interrupted.

'If you have this much involvement with all your little creations, you must be a very busy man. I'm sure I'm not your only patient to have miscarried through some accident.'

The creaking of the floor overhead ceased and I could hear Adam's footsteps moving through the old house.

'Here he comes,' Larry announced. 'Why don't you go outside with him? He'd love it.'

Adam entered the kitchen. He was wearing a miniature

pair of jeans and a red sweatshirt with *Boston Red Sox* printed on it in white.

'Hello, Uncle Dom,' he said. 'I got this sweatshirt in America.'

'And what is a Boston Red Sox?' I asked.

'It's a baseball team. They play baseball in America.'

'Do you like baseball?'

Before he could reply, Larry suggested, 'Why don't you take Uncle Dom to see the pond?'

'Yes,' the child agreed and, taking my hand, led me out of my seat and towards the door.

'Are you glad to be home?' I asked as we crossed the lawn.

'Yes. I wanted to come back.'

'Didn't you like America?'

'It was all right. But . . . but I wanted to be back here.'

'Do you remember it all?'

He thought for a minute before replying, 'Yes. Almost all. I remember you.'

We reached the pond. Whereas it had once been a stillwater pool, there was now a small tributary from the stream leading into it and the surface must have increased twofold. At the downstream end, a sluice had been constructed, the water rilling over it as if across a model weir.

'The fishes are still here,' Adam announced. 'I saw them yesterday. And some frogs and . . .'

'Newts?' I prompted him.

'Are those the lizard things?'

'Yes, those are the ones. They live in water but can come on land. They are amphibians.'

'I saw lizards in Arizona,' Adam declared. 'In America, lizards which live in water are called salamanders.' He spoke with a certain pride in his knowledge, paused then added, 'Newts is a better word.'

We stood by the edge of the pond, at the very spot where he had called the fish in.

'Can you still talk to the fish?' I asked.

185

Adam turned his head and looked me straight in the eye.
It was disconcerting, as if he was, from somewhere deep in his
soul, accusing me of something. 'I don't talk to them,' he said
quietly. 'I . . . I know them. And,' he glanced in the direction
of the house, 'you won't tell Mummy or Daddy?'

It was a question yet it sounded also like a command.

'No,' I promised, 'I won't tell Mummy or Daddy. It'll be
our secret.'

'Are you sure?'

'Quite sure.'

'Do you want me to know them now?' he asked.

'No,' I said. 'Another time.'

'I knowed them yesterday,' he declared. 'They aren't very
happy.'

For a moment, I was at a loss as to how to reply: such a
bald statement from any other child would have prompted a
patronizing response but this was Adam. 'Maybe,' I proposed,
'they don't like the stream coming in.'

He was thoughtful for a moment then said, 'Yes. Maybe.
It's because the water . . .' He searched for a word. 'Tastes
funny.'

'What do you mean?'

'The frogs don't like it,' he answered. 'And the fish
don't, too.'

He turned and looked in the direction of the gravel drive.

'Napoleon's come back,' he stated.

No sooner had he spoken than the cat appeared. It
stopped, looked around the garden then came in a direct line
towards Adam to curl around his legs as he stroked it.

'He's an old cat now,' Adam said. 'His bones ache.'

'How can you tell?'

'I know him, too.'

I was quite shaken by this conversation. Adam was a child
but with the attitudes of an adult and the perceptions, I had to
admit to myself, of one possessing supernatural powers: yet he
was not precocious and objectionable as some bright children
could be.

After tea, Brian and I sat in the kitchen while Larry prepared the supper. As we chatted about America, about their plans for the future, Brian's hopes for his practice and the dental technology he had picked up at the cutting edge of his discipline, as he put it, Adam came in and stood by my side. He did not interrupt or tug on my sleeve as children are wont to do. He just bided his time until there was a lull in the conversation.

'Uncle Dom,' he said, 'would you like to see my room?'

'I'd love to,' I replied and, leaving the kitchen, followed him up the stairs.

As we passed the old photo, Adam remarked, 'That's our house a long time ago. The little boy is what I am now.'

'What do you mean?'

'Well, he lived here and now I live here.'

His bedroom was typical for a child of his age: the wall was painted white and hung with pictures of the sort of things to interest small boys – aircraft, cars, a NASA poster of the space shuttle. A pine chest in the corner lay open containing an assortment of toys whilst on a shelf by the bed were ranked books of stories and thin volumes about dinosaurs, the Ancient Egyptians, insects and baseball. I noticed the books I had sent him were kept separate, in their own little section between two bookends of heavy, gruff-faced bison carved out of stone.

'It's a very nice room,' I complimented him.

'Would you like to see my drawings?' he asked.

I said I would and he pulled an art folder out from beneath his bed, untying the ribbons which held it shut.

'These are my best ones,' he declared.

One by one, he handed me drawings and paintings on cartridge paper: some were in pencil, some in felt-tip with about half a dozen of them crudely tinted by water-colours. I was not quite sure what to expect but what I saw was certainly a surprise.

Whereas most children draw stick men, stick houses, stick animals, stick trees, these were different. They lacked any sense of perspective and the figures were predominantly stick-like but much thicker. I could see where Adam had drawn a single line and then, moving his hand, drawn parallel ones to give more body.

'Do you like them?' he enquired.

'They are very good,' I praised him.

'Would you like one?'

'I'd love one,' I said.

'You can have six,' he told me. 'You can choose.'

I turned them over in the folder, one by one. They were remarkable for quite a few were compositions of stick animals, men and trees. One or two contained what were obviously houses which looked as if they were half-timbered, built like any of the old cottages in the village. The pictures had a robust quality to them, a primitivity more than just a child's early attempts at art. I could not put my finger on it but, to me, the figures had movement, substance.

'Where did you draw this?' I asked, holding up a house.

'In America. I did them all in America. I haven't started here yet.'

I chose a house with a man, a single stick man and four compositions. Adam approved of my choices. 'You've got the best ones,' he declared.

'I shall have them framed and hang three in my cottage and three in my office in London,' I said.

When I returned to my practice on the Sunday evening, I scanned the drawings with a computer hand scanner and added them to the Mouette database hidden file. The next morning, Molly sent the originals to a framer in Holland Park.

◆

I have been steadily running out of supplies.

In accordance with Dr Suarez's instructions, once I had the confidence of the people of the clearing, I set in motion a programme of immunization against tuberculosis, diphtheria and measles. However, there has been an unforeseen complication:

as soon as I commenced my work, one of the men, whilst out hunting, informed the people of the settlement above the falls of what I was doing and, in a steady trickle, I have been visited by them. The result is I am now out of the TB vaccine and almost out of hypodermic needles and syringes. Other basics are also running very low: disposable scalpels, scalpel blades, iodine and antiseptic cream, Band Aids and throat swabs. I have bandaged numerous abrasions, set three broken bones, lanced more boils and ulcers than I can remember, treated umpteen skin complaints and seven cases of *pian*, sutured four nasty *piraña* bites, burned out jiggers with a red hot needle and cut out subcutaneously established bot-fly larvæ.

Only one of the forest folk has been beyond my ministrations. A small, comatose child arrived one day from deep in the forest, brought to me on a litter carried between two men, its mother walking behind in mute sorrow. The poor mite's flesh was firm and dark mauve as if a huge bruise had covered its entire body: the lips were swollen and the eyes puffed and closed.

'What has done this?' I enquired.

The man at the head of the litter, who was the child's father, replied enigmatically, '*Abejas, señor.*'

I nodded. Dr Suarez had warned me of the vicious African honey-bees brought over by slaves and slavers and now indigenous throughout the whole of South America. Once aroused, a swarm would attack relentlessly, even braving dense smoke to get at the object of the antagonism.

There was nothing I could do. I gave the child an injection of morphine to ease the pain but saw no sign the drug had any effect. It died in the night, throwing a tiny spasm and waving its hands briefly in the air as if, in those last moments, trying to fight off the remnants of the swarm.

When I anticipated the problem of prematurely dwindling supplies, I sent word to Santo Antonio do Içá: Chuhi took my note to the settlement above the falls whence, I assume, it was sent on by a chain of runners, hunters, canoe paddlers, jungle walkers and traders. As was arranged between Dr Suarez and myself, the note bore no address and was written in English but signed in code: I was Father Dominic.

Dr Suarez is a good man, one of those saintly men for whom the suffering of others is a torment shared, be it as a result of disease or their own stupidities and weaknesses. He runs a clinic, curing those whose lives the *gringos* have destroyed with whisky, mercuric oxide from the gold mine or the pox. Where I am concerned, he has taken pity upon me, not because I am sick of body but of spirit. He knows what I have done for he is my father confessor to whom I have admitted everything; and he sympathizes without moralizing, without criticizing me. Dr Suarez is a man for whom my sinning is not a frailty but an obstacle over which I have tripped.

How long my message would take to reach the doctor's hands was anybody's guess. It might have taken a fortnight, it may have taken three months.

Matters got so bad I tried sterilizing my disposable scalpel blades and, although I was satisfied they were sterilized in a boiling pot of water over a fire, they were also blunted by being heated. The disposable syringes, being made of surgical plastic, would not sterilize but simply warped in the heat. The needles lost their plastic bases. At last, in near desperation, I sat down one morning to try and sharpen a scalpel blade on a smooth stone picked up from the edge of the river and boiled clean. No sooner had I begun the task than Urú came running towards me.

'*¡Señor! ¡Vienen dos hombres! ¡Vienen para verte!*'

'*¿Gringos?*' I asked.

She thought for a moment. '*No, señor.*'

Inevitably, twenty minutes later, a wide-hulled canoe powered by a large Evinrude outboard motor turned into the shore and was run up on the bank by two men. One was dressed only in the loincloth of a native but the other sported a pair of jeans cut off at the knees and a grimy T-shirt on which was printed a laughing cartoon grizzly wearing a Mounties' hat around which was printed the legend *Support my Right to Arm Bears*. Both men were barefoot but the jeans owner carried a pair of worn tennis shoes round his neck, suspended by their laces. As soon as he stepped on to the river bank, he put these on with evident pride and ceremony.

'*¿Padre Domenico?*' the shoe owner enquired, getting to his feet as I approached.

'Yes,' I replied in English, 'I am Father Dominic.'

'And I am Miguél, *señor*. He,' he pointed to his companion, 'is Fernandez. We are from Dr Suarez.' He shook my hand. 'We have brought the boxes.'

'Good,' I exclaimed. 'Thank you very much, Miguél.'

Chuhi joined us, Keewei and a few others hovered in the background, the women watching almost nervously from the shade of the long-houses. I sensed perhaps these two visitors were from a tribe considered unfriendly to the people of the clearing.

'Chuhi,' I requested in the way I thought a priest might address his convert, '*me gustaría que descargaras las cajas.*'

'*Sí, señor,*' Chuhi responded.

The two newcomers exchanged glances.

'*Padre,*' I said, as if reminding Chuhi.

He thought about it for a moment, winked surreptitiously at me and replied, '*Sí, padre.*'

The wooden boxes were taken by six or seven men up to my hut and piled on the porch. Several of them were heavy and required two carriers. All the lids were nailed down and banded with nylon tape joined by metal seals.

'Father,' said Fernandez, reaching into a canvas satchel in the canoe and removing an envelope wrapped in polythene, 'Dr Suarez has sent a letter for you.'

'Thank you,' I said and took it from him. I wondered if I ought to add, *my son*, but it seemed to stretch both my disguise and hypocrisy beyond necessity.

After their craft was unloaded, the two boatmen sat on their haunches by the river bank. They removed some sort of pemmican from the satchel and chewed it, cutting hunks off with a sheath knife which they flashed ostentatiously in the air so Chuhi and the others could see they were armed.

Only when their meal was over, and they had drunk a bottle of beer between them, did they get into their canoe and push off from the bank. Within a minute, they were lost to sight.

'*Hombres malo*,' Chuhi remarked as he walked past my hut on his way to the forest glade used as a latrine.

'*¿Porqué?*' I replied.

'*Javee*,' he said and farted loudly to give emphasis to his hatred of the Javees.

I took all the boxes inside my hut, stacked them neatly against the wall and then, returning to the porch, slit open the polythene and the envelope within it with the scalpel blade I had been attempting to hone. Dr Suarez's letter was brief and to the point.

Dear Doctor Father Domenico,

Here are the supplies for which you requested. You are doing sterling work for our clinic and ministry in your area. I have added more of the vaccine you asked for. There seems to be a greater call for it than we anticipated. Also, you will find more equipment and some dentistry tools. Just in case.

Also, there is a Polaroid Land Camera with a dozen films. If you should see some interesting medical conditions, perhaps you would photograph them and return same with your notes. It would help.

Your work is not going unnoticed by me. I have word from the bearer of your message you are a good man and kind. The Huambas people like you and maybe they love you. This is the way for it to be.

Finally, my Doctor friend. There are three men here in Santo Antonio do Içá who ask after you. No one talks, of course. But they are very persistent and they have gifts for those who may have a loose tongue when they are in whiskey. One of these men is a Brazilian official, maybe a police. Who can tell? The other two are, like yourself, Englishmen.

I think you should know this.

We pray you will be well and that the Good God watches over you.
Your friend and comrade,

Felipe Suarez MD

It is only a matter of time now. They will come and they will find me. Such is the world today there are no corners left in which to hide and no letting up when a society takes it upon itself to hound out the good or the bad, the beautiful or the ugly, the innocent and the guilty. In the long run, everyone must pay his due, accept his punishment, and be damned.

◆

Over two months, I encouraged Adam to draw more pictures for me. I sensed, in some way beyond my comprehension, they were special. One, in particular, took my fancy to such an extent I had it framed and hung directly in front of my desk. It showed a rickety frame building, several stick men and a stick dog. Several patients commented upon it and asked who had drawn it. Depending upon the enquirer, I lied accordingly, pandering to their nationalities or backgrounds. For a Portuguese patient, it was an unsigned Picasso sketch, a study for a later painting: she cooed appreciatively and I could tell she envied me it. To an American patient, I claimed it was a Warhol doodle and showed her a few of the others, suggesting I had the complete set: she offered to buy them from me for a ludicrously large sum but I politely declined. Signor Riccione, an Italian banker with a wife twenty-two years his junior, was told it was a sketch by Alberto Giacometti, in preparation for one of his emaciated sculptures.

Molly, who knew the pictures were by a child but not which one, devised a little game with me, trying to decide by which artist to represent the drawings to which patient. We ran through a whole gamut of twentieth-century names –

Dufy, Braque, Metzinger, Kandinsky, Feininger, Bacon, Dali
– trying to fit each to an appropriate patient much as one does
in the dog game, matching dogs running in the park with their
owners strolling on the paths or sitting reading the paper whilst
their pets cavort, carouse and crap on the grass.

All went well, and provided us with some fine and
harmless entertainment, until the morning Colonel Pratt-
Whittcombe arrived with his wife. He was a surprisingly
short man and I wondered facetiously if, perhaps, he had
been a sapper. Every movement he made was calculated, as
if he was living his life by numbers. His wife was dumpy to the
point of being rotund, the image not being enhanced by the fact
she wore a voluminous dress like a tent and a fluffy pullover.
What underclothing she wore was a subject for speculation: she
took longer to undress than any patient I can recall.

It was while waiting for her to disrobe that her husband,
wanting to make small talk, commented upon the pictures.

It was raining hard. I should have taken the warning and
let the game go that day.

'I say,' he began, his head snapping up, his eye fastening
on the picture, 'where d'you find that? Fine execution. Damn
fine copy. Wouldn't mind one myself. Very expensive, was it?
Hope you don't mind my asking.'

I wanted to laugh. The man was a parody of himself, a
military figure on day release from a Gilbert and Sullivan opera.
Then his words registered. 'A copy?' I replied.

'Can't be an original, can it, sir? Not on paper, anyway.'
He snorted briefly at his own humour. 'On bark, perhaps. Who
knows, eh?'

'In fact,' I said, abandoning the artist game, 'it was drawn
by one of my children.'

'Fancy that! Your son or daughter?'

It was my turn to smile.

'I am not married. When I refer to my children, I mean
one I have caused . . . '

'Ah! Yes, test-tube baby man as well, aren't you? Must
bring lots of joy to miserable couples, I don't doubt. Not,' he

194

leaned forward stiffly as if confiding a secret, 'what we're here for, Daphne and myself. Bit past it. She's got trouble with her down-belows, poor lass.'

'Yes, I know,' I said, looking down at the referral papers on my desk. I was becoming mildly annoyed by his mannered speech and military bearing.

'Remarkable copy, though,' he commented again.

'A copy of what?'

'Don't suppose you have much time for museums and such. We do, you know. Being retired. Like to wander the galleries, see what we see. As for your picture here – well, I suggest you visit the British Museum. There's an exhibition on . . . '

At that moment, Angela knocked and entered. Daphne Pratt-Whittcombe, it seemed, was finally reduced to flesh and a fresh cotton surgical smock.

All through my examination of her, I could not drive the thought of her husband's words from my mind. Even my sorrow at the suspicion the poor woman had cancer of the ovaries could not entirely eradicate his voice.

At three-thirty, my last patient seen out by Molly and the tissue samples taken from the colonel's wife despatched to a pathology laboratory in Hendon, I printed out a copy of the picture from the computer, put on my coat and walked towards the British Museum through streets damp with drizzle. The colonnaded façade loomed up at me as I made my way through the wrought-iron pedestrian entrance and across the forecourt.

As the colonel had not told me the location of the original of Adam's picture, and I had not thought to ask it, I went to the information desk. The young woman in a museum uniform took one look at my hard copy printout and pointed to a tall doorway to her left. 'You can't miss it, sir,' she advised me. 'Just follow the signs to the Camunian Exhibition.'

As instructed, I strolled through halls of Roman pillars, Greek statuary, Egyptian artefacts and mummy cases, Phoenician pots and models of early sailing craft. Each step took me back a decade in human civilization. At the end of

the Hittite collection, a signboard over a side door announced
The Camunians – Art in Artefact.

I was filled with a sense of both excitement and apprehension. In my pocket, my hand crumpled the copy.

The exhibition room was in semi-darkness, display cabinets lining the walls and containing their own integral lighting. On a central easel was a series of contour maps of northern Italy, the kind used by the military with every detail indicated. Markers on the map related to display cabinets. All around it were photographs of Bronze Age depictions of weapons, tools and domestic equipment with an explanatory statement: the exhibition consisted of reproduction Bronze Age implements based upon illustrations and designs found in rock carvings.

I started at the first cabinet. Within were a number of reproduction daggers, some fashioned from flint, others from bronze. Behind them was a marked fragment of the main map and a simplistic drawing of the daggers. A card stated:

The dagger (a) is cast from bronze. The handle consists of leather thongs bound tightly around a bronze shaft, covered by twine strengthened with beeswax. The design is similar to style IIIA, reminiscent of the Remedellian subtriangular bladed daggers.
Site: Cemmo.

I did not bother with the other cabinets and moved swiftly along, going by more daggers, spears, arrows, lances, hammers, axes and halberds. Finally, I reached a life-size display. Cordoned off behind a rope was a mock-up of a Bronze Age house. In it, mannequins dressed in leather and animal skin clothing illustrated everyday chores. A woman was seated by a fire sewing a garment, a man stood as if arrived from the hunt, two stuffed rabbits hanging from his belt, a dagger in his hand. A tousle-headed child stroked a stuffed dog whilst a stuffed goat chewed on some hay hanging in a net.

The building was two-storeyed, the upper level containing a pile of pelts as a mattress. Here and there stood earthenware pots and, by the fire, a mould for an axe head. On the wall by the tableau was another explanatory sign. Printed above it was a picture of the house upon which the display was based. I stared at it: almost as a reflex, I removed Adam's picture from my pocket, smoothing out the creases. Both were identical.

There was no seat in the gallery. I leaned against the wall, my heart pounding as if I had run there from the practice. For a moment, I wondered if I might suffer a stroke: had I a history of cardiomyopathy, now would have been the time I suffered heart failure. I must have looked ill for a museum guard, walking round to check on displays, came up to me.

'You OK, sir?' he asked in a cockney accent.

'I'm fine,' I replied, gaining my breath and composure. 'Fine. It was just a turn. I'm on medication.'

'Can I fetch you a doctor, sir?'

I smiled and said, 'That's quite all right. I am a doctor.'

At the museum bookshop, I bought the publication accompanying the exhibition but did not open the covers until I was back in my apartment, a whisky and soda on the table by my armchair.

There was little need for me to read the scholarly text. Reproduced throughout the lavishly illustrated pages were hundreds of Bronze Age drawings. Some of these were simplistic images of human figures and common domestic animals, a number of them very similar to Adam's drawings. From these the art progressed slightly to more complex drawings of figures working looms, building houses, driving carts and hammering anvils. Others evinced strange men with extra limbs projecting from their torsos, diffused antlers sprouting from their heads or with square, handled objects in their fists which the catalogue listed as magic paddles. The most idiosyncratic of the pictures were listed as anthropomorphic labyrinths. In each of these, a stick man's arms and legs extended out from his body to weave in circles and spirals around him, the finished picture giving the appearance of a childishly drawn maze with the figure in the centre. Putting the book down, I telephoned Harbury. Larry answered the telephone.

'Hello, Larry?' I said. 'It's Dom. I need to ask you a few questions about Adam.'

My immediacy alarmed her.

'Is there something wrong?'

'No, no,' I reassured her hurriedly. 'Just a precaution. When you were on your travels, did you go anywhere else in Italy but to Rome?'

'We went to Florence.'

'Did you take Adam into any of the art galleries?'

'Yes, of course. The Uffizi and . . . What are you getting at, Dom?'

I had to think fast: my excuse was not premeditated, in such a hurry was I to ascertain if Adam had seen such pictures. 'Flu,' I said, grasping on the obvious pretext. 'There's a nasty strain arrived in Italy. I thought, in the light of Adam's bout in the States . . .'

'I see,' Larry interrupted. 'Do you think he needs immunization?'

'No,' I continued, 'I don't think so. You probably left before the outbreak began. It was just a thought I had. Better to keep an eye on him over the next few weeks.'

'I will,' Larry said.

'How did he like the art galleries?'

'Very much. He is fascinated by drawing. As you well know. You can't tear his crayons away from him.'

'Did you visit any prehistoric art exhibitions?' I enquired, my voice as nonchalant as possible.

'No. Only the big ones. We did go to a lot of Roman exhibitions in Rome.' She laughed. 'Where else? When in Rome! But the Romans aren't prehistoric.'

We chatted on a for a few minutes before I proposed I might take Adam out for the afternoon when I was next down in Harbury.

'A visit to a zoo or something,' I suggested.

'You are a poppet, Dom!' Larry exclaimed. 'I'm sure Adam would love it.'

'Godfather's duty, more or less,' I said. 'Museums and

such. I first went to the Science Museum with my godfather and London Zoo with my godmother.'

We compared our diaries and it was agreed I should take Adam out in a fortnight.

◆

The traffic was blocked at Marble Arch where a bus had collided with an articulated lorry and a motor cyclist: consequently, I arrived a few minutes late. Ruth was standing by the W.H. Smith bookshop in Paddington Station, looking around the crowd of mid-morning shoppers. Her train from Oxford had been crammed with day trippers. I apologized for my lack of punctuality and guided her towards the Porsche parked by the taxi rank.

'I was somewhat surprised to hear from you, Dom,' she said as I drove out of the station and turned left along Praed Street. The sun was bright overhead, the sky clear blue but the air chill. 'It's been three years. How have you been keeping?'

'Fine,' I replied. 'And you?'

'Life goes on.' She looked out of the window and added, 'I would've liked to have seen you.'

I made no answer but concentrated on my driving. Fortunately, the traffic was heavy on the Edgware Road and in St John's Wood Road, giving me the opportunity for silence.

'Where are we going?' Ruth asked at length.

'A little restaurant I know,' I said noncommittally.

'This had better be important? I'm supposed to be at an inter-departmental conference . . . '

'Yes, it is.'

'You sounded very tight-lipped on the telephone.'

After fifteen minutes, I reversed the car into a space in the maze of narrow streets near Primrose Hill and, locking it and setting the alarm, steered Ruth towards The Vine Leaf, a small Greek restaurant in Chalcot Square. It was not until we were seated at a corner table with our drinks ordered I chose to talk about my summoning her to London.

'I was tight-lipped,' I admitted, 'and I'm sorry. I've had a lot on my plate recently.'

'And, as you British put it, I'm on the skive. I've had to make a pretty far-fetched excuse to be here today.'

'What was it?'

'I told the chairman of the conference my half-brother was passing through Heathrow and wanted to see me. We hadn't met in years: it was my only chance: he normally lived in Saigon. That sort of thing. If they check my records – and you can be damn sure, Dom, they will – they'll see I have a half-brother. My mother married twice.'

The waiter brought us our drinks and took our order.

'Now what's it all about?'

'I need to ask you something and I want you to reply without asking the reasons for my questioning.'

'That's asking a bit much,' Ruth said sharply. 'You call me out of the shires and up to the city, whisk me through traffic without a damn word of explanation, sit me down here and expect me comply. Hell, no! If you want information, I want reasons.'

'At this time,' I replied, consciously using an American-ism, 'I cannot. In a few weeks, I will be at liberty to tell you more. But not now.'

'You sound like Institute security,' she rebuked me.

'I'm sorry for that, too,' I said and sipped my dry martini.

She picked up her own glass, a Pimms, and put it to her lips but did not drink.

'What're you up to, Dom?'

'I can't say unless you agree to my terms.'

'So!' She put her Pimms down with a jolt on the table. A mint leaf fell off the rim of her glass but she did not pick it up. 'I'm presented with a *fait accompli*. I either do as you ask or I've skipped work and travelled all the way to London in the company of shop-till-you-drop tea louts. And for nothing.'

'You are having lunch,' I teased her, putting my glass down gently next to hers.

'A lunch, sure!' she exclaimed angrily then her animosity caved in. 'OK. You win, Dom. Teasing as usual. I won't ask questions. But this had better be damn good.'

From my pocket, I removed an envelope containing copies of Adam's pictures. She opened it with her knife and started to sift through them.

'Where did you get these, Dom?'

'They're copies.'

'That much I see! They can hardly be the originals.'

I was briefly reminded of Colonel Pratt-Whittcombe and his voluminous spouse.

'What can you tell me about them?'

'They're copies of Bronze Age drawings. Of men, a horned animal,' she turned them over as she spoke, 'a house . . . ' Then she stopped, Adam's drawing of the house in her hand.

'Do you know anything about them, Ruth?'

She did not reply. Instead, she studied several of the pictures, shifting them from one hand to the other, a pensive look on her face.

'Where was the axeman found?' I asked.

She did not immediately answer but had another shuffle through the pictures. 'Have you been digging about, Dom?'

'No,' I said. 'I'm not an archaeologist. You're the one to go digging.'

'You know what I mean, Dom,' she snapped.

'Yes,' I answered, 'I'm sorry. I didn't mean to be clever.' I picked up my glass again and added, 'So what do you know about these?'

'These pictures come from the Camonica Valley,' she commenced. 'It's famous for its Bronze Age art. The valley's eighty kilometres long, north of Brescia and north-east of Bergamo. At the southern end is Lake Iseo, at an altitude of about 250 metres. It rises to around 1750 in the Tonale Pass. Down the valley runs the River Oglio. The Romans occupied the valley, building a road along one side of it. Today's settlements straddle that road. Before the Romans, there was Iron Age settlement and before that . . . '

'Bronze Age,' I interjected.

She nodded and went on, 'Bronze Age. Not a lot of settlement sites are extant but pottery, querns, pestles, stone walls are known. A number of Bronze Age tools and so forth have also been discovered and are held in a little museum in the town of Breno. An Iron Age necropolis was excavated in, I think, the late forties and there are a number of *castellieri* in the valley. That's the local name for fortified hamlets dating to the third century BC. Other than this evidence . . . '

I looked at her. She was gazing at the pictures as if mesmerized by them. 'Have you copied these from a book, Dom?'

'No,' I said, 'and you've promised not to ask questions.'

'The valley's famous for its Bronze Age art. Rock carvings. There are thousands in the valley and they afford one of the most complete pictorial guides to Bronze Age life known to us. The pictures cover not just animals and people but houses, buildings, weapons and tools, geometric mazes common in Bronze Age art, symbols as yet uncoded, even depictions of smithing, weaving and perverted sexual practices. There is one example I can recall of a man fucking a goat.'

'And where,' I asked, reverting to an earlier question, 'was your axeman found?'

Ruth avoided my question.

'Have you been to Breno?'

I shook my head and admitted, 'No, but I have been to the British Museum, to verify these. And you are equivocating. Where was the axeman found?'

'In the mountains near Tirano. About thirty-five kilometres from the Camonica Valley. It's odds on he came from that community.'

It was my turn to fall silent. The implication was staggering: Adam was not just gifted with the ability to 'know' animals, as he put it, but he had buried in him memories thousands of years old.

How this was possible was beyond me. I had read of studies in which people claimed to have had knowledge of a former life, were familiar with places they had never visited, intimate with people whom they had never met but I put all the reports down to spuriocity, a branch of the chicanery of mediums, paranormal investigators and confidence tricksters. My disbelief was almost as great as my hatred for these cruel cozeners who preyed upon the misery of those bereaved or desperate for some kind of inner peace. Now, however, I was being presented with a possible proof that memory could be passed down from one generation to the next. It seemed too fantastical to consider but I could see no alternative.

'Who drew these pictures, Dom?'

'Nobody drew them,' I lied and developed what I hoped was a convincing provenance for them. 'Not exactly. They are copies. I obtained them from the husband of a patient of mine whose father had fought in the war and been captured by the Italians. He was incarcerated in a prisoner-of-war camp near Milan but had escaped. In the course of heading for neutral Switzerland, he stumbled upon rocks covered in carvings and, being forced to hide for several days due to atrocious weather and German patrols, passed his time away copying some of the ideograms. I mentioned I knew of someone – that's you – working on Bronze Age remains and he offered me copies to show to you.'

'So why all the secrecy, Dom? Why the all-fired goddamn rush to get me out of a pretty vital conference and up to London? You could have written me.'

'Yes, I could have. I'm sorry I didn't,' I said. 'Seeing the pictures in the museum reminded me how long it's been since we last met. It seemed a good chance to get in touch again.'

It was all bunkum but it served its purpose.

'And that's it?'

'And I wanted to give you no chance to procrastinate,' I continued. 'I wanted to know where the axeman came from.

You hadn't told me and you dodged the question when I've asked it. So . . .'

She looked at me for a moment then sipped her drink. 'You've something else up your sleeve,' she determined. 'I don't know what it is, but . . .'

I handed her another, smaller envelope. 'Royal Shakespeare Company.' I pointed to the contents of the envelope. '*King Lear*. Tonight. A box.'

She laughed and said, 'All this subterfuge just to get me to go to the theatre. And you know I love Shakespeare. That's very sweet of you, Dom.'

Then she leaned over the table and kissed me.

◆

The old crone has died. She was suffering, as near as I could guess, from some kind of brain disorder, perhaps a tumour. Her shaking hands grew considerably worse over the space of a few days and the other women avoided her as if wishing not to be tainted by her imminent death. It was not long in coming. Like animals, these people seem to be fit for a long while but then very quickly degenerate and die. They age, of course, but they do not gradually deteriorate, grow moribund and linger. For them, death is a quick passage.

Once she was ostracized, the old woman must have known the end was near. Perhaps her rejection speeded it, her mind surrendering to the inevitable. A few hours before her death, she visited my hut and sat awkwardly on the edge of the porch. She did not speak, even when I went outside and asked her what she wanted of me.

'*Nada*,' was the only word she uttered.

'*¿Te duele?*' I enquired, for had I known where she was pained I might have alleviated it.

She did not answer.

'*¿Quieres beber algo?*' I asked, holding out a mug of sugared water of which the people of the clearing are fond.

Again, she ignored me but, turning her head, gazed up at my face with a puzzled look. Her left hand began to shake uncontrollably. I knelt by her side and took hold of it. The flesh was wracked with twitching, every muscle flexing and relaxing, bunching and stretching involuntarily. I tried a gentle massage but it had no effect. All the while she looked into my face with consternation and I wondered if she was afraid of death.

'*Espera aquí,*' I ordered her and went into the hut.

For some reason, for it had not been on my list of requirements, Dr Suarez had sent me a bottle of Valium. I removed two of the tablets, returning to the porch with the mug. The old woman was gone. She was not hobbling across the clearing so I assumed she must have gone into the forest near the hut. As she could not have gone far, I looked for her through the trees but could not see her.

The first I knew of her death was when I spied Chuhi, Q'eke and several other men frantically hacking at a tree trunk, hollowing it out with axes and adzes. They worked feverishly, not talking as they usually did when doing chores, their tools rising and falling rhythmically. When he caught sight of me, Chuhi put down his axe and came towards me. '*La abuela esta muerta,*' he said, his voice more distant than grieving.

'*Lo siento,*' I replied by way of condolence.

'*Ahora, es una casa de diablos,*' he declared matter-of-factly. '*Debemos actuar rápidamente.*'

He returned to the log and set to work, fitting in with the others. I felt suddenly very sad the old woman, for so long a member of the community of the clearing, had died alone and was now classified as a houseful of devils which had to be dealt with as speedily as possible.

I wondered what I should do as a part of the community. So far as I knew, there was no priest within a week's travel and I considered offering my own services in lieu but I need not have concerned myself. The old woman was not to undergo a semi-Christian burial in a bark or cotton shroud and placed in a grave with a wooden cross. Her send-off was to be traditional.

As soon as the rough coffin was hewn, the men entered the jungle and, about a hundred metres off, hacked out a circular clearing about ten metres in diameter. In the centre was erected a makeshift bivouac of branches beneath which a simple trestle was made. The coffin was placed upon this and, in mid-afternoon, the old woman's body was carried to her simple burial chamber and lain on its back. Several strings of glass beads decorated her neck and shrivelled breasts, her hair adorned with garish feathers. A fire was lit under the coffin, but not to cremate her: certain green branches and leaves were put on it by Keewei, producing dense billows of acrid smoke. They might have been intended to keep off the flies but I was sure they were for cleansing the devils.

The funeral rites were observed by the whole village. No one cried, wailed or seemed to lament at all. They merely stood in a sombre, almost dazed fashion. At nightfall, the fire was stoked up and a bowl of *yamanachi* was passed around with handfuls of what I assumed to be flakes of dried fungi which the men masticated solemnly, passing into a light state of euphoria. At last, as the moon rose, Keewei chanted for a few minutes then everyone returned to the clearing, taking up their normal evening routines as if nothing had happened.

'*¿Cuánto tiempo la dejas en la selva?*' I asked Chuhi. I was a little concerned. If the body was to remain in the proximity of the clearing for more than a few days it would pose a serious health hazard not only to the people of the clearing but also to myself.

'*Hasta que no haya carne.*'

It had such an ominous ring: until the flesh is no more. It sounded so final and depressed me. At such moments, the people of the clearing did not grieve and look to the future but I did. One of my many civilized failings is the cursed ability to fear what might happen. What will happen. What had happened, keeping me away from the boulders and risking the uneven bridge across the creek.

'*¿Y pues?*'

Chuhi smiled broadly and replied, 'She weel go up the mung-tayne.'

'Will you go to see her?' I enquired, pointing in the direction of the mountain.

Chuhi thought for a moment before answering. '¿Porqué, señor? She go,' he said starkly, his right hand waving dismissively.

So it was with these simple folk. Life is for living and death is the end of it. The breath ceases, the door shuts and that is it. The dead are given no more thought. So it was with the little child stung by bees. No one referred to her again. She was here and now she is not. She has become a myth, an ancestor, a humming-bird in the flowering bushes of the jungle. So it was with my own terrible sadness to which I am sure they give no thought but which haunts me daily.

This is my failing. I have a past and my civilized sophistication cannot rid me of it. It rides on my back like an incubus, digging its talons into my pectorals and sucking at my soul. Sometimes, I wonder what it might look like if it were to take shape: the most bizarre cathedral gargoyle would be handsome by comparison.

I felt cold that evening, sitting on the porch watching the insects cavort around the oil lamp. Amongst their number was a huge moth, its wingspan at least fifteen centimetres. Its body was furred as if coated in a fine fungus, its antennae like short, twitching feathers, each of its legs hairy and grotesque. The general colouring of the insect was a mottled brown but in the centre of its hind wings was a round spot the size of a man's thumbprint. It bore no colouring but was transparent, like a little window.

I could not help wondering if the old woman's spirit was in the moth. It made no attempt to advance on the lamp and be singed, as many of the smaller moths and flying bugs had been, but seemed quite content to rest on one of the roof supports, occasionally shimmering its wings as if it too was cold.

An hour or two after moonrise, I felt suddenly chilled. The night was warm but a shiver of something I could not name froze me. My skin rose in goose-pimples and the hair on the back of my neck prickled as if I had a rash. I even turned round, half expecting to be confronted by the old woman's devils or, at least, the moth in flight heading for my face. Yet there was nothing, just the hut window with its shutters opened.

The insect orchestra which fills every night went silent. For fully ninety seconds, nothing stirred, sawed, sang, zizzed or scratched in my vicinity.

There was a reason for this sudden silence: a jaguar might have been prowling in the undergrowth or a night bird of prey settled in a branch. Maybe, as happens to humans at cocktail parties, all the insects suddenly ran out of conversation simultaneously. I could not know and, lacking the explanation, was afraid.

I suppose the fear of death was haunting me that night, spurred on by the old crone's mortality and the realization I was going to die and, like as not, in the not-too-distant future.

◆

The wildlife park was situated in two thousand acres of what had been the grounds of a stately home. Rolling hills, woods, gentle valleys and streams were criss-crossed with paths, walks and the track of a miniature railway system linking the various areas of interest. In some of the wide-open spaces, large paddocks had been established containing animals which might be approached whilst the most dangerous or unpredictable were housed in large cages in a complex once the extensive walled gardens near the mansion building. In every copse stood a small herd of deer whilst, on the edge of a large lake, a flock of flamingos strutted in the company of black and white swans, crowned cranes, Canada geese and vast numbers of smaller water-fowl. In the next lake, the sides of which had been lined with stone, seals swam like torpedoes or basked lazily upon a rocky island.

From the moment I switched off the engine of the Porsche,

Adam seemed to be a different person. Most children, I thought, would have been excited to the point of hysteria by the proximity of their first zoo and yet he was composed and pensive.

'Are you looking forward to your visit?' I asked as I locked the car and set the alarm.

'Yes, Uncle Dom, I am,' he said quietly.

'Are you quite sure? We can go to the seaside if you'd prefer. It's only another twenty minutes in the car.'

'No,' he answered quite emphatically. 'I want to go here.'

He took my hand as we went along the road to the car-park, gripping tightly as a car drove past us. A coach filled with elderly people on an outing caused him to step on to the grass verge although there was ample room for pedestrians. I had the impression the child was not so much afraid of the vehicles but somehow respectful of them, aware of their potential rather than the actual danger they posed him.

We walked towards the pay kiosk where I handed over the entrance fee and bought Adam a guide book. He was offered a paper baseball cap to wear but politely refused it.

'It's free,' the lady in the kiosk announced.

'No, thank you,' Adam insisted. 'I don't need a hat.'

The woman gave a light shrug in my direction and replaced the hat in its box. We pushed through the turnstile and into the former walled gardens.

'I don't need a hat,' Adam said once we were out of the earshot of the entrance. 'I've got hair. That's instead of a hat.'

'What animal would you like to see first?' I asked, at a loss to make a comment on his observation. 'We have all day so there's no hurry.'

'Can we just walk about, Uncle Dom?'

I agreed and we set off at a leisurely pace. Adam did not hold my hand but walked by my side clutching the guide book.

Some smaller animals were contained not in cages but smooth concrete-lined enclosures surrounded by a dry ditch. Adam cursorily glanced into each of these, referring to the illustrations in his guide book if the occupants were out of sight in a burrow or other shelter. It was not until we reached some racoons he stopped. Three or four were feeding on fruit dumped over the wall into the ditch whilst another sat in a dead tree erected well away from the concrete sides. Adam did not speak but intently observed them for some minutes, leaning over the wall to get a better view. At length, he set himself on his feet again and stared at the sign beneath the dead tree.

'They're called racoons,' he informed me.

'They are,' I said. 'They live in North America. Did you see any when you were there?'

'Yes, sometimes. They got run over on the road and they stole the rubbish. But we didn't see many. Only when we went to stay with Uncle Bill and Auntie Han in Brockport. That's in New York State. Then we saw lots.'

Leaving the racoons to their feast, we sauntered on. Adam was in no hurry to get to the next animal, unlike a party of slightly older children, visiting the place on a school trip. They rushed hither and thither, calling to each other and scribbling on notepads. Their teachers made no effort to discipline this rabble and I was glad when they had moved on.

'Do you know why they are eating?' Adam asked suddenly.

'The racoons?' I replied. 'They're hungry, I expect.'

'But they shouldn't eat now. It's morning. They are night animals. They ought to eat in the dark.'

'I don't expect the keepers are on duty at night.'

'That's not fair,' Adam said.

We went by moribund tortoises, a sleeping coati, fidgeting wallabies, some cages of wide-eyed lemurs swinging to and fro in a network of ropes and boughs and a large cage containing a sleeping caracal. Adam paid scant attention to these creatures and did not stop again until we reached an area of aviaries. In one cage, on a guano-spattered branch, sat hunched a professorial-looking owl. Its plumage was mottled brown, its eyes deep golden and its hooked beak buff-coloured. Being a large bird, the mesh containing it was quite wide and sparrows had infiltrated its territory to hop about in the leaves under its perch.

Adam watched the owl intensely. From time to time, it watched him when not swivelling its head to keep an eye on the sparrows. Apart from slight movements of its skull, it was motionless.

'Watch,' said Adam softly.

I was not sure what I was meant to watch, him or the morose owl.

For at least fifteen seconds, Adam stared intently at the owl. The owl stared back in the myopic fashion of its kind: then, without warning, it flung its wings out and hooted loudly. The sparrows scattered, squeezing frantically through the mesh in their escape. Adam smiled to himself.

'Did you make him do that?' I enquired.

'I know him,' the child remarked noncommittally.

The next cage Adam chose to halt before contained a rather beautiful monkey. It had a black head, legs and tail with a deep grey body and a reddish-brown rump, its chest and neck white. Across its brow was a thin white line from beneath which its black eyes disdainfully surveyed the passers-by.

'What is this animal?' Adam enquired, the notice being rather too high for him.

'It's called a Diana monkey,' I read. 'A guenon or long-tailed monkey. Habitat: rain forest – Sierra Leone, Liberia, Ivory Coast. In other words, Adam, it comes from the jungle in western Africa. Arboreal. Lives in troops of up to thirty. Naturally inquisitive and very vocal. The long tail is used for balancing and hanging.'

'What does inquisitive and vocal mean, Uncle Dom?'

'Inquisitive means it's nosy, curious, always looking into things and vocal means it makes a lot of noise.'

Adam looked at the little primate. It was sitting on the ground turning over a piece of dead bark in its hands. 'He's not very inquisitive or vocal now, is he, Uncle?'

'No, not very,' I concurred.

'And what does arbriale mean?'

211

'Arboreal,' I corrected him. 'It means living in trees.'

'He's bored,' Adam declared, looking at the monkey. 'He's got nothing to do. And he's sad.'

'How do you know?'

'I get sad like that sometimes. He's sad because there aren't any trees in his cage.'

I squatted down and looked at the monkey from Adam's perspective. It glanced up in the way monkeys have, of avoiding direct recognition, dropped the bark, kicked it and picked it up again.

'He does seem to be a bit miserable,' I agreed.

Adam took a step nearer to the wire of the cage. A steel barrier prevented too close an approach but Adam was undeterred by it, ducking beneath the bar.

'I think you'd better stay this side,' I said, reaching for him.

'It's all right, Uncle,' he replied, not turning round. 'He's my friend.'

Something in the child's confidence reached through to me and I let him take the three steps to the wire, casting a quick look around to make sure there was no keeper present and moving to the side so I was close enough to snatch at Adam should anything happen, at the same time being in a position to observe his face. I was more than eager to see how this encounter might develop.

The monkey, not much more than a metre away, dropped the bark as Adam's hands touched the wire. It opened its eyes and stared roundly at the child. Adam made a small sucking noise with his lips, moving his mouth as if he was kissing the air. The monkey ceased staring and started to chatter its teeth together as if it was shivering. Adam followed suit. After a moment, the monkey then looked away and Adam did likewise.

Throughout this display, I kept alert. There was no way of telling what the monkey might do and a warning on the wire now caught my eye: *Do not feed these monkeys. Your food may kill them. Do not attempt to touch them: they bite!*

'Adam,' I whispered so as not to alarm the monkey, 'I think we should go away now.'

'It's all right, Uncle Dom,' Adam replied.

He and the monkey looked at each other again, the latter moving up to the wire. It had its mouth half open and I could see a row of small, needle-sharp teeth.

'It's all right,' Adam said again, as if to allay my rising fear.

He pushed his hand through the cage wire and the monkey, turning sideways on to him, allowed him to ruffle his fingers in its fur. This activity went on for at least a minute before the monkey turned again and started to stroke and investigate Adam's arm.

I was utterly captivated and forgot all about the warning notice, the risk of being caught breaking the rules. Adam was quite clearly in complete harmony with the monkey and yet how he could be, how he could understand the skills of communication with the animal was beyond me. Even if he was, I considered, the possessor of inherited communications skills with animals surely his knowledge would be restricted to creatures with which his forebears were familiar: I could not recall any mention of monkeys being indigenous to southern Europe in the Bronze Age.

With a slow, measured gentleness, the monkey reached full stretch through the cage and ran its fingers lightly over Adam's cheek. It was, I thought, more like the touch of a lover than a wild animal penned in captivity.

At this, Adam chuckled under his breath and slowly withdrew his arm. The monkey did likewise, let out a high-pitched chirrup, like a little bird, which Adam imitated perfectly.

'He's happier now,' the child said decisively and left the cage.

'Have you seen monkeys before, Adam?' I asked as we walked away.

'I've seen them on television,' he admitted.

'But you've never seen one alive? In a cage or as someone's pet. In America, perhaps?'

'Daddy has a friend with a pet lizard,' Adam replied.

'But no monkeys?'

'No, no monkeys, Uncle Dom.'

Adam passed without stopping through the reptile house, stayed only momentarily in front of a huge cage containing a pair of African leopards and paid no heed to an alligator in a heated pool. He ignored more aviaries and two strutting peacocks displaying on a lawn but he stayed for ten minutes laughing loudly at the antics of some otters in a waterfall and artificial stream, declaring they were happier than the monkey.

Finally, we came to what had once been a large orangery when the mansion had been a gracious seventeenth-century home rather than a day-tripper's destination. By the door was a sign reading: *Tropical Forest House*. We entered to discover ourselves in the humid, dank, warm atmosphere of a miniature jungle. Huge gaudy butterflies flew languorously between lianas, banana trees, palms and dense foliage. Brushing against a lantana bush, I scattered a blizzard of bright blue wings and smelled the scent like cat's urine the leaves give off. Small birds hopped and ran beneath the plants whilst, in a pool, orange and white Koi carp over a foot long turned lazily against the weak current.

Adam watched the butterflies closely. Decaying fruit had been placed on wooden platforms under the trees, butterflies landing on them to feed on the juices.

'Do they eat the fruit?' he asked.

'They suck the juices,' I replied

'I thought butterflies ate flowers.'

'Not exactly. They eat nectar.'

'What's neck-tar?' he asked.

'A sort of flower syrup,' I replied. 'In England, they lick it with their long tongues, but in tropical – in hot – countries, they sometimes eat rotting fruit as well. This building is supposed to represent a hot country.'

'Is that for butterflies, too?' Adam said, pointing to an

inverted bottle nailed to a stake, the glass mouth stuffed with foam.

Before I could answer, a light breeze tickled my cheek, as if someone had blown on it, and a deep emerald humming-bird materialized at the base of the bottle, inserting its beak into the foam. Its tiny wings blurred on either side of its body which could not have been as large as my thumb.

'Oh, look, Uncle Dom!' Adam exclaimed, entranced by the bird. 'What is it?'

'It's a humming-bird. They drink nectar from flowers, too. Like butterflies.'

The bird vanished. I did not see its line of flight: it merely dematerialized.

'It will come again, won't it?' Adam almost begged.

'Yes,' I promised and, no sooner had I spoken than it did.

We remained in the hothouse for half an hour. Adam discovered a bench near another bird-feeding station and sat on it, enraptured by the humming-birds of which there were, it transpired, several species present.

As he watched the birds in wonderment, I watched him with a similar amazement. He had remarkable, almost miraculous gifts and yet he was quite matter-of-fact about them. Clearly, he did not regard himself as out of the ordinary and was not yet old enough to appreciate how unique his powers were. That he had inherited them seemed beyond doubt. I could see no other conduit through which he could have attained such skills. His upbringing was hardly responsible: had his father been a naturalist, a conservationist, a white hunter or a wildlife photographer, I might have been able to understand the child. As it was, he was a little boy who had lived, for a while, in suburban America, the son of an English dentist and an art historian.

At least, he was the son, but not the offspring.

Eventually, we left the tropical forest and went to a café in the centre of the walled garden. I ordered myself a lemonade whilst Adam requested a Coca Cola and an ice-cream. We sat at a table on a patio outside. The sun was warm and the peacocks moved around us, mewing and wheeping. A light breeze rippled the leaves of beech trees planted in the lawns, surrounded by neat borders of marigolds and forget-me-nots.

'Adam,' I said, 'how did you learn to . . . ?' I was at a loss for words to describe what he could do.

'Know animals?'

'Yes,' I said, ' know animals. It's almost as if you can talk to them. You and the monkey got along famously but you've never seen one. Who taught you how to do that?'

'No one, Uncle Dom,' he said with such openness I knew he was telling the truth. 'I just know it.' He took a spoonful of his ice-cream. 'It's like the pictures. And the clouds. I just know it.'

'Can you do it with any animal?' I asked.

'No. Not any animal. Just some.'

I made no reply but drank my lemonade. It was very cold, ice cubes bobbing in it, and gave me a slight headache after the intense closeness of the orangery.

A grey squirrel appeared on the edge of the patio, sat up on its hind legs and looked quickly around, its tail twitching with fear or excitement.

'That's a squirrel,' Adam declared.

'Can you talk to him?'

'I'll try.'

He put down his ice-cream spoon and turned in his seat to face the squirrel. It was eyeing some crumbs under the next but one table to our own. I scrutinized every movement Adam made but these were minimal. He did not, to my hearing, make a noise nor did he open his mouth. His hands lay relaxed in his lap and his feet were still upon a bar under his chair. The breeze ruffled his hair. Not for one moment did he take his eyes off the squirrel but I noticed he blinked more than one might expect.

At first, the squirrel made no sign of being affected then, quite suddenly, it ran in its endearing, undulating way right up to Adam's chair. I kept perfectly still. It sat up again, rubbed its front paws over its face and leapt on to the table beside Adam's ice-cream. I could hardly believe it. Very slowly, Adam put out his hand and tickled the creature's belly with his finger. It made a churring noise, looked him full in the face, ran across the table, jumped on to my shoulder, stepped on to the back of my chair and made off across the patio.

'I can talk to squirrels,' Adam announced, a certain pleasure in his voice and picked up his ice-cream spoon.

For the next hour, we wandered the grounds of the country house, saw a pair of Indian elephants, ostriches, zebras and camels. Along one path, we came face to face with four giraffe, one of which bent its neck down and allowed Adam to put his hand on its nose.

'He's very tame,' the child said as we moved on.

I wondered if perhaps he had managed to communicate with it.

Towards four o'clock, we started to make our way back to the car-park. I had promised Larry we would be home by six. An agitated crowd was gathered at the end of the row of cars in which I had parked. People were yelling and waving their hands. A woman in her late fifties was screaming and crying hysterically. Two men, one armed with an umbrella and the other with a car-parking signpost were thrashing at something I could not see.

'Run, Uncle Dom!' Adam suddenly shouted and darted away. He reached the crowd a good few metres ahead of me and pushed his way through. I followed in hot pursuit, worried as to what the child was up to.

In the circle of people, two dogs were fighting. A snarling Alsatian, its hackles raised in anger and defiance, had a smaller, nondescript mongrel pinned to the ground by the throat. As I arrived, it shook the mongrel viciously, the little dog gasping for breath and whimpering. One of the men beat the Alsatian on its rump with the post but the dog was oblivious to it.

Adam, after pausing for a moment as if assessing the situation, stepped forward.

'Get that fucking child out of here!' bellowed the man with the umbrella.

'Oh, my God!' screamed a woman and she reached for Adam but failed to grab him.

'Get the child! The dog'll turn on him!' bellowed another man.

I stepped out behind Adam but made no attempt to interfere. I had the utmost confidence in him, was quite sure he knew what he was doing.

'Grab the boy!' a voice hollered near me but I just raised my hand as if acknowledging this advice.

Adam whistled. It was a thin, shrill but tiny noise, the same as he had made when calling to the blackbird as an infant. For a moment, nothing happened. The Alsatian kept its grip on the mongrel which was suffocating. The elderly woman was sobbing loudly but the rest of the crowd had fallen silent. Gradually, the Alsatian's hackles fell, it loosened its grip then let go of the mongrel altogether, sitting down as obediently as if it had been in dog training class. The mongrel lay on its side, panting for breath. Its neck was flecked with the larger dog's saliva and it was bleeding from a torn ear.

The crowd murmured. I crouched down beside Adam and put my hand on his shoulder. He made another little noise, barely audible. The Alsatian and the mongrel both stood up and came towards him, their heads hung down with canine shame. Adam took a step towards them and put each of his hands on the dogs' heads. He said nothing to them but I knew he was gazing into their eyes.

'Well, I'm damned!' I heard a voice say behind me.

Letting go of the dogs, Adam turned to me, smiled and walked out of the gathering. The elderly woman picked up her mongrel and cuddled it, pressing a wadge of Kleenex to its ear. The Alsatian moved off and lay down in front of the man with the umbrella.

'How the hell did your little boy do that?' the man with the car-parking signpost asked me, putting his hand on my arm.

'He has a way with animals,' I replied, smiling gently. 'Now, if you'll excuse me.' As I walked away, I felt the eyes of the crowd on me and heard a subdued bubble of conversation break out.

Adam was standing by the Porsche. I took out my handkerchief and wiped the smears of mongrel's blood off his little fingers. 'You were very brave, Adam,' I praised him. 'And it was a very good thing you did.'

'Animals shouldn't fight, Uncle Dom. Not like that. And I can talk to dogs.'

◆

I saw a man coming. He was making his way down the steep pathway beside the falls. I hid myself in the shadows but, as he drew nearer, I recognized him as one of the men from the settlement up-river from the cascade whom I had injected against TB a while back. Confident as to his identity, I stepped out of my hiding place.

'*Buenos días, señor,*' he said, his Spanish very accented: I guessed he mostly spoke the local Huambas dialect.

I nodded and replied, '*¡Buenos días!*'

At this, and to my astonishment, he took me by the hand and, as if I was a child, led me quickly down the riverside path. I did not protest nor hang back: in fact, I was a little afraid. The people of the clearing do not hold hands and I assumed others in the forest would behave likewise: this man was either an eccentric or the reason for his visit was serious. As we hurried along, brushing against plants in our haste, he quickened his step, looking back several times. I did likewise but could discern no one following us, his action considerably disquieting me.

On reaching the clearing, he did not release my hand but positively dragged me towards the long-houses. Keewei appeared at the door of one, saw us and shouted. Chuhi and five or six others appeared as if from nowhere, each of them armed with a weapon of some sort.

Still holding my hand, the newcomer started to talk volubly, expressing with his free hand but not letting me go. I wondered what etiquette I had transgressed and grew increasingly concerned although I put on a brave face, feigning interest in what they were saying although I was unable to comprehend so much as a syllable.

At last, he let my hand go and everyone stared momentarily at me. I felt like a gatecrasher must at one of Thomas Arkassian's parties: those heady days seemed suddenly so very distant. I must have smiled at the reminiscence of them for Chuhi shook his head.

'¡No!' he exclaimed and grimaced. 'No rie.' His voice was so serious, so taut with emotion I felt any sense of ironic humour drain from me.

'What's the matter?' I asked, forgetting myself for a moment then adding, '¿Qué pasa?'

Yet before he could answer, I knew. The look on Urú's face gave me the news. Chuhi pointed to my hut then started to speak rapidly to the men. They ran for the long-houses, calling in quiet, urgent voices to the women and children. Within a minute, the families had vanished into the forest.

I made quickly for my hut, entered it and closed the door, bolting it for the first time since I had arrived in the clearing. I fixed the shutters down on my windows but left one ajar: although I was afraid, it was with a fear of excitement as much as of loathing or incomprehension. It was a fear such as I supposed racing car drivers experienced as they waited for the lights to change and start the race, as I had experienced the first time I put a scalpel to living flesh and watched as the thin line of blood drew itself out. It was unassimilable, exquisite even.

For a while, nothing stirred in the clearing save for one of the dogs which sauntered about, seeking a new patch of shade. At last, as I was beginning to think perhaps it was a false alarm or the threat had passed by on the river, a bird broke cover and set up a squawking alarm call. Others took it up as they flew across the clearing into the jungle. The dogs looked up at the birds' tocsin. One by one they began to rise and turn their lips back. They did not bark but stared in the direction of the river path, growling ominously. I could not see the object of their loathing but used their behaviour as an indication of what it was doing.

Gradually, the dogs began to retreat, their heads low and their hackles raised, their ears flat and their tails hanging down immobile.

A man came into my field of vision. He was a native wearing a loincloth but carrying a rifle. He was soon followed by another and a third, also armed. They fanned out across the clearing, moving cautiously like animals hunting, their feet lifting slowly, placing them with precision as if they were taking part in a languid ritual dance.

Finally, another man entered my restricted sight. It was Rodriguez, the amber trader. He stood in the centre of the clearing, his automatic pistol balanced easily in his hand. For a long moment, he surveyed the clearing, his head turning little by little, his eyes absorbing every detail. Satisfied he was reasonably safe, he turned and faced my hut.

'¿Señor? ¿Doctor? ¿Donde estás?'

His voice was wheedling, like that of a school bully taunting the butt of his cruelty.

'¡Señor!' he shouted again, changing to pidgin English. 'Where you are? You come. Come to see me, doctor.'

I made no reply. Hopefully, he would think I had run into the forest with the others.

'Doctor! We no you keell. We no wan' keell you. You OK with us.'

Quickly scanning the hut, I wondered what weapon I might have to defend myself. There was nothing of use except perhaps in close quarters combat: a man with an automatic pistol has no need to join closely with his enemy.

'Come, doctor!' he taunted again. 'You in the house. I know you in the house.' His voice lowered to a deep threat. 'You come out. I no keell you.'

I felt sweat running down my spine, tickling as it went. A panic began to swell in me. I wanted to scream, even to cough loudly, anything to relieve the tension; but I knew to make the slightest noise would bring him on. Yet, at the same moment, I knew it was only a matter of time before he found me.

'Doctor! You come.'

He raised his arm, slightly bent at the elbow and vaguely aimed the pistol. His three companions stood behind him, two watching his back, the other facing towards the hut.

'Doctor! You come.'

I heard rather than saw him cock the weapon. It was a metallic series of clicks not unlike those made by the jungle multitude of tree frogs but somehow horrifying. He fired. I winced but did not move. The report was not as loud as I had anticipated. The bullet smacked into the tin wall fifty centimetres to my left, penetrated it as easily as it might a sheet of cardboard. It smacked against the rear wall, shattering a mug hanging on a hook. The china exploded into shards, the handle remaining grotesquely swinging from its hook.

The cocking mechanism clicked again.

'You no can go a place, doctor,' he mocked.

The next shot struck the door frame, splintering the wood. A sliver hit me on the thigh. The pain was like a frozen needle going in. I gritted my teeth. Tears filled my eyes. I quickly rubbed them dry with my thumb and peered out through the crack in the shutter.

Rodriguez was walking slowly towards the hut, his pistol at the ready, held out before him and wavering slightly from side to side to cover the door and window. He no doubt feared I might have a gun.

'I come to you, doctor. You no can go a place.'

Five paces from the porch he halted, studying every square inch of the hut. I moved slightly back from the crack but he knew I was there. His eyes sought me out and found me. I sensed him become aware of my presence.

'Come, doctor.' He spoke quietly, well aware I was only a few metres from him. 'I no keell you,' he added improbably. He raised the pistol before his face. His thumb moved. The cocking mechanism clicked. He looked down the short barrel at me. I closed my eyes and began to crouch.

There was a soft noise, like air being released from a half-inflated cushion, followed by a clatter. I stood up and opened my eyes.

Rodriguez was leaning against the porch roof support nearest the door. His automatic was on the top step. His left hand clenched the wooden pillar. Protruding from his throat, just below his thyroid, was an arrow. As I watched him, he gripped the shaft with his right hand and tried to draw it out.

There was a rifle shot. I saw, behind Rodriguez, one of his native followers spin round and fall in a heap, the barrel of his rifle smoking and his legs kicking involuntarily. Another lay still. The third was nowhere to be seen.

Very cautiously, I opened the hut door. My action drew no gunfire. I peered out. Chuhi and the other men were advancing in a line across the clearing, crouching to run or bobbing up to see ahead. Each had his bow and arrow at the ready.

Rodriguez was alive still, slumped against the wooden post, one arm around it, the other limp at his side. He had succeeded in bending the arrow shaft but not in breaking it off: not that this would have aided him. At least ten centimetres of the shaft and the fletchings protruded from the nape of his neck whilst just behind the bloodied arrowhead was a dark smearing of poison.

He was breathing hard, in short, hungry gusts, bubbles of blood and saliva forming and bursting around the point where the arrow protruded from his neck. I picked up his automatic pistol and unloaded it, my every move watched by him. His lips moved. It occurred to me he might have been asking for mercy, for medical aid or to be put out of his misery.

Chuhi and Mayno approached.

'*Gracias*,' I said, my voice little more than a whisper.

The two of them grinned broadly then Chuhi stepped up and offered me a large knife, handle first, nodding in the direction of Rodriguez. From somewhere in the jungle came a blood-curdling yell. The third of Rodriguez's men had been discovered. Chuhi and his brother exchanged glances and grinned all the more expansively.

I looked down at the amber dealer. His eyes were beginning to glaze with pain. He was slipping into unconsciousness, into the sweet abyss of oblivion.

'No,' I said and I gave the knife back to Chuhi. He and Mayno grabbed Rodriguez by the arms and dragged him over to the logs around the fire hearth. In the bright sunlight, they sat him against one of the trunks and very slowly, very methodically, severed his head.

◆

There was a knock on the cottage door. I was not long up. The night before, an emergency had kept me in London: it was midnight before I felt I could leave and three in the morning before I reached Cobb End.

Putting my slice of buttered toast down, I slid the bolts on the kitchen door and opened it to discover Adam standing before me holding a manila envelope.

'Hello, Uncle Dom,' he greeted me. 'Mummy said I could come. But she said I had to ask if I was distrubbing you.'

I tightened my dressing-gown. 'No, Adam,' I replied, smiling. 'You are not distrubbing me.'

He came in and stood by the kitchen table. 'Are you having your breakfast?'

'I am. I went to bed very late last night.'

'Why?'

'Well, I didn't leave London until midnight because I had a sick lady to look after.'

'Is she all right now?'

'I think so,' I answered. 'Would you like some toast?'

'No, thank you, Uncle Dom. I mustn't spoil my lunch.'

'Do you mind if I finish mine?'

He shook his head and perched himself on a chair across the table from me.

'Would you like a drink?' I enquired.

Again, he shook his head.

'Does Daddy let you walk up the lane on your own?'
I asked.

'Yes,' Adam answered proudly. 'But he watches from the gate. And if you weren't in, I had to go straight home.'

'Well,' I advised, 'do be careful of cars, won't you?'

He nodded and pushed the envelope across the table.

'I've done some more pictures for you.'

I wiped my hands on a dishcloth, moved my plate aside and set my cup of coffee off to my right. The envelope was closed with a reusable flap which I eased open. Within were nearly three dozen pictures, all drawn in pencil or child's wax crayon upon A4 typing paper. I spread a dozen or so out across the table. They were not single figure sketches but tableaux of men and animals, fantastic shapes and abstracts. All were very similar in style to those I had seen in the British Museum.

'Are you going to tell me about some of the pictures?' I asked. 'What's this one about?'

'It's a picture of . . . ' he began but paused to consider his response.

I studied it. Two figures were seated on horses, the bodies of which were fleshed out from sticks. One man had a black circle in his left hand, the other a spear in one and a sickle in the other. A number of animals I took for deer, for they had antlers, and smaller creatures which might have been dogs or rabbits for they bore big ears, were drawn scattered about the page between squares criss-crossed like a flag.

'I don't really know what it's of,' Adam admitted.

'Well,' I suggested, 'aren't the men hunting?'

'No,' he replied quite emphatically but did not offer an alternative.

The next picture was composed of individual objects and seemed not to make up a coherent scene. A kind of circular dish was the centrepiece, but other depictions showed a stick man on what was obviously the frame of a hut, another wielding a hammer over a wheel, a third balancing on a horse waving a stick. The horse was galloping and, within the restrictions of the style, showed movement and agility. Other facets of the picture were less obvious: a six-legged rabbit, a square box with dots under it and bars in the centre, a number of sickle-like objects, straight lines surrounded by dots and what might have been simplistic birds.

'What's this one about?'

'I don't know,' he answered. 'It's just things.'

I admired the pictures, passing a praising comment or two and drinking my coffee.

'There's some more,' Adam reminded me.

I removed all that was left in the envelope and started to go through them. They were like those already set out, crowded with stick figures of humans, and animals, abstracts and unrecognizable objects. It was not until I reached the bottom of the pile I discovered the most fascinating picture of all.

Adam had started to draw a stick man but instead of being satisfied with this, he had doodled with the arms, wrapping them round and round the figure in a continuous whirling spiral which broke up, bisected and turned back on itself. It was exactly like the pictures listed as anthropomorphic labyrinths in the museum catalogue.

'Where do you . . . ?' I began, yet Adam foresaw my question.

'They're . . . They're dream pictures, Uncle Dom.'

'Dream pictures?' I responded.

'Yes. I don't know why. At night, I dream them up and in the morning, I draw them.'

'I see,' was all I could say.

'Sometimes, I see other things, too. But they're not easy.'

'Tell me,' I asked after a moment's thought, 'do you dream them in colour?'

'No,' he replied, 'I dream them like that. Sometimes, I dream lots of other things.'

'Tell me about them,' I said, pouring myself another coffee. 'And would you like a glass of milk?'

He shook his head and looked at the pictures.

'I dream all sorts of things. Once, I saw a man hitting a stone with a hammer and another time, I saw him throwing something on an animal. Sometimes they walk along with other animals. Sometimes, they've got little carts. Sometimes, they do funny things.'

'What sort of funny things?'

'Last night, a man kept hitting an animal with his thingy.'

'His thingy?' I questioned.

'Yes. His thingy,' Adam repeated, his cheeks blushing a little. 'His weeing thingy.'

As he spoke, I heard Ruth's voice saying, quite distinctly, *There is one of a man fucking a goat.* The hair prickled on the nape of my neck. 'Did the man say anything?' I enquired.

'No,' Adam said, 'They don't make noises. Never.'

'What other funny things have you seen?'

'A man dancing. He had a funny dress on.'

'A dress?'

'Like a dress. Not tight like Mummy's but sort of loose and made of bits of string. And I saw another man with a deer's head on his head.' His voice became much quieter. 'Last week, I saw a man kill another man. That wasn't funny.'

'How did he do it?'

'One man was fallen over and the other man who wasn't fallen over hit him on the head with a stick and his head came off.'

Adam had a faraway look in his eyes as if he was, once more, witnessing the murder.

'What about this man?' I asked, turning the picture of the spiral-armed figure around.

'He's a magic man,' Adam said with certainty. 'He's . . .' He looked embarrassed, guilty in the way children feel when they are not sure if they have committed a wrong.

'He's...?' I prompted.

'He's my friend, that one. I know him.'

'What's his name?'

'He doesn't have a real name. I call him Da.'

'Do you ever show your drawings to Mummy and Daddy?'

'No.' He was a little reticent.

227

Don't they ask about them? After all, you do lots of them.'

'Sometimes. Mummy says "That's a pretty picture" but . . . ' He looked out of the window. 'She doesn't understand them. She doesn't know them.' He paused. 'This is still our secret, isn't it, Uncle Dom?'

'Yes, Adam,' I assured him. 'It's still our secret, like the fishes.'

The kitchen door opened so suddenly, I started.

'You still here!' Larry exclaimed. 'I am sorry, Dom. He insisted on showing you his pictures and . . . ' She looked at my dressing-gown. 'Now Adam, that was naughty. I said you were not to disturb Uncle Dom if he . . . '

'It's all right, Larry,' I said. 'I was up and, besides, I've got to phone London to check up on my latest patient. It was a long night.'

'See you for tea?' Larry enquired.

'See you for tea,' I confirmed and I started to put the pictures back in the envelope.

'You can keep them, Uncle Dom,' Adam said. 'They're for you.'

'Thank you, Adam,' I said. 'I'll treasure them.'

'Now run along,' Larry commanded. 'Get in the car. We've got to go shopping.'

Adam looked hard at me for a moment as if to say not to forget our secret then ran out.

'Dom,' Larry said, 'don't feel you have to keep all his scribbles. You must have hundreds by now. You can get rid of them. He'll not remember and you'll get a load more soon enough, I'm sure.'

'He certainly is the little artist,' I agreed humorously.

'He's always drawing,' Larry continued. 'Sometimes, he totally ignores his toys. If I tell him to stop, he – well, he doesn't exactly sulk but you can tell he's unhappy. He doesn't complain at all, he's a good little boy, but . . . ' She looked at her watch. 'I must be off. You know, Dom, he seems to live in a complete make-believe world much of the time.'

'That's normal,' I said, 'and he has a good imagination.'

'I must rush!' she exclaimed, waved her hand and was gone.

I did not go to tea that afternoon. There was a minor complication with my patient and I returned to London around midday.

Driving across the southern counties, I could not stop thinking of Adam and his dreams. The revelation that he dreamt all his pictures was staggering. It was not just a matter of him having some inherited skill but I was now convinced he also had an inherited memory. It was abundantly clear to me he was dreaming of the Bronze Age.

As soon as I could, I left my patient, returned to my practice and spent the rest of the weekend typing up my notes, reading through the past case history in the Mouette file and comparing Adam's drawings with those over three millennia old in the catalogue. In many instances, they were so similar as to be almost copies.

It was not until I reached the end of the notes on my breakfast meeting with Adam it registered.

He called the man Da.

How many times, I thought, had I heard children in my surgery call their fathers Dad – or Da.

◆

The dinner was, by Thomas Arkassian's standards, a small gathering. There were just ten guests in addition to Thomas and Marie. As was to be expected, the food was excellent and the wines, different with each course, well chosen and of the best vintages. The conversation was lively. Amongst the others around the table were a famous actor and his Polynesian wife, a criminal barrister specializing in what he termed Oriental criminal cases and an eminent woman jockey whom Thomas had seated next to me. I was reminded, on hearing her profession, of a friend's comment about a former mistress of his: he had declared she was a horsewoman, more horse than woman. My misgivings, however, were unfounded. Her fund of stories, few of which were based on the turf, were hilarious and we were kept in good humour until my pager sounded.

'Oh, Dominic!' Marie chastised me: she only used my full name when annoyed with me or teasing. 'You've not brought your work with you?'

'I'm afraid I've had to,' I replied. 'May I use your phone?'

'At least you haven't brought one of those bloody mobiles with you. They cheep like birds.'

I dialled the practice number, the receiver lifting at the second ring.

'Hello,' I said, curious to know who was on my phone. It was Molly.

'What's the problem, Molly?'

'I think you'd best come back here, Dr Lyall,' she said. 'It's rather urgent.'

'Mrs Quennell . . . ?' I began.

'It's not a medical matter, sir,' Molly interrupted. 'The police are here.'

I could feel the blood drain from my face, the telephone receiver vibrating against my ear. Excusing myself from the dinner, I left the Arkassians' house and drove as quickly as I could through London. Every red traffic light frustrated me: I banged on the steering-wheel with the ball of my thumb, blared my car horn at anyone slow to draw away at the green light. I wanted to get to the mews as fast as I could: and yet I also gave a mild thanks for the temporary respite from fate each hold-up offered.

There was, I felt sure, no way in which anyone could have readily discovered the Mouette file in the computer and there was nothing in the filing cabinet to arouse suspicion. The only function of the manila folder was to cover for the material in the freezing unit.

Molly, I was certain, could not have delved into the entrails of the hard disk for she was not sufficiently computer literate to uncover hidden files: her only use for the machine was as a database and word processor. The other members of my staff would similarly not have been so inquisitive: even, I was convinced, if any of my employees had uncovered the file, they would not read it unless it was an active file on someone currently undergoing treatment, appreciating the patients' privacy.

On the other hand, I considered, what if the HFEA had returned out of hours, Hodson and his pals arrived again for a snap inspection. I tried to recall if they were allowed by their code of practice to act in such a way. Yet surely, I reasoned, they would not make an evening raid, out of office hours, merely because my administration had once been slightly lax and the floor not demarcated like a basketball court. By the time I turned off Oxford Street, my mind was in a turmoil.

At the entrance to the mews, I was met by a phalanx of flashing blue strobe lights and cars with reflective strips on them. The door to the practice was open, Molly standing in it wearing a terrified smile. She looked as if she'd been crying.

'What's happened?' I asked.

'There's been a break-in.'

I went quickly up the stairs. A plain-clothes police officer was sitting at the reception desk. The office was turned upside down. Two other policemen were dusting the filing cabinet, the window-sill, and the walls by the door with a fine powder.

'Dr Lyall?' the officer asked unnecessarily, rising from the typing chair. 'I'm Inspector Rhys. I'm afraid you've had a burglary.'

'Yes,' I replied, numbed by the sign of the damage. The desk drawers hung open, the filing-cabinet lock prised out with a jemmy. The window overlooking the courtyard at the rear was smashed.

Without saying more, I went to the laboratory. Nothing had been touched. I leaned against the microscope bench and felt suddenly very weak. If the freezing unit had been damaged countless couples could be rendered childless, countless tests and pathology work have to be repeated. Hundreds of hours of work would have been lost.

'Always a bit of a shock, sir,' the inspector remarked.

I nodded, at a loss to reply.

'I wonder, sir,' the inspector went on, 'if you could please check . . . ?'

He did not need to say more. I opened the freezer. It was obvious the contents had not been disturbed. Some samples of tissue in a petri dish, taken from Mrs Quennell earlier in the day, lay at the front of the top shelf, exactly where I had placed them in readiness for forwarding for pathological investigation the next day.

'I'm sure the freezer has not been tampered with,' I said.

'All your test-tube babies in there?' the inspector enquired, peering curiously through the door.

'Yes.'

'Glad to hear they're all safe, sir. Though I'm afraid you've got a lot of files missing from your cabinet. It'll take a lot of time sorting out the inventory and getting them rewritten. Hope it's all on computer as well.'

'Yes,' I said bleakly, 'it is.'

The strain must have showed on my face for the inspector smiled in a kindly fashion and suggested, 'Like a nice cup of tea, sir? Settle the nerves?'

'No, thank you,' I replied vaguely as if he was offering to make me one. 'Will you be long in your . . . ?'

'We'll be done in half an hour or so, sir,' the inspector said.

'What have they done to my apartment?' I asked, dreading his reply.

'Broken into your safe. Nothing more save a few knocked over ornaments and the like. Nowhere near as bad as the office. This was a professional job, Dr Lyall. Not two yobs with a crowbar. They disabled the alarm system by filling the bell housing with wall insulation foam.'

I was a little puzzled.

'You mean I still have a TV set and a hi-fi?'

'This was not a robbery for your expensive belongings, Dr Lyall,' he explained. 'You'll find your bedroom much as you left it save the damage to the wall and a bit of a mess on the bed and carpet. They've not so much as touched your cufflink box. This is what might be termed a celebrity burglary.'

I laughed emptily and replied, 'I'm a gynaecologist, not a famous footballer or a film star.'

'I'm aware of that,' the inspector answered ironically, 'and so are the thieves, but your patients are famous. Or may be. This is what they're after. This kind of thief breaks into doctors' surgeries, solicitors' offices, that sort of place. They're after data, not diamonds. Consider this: you may be treating a famous industrialist's wife for VD. The scandal can shake his company. You're treating a macho actor – an Arnold Schwarzenegger type – for impotence. It can have adverse effects on his career. *Hulk Cowboy Star Hank Shoots Blanks*. Such a tabloid headline destroys reputations. Abortion details on famous film stars. The blackmail potential held in even the files of a gynaecologist can be substantial.'

We returned to the reception room. The forensic inspection was ended, the two officers packing away their equipment.

'Got much?' the inspector asked.

'Doubt it, sir. We've lifted four sets.' The forensic officer turned to me. 'How many people're likely to go to this filing cabinet?'

'Three or four.'

'We'll take your fingerprints if we may, sir. For comparison and elimination. And the young lady's here. And your other staff when they come in tomorrow, but I doubt we'll get anything. It's a professional job. No doubt about it.'

The inspector took me aside, out of Molly's earshot and said, 'You may be contacted by Johnny Burglar. In a week or so. If he's going to get in touch, he'll let you sweat a bit first. Might try to flog you back your records. Or, of course, he might just go straight to some of your patients. Anyway, should he get in touch, do let me know.'

I nodded my agreement.

'Is there anything else I can do?' I enquired.

'Not a lot. Until he makes his first move, we're stuck.'

Before the inspector left, he asked me to take a quick inventory of the practice to see if there was any identifiable equipment missing. Molly and I looked round. There was nothing stolen: the telephones, the expensive light fittings, the pictures on the wall by both established artists and Adam, the ansaphone were all there. The surgery had not been touched, the operating room likewise. As the inspector had said, only my safe was damaged in the apartment and rifled through. Some money was missing from Molly's desk and my safe but travellers' cheques remaining from my last trip abroad, my passport and personal papers were untouched. Only the filing-cabinet drawers in reception were half empty.

'They've not even taken the IBM,' Molly remarked.

As soon as she spoke, I looked at the computer. Lying next to it on her desk was an empty, black, TDK floppy-disk box. I instantly knew what it meant. The thieves had downloaded a copy of the contents of the hard disk.

◆

'He is go,' Chuhi stated matter-of-factly.

I looked at the surface of the river, rippling in the early morning sunlight. The moon still hung in the sky over the far bank, an etiolated circle on which the pock-marks of craters were just visible. Water dripped from the branches of the trees: there had been an hour of heavy rainfall during the night which had cleaned the air and diluted the blood stains in the earth. About five metres out from the bank, the last of the bodies was gyrating slowly as the currents began to reach for it.

'*¡Mire, señor!*' Q'eke ordered.

I watched.

A current caught hold of an arm and moved it out from the body: then, suddenly, the water was agitated by the corpse's midriff. For a moment, it settled then the dancing sunlight was shattered into spray.

'*Piraña*,' Chuhi remarked stoically and set off towards the long-houses.

I watched as the body shivered under the impact of fish and teeth, swung about and was suddenly caught by the river which took it swiftly away.

Urú came up to me then and put her hand in mine. She did not speak but looked up at me with her dark, deep eyes. I smiled down at her but she did not return it. Instead, she squeezed my hand then, letting it go, walked off.

Equipping myself with a water-bottle and a knife, I left the clearing and set off on the path leading to the mountain. I did not hurry and arrived on the corpse platform just before noon. The rocks were hot from the sun, silver flecks of mica glinting in them. As I arrived, over a dozen green iguanas ran for cover in the rocks, their pointed spinal scales swaying as they fled. I was curious as to why they were there for I had not previously encountered even a single iguana on the hill. They were usually to be discovered nearer the river, lounging on branches or rocks from which they slid or fell when disturbed, swimming away to safety.

My curiosity was soon satisfied. At the far end of the rock platform were the remains of the old lady. I knew, after some time in her coffin in the funereal clearing, her cadaver had been removed: the sweet stink of putrid flesh has vanished from that part of the clearing. My assumption had been she was buried. Plainly, this was not so although when she had been brought here and by whom I could not guess. I had not seen a procession setting off.

After the last iguana had vanished, its feet and dry scales rattling upon the rock, I approached the old lady's remnants. All I could see left of her were bones and a hank of hair with a crimson, bedraggled feather matted in it. A few of her glass beads glinted in the sunlight but most had disappeared, scattered by wings or claws. The flesh had been stripped from her both by birds and insects and, I guessed, it was these which had attracted the iguanas. When her body was freshly dead, the whole summit of the hill must have been alive with voracious hunting lizards preying upon the devourers of human flesh.

That birds had partaken of the feast was indicated by the scattering of the bones. Larger predators would have gnawn upon them or carried off some of the limbs but this was not the case. Her entire skeleton was still there, yet most of the smaller bones – those of the fingers and the toes, some of the ribs – had been displaced and lay up to a metre from the vertebrae and pelvis.

Bending to study the bones more closely, I saw through one of the orbits in the skull, whilst the bones were stripped, there lingered in the cranium some of the flesh of the old lady's brain. As my eyes adjusted to the darkness inside her skull, I saw the flesh move. It was as if her dreams were coming alive once more. Yet it was nothing more than a battalion of large ants each biting free a microscopic fragment of the desiccated tissue which they took on a trail out through a fracture in the lambdoid suture and into a fissure in the rocks.

So much, I thought, for immortality and stood up. Just then, a small anonymous brown bird hopped along the rock, daintily picked up a skein of hair and few off with it. It struck me as quite beautiful, that the old lady's hair would line the nest of a jungle songbird.

Taking my customary seat at the end of the platform, I gazed out over the fragile bones being gradually bleached by the sun to the undulating ocean of jungle, the gentle roll of the canopy like a still tide, the waves of which had been caught in time. The scene, I thought, could hardly have changed since the first man walked here. Like nowhere else on earth, I considered, the primeval jungle is the most timeless of places.

Sitting with the sun beating down on me and what was left of the old woman, I allowed my mind to empty of all thoughts. Only in this way am I truly able to find peace.

After a while, my attention was brought back by a small flower blossoming from a crevice in the rock. It was little more than a daisy, a tiny star of petals in the arid stone. There was no other plant apart from a lichen growing anywhere on the platform and it occurred to me its seed may have been germinated and nourished by the bodily fluids of the corpse. As a warm breeze shimmied the petals, my mind dredged up a line of verse from some distant poetry lesson in school or an hour's reading in the romantic years of late youth. It was by Omar Khayyám.

> One thing is certain and the rest is Lies;
> The Flower that once has blown for ever dies.

◆

'Hello?' I said loudly and for the third time. 'I'm afraid it's not a very good line. I can't hear you.'

'You don't need to shout, Dr Lyall. I can hear you well enough.'

The voice spoke in a flat, London accent, the response so unexpected it took me aback. I sat up in bed and pulled the telephone on to the duvet.

'Who is this?' I was abrupt. It was past two o'clock in the morning and I had been asleep for at least three hours.

'You've been a bit of a naughty boy, haven't you, doctor?'

'I beg your pardon!' I exclaimed. I was fully awake now and angry, but not fully aware.

'A bit of a naughty boy. At least,' the voice continued, 'a bit of an unethical boy.'

'I'm sure I don't know what you mean,' I snapped. 'Who are you?'

Yet I knew. Before he said another word.

'Computers aren't foolproof, you know,' he said, his flat voice even and in command. 'Like any machine, what you put in you can get out. Every little byte.' He briefly chuckled at his pun. I made no response but gained control of myself.

'I think you'd better explain yourself,' I said at length.

'It's quite simple,' the voice replied. 'You've a lot of money and I want some of it. You'll give me a fair sum to get your files back. Not just those in the filing cabinet, of course, but those on the computer, too.'

'I fail to see what proof you have,' I said.

It was a stall. He was so confident he had to know something about someone. I prayed he was referring to a case file where he had misread the information. If a file stated I had used a third party's oöcyte to assist a couple, this might be construed by a layman to be unethical.

'Let's put it this way, Dr Lyall,' the voice replied. 'I've got an A to Z guide and there's no Havingdene Rd, London SE28. Therefore there's no Mr and Mrs Childless Mouette is there?'

'You'll find a number of false names in my files,' I bluffed. 'They are there to protect the famous. There is no Mouette, as you say. Yet it does refer to a patient.'

'Not one called Ruth?'

My heart thumped. Adrenalin coursed through me.

'I have no patient called Ruth whom I can recall.'

The voice turned sharp, curt and efficient.

'Don't fuck about with me, doctor.' He stressed the last word with as much irony as he could muster. 'I know you've been pissing around. You know it. And you know I know it. Bit of a checkmate situation, I'd say.'

'You have to prove it,' I said. 'Hearsay's no good.'

'I don't know. Hearsay's screwed many a better man than you, Dr Lyall. And you're not alone in the shit. I know you and Ruth Schroeder have been up to something. I know what it is, too.'

'You leave her out of this!' I said, my voice as threatening as I hoped I could make it in the circumstances.

'So far I have. She's not a medical doctor. Least, not on the BMA lists. But I'll find her. As for leaving her out of it, that's my decision, not yours.'

'If you . . .' I began.

'If I, Dr Lyall?' he cut in. 'If I . . . ?' His voice turned:

until now it had been comparatively suave. 'Now you listen to me, you cock- and cunt-fingering quack. I know about the dead man's spunk and I know some poor bitch had it shoved up her. Who this Mouette is, I don't know. But I'll find out. Easy to do. Your computer file's dated automatically so all I've got to do is go through the rest of your patients and look for another file started – or acted upon – about the same time. Odds are you write up your notes pretty efficiently. After all, you've been pretty damn detailed about the Mouettes and their kid. What's his name?' There was a pause and I heard papers shuffled. 'Adam, that's it. Of course, there may be five or six patients around the time so I'd have to write to them all now, wouldn't I?'

I did not answer and he interpreted my silence correctly.

'Bit thunder-struck, aren't you? You should be. Now, pay attention. I'll be in touch. I'll tell you how much I want and I'll give you time to get it. You'll get your data back if you do as you're told. No tricks, no Bill. If I see a uniform within a hundred miles of this, I'll be the one to blow the police whistle. And you'll be the one who loses out. And remember, this isn't a kidnap. No one's going to snuff it. The ransom's for a lot of bits of paper. And a disk or two.' He laughed sourly. 'The only thing to snuff it if you don't play ball is you. You and the certificate swinging from your office wall.'

He hung up before I could reply.

I lay back on the pillow. My hair itched with sweat, my hands uncontrollable. I was not so much scared as furious with the man for his artifice, with myself for my sheer bloody stupidity. That there was nothing at all I could do frustrated and enraged me even further: I was at the man's mercy, he knew it and was sure to give no quarter in his dealings with me. In his hands, I was impotent, a pawn for him to play with as he would.

For the rest of the night, I did not sleep but lay awake trying to figure out some way of escaping my fate. I considered calling the police as the inspector had requested but decided

against it. Instead, I tried to assess the chances of bluffing
it out. I even thought of requesting a favour of Archie
Hammerton whose fourth wife had been one of my patients
in the early days.

Archie was in his sixties when I first met him, Junie in her
mid-twenties. He had been, in the heyday of London gangsters,
one of the most feared men in the city who had done birdd, as
he put it, for a number of offences, all of which were violent.
He had broken fingers with a pair of pliers, thrown enemies
out of cars at speed, smashed his way into Hatton Garden
diamond dealers and taken part in a killing in a night-club
in 1959. As I was examining what he variously referred to in
his blunt East End accent as his tosher, bishop or plonker, he
asked me to 'go careful with me orchestra stalls' and told me,
quite matter-of-factly, how he had once wired an opposing gang
member's testicles to an army field telephone and cranked the
bell handle to send fifty volts through his Hampton Wick. After
an epidydimal aspiration – Archie was the first I ever carried
out this procedure on – Junie presented him with twins. He
presented me with a gold Parker pen set in addition to my fee
and, as we left the delivery suite in the private hospital, took
my by the elbow.

'You done good, doctor,' he said gruffly, close to tears. I
was surprised to see this notorious gangster emotional.

'I've done my best,' I replied.

'Yeah, you 'ave,' he agreed then, leaning closer to me, said
quietly, 'if you ever need a favour, someone gives you gyp or
don't pay up, or you get a spot of bovver, just give me a bell.
Understand?'

I nodded, the hairs on the nape of my neck rising. I
knew enough about male genitalia to imagine what a fifty
volt current might do to testicular tissue and the transversus
perinæi.

Now, lying in bed with my thoughts confused, I wondered
if I might still call in his card. I gave no thought to the
consequences, to the morality of hiring a hit man and reached
for the telephone although it was only 4 o'clock. I even raised

the receiver, but I did not dial directory enquiries. There had to be another way.

Three days later, I was examining a patient when Molly came in. 'There's an urgent call for you, doctor,' she said, smiling apologetically to my patient. 'I can't put it through. Line one's faulty again.'

I went into my office, picked up the receiver and pressed the number one button. My hand shook. For the past three days, I had not slept without giving myself a stiff dose of benzodiazepine. My nerves tautened every time the telephone rang, especially at night.

'Hello,' I said tentatively.

It was Ruth. 'Dom? I must see you. Immediately.'

I did not ask her why. I knew. 'Where are you?'

'I'm in a phone box at Paddington Station. Can I come to your practice?'

'Best not,' I said. 'I'll meet you for lunch . . . '

'I don't want any goddamn lunch!' she exclaimed. 'I want . . . '

'Get a hold of yourself,' I said sternly. 'I'll meet you . . . ' I thought for a moment of an appropriate rendezvous but came up with none. 'At Speaker's Corner in Hyde Park.' I glanced at my appointment schedule. 'Give me an hour,' I told her and I put the receiver down before she could reply.

She was standing alone, some metres from a man in a shabby trench coat balancing drunkenly on a blue plastic beer crate and sounding off to a small crowd about the injustices of the government of El Salvador. A few of his audience jeered and heckled but the rest gazed indifferently at him. A Japanese tourist had his camera out, the power wind humming every time the proclaimer gestured.

'What have you done?' were her first, strained words.

Taking her by the elbow, I guided her away in the direction of the tea-house half-way to the Serpentine. I walked slowly but she was agitated and wanted to speed up, as if by walking faster she might pass time the quicker and get out of her predicament all the sooner.

'I have not done anything,' I replied.

'I've been phoned . . . ' she began, but I put my hand up to silence her.

'You have been telephoned by a blackmailer,' I explained. 'So have I. My offices were burgled for files on patients. It's apparently a common crime. Blackmailers do it to get information. I'm assuming this man, whose name I do not know as yet, has discovered I assisted in your Bronze Age man's medical investigation and believes it to be unethical – a doctor of the living dealing with a corpse, the responsibility of a pathologist, coroner or mortician. He is, of course, wrong.'

'But he's got papers. About a Mr Mouette and his wife,' she babbled. 'What have they to do with it? I don't see . . . '

'I have kept a record,' I lied, 'of what we did together. Purely for scientific interest. Nothing more. I have nothing to be ashamed of and nothing to hide save to protect me against the misgivings of a few patients. I told you when I did the work I wanted to keep my name out of it for that reason. Now this matter hinges around my office equipment. All my information is kept in the computer and to do that, I have to give each file a name. I gave this one the fictitious name of Mouette, with a fictitious address. Without the name and address, the database will not accept the information . . . '

I went on to explain how I had recorded all our work together. It was so easy to fabricate, to lie to her. She seemed to believe everything and, by the time we reached the tea-house, was much calmer, much more relaxed. We entered the building, sat at a table. I ordered a pot of coffee.

'He's demanding money from me,' she declared, keeping her voice low although only a few of the other tables were occupied and those which were accommodated a Japanese tour party of which the photographer was one.

'And from me,' I confirmed. 'I think the best thing we can do is pay up, get him to shut up and get the files back. I have to do that, in any case, to protect my patients. He has, I feel, little he can use against any of my clients but one never knows. I suggest,' I went on, 'you leave it all to me.'

'But how did he get my name?'

'You're entered in the file. He only had to look up lists of scientists. I assume you're licensed to . . .'

'That will have been it!' Her voice betrayed her relief. 'I was thinking he was hanging around my house . . .'

'He's not that sort of man,' I said. 'He's a mercenary bastard but he's not in this to physically harm you. Or me. He just wants money.'

'Do you know how much?'

'Not yet. He's keeping me sweating for a bit.'

I had not realized it until then but the man's delay in contacting me was surely intended to unnerve me, get me wound up so I would meet his demands without equivocation. He was, I thought, a clever psychologist as well as a thief, a man who probably knew his trade as well as I did my own profession. I resolved there and then to resist his psychological ploys.

'He's asked me for fifteen thousand pounds. I simply haven't got that kind of cash.'

'Well, I have,' I replied, 'and I'll pay for both of us. I'll tell him that.'

'He'll want a lot more from you. He knows I'm only an archaeologist but you're a society doctor.'

A pot of coffee arrived. Ruth poured it and handed me a cup.

'I'm hardly a society doctor,' I said. 'I just deal with rich patients.'

'He's not to know that. He'll get you for every dime he can.'

I thought, as she sipped her coffee, how wrong she was. He knew exactly what I was and he was going to make me pay for it.

'Look,' I said, 'you've had a long journey up to town today, had a nasty shock from this damned blackmailer and you must be dead-beat. Can I suggest I take you out to dinner, you stay overnight at my place and go back to Oxford tomorrow?'

'I'm not exactly dressed for company,' she remarked, looking down at her jeans.

'In that case,' I replied, 'we'll keep clear of the classier joints.'

'It isn't necessary to take me out . . . ' she began.

'No,' I agreed, 'but I'd like to. A piece of sugar after the bitter pill.'

That night, we slept together. She was, I could tell, still afraid deep down inside herself. Making love released some of her fear but not all of it. Afterwards, she fell into a light and troubled sleep.

I lay on my back next to her, her head on my shoulder, staring at the ceiling and wondering if he knew she was here, was watching the practice in case I had called the police. Casting my mind back to our return from the restaurant, I tried to visualize what cars were parked in the mews and if any one of them was unusual.

Gradually, my thoughts moved back to the predicament I was in. If it all went wrong, if the information was leaked, if it all blew up, if the blackmailer managed to guess Mouette was all but synonymous with Cordiner, if Brian and Larry learnt the truth, it would not be me to suffer. Not ultimately. I would lose my practice, my profession, my reputation. I would be abandoned by the Arkassians. I would make tabloid headlines for a while and I would have to flee before the inevitability of a show trial, a critical summing up, an appearance before the ethics committee of the British Medical Association and, I doubted not, a term of imprisonment.

Yet the one who would suffer most would be Adam. I would lose my past but he would be robbed of his future.

◆

It was all so simple.

Four days after Ruth and I met, I again received a telephone call late at night.

'Dr Lyall?' the voice said.

I was not shocked. I was expecting it, was ready for him now. My mind was prepared and my decisions made.

'Yes,' I answered bluntly.

'Sure you haven't called the Bill, Dr Lyall? I'd hate for all this to go wrong. For your sake as much as mine.'

'I have not called the police,' I assured him.

'What about your little pet Yankie fuck? Do you think she has?'

'She has not,' I responded, feeling my anger rise but controlling it. It was imperative he did not see I was rattled. Nothing would be achieved if I gave way to my emotions.

'Good. Very good. Now, here are your instructions . . .'

'First,' I interrupted, 'I will be dealing on both Dr Schroeder's and my own behalf. I do not want you bothering her again. You may refer all your demands to her on to me.'

'Very gallant, doctor.' His irony was cruel and cutting. 'And although you're in no position to make terms, I'll accept. Your cash is as good as hers.'

'Second,' I continued, 'what guarantee do I have once I've paid you will return everything to me and that'll be the end of it?'

It was such a naïve question. And yet I had to ask it. He might have sensed something wrong had I not.

'None,' the voice said. 'You will have to trust me. The trust of one bent fucker for another.'

'I see,' I said flatly.

'Honour amongst gentlemen, Dr Lyall.' He laughed briefly, humourlessly. 'Now, these are your instructions. I want £75,000, all in £50 notes, all used, no sequential numbers. Don't withdraw it all on the same day. Spread it out over four days starting next Monday. Don't think you can dupe me. I've access to your bank account so I can check. I hope,' he added as an aside, 'you appreciate I'm not unduly stretching your resources. This'll leave you with . . . ' – there was a pause: I heard a computer keyboard clicking – ' . . . plenty in hand in your personal accounts.'

'How do you . . . ?'

'Don't underestimate me, Dr Lyall. And don't waste my time. Just pay attention. The money's to be banded as the bank provides it. That's thirty bundles, fifty notes in each. When you get them, they'll be in plastic bags. Remove those. Place it all in a used briefcase and don't lock it. Don't try and tamper with the money. No gentian violet, no malacite green. No trick locks, no explosive charges, no CI solvent red. You'll be opening the case before I do. You got all that?'

I reiterated his instructions.

'Good. I'll be in touch,' he said and instantly hung up.

As requested, I started to withdraw the money on the Monday morning, visiting my branch of Barclays Bank in Oxford Street. Due to a busy day on the Thursday, my final withdrawal was on the Wednesday lunch-time. He must have been scanning the bank computer on a regular basis for, no sooner had Molly left that evening than he rang.

'I said four days,' were his first words.

'I'm operating all tomorrow,' I replied, 'with no breaks.'

'OK.' He paused as a schoolmaster might listening to a miscreant pupil's weak excuse for cutting a lesson. 'I'll let it pass this time but don't go off on your own again. Understand?'

'I understand,' I said, gritting my teeth.

'Right, now we've got that over, listen carefully. Friday afternoon. You leave your office at two sharp. Take the tube to Hampstead. Go down Flask Walk into Well Walk. At the end, cross Heath Road and go across the heath towards Highgate Ponds. If I smell so much as a whiff of a rat, you're fucked.'

With that, he slammed the phone down.

As he requested, at two o'clock on Friday, I followed the route he dictated. It was a sunny afternoon, ideal for a walk across Hampstead Heath. I wore a dark grey suit, black shoes and matching calfskin gloves, the leather thin and supple. My briefcase was also black, quite heavy with its contents. To even the most observant onlooker, I must have appeared no more than a businessman breaking his day in the office with a constitutional or walking to an afternoon meeting having taken luncheon in one of the Hampstead pubs or restaurants.

The heath was busy with people walking their dogs, children running about, students sitting on the grass and lovers lying side by side under the trees. I reached the middle of the heath without anyone approaching me. From time to time, I looked around to see if I was being followed but there was no one on my tail. It was not until I started down the hill towards the ponds I became aware I was being watched. A man in jogging gear was keeping pace with me on a parallel pathway. His tracksuit top had a hood fitted to it which he had drawn over his head. His eyes were covered by wide, reflective sunglasses. Hanging from his shoulders was a rucksack which appeared to be half empty.

At a point where the paths converged, he came towards me.

'Afternoon, Dr Lyall.'

There was no mistaking his voice.

'Go down to the bench by the pond.' He pointed with a gloved hand. 'The one next to the litter bin.'

I set off as ordered. He jogged away. On reaching the bench, I sat down, a small flotilla of ducks heading towards me in expectancy of crumbs of sandwiches or stale crusts. There was no one close and the ducks regarded me as their only source of potential sustenance. Within a few minutes, the jogger appeared again and, moving behind the bench, ran his hands over the upper half of my body, feeling briefly under my armpits, patting cursorily at my pockets and the waistband of my trousers: then he sat at the end of the bench.

'Good boy,' he said patronizingly, as if to a pet dog. 'Glad to see you came alone. No friends and no heroics. Pity if you had a gun. I might have had to do something else. Still, no harm done. You know it makes sense, don't you?'

His lips curved in a grin. I made no reply but tried to penetrate his dark glasses. I did not want to see him to recognize him but just to know my enemy, to know what this bastard looked like, who had ruined everything.

He nodded in the direction of the case. 'Turn it round so it faces me. Open it. Not too wide, just half-way.'

I did as he asked. He looked into it for a long moment then slipped his hand under the lid. I heard his fingers flick through a bundle of notes.

'Looks all right. But then you wouldn't cheat me, would you? Not a doctor.'

'Seventy-five thousand,' I said. 'Plus fifteen for Dr Schroeder.'

'I won't count it. Not here. Now, close the lid slowly, reach over and snap the catches.'

I did as he commanded but, when he then reached for the case I drew it back.

'Where are my files?' I demanded.

He slung his knapsack off his shoulders, undid the plastic buckles and removed a fat, A4 sized bundle sealed with Sellotape and tied about with parcel string. This he placed next to the briefcase, propping it against the bars of the back of the bench but keeping his hand on it.

'Is that all the files?' I enquired.

'Most of them. The file on Mysterious Mr & Mrs Mouette is here,' he said. 'And the floppy disks.'

'How do I know you've not kept a back-up copy of the computer information?'

His lips curled in a half-smile again as he answered, 'You don't.'

'And the rest of the files?'

'They're mine, Dr Lyall. Just three or four. They've got some interesting stuff in them.'

'But . . . ' I began to stutter.

'But, shit!' he retorted. 'You're buying your peace of mind, Dr Lyall. Your little bit of the action and all the dross, the crap with nothing in it of interest. The rest'll run for a while yet. Now, you take this or you leave it?'

I had no choice. I closed the briefcase, pushed it along the bench and reached for the bundle. He let it go and started to slide the briefcase into the rucksack.

It was now or never. I glanced round to ensure we were still alone, reached into my pocket and took out the syringe with a wide bore hypodermic needle glued to it with a super-strength adhesive. Handling it through the calfskin was no more difficult than if I had been using it with surgical gloves in an operating theatre.

Flicking off the green plastic needle sheath, I leaned quickly towards him and rammed the needle through the material of his tracksuit and into the side of his belly. For a split second, I felt the nylon of his clothing resist the point but then it was through and in. I depressed the syringe, leaving it in his side. It all happened so quickly he was quite taken by surprise. Having ascertained I was not armed, he was at a loss.

'What the fuck . . . ?' he began, involuntarily plucking the syringe out and dropping it on the bench where it slipped through the wooden slats to the ground.

Immobilon is a veterinary drug, a mixture of etorphine hydrochloride, a morphine derivative and acepromazine maleate, a tranquillizer. It is the stuff used to sedate horses, dart elephants and, sometimes, to put down senile or dangerous animals.

Obtaining a vial of the drug had been simple. I captured one of the oldest of the mangy alley cats which hung around the dustbins at the end of the mews and, playing the part of a concerned owner, took it to a vet in Maida Vale. He agreed to put it down and, whilst his back was turned doing the deed, I removed one 5ml dosage bottle from the polystyrene box in his cabinet.

The solution I had injected into the blackmailer was enough to kill a bull. There is an antidote called Revivon but I had stolen none of that and, besides, it would have to have been administered within a minute to be effective.

He made no other comment. His breathing suddenly shortened, one hand going to his throat and the other to his side. I leaned over and took the briefcase out of his rucksack.

It was not thirty seconds since the needle had punctured him. His face was red. I could actually hear his heart racing.

He tore his gloves off, snatched at his hood and flung his sunglasses aside.

I stared at him. He was such an ordinary-looking young man. His hair was ginger-ish and wavy, cut short and quite wiry. His face was freckled and his eyes dark blue. He was clean-shaven and wore a small gold stud ear-ring.

The veins on his neck, on his face, on his hands stood out like cords. His brow oozed sweat and he fought for breath. His legs began to jerk and his arms started to spasm.

How strange it was, watching a man die after so many years. Death had not visited me since my sleepless nights on the emergency wards. My world had become one of creation, not destruction. Whenever a patient miscarried or a baby was stillborn, I did not somehow regard it as a death but simply as a hurdle on the path to eventual being: my every action was dispassionately and logically directed towards creating life. Yet now I was taking it away just as dispassionately and, I told myself as he gurgled incoherently, in order to continue with the process. It was not just my selfish motivation of which I was aware: by killing this ginger-haired thief I was protecting Adam.

There was no regret in me. I considered the blackmailer now not as a man, as a thing of creation, but as a mere obstacle, another hurdle to be jumped. He was little more to me than a sample of human tissue winding down and ceasing its activity. He might have been a tumour in a kidney dish, heading for the hospital incinerator.

As his fingers flexed open and shut, a marvellous and omniscient power came over me. I thought, with a cold detachment, this was how it truly felt to be a god.

I stood up, said nothing to him and retrieved the syringe from under the bench, replacing the sheath and putting it back in my pocket. This done, I picked up the briefcase, bundle of files and computer disks, walking away along the edge of the pond, the ducks following me as if knowing he was unlikely to throw them anything. Within a few minutes, I was in Fitzroy Park where I had left the Porsche.

Starting the engine, I drove south to Kentish Town, halting at a telephone box.

My hands did not shake, my mind was clear. For a while, I sat calmly behind the steering-wheel and considered my situation quite dispassionately, much as I might step back from the operating table and look down not upon a human breathing shallowly under an anaesthetic but upon a problem to the solving of which I held the key.

Like any assassin, I was sure I would not be discovered. I had worn gloves so there were no fingerprints on the park bench, on the rucksack. No one had been close enough to observe our meeting. The pathway round the pond was metalled and I had left no footprints. I had my files in my possession. When the police finally traced the man's background, it was possible they might find the few files he had stolen from me and retained, but that was insufficient to link me to his death and a risk I was obliged to accept: besides, he most probably had data stolen from other sources and I would be but one of a number of victims.

Nevertheless, for fifteen minutes or so I considered my options and went over my plans, my excuses, my alibi.

At last, locking the car, I made just the one call.

'Ruth?' I said.

'Yes.' Her voice was tentative, like a patient awaiting the results of a laboratory test which might have been good but could have been bad.

'It's Dom,' I continued unnecessarily. 'There's nothing to worry about now. I've paid him. He won't bother us again.'

'Are you certain?'

'Yes,' I assured her, 'I'm quite certain.'

I heard her sigh. It was not so much a release of tension as a huge, deep, clean breath. She might have been sucking in her first gulp of mountain air after a month in the city.

Hanging up, I noticed the ground behind the telephone box was littered with the garbage of urban desolation – cigarette ends and crumpled packets, dog turds, broken bottles and jagged cans, sweet wrappers, wind-blown newspaper and several addicts' syringes: to this detritus I added my own, dropping my hypodermic amongst the others.

Returning to the car, a wave of almost placid euphoria swept over me. Ruth and I were now safe but so, I told myself, was Adam. The secret was laid to rest once more.

◆

It all began with a snake.

For three days, Chuhi was absent from the clearing. He had set off on his own into the jungle without so much as a backward glance. No one waved him off or wished him luck. He merely walked into the shadow of the trees and was gone. When he finally returned, late on the afternoon of the third day, he carried a boa constrictor about three metres long wrapped around his shoulder like a coil of rope. Its back was decorated by roughly triangular, dark brown patches like saddles with lighter, buff-coloured centres and diamond shapes of the same colouring down its sides. The snake's tail was a dark pink with the diamonds towards its tip turning from pale brown to weak scarlet. It had recently sloughed its skin and shone as if polished. Even in death it had lost none of its sheen.

Upon seeing him, the people of the clearing became unaccountably excited. I mused at this. They frequently saw snakes and often caught or killed them without so much as a second thought yet this one prompted a near frenzy of chatter. Only Keewei seemed to remain aloof from the general hubbub.

A fire was lit in the communal hearth in the centre of the clearing, a smoke-blackened iron cauldron I had not previously seen placed upon it, and filled with water. When it was boiling, the snake was coiled into it like a bizarre stick of spaghetti. All the people, from the youngest babe in arms to a wizened old man called Pa'ui, gathered round the fire.

The sun went down but no one left the circle. Women sidled off on occasion, but only to return with firewood or small strips of dried fish or meat which the men and children sucked. No one spoke. It was eerie. The people, normally so full of conversation amongst themselves, were subdued as if entranced. Even the dogs moved about in silence, not snarling at each other or contesting scraps or sleeping hollows in the dirt.

I watched all this from my porch. No one invited me to join in and I considered it best not to saunter over. This was clearly no ordinary gathering. It was not until the evening was almost turned to night that someone departed the circle and came towards me. It was, as usual, Chuhi.

'*Señor*,' he said, '*ven*,' and he beckoned.

I followed him across to the fire where a space was found for me in the circle. A few of the men nodded briefly to acknowledge my arrival but that was all. I politely nodded back, wondering what was going to happen next.

At first, we just sat staring at the flames under the cauldron but then, once it was quite dark, Keewei left the gathering, went towards the long-houses and returned dressed in his jaguar skin pillbox hat and unlaced violet trimmed Reeboks. Whatever was going to happen, it was obviously an event of importance. For a moment, I felt I should rise myself to fetch my stethoscope and white coat, at least pin my useless dosimeter to my shirt, but I sensed to leave the gathering would be frowned upon, somehow break a spell which was beginning to weave itself about us.

In front of him, Keewei carried a bundle held almost reverentially in two hands which he placed on the smooth fireside stone: the wrapping of intertwined leaves fell away to reveal Rodriguez's head, his shoulder-length hair tied into a top-knot with a cord. I was instantly reminded of the woman swinging the howler monkey's head on to the same stone and the crack of its skull.

Q'eke and Manyo knelt beside the head, their fingers lightly caressing it then suddenly flicking to one side into the fire as if they were taking moisture from the grotesque thing. For several minutes, they performed this rite, everyone watching them intently. This done, Manyo raised the head up and, with deft movements of a knife, Q'eke sliced the skin below the right ear, sliding the blade under it to cut it loose. I was reminded of a face-lift operation I had once observed. With quick jerks and more nicks and cuts, he peeled the skin off the head as easily as one might skin a cat. He paused only at the eyes, nose and lips, to cut round them so they should not snag the operation: the eyes themselves he gouged out and tossed in the fire where they hissed and shrivelled. The people sighed at this as if the act was releasing them from some terrible, pent-up emotion. When the skull was flayed, Chuhi took it away: a few moments later came a splash from the river. The people sighed again.

The skin, which had come off inside-out, was reversed and, a stick passed through the hair, it was lowered into the cauldron by Keewei who chanted incoherently as he did so. Every so often, he lifted it clear of the water, muttered a louder incantation and let it drop into the liquid again. From the pot rose a faint waxy smell which, despite the experiences of a medical career, turned my stomach.

Chuhi noticed my discomfiture and passed me a broad, smooth leaf, indicating I chew upon it. I took it and put it in my mouth wondering, as I did so, if he had washed his hands since tossing the head in the water. The leaf was acidic but sweet, like a pear drop, and it quickly soothed my stomach. Others around the fire, I now noticed, were also chewing on leaves. Clearly, I thought, I was not the only one to feel queasy.

After about half an hour, the cauldron was removed from the flames, the scalp removed and spread on the smooth stone where it quickly dried.

As soon as the thing was drying, the people started to chatter normally and a large fish was roasted over the flames, people breaking pieces off as it cooked and eating them. A bowl of *yamanachi* began to circulate and I shared in this, spitting the masticated leaf into the fire as the others were doing.

As we ate, Q'eke and Manyo disappeared, returning stark naked, their bodies oiled and glistening by the light of a three-quarter moon which had risen to compete with the fire. Along the profile of their ribs and arm bones they had painted black lines, their faces darkened save around the eyes and mouth.

'*Hombres muertos*,' Chuhi muttered, adding, 'He ees die.'

Rodriguez's scalp was removed from the stone: it looked like a piece of flaccid pale leather. Keewei pierced holes around the cut below the ear and around the neck, threading a length of twine through them so the head became a sort of draw-string bag. I was reminded instantly of a bizarre comparison: it was not unlike the little canvas bag containing marbles I had owned as a child. This done, he sewed the mouth, eyelids and nose up tight, the skin pinching in.

I watched with a cool, morbid fascination. I was not disgusted nor was I afraid this might one day be my fate; nor was I sorry, for Rodriguez had tried to kill me. If anything, I was resigned to this brutality. And, in any case, I could hardly censure it. I had myself killed a man and, I considered as Keewei did his grotesque sewing, in a far more calculated and violent fashion than that in which Chuhi and the others had disposed of Rodriguez. They had assassinated the amber trader in order to protect me, to defend their friend or one of their number whereas I had murdered my victim for only one reason – malicious self-preservation. Of course, I told myself, I also did it for Adam but this was a partial excuse, an aside after the fact.

Watching Keewei at work was, I supposed, an instructive punishment of sorts, a lesson by which I might learn and come to terms with my own wickedness, a trial I had to endure in preparation for my entry into hell. For, as I sat around the fire with the people of the clearing staring fixedly at the head-bag, I realized I was no different from them. They hated and killed, loved and treasured just as I did. They lacked only my technological skill, the knowledge that had, in so many ways, been my downfall. Under it all, we were one, driven by the same urge to survive, to test the world around us, to somehow control it and make it obey. The only other difference was they worshipped their gods and I played at being mine.

A flat iron plate was placed upon the fire by two women who then poured river sand on to it from a basket, spreading it out with a stick. For a short while it steamed then became dry and started to crackle. Keewei inverted the head, holding it open like a little sack. With a wooden spatula, Q'eke tipped the hot sand into it, Keewei shaking it vigorously to let it settle into every fold and cranny of the skin. They did not stop until the head was full. Keewei drew the twine tight around the neck. Drops of liquid started to ooze from the skin as if the dead man's soul was sweating. I looked at where it splashed upon the smooth stone. It was fat seeping out through the pores.

When no more liquid appeared, the three men set about kneading and shaping the head as children might a ball of plasticine. They pressed and smoothed with their thumbs, massaged and pulled with their fingers, polished it with the balls of their palms. At last, the head looked like a caricature of Rodriguez.

I no longer wanted to be a part of this ceremony. I had seen enough to recognize myself in the clearing folk, to know I was nothing more than they were, a confused jumble of primitive hatred and fears, ambitions and determinations, none of which I wanted to acknowledge.

I went to my hut and lay fully clothed upon my bed, staring up at the ceiling. Later, I fell into a restless sleep in which Rodriguez stood in the mews with a bundle of files in his hand and Adam, dressed like a miniature *gaucho*, toyed with a pistol he pointed at my head: and when Rodriguez spoke, it was with Ruth's voice.

◆

It was a miserable morning, a dreary London drizzle falling which was not light enough to be fog but not heavy enough to be rain. It had settled in raised bubbles on the polished bonnet of the Porsche which I had not stored in the lock-up garage I rented at the end of the mews. I had not come home until after three, having attended to a multiple birth at a private clinic near Woking. There had been complications and I had thought I might have had to carry out a caesarean but, in the end, it was unnecessary. Both babies appeared to be hale and well on their way to their first Polaroid photograph and my noticeboard.

I was just dressing when there was a ring on the bell. I glanced at my alarm clock: it was just after seven. Ever since my encounter on Hampstead Heath, I had become a little nervous of unexpected events. During the bustle of the working day, I was unruffled but a wrong number late at night, a call from a worried patient out of surgery hours or the sound of a vehicle in the mews in the early hours set my nerves momentarily on edge.

The discovery of the corpse slouching on the bench, by a father and his son sailing boats upon the pond, had made the headlines in the evening press and on local radio news. The newspapers suggested, as the ginger-haired man was a known felon, sometime heroin dealer and member of the underworld, his death by lethal injection was probably an act of bizarre retribution within the criminal fraternity and, as the days passed, the story was overtaken by other events. As no police officer visited me on the matter, I presumed nothing had been uncovered to tie me in to the blackmailer's death just as, according to Inspector Rhys, no progress had been made on discovering who had burgled my surgery.

From time to time, I wondered if perhaps it would not be the police but some shady confederate of the corpse who would seek me out, that I might be the victim of an underworld killing rather than my erstwhile protagonist but, gradually, this fear faded in me just as all irrationalities tend to do.

Nevertheless, I very cautiously edged the curtains of my window aside but could see nothing to concern me in the mews.

Assuming it to be the postman, for he frequently called before eight, I went down the stairs and opened the door to discover Ruth standing close in to the door, a battered briefcase under her arm.

'Ruth!' I exclaimed and looked at my watch to confirm the time. 'What are you doing here at this hour? I . . . '

'I want to talk to you.' Her voice was little more than a mutter. 'Now.'

She pushed past me and went up the stairs. I followed with a growing apprehension. She did not stop in the surgery but went through into my apartment where she stood in the sitting-room. Hanging on the wall behind her was Adam's best picture.

'You bastard!' she exclaimed quietly. 'You unscrupulous, total asshole.' Her face was tight with anger, her eyes dull, the corner of her mouth twitching ever so slightly.

'What is the matter?' I asked. 'Please, sit down.'

She remained on her feet.

'What is the matter?' she mimicked my accent before slipping back into her own. 'You knowing fucking well.'

She was near to breaking, her hands clenching on her briefcase which she now held before her. I knew I had to calm her down for I would no more be able to reason with her hysterical anger than I could with the hysterical despair of patients whom I, and god and nature, had let down.

'Unless you tell me,' I said, 'I can hardly help you.'

'I don't need your goddamn help. Nor your goddamn patronizing. I want . . . ' She paused, taking a deep breath: I wondered if her rage was about to collapse but I was wrong.

'You want what?' I enquired, keeping as calm as I could.

'Who are the Mouettes?'

'They are patients of mine,' I bluffed, sitting down across a low coffee-table from her. 'I cannot discuss their affairs.'

'The fuck they are!' she almost shouted. 'Mouette! No such person.' She flung her briefcase on the table, the buckles scratching the wood. I could hear the blackmailer's voice speaking through her. 'And no address either. There's no

Havingdene Road in London. You've been up to something, you son of a bitch. And I've a shrewd idea what.'

She sat down then and was silent for a moment, breathing hard as if her tirade had actually exhausted her, like a quick sprint or a run up a long flight of steps. I said nothing for I thought the longer I remained silent, the more the play in this confrontation would fall to my advantage. When she seemed somewhat more composed, I spoke. 'What is it you think I've done?'

'I'll tell you what you've done. I don't think it, I know it. You took a sample from my axeman and you cultured it. You wouldn't do that for me, you bastard, but you did it for yourself. You fertilized an oöcyte with it. Maybe more than one. You managed to get it to work.' She slammed her hand hard down on her briefcase, skidding the buckles on the table again. 'And then . . .'

'And then?' I asked.

'I don't know. Maybe you . . . Perhaps . . . ' She was either trying to come to terms with her imagination, or the possibility of my actions, or hoping to have me confess there and then.

'If you don't know,' I replied, speaking evenly and quietly, 'you shouldn't jump to conclusions.'

She made no response but stared at her briefcase with such loathing I wondered what it might contain.

'This much I will tell you,' I began. 'I did take a sample from your axeman. Only out of curiosity. And I did try to fertilize a number of oöcytes with it. The material, of course, was not motile being long dead. I injected the equivalent of one sperm through the cellular membrane. It's not an uncommon technique where a patient's sperm is of reasonable quality but unable of its own volition to penetrate the oöcyte. And yes, the oöcyte was fertilized. But . . . '

'Enough!' she said, but her voice was low and almost threatening. 'Just tell me this. When do you intend to publish?'

'I did not and do not intend publication,' I replied. 'Indeed, this was never my intention. I merely wanted to see, from academic or professional curiosity, if you will, if it was possible.'

'And then?'

'When my work was complete, I would have let you know. You could have had the data and used it to repeat the experiments, taking them . . . ' I halted. 'Taking them to whatever conclusion you wished. I could not possibly . . . ' I let my words hang in the air.

'Why didn't you trust me?' she asked.

It was my turn to saying nothing. In truth, I could not answer her for I did not really know. Perhaps it was vanity, a fear of being accused of impropriety and facing the ethics committee, a desire to tread new ground myself, a distrust of her after all. She was not my mistress, my partner. I had no reason to believe I could safely confide in her. There again, perhaps it was not the knowledge but the power I had discovered over creation which I did not want to share.

'So what did you do with the oöcytes. Where are they now?' Ruth enquired. 'Did you section them? Freeze them? Keep a record of them? Have a DNA analysis?'

I said nothing.

'What did you do with them?' she asked again.

I evaded her question and answered, 'How did you discover all this?'

'I was sent some photocopies. Of printouts. By registered post.' She pointed to her briefcase. I turned it over, undid the buckles and removed a large manila envelope bearing several high denomination stamps and a recorded delivery label. I did not need to look inside the envelope.

'The blackmailer must have sent them,' she declared.

I looked closely at the smudged postmark on the envelope: the date was discernible and I did a quick calculation. Whoever had posted it had done so two days after I had walked across Hampstead Heath cautiously nursing a hypodermic syringe full of Immobilon in my pocket.

Sitting back in my chair, I let the envelope drop to the table. My head felt light, as if I was coming round from a fainting attack. My hands weighed nothing and the room around me appeared strange, as if I was waking in an unfamiliar place. My cheeks were cold.

It wasn't over. The blackmailer had an accomplice with access to my stolen files. The material had not been in the blackmailer's hideaway for the police to find and for this reason they had not been able to link the corpse by the pond to me: but this someone could, and he was calling the game now. My early afternoon stroll in the park had been in vain.

'Are you all right, Dom?' It was Ruth's voice. I looked at her. I must have been ashen for she put her hand against my temple to test my temperature.

'You've gone quite white,' she stated.

I gathered my wits.

'Have you shown these papers to anyone else?'

'No,' she said.

I picked up the envelope and got up. I felt a little giddy but under control. 'Wait here,' I ordered, left the room, went to Molly's reception desk and switched the shredder on. It sucked through the envelope and its contents, depositing them as tangled ribbons in the bin below.

When I returned, Ruth was sitting where I had left her, her hands on the arms of the chair.

'There's nothing to fear now. I have my disks. In exchange for the ransom. You may take them and use the data as you will. But it's best not to have a printout floating around.'

She nodded her agreement and said, 'I thought you were going to undermine my research. Publish ahead of me. That sort of thing.'

'No,' I assured her, and it was the truth, 'I was not. Now,' I looked at my watch, 'my staff will be arriving soon and I've a heavy day's schedule. Can I suggest we meet later? Will you be in town all day?'

'I'm going back to Oxford,' she said and she stood up, bending down to take her briefcase.

'I'll be in touch,' I promised, yet I somehow knew it was a lie.

She turned and then saw Adam's drawing. For a moment,

she looked away and took one step towards the door. Then she stopped and looked hard at the picture again.

'Dom . . . ' she said in a near whisper, not turning around.

'Yes.'

'You did it, didn't you?'

'Did it?' I repeated.

'Mr and Mrs Mouette.'

'Yes,' I admitted, 'I did it.' There was no longer any reason to deny it.

'And it worked,' she said: it was not a question but a statement.

I did not see any point in responding.

Still, Ruth did not look at me but gazed at the picture. At least a minute must have passed with her staring at the wall and me looking at her back.

'Do they know?'

'They do not.'

'We must tell them,' she said after a lengthy pause. 'They must know.'

'No,' I declared. 'They must not.'

She turned round quickly, her eyes sharp with tears. 'Yes, they must! It isn't fair otherwise. Their child . . . '

'If this knowledge gets out,' I said flatly, 'the child will be regarded as a freak. Every paediatrician, scientist, DNA lab, professor and the rest will want to see him. Every journalist, every camera crew in the world will want to photograph him, interview him, study him. He'll be little more than a scientific curiosity, a wonder, a test bed for experiments, a walking gene pool dating back . . . '

Ruth put her hand on my arm. It was not a gentle touch. 'That,' she said, 'is something you should have thought about.' She let go of me, opened the door and went out. I followed her down to the entrance.

'I'll be in touch, Dom,' she said.

I detected a terrible coldness in her words and sensed what she was thinking. At last, she had within her grasp a discovery so remarkable, so terrifyingly incredible, she hardly dared believe it. Perhaps she was afraid to, yet she did.

Watching her as she unlocked her car, I knew the awesome truth of her last words. She was certain to be in touch, would never be satisfied now, not until she had met Adam, seen him standing before her, put her hand on him, taken her samples and focused her microscope, set her DNA machine to busily churn out its fuzzy bar code pictures.

She got into her car which she had parked at the entrance to the mews, started the engine, drove by me to the far end of the mews and reversed around, careful to avoid my neighbour's brand-new Daimler. Returning towards the street, she stopped by me and wound down the window. 'Do you know what it means?' she asked.

I nodded. 'Yes,' I replied.

And I did. It meant the end of everything was drawing near.

◆

The call, when it came, was curt and to the point. Molly put it through to me just before the morning's first appointment so there was no coded warning, no time for me to prepare myself for it.

'Dr Lyall?' the voice said. It had the tone of efficient officiousness about it.

'Yes, speaking,' I responded.

'Good morning, Dr Lyall. My name's Jonathan Clague,' he introduced himself, adding, 'I'm a journalist.' He paused, perhaps to put me off my guard but by now I was ready for him, whoever he was.

'I see,' I replied. 'And what may I do for you?'

'I'm a journalist on the *Sunday Times* Insight team,' he continued. 'We've received a package of documents purporting to be printouts from your computer.' His voice was even, urbane yet inquisitorial.

'May I ask how you obtained these?' I enquired, but the question was rhetorical: I knew where they had come from. The accomplice had sent them.

'They came anonymously but they look to be genuine. I understand you had a robbery lately?'

'Yes,' I admitted, 'I did.'

'And the police have drawn a blank?'

'So far,' I concurred, 'they have.'

He paused again. I could hear him shuffling the pages of a notebook and wondered what he knew that he was withholding.

'May I ask, have you been contacted by a blackmailer?'

'No, I have not as yet had any approach,' I lied then, feeling I should take the offensive, added, 'If the material you hold is genuine, I must ask you to treat it with the utmost confidentiality. Not for my own sake, you understand, but for that of my patients. The files I maintain include a good deal of sensitive information . . .'

'Quite,' he interrupted. 'I understand. And, in connection with this, I wonder if you would be so good as to grant me an interview. I appreciate your time may be at a premium but I can fit in to see you at your convenience.'

'I shall be free towards the start of next week,' I stalled. 'Perhaps Monday, late afternoon?'

'I was hoping to see you before then,' he said. 'It is important we clear the matter up and I should return these papers to you. But I have some questions to ask you about one of your patients.'

He did not need to give me the name. I knew it already. Suddenly, I felt tired, resigned, bored with the whole subterfuge but I had to maintain it.

'Might I drop by to see you later today?' Clague continued. 'About six, perhaps? After your surgery closes, of course.'

I waited for a moment as if studying my diary then conceded. 'I'm afraid I'm otherwise engaged tonight. Perhaps tomorrow evening?' I asked, buying as much time as possible. 'Could you make, say, seven o'clock?'

He agreed. I put down the phone. My mind was quite set. I was not afraid. With my hand now being forced, I put into operation the plan I had determined after the murder for just this eventuality.

◆

A stern voice behind me said, 'May I help you?' in the kind of tone one might usually associate with fractious mothers superior, hospital matrons and buxom traffic wardens with sore feet. I turned to face a woman in her early middle age dressed in a pair of denim dungarees, her hair knotted into an unkempt bun and a child's watch upon her wrist. On the wall behind her was a puerile painting of a woman which could conceivably have been a caricature of her.

'This is St Catherine's Junior School?' I enquired, although I knew full well it was from the sign by the gate to the playground.

I was acting the ignorant in order to strengthen my hand: a man double-checking the most obvious of details is always to be trusted. That was something medical school taught me or, to be more precise, a Dr Hämmerstrom who decreed a patient who saw a surgeon meticulously going over pre-op details which he knew off by heart was filled with confidence and went to the table a happier man: that, as the tutor pointed out in his sing-song Scandinavian accent, was a part of the 'show-biz of medical practice' and applied whether one had carried out the procedure a thousand times or if this was one's first look at a spleen, pancreas or whatever.

'Yes, this is St Catherine's,' she snapped. 'May I ask you what you want?'

'I'm Dr Lyall, Adam Cordiner's godfather,' I said. 'I telephoned the school about half an hour ago.'

She thought for a moment before replying, 'Ah, yes, of

course. Do you have identification? We can't be too careful these days, you know.'

'Quite so,' I agreed and, smiling at the irony of her statement, handed her a security pass to one of the hospitals I sometimes visited. With the perspicacity of a zealous border guard in a banana republic, she studied the card and my signature, muttering my address to herself as if vocalizing it gave it some kind of bona fides and glancing up to compare my face to the photograph imbedded in the clear plastic. 'This seems to be in order,' she decided. 'Can you give me the details once more?'

'Mr and Mrs Cordiner have been called away today to the bedside of a sick relative. I have a cottage in the village and have agreed to look after Adam in their absence. However, I also have a patient to attend to in Musgrove Park Hospital, Taunton and will not be able to pick Adam up when school closes. I have, therefore, come for him now. He will,' I added, seeing the woman was about to question me, 'be properly cared for by my housekeeper whilst I see to my patient. I am a private practitioner.'

It was all a fabrication. Brian was in his dental surgery and Larry, I knew, had gone to Bath: she had, since the start of the academic term, been travelling once a week to the university to teach an extra-mural class in art history. At no time had I ever set foot in the Taunton hospital. However, any doubts the teacher may have had were assuaged by my last sentence.

'I'll fetch Adam now, sir,' she stated abruptly and began to turn away.

'Before you do,' I said hurriedly, 'can you tell me how he is at school? As his godfather . . . '

She softened a little and replied, 'He is, quite frankly, a remarkable child, doctor. He mixes well with the other children, has many friends and is surprisingly even-tempered for his age. Never throws a tantrum, never fights at playtime. Indeed, the other boys seem to look up to him, even those in the year above, but he does not seek to become the leader of his little gang. On the contrary, he can be quite withdrawn and I wonder if he's happy but he soon snaps out of it. It's nothing to worry about, not unusual in gifted children. They can slip into a fantasy world. He has,' she paused to choose her words, 'a certain charisma. Quite charming in one so young. An exemplary pupil. Not precocious, though. I would predict, as much as one can at this age, he will go far. A very clever little boy.'

'Clever in what ways?' I enquired.

'His ability with language is excellent and he has a vocabulary well beyond his age. His reading is that of a nine-year-old at least. He is mathematically aware and his art work – well, as you can see, we place a lot in a child's ability with the brush and crayon.' She looked at the wall to give her next statement credence. 'Art is a great social leveller, doctor. It allows the not-so-well advantaged to shine in the light of others' perhaps more developed skills.'

With that, she was gone. An electric bell sounded on the wall. From a classroom came the sound of childish prattle, a woman's voice raised above it, subduing it slightly. Down a long corridor lined with primary school-sized chairs echoed a chant of some sort whilst a piano tinkled distantly.

I turned my attention to the paintings on the wall. They were untidy, childish, the paint ran on some of them. Bright yellow suns shone on black and white animals which might have been cows. Trees looked like green lollipops and clouds were tufts of cotton wool glued to the paper. A portrait of a dog was made from pieces of hessian stuck to the drawn outline of a kennel.

After a few minutes, the teacher reappeared with Adam. He saw me and skipped towards me.

'Hello, Uncle Dom,' he called out.

I watched the teacher's face: this response was what she had been looking for, a far better set of credentials than my hospital pass.

Greeting him, I thanked the teacher for fetching him and apologized for the inconvenience: then, taking his hand, I walked him out of the building, across the playground and over to the Porsche. I sensed the teacher watching us, felt the moment when she looked away, finally satisfied by my expensive car.

'What is happening? Where are we going?' Adam enquired as I started the engine.

'It's a huge surprise,' I said. 'You and I are going on a holiday together. It's for your birthday.'

'My birthday's not yet,' Adam replied.

'True,' I conceded, 'but when it is your birthday, I shall be away and not able to give you a present. You'll be seven and that's big. So this is an early present. Instead of one then.'

'I'll have to pack my case,' he declared.

'All done,' I told him. 'You don't need English clothes where we're going. More . . . '

'Are we going in a plane?' Adam asked, his voice shrill with excitement.

'We are. Several planes.'

We reached a main road and I turned left towards the motorway. It would take us less than an hour to reach Bristol airport.

'Shouldn't we say good-bye to Mummy and Daddy?' Adam said.

A wave of sudden terror ran up my spine, a jab of sorrow so hard, so vicious, it was of the sort which might have been caused by his father probing an unanæsthetised nerve in a rotten molar. For a long moment, I was silent, then I said, 'No. They know. It's all part of the surprise.'

I had made my preparations for this day, for the rest of my life – our lives – with all the meticulous attention of a theatre sister setting out the equipment for a particularly testing operation.

When starting my planning, my biggest fear was how I might obtain a passport for Adam but, to my amazement, this was the easiest part of the whole process. All I had to do was to add his name to my own passport in a hand not too similar to my everyday writing. I packed some books into parcels, ensuring whilst some of them were basic medical tomes, others might be of some vague interest to me in the future, useful to while away the years ahead: my collected Dickens, the tragedies of Shakespeare, an edition of *The Golden Treasury*, the only poetry book I possessed. With these I placed such basic equipment as my stethoscope, a few thermometers and the like, mailing everything poste restante to Santo Antonio do Içá. In addition, I sent several parcels of clothes, both for myself and for Adam. I toyed with the idea of including some educational materials – pens, pencils, crayons, a few junior school textbooks or exercise pads – but decided against it. What education Adam might need was to suit him for his new world, not the old one.

Having destroyed the back-up disk kept at Cobb End and shredded the folder from the filing cabinet, my final task was to take a printout of the entire hidden file in the computer. Switching on the printer, I logged on to the appropriate file name and typed *print c: Mouette.doc*. It was as simple as that. Within twenty minutes, the entire contents of the file existed as a stack of neat pages. This done, I returned to the computer and typed *del c: Mouette.doc*. For a moment, I paused before hitting the enter key: just the touch of my finger would erase it all. I pressed the key. *Are you sure?* the computer enquired, in a single bleak line on the screen. I touched Y. The disk hummed for several seconds and that was it. A disk compression then assured the disk space where the file had resided was over-written by other data.

Santo Antonio do Içá was chosen more or less at random, searching through the *Times* atlas for somewhere remote, lost to the world. Like any serious sinner, I was not prepared to surrender, or die, or admit my wrongdoings, but to hide.

I had no plans for our future but sensed, as a man of medicine, I would be able to find work. Wherever men live in poverty the priest and the doctor can be assured of employment, one to kill the pains of the living, the other to assuage the anguish of death.

A few miles from the airport, I stopped the car, removed a large brown envelope from the glove compartment and, telling

Adam I'd only be a minute, entered a village post office. It was small, crowded with racks of postcards and birthday cards, shelves of envelopes and stationery, boxes of yellow Bic pens and tins of coloured pencils, rolls of brown paper and packets of labels. The postmaster stood behind a toughened glass screen on to which were stuck notices about pensions, a forthcoming rise in the cost of stamps, an advertisement for television licences and a warning of future public holiday closing hours. On the counter were piled Post Office leaflets and a set of bus timetables.

'Can I 'elp you?' he asked.

I must have been hesitant for he looked at me most suspiciously, wondering if I was there to buy stamps or hold him up.

'I want to post a first-class letter,' I said, pushing the envelope under the glass screen, 'by recorded delivery.'

The postmaster dropped the envelope on a set of scales. 'Bit 'eavy,' he remarked. 'That'll be sixty-seven pee plus fifty-five pee recorded.'

I slid a £5 note under the screen and he pushed a recorded delivery label back at me. 'Fill it in,' he said and he tore off the required stamps from sheets in a folder.

'You ain't filled in the sender's address,' he admonished me as I returned the label to him. 'Can't accept it unless it's got it.'

I did not argue: I just wrote a fictitious sender's address. He stuck the stamps on the envelope, franked the posting certificate and thrust it back to me with my change. I looked down at the address on the slip: *Mr & Mrs B. Cordiner*, I read, *Dell Cottage, Harbury, Somerset TA14 2NN*.

Soon, I thought, they would know everything, what I had done and why I had done it. I made no excuses. An excuse is a cowardly device, one of man's greatest failings: it is better to seek a remedy to self-inflicted misfortune rather than make an excuse. I think I may have written as much in my letter.

Leaving the post office and its breviloquent owner, I

returned to the car with the sense of having lightened my load a little. There was, of course, no justification in this: I had ruined the lives of two friends, destroyed them unequivocally and irreparably. My emotion was really one of pure, unadulterated selfishness but I would never have admitted as much to myself. Not then.

We checked in at the airline desk. The flight coupons were in order. The ticketing clerk, a pretty brunette in an airline uniform, smiled politely and wished us a good flight. At the departure hall entrance, as the immigration officer took my passport, I had a strong desire – just for a moment – to turn back, admit everything, stop the charade, halt the merry-go-round of fate upon which I was embarking. Yet, looking down at Adam standing by my side, a little in-flight bag I had bought for him in his hand and his face bright with boyish wonder and excitement, I knew I had to do it. For him, if not for me.

There were several instances when I wondered if I might be found out, if the official checking boarding passes at the entrance to the departure lounge might smell a rat or the x-ray security machine indicate the bundles of used banknotes in my briefcase. When the immigration officer, holding my passport open, scanned a printed list on a clipboard I sensed my heart rate increase noticeably. He saw me watching him, smiled and said, 'Abscondees. Custody cases and so on.'

'Of course,' I replied and thought how, within the next twenty-four hours, my name would be on his register.

I had timed it all very carefully. We had less than thirty minutes to wait to board the commuter flight to Brussels. Adam wandered into the duty free shop but he did not wish to buy anything: unlike the other children in the departure lounge, heading off on holiday and eager to buy with the acquisitive habit of their like, he was satisfied just to look. When the flight was called, we boarded and, as the aircraft jets whined up a note and the fuselage started to shake then roll forwards, a strange peace came upon me.

The adventure was embarked upon, the escape was made. All there was now was the future and the process of existing.

The aircraft banked and climbed. Far below, the patchwork of English fields, villages, roads and railway lines grew smaller then became dimmed by fleecy clouds. I would not, I thought, ever see them again. Not like this. If I was to return, if fate was to be that cruel to us both, it would be to years in a stone box, slopping out my cell in the company of men with no imagination, no sense of direction. My days would be filled with endless games of snooker, lessons in skills I neither needed nor wanted, an eternity of echoing halls and closing locks.

An air hostess passed us by with a drinks trolley. I accepted a plain tonic water and Adam requested a Coca Cola: we were both of us given the statutory packet of dried peanuts which taints the breath of every airline passenger the world over.

As I sipped my drink Adam, who was looking out of the window, suddenly turned to me and said, 'We're not coming back, are we, Uncle Dom?'

I was speechless and just looked at him.

'I don't mind,' he said. 'I'd rather be with you. You understand how I know things.'

He was looking up at me, smiling very faintly with such an adult stoicism I was shocked. I felt tears welling into my eyes, put my drink down and wiped my cheeks with the napkin.

Adam put his hand in mine, like a child being taken across a busy road, and said, 'You don't need to be sad, Uncle Dom. I think it'll be really . . .' – he looked for a word – '. . . fun.'

◆

From the start Adam, Urú and Yammi were friends. I sat on the porch of the hut and watched them. Some days, when no one visited me for medical attention, I observed them for hours on end. Every so often, Adam would look up in my direction and wave or smile and I would wave back or wink at him. This always made him laugh. For some reason, he could not wink without screwing up one side of his face. It was not that he required my approbation for whatever he was doing but he wanted me to share in it somehow, to be a part of his new existence.

In a very short time, he picked up both Spanish and the Huambas dialect, freely skipping from one language to the next at whim and, within a matter of weeks, he was able to act as my translator in most simple intercourse and took a delight in this activity. The women of the clearing were quick to be captivated by him. They called him Aracás which meant *The Singer*. For Adam was always singing, humming to himself in a tuneless yet melodious fashion, pronouncing words I thought he had picked up from Urú and the others, but they were not. None of us understood this in him.

When not being spoilt by the women, Adam was taken in by the men folk. Chuhi showed him how to fire a bow although he was not strong enough to do so: in lieu of this, Chuhi taught him the basics of using a sling-shot. Adam was soon very proficient, knocking quite small targets off a riverside log from a distance of up to twenty metres.

For my part, I enjoyed his company, was made happy by his gaiety and kept my notes up to date, writing them each day with the religiosity of a fanatical diarist, working on them by the light of the oil lamp whilst Adam slept blissfully in his little bunk across the hut from my table.

One day, in our second month, I returned from a short walk up the river to see Adam sitting alone by the river, a little distance from the clearing. He was squatting at the water's edge on a narrow beach of sandy mud, staring into the water, the reflections of the sun dancing upon his forehead.

'What are you doing, Adam?' I asked.

273

For a moment, he did not reply and I wondered if he had heard me. I was about to speak again when he stood up and faced me. 'It's very interesting, Dom,' he said quietly: he had recently dropped the prefix of *uncle*, not at my request but as a natural progression of our relationship.

'What is?'

'I know these fish. Not all of them but some of them. I know the *piraiba*. I shouldn't really, should I? I mean, I didn't come from here. Did I?'

I sat down on a fallen tree, brushing it first with my handkerchief to rid it of ants. 'No,' I said, 'you did not come from here.'

'Where did I come from?'

He was standing before me, his hands loose at his sides and his head tipped slightly. The harsh sun, bouncing off the river, turned his hair into a halo of hazy light.

'Your mother is Larry,' I told him, 'but your father is not Brian.'

'I thought so. Mummy seemed . . . I knew Mummy. But I never knew Daddy. And she was so like him . . . ' There was no misery in his voice, more a sense of reluctant sorrow as if he would have had it otherwise but was aware he could not. 'That was what was not nice. I couldn't tell Mummy things.'

'No,' I replied. 'I know you couldn't.'

'But I could tell you.'

'Yes, you could. And you still can.'

There was a rustling behind me. I glanced around sharply. It was in those early days when I was still concerned about jaguars and anacondas, pit vipers and caimans.

'It's just a lizard,' Adam reassured me. 'One of the big green ones like dinosaurs.' He picked up a pebble and flicked it into the undergrowth. There was a scrabbling of leaf litter then silence.

'Can I ask you something, Dom?' he said.

'Of course you can,' I answered, lifting my face and shielding the sun from my eyes with my hand: he was looking straight at me.

'Are you my real daddy?'

'No, Adam, I am not.'

I paused. He would have to know. There was no alternative left to me. At the same time, I knew there was nothing to be scared of any more. The secret was out to everyone but Adam, whose secret it was.

'I am not your father but,' I continued, no longer afraid of speaking of what I had done, 'I made you. As a doctor, I was able to make babies. It was my job. Some people can't have them because the bits of their bodies which come together to make a baby don't work properly. I fixed the problem. Usually, I took the right bit of the woman and the right bit of her husband and put them together in a glass container. They joined, I put them back in the woman's tummy and the baby grew like normal. You know,' I added as an aside, 'babies are made in their mummy's tummies?'

'Yes. I know that.'

'Well, in your case, I took a bit of your mummy but a bit of some other man to be your daddy. Brian's bits didn't want to work with Larry's.'

Adam thought about this for a moment. I wondered if perhaps I had confused him but it seemed not. 'So who is my real daddy? Will I ever meet him?'

'No. You won't. Your daddy died. Over three thousand years ago. But the bit of him which made babies was still alive.'

Adam turned and faced the river. It was some minutes before he spoke again, minutes which were, for me, filled with dread. I could not know if I had done the right thing by telling him. He was but a child. Perhaps I should have waited until he was older, more equipped to handle the burden of knowledge.

At last, Adam moved round to look at me again.

'Do you think,' he asked, 'my daddy, my real daddy, knew the animals?'

I hugged him close. I do not think I have ever felt such love for another human being as I did at that moment. Nor do

I think I ever shall again. For his part, he put his arms around me and pulled himself into me.

'Tell me,' I asked as I let him go, 'which one is the *piraiba*?'

He put his hand in the water, made his little noise and, within a matter of thirty seconds, a huge fish appeared over the muddy submerged siope of the beach. It hung in the water like a waterlogged tree branch. I reckoned it must have been at least two metres long.

'That's a *piraiba*,' Adam declared. 'It's got a beard of four funny hair things on its chin and two sticking out from its lips.'

I knelt on the beach and studied the fish. It must have weighed at least a hundred kilograms. Its body was solid but slightly flattened horizontally, its eyes reminding me of those of a shark, blankly staring in the sightless fashion of a blind beggar's. The dorsal fin, when it was raised, cut the surface and was the size of a Victorian madam's fan. Adam reached forward and stroked the fish's head. The creature made no response.

'Is it a dangerous fish?' I enquired.

'It hasn't any big teeth but Urú says it can grab you by the leg and drown you. She says it then pulls you under and stores your body in the mud so it can eat you later.'

'I think,' I advised, 'you had better take your hand out now.'

'It's all right, Dom. I know him,' he replied.

It was not long after this Adam taught Urú how to know the *piraiba*. In exchange, she imparted to him her skill of listening to the gods with wings which, I soon realized, was an extension of the skill he already possessed and which I had first seen when he predicted the arrival of Napoleon the cat.

By the end of our third month in the clearing, Adam's body was as nut brown as those of the other children. He took, on occasion, to wearing their dress, exchanging his clothes with them. There were times when, looking out between the shutters of the hut, I could not tell at a distance which child was which.

One mid-morning in our fifth month, Adam came and sat next to me on the porch. I was, I remember, inexpertly sketching.

'What are you drawing, Dom?' he enquired.

'The long-houses,' I said. 'At least, I'm trying to.'

He leaned over my arm and looked briefly at the drawing without passing comment. After a few moments' silence, he suddenly asked, 'You aren't going to go away, are you, Dom?'

'No,' I exclaimed, putting down my drawing and pencil, 'I am not. Ever.'

He smiled in the engaging way children have when they are still innocent of adult subterfuge.

'I don't want to go away,' he stated bluntly. 'I like the clearing.'

'Why?' I queried.

He thought before replying. 'It's nice here. I've got lots of friends. And . . . And I think my daddy might be here, too.'

In the sixth month, I was making my way along the up-river path to the waterfall when I chanced upon Adam in the area of huge moss-covered boulders along the narrow creek. He was alone, sitting cross-legged on the jungle floor, humming absent-mindedly to himself. In his left hand he held a grey rock the size of a grapefruit whilst, in his right, he grasped another, smaller and much blacker stone. As I set eyes on him, he struck the grey stone with the black, sparks jumping up and a shard of the former breaking free. I wondered if he was trying to make a fire and was about to warn him against this, despite the dampness of the jungle, when he began to methodically strike the stones together, keeping time with his humming melody. For fully five minutes, I studied him. At last, he had fashioned a very rough stone axe.

'Do you like my axe?' he asked, not looking up.

I was taken aback: for some reason, I had assumed he was not aware of my presence. I should have known better.

'It's very good,' I complimented him. 'Did Chuhi teach you how to make it?'

'I know how,' he responded and began to hum again.

Just as Adam was turning into one of the people of the clearing so, too, was I. In my own way. It was not as drastic nor as magically wonderful a transformation as Adam made but it was distinctive. I came to keep their timetable, rising at dawn and settling to sleep just an hour or so after dark, eating my food only in the early morning and the evening. My diet soon became a pale imitation of their own as my food stocks began to dwindle and I was forced to become more reliant upon the jungle fare and the little market garden the people maintained. My fear of the jungle gradually evaporated: more accurately, it became reasoned, logical.

The people accepted me. That was the most wonderful thing of all. From almost the first day – certainly the first week – I was considered one of them. Adam, I am sure, helped pave the way for this acceptance. Life looked good.

At the end of the eighth month, I woke one morning to discover Adam still in his bunk. Normally, he was out with the first bird-song, rendezvousing with Urú and the others. I touched his brow. It was hot. Taking a thermometer from the shelf, I shook the mercury down and placed it under his armpit, pushing the flesh close around it. Under my thumb, his pulse raced, jumped, slowed. When I removed the thermometer, the mercury read 105°.

'Adam!' I said sharply, agitating his little shoulder. 'Wake up!'

He stirred and muttered something. I stripped the sheet under which he slept off his little naked, tanned body. It was cold with the night's sweat. He looked so peaceful, so utterly innocent.

Moving him gently on to his back, I examined him thoroughly. His breathing was shallow, the skin of his belly slightly clammy to my touch. Pressing my fingers gently around his abdomen, I discovered his liver was enlarged.

Trying to get him to drink was impossible for Adam seemed not to be able to swallow, any liquid dribbling from his mouth: yet I had to rehydrate him somehow. I threw a length of string over the beam above his bunk and tied a bag of saline to it, inserting a drip in his left forearm.

The symptoms puzzled me. It seemed as though Adam was suffering from malaria but he had not complained of headaches or muscular pains in the previous days. The lack of a shivering fever concerned me: if this was malaria, I thought, it was the malignant tertian type, the most dangerous, meningital form of the four types.

Taking a pin-prick of blood from his thumb, I slid it under Dr Suarez's ancient microscope, turning the brass knobs to focus the lens on the glass slide. It was malaria, Adam's red blood cells heavily infected with merozoites: also present were gametocytes, showing that he must have suffered from the disease for some days without showing any symptoms. This, I knew, was theoretically impossible yet here was the proof before my very eyes. It occurred to me Adam perhaps had some mechanism present in his body which inhibited the disease but had not succeeded in conquering it. This realization brought back such memories: I could see Ruth sitting in the kitchen at Cobb End, hear her voice – *No more ADA, no more SCID. No more Huntingdon's chorea, Alzheimer's. The sky's the limit.*

Looking down on him lying before me without moving save to breathe in a shallow, almost tentative, manner, I wondered what other secrets Adam harboured within himself, what other skills he had yet to display which might have achieved so much had I left him to his fate instead of taking him away to share mine.

I frantically thumbed through my tropical diseases reference book but, to my frustration, there was little I could do, despite my expertise. To administer quinine from my medical supplies could very easily worsen the situation and cause it to develop into blackwater fever: my only option was to leave the disease to run its course.

Throughout the morning, I sat by his side, watching him, dabbing the sweat from his brow and, over and over again, checking the drip.

Around noon, he opened his eyes, quite suddenly.

'Hello,' I greeted him quietly as I might once have welcomed a patient back from an hour under sedation. 'How are you feeling?'

'Very tired.'

Outside, somewhere above the galvanized iron roof, the damnable *seringueiro* was whistling. Adam looked up at the roof, a faraway look in his eyes. Foolishly, I wondered briefly if he was looking through the tin sheeting.

'The bird says the sun is high,' he remarked softly. 'We're more than half-way to night.'

'Just rest, Adam,' I said. 'Try not to move.'

He looked at the needle in his arm.

'I'm very thirsty, Dom,' he whispered.

I held a cup to his lips. He sucked on it but had difficulty swallowing. In a short while, he dozed off again, his head turned to one side on his pillow.

Adam's absence from the clearing during the morning soon had the children and then the adults, crowding silently on to the porch. They looked round the door and through the windows, a mute stillness settled upon them. When they moved, they did so with the caution of one stalking a wild animal. Hardly a plank squeaked.

In the late afternoon, he awoke once more, asking for another drink. As I propped him up to put the cup to his lips, he caught sight of the faces looking in.

'All my friends are here,' he murmured.

Keewai entered as he spoke, a smoking swatch of dried leaves and bark in his hand. He wafted it about over Adam's head, muttering to himself. I made no attempt to restrain him. He could do no harm now.

'*Dejale dormir en paz*,' I heard Chuhi say from the door.

Within minutes, Adam was asleep once more, a faint smile upon his lips. He did not wake again.

Chuhi, Mayno and Q'eke helped me carry him in a coffin I constructed out of the timber from one of the supplies boxes.

We did not take him to the mountain but, at my suggestion and their agreement, we made for the boulders by the creek. I dug a shallow hole and, I think, I may have muttered a few words over it as I gazed down on the wooden lid ironically stencilled with a faded red cross. Standing about in the jungle shadows, perched on the boulders and waiting on the pathway, all the people of the clearing remained without speaking. Overhead, birds sang obliviously.

Chuhi and the people left then. I remained for an hour or two, crying and cursing myself. Then I covered him with earth, placed his rough-hewn axe on the mound and vowed I would take the bridge over the creek from then on.

During the night, in the company of Chuhi, Keewei and Mayno, I burned all my notes.

◆

The sun has gone by its meridian. I would guess it to be about half past two. Smoke from a cooking fire wraiths in the trees, catching shafts of light. A troop of howler monkeys is calling somewhere far off. The birds around the clearing are not as vociferous with the sun high.

Down by the river, Urú is helping her mother launder some clothes. Yammi is teasing one of the dogs with a *buriti* palm leaf frond left over from a morning's basket weaving whilst another boy is whittling a flute out of a reed stalk. Chuhi has gone hunting, the other men are off fishing. Keewei remains in the clearing but he is dozing outside the long-house nearest the river.

If I could I would be like these people of the clearing but I cannot, no matter how much I fool myself. They are simple, honest folk living without shame, not because they have no concept of it but because they are without blame. Not one of them transgresses the laws of the clearing. No one thieves from his neighbour, no one seduces his friend's partner, no one cheats. They have no guilty consciences because they have no need of them.

I am beyond such human simplicity, being a man of stealth and guile, of cunning and selfishness. I may have abandoned my own world but I cannot leave it behind and, though I would smother my guilt if I could, I am unable to eradicate it. Of course, it is only a matter of time until my past catches up with me. As sure as day follows night, there will come a moment when Urú looks up, shouts, waves at me and points to the jungle. When the moment happens, I have decided I shall not run. I shall sit in my chair on the porch and wait. There is nothing I can do about it. The people of the clearing will be nonplussed. Chuhi will yell for me to hide. Keewei will flap his old arms about. Mayno, Q'eke and the others may rush for their bows and poisoned arrows. I shall call to them *¡No luchar! ¡No luchar!* for they should not risk their lives in a battle on my account.

This is the greatest advantage they have over me. For them, there is no past and no future, save in mythologies and the wind. Or, perhaps, the gods with wings.

From the rafter to the left of the crack in the hut wall through which the bats exit from their roost hangs Rodriguez's shrunken head. Keewei presented it to me, a considerable honour. It is about the size of a small coconut, shrunk to approximately a quarter of its original size. The hair is long and has been combed straight. The eyes are mere slits: the cheeks have been rouged with a reddish dye called *pee-ah-ko*, the significance of which I have been unable to ascertain. Into the mouth has been inserted a sliver of bleached wood which, being criss-crossed by the black twine binding the lips almost shut, gives the impression of a line of teeth. In the deep shade of the porch, I sometimes wonder if the bizarre thing is grinning. Whether this is so or not I cannot tell, being neither a man of great imagination nor, any longer, of fear. All I do know is, if I glance quickly at it or catch sight of its shrunken, morbid features hanging there in the evening twilight, it hauntingly reminds me of the axeman.

And he, I am quite sure, is mocking me.